For th
Tycoon's Pleasure

LUCY MONROE
LUCY GORDON
NATALIE RIVERS

Published in Great Britain 2014
by Mills & Boon, an imprint of Harlequin (UK) Limited,
Eton House, 18-24 Paradise Road, Richmond, Surrey, TW9 1SR

The Greek's Pregnant Lover, The Greek Tycoon's Achilles Heel and *The Kristallis Baby* were first published in Great Britain by Harlequin (UK) Limited.

ISBN: 978 0 263 91179 4
eBook ISBN: 978 1 472 04474 7

05-0414

Harlequin (UK) Limited's policy is to use papers that are natural, renewable and recyclable products and made from wood grown in sustainable forests. The logging and manufacturing processes conform to the legal environmental regulations of the country of origin.

Printed and bound in Spain
by Blackprint CPI, Barcelona

THE GREEK'S PREGNANT LOVER

BY
LUCY MONROE

Lucy Monroe started reading at the age of four. After going through the childrens' books at home, her mother caught her reading adult novels pilfered from the higher shelves on the bookcase…alas, it was nine years before she got her hands on a Mills & Boon® romance her older sister had brought home. She loves to create the strong alpha males and independent women who people Mills & Boon books. When she's not immersed in a romance novel (whether reading or writing it), she enjoys travel with her family, having tea with the neighbours, gardening, and visits from her numerous nieces and nephews.

Lucy loves to hear from her readers: e-mail LucyMonroe@LucyMonroe.com or visit www.LucyMonroe.com.

For my beautiful daughter Sabrina,
her wonderful husband Kyle, and their precious child Nevaeh. I love you all so much, and am so very, very, VERY proud of you. I thank God to have you as blessings in my life. Kyle and Sabrina, you have a love worth memorializing and prove the truth that romance is more than fiction. I pray you are blessed with as much or even more love and happiness as your dad and I share for many years to come.

PROLOGUE

ZEPHYR NIKOS looked out over the Port of Seattle, remembering his arrival here with Neo Stamos over a decade before. Things had been very different then. Everything Zephyr owned fit in the single tattered duffel bag he'd carried. He still had that duffel bag stored in the back of his oversized walk-in closet, behind the designer suits and top-of-the-line workout gear.

It was a small reminder of where he had come from, and where he would never be again.

They had been so sure this was the place to start their new life, the one that would move them as far from the backstreets of Athens as a man could get. And they'd been right.

Two Greek boys from the wrong side of the tracks had built not just a business, but an empire worth billions of dollars. They dined in the finest restaurants, traveled by private jet and rubbed shoulders with the richest and most powerful people in the world. They'd realized their dreams and then some.

And now Neo was in love and getting married.

As much as everyone else saw Zephyr as more easygoing than Neo, *he* wasn't surprised his friend had found domestic bliss first. Zephyr wasn't sure he would ever find anything like it. In fact, he was near positive he wouldn't. Oh, he might marry someday, but it wouldn't be a hearts-and-flowers event, just another business transaction. Just like how he'd been conceived.

He had learned early that a smile made as effective a mask as a blank stare, but that's all it was…a mask.

His heart had turned to stone a long time ago, though he guarded that secret as well as he guarded all his others. Secrets he would never allow into the light of day.

Even Neo did not know the painful truth about Zephyr's past. His friend and business partner believed Zephyr had had a similar childhood to his own before they'd met in the orphanage at the age of ten. Neo could not imagine anything worse than his own messed-up childhood and Zephyr wanted to keep it that way. The pain and shame of his past had no place in the new life he'd built for himself.

Neo had hated the orphanage. However, once Zephyr accepted his mother was not coming back for him, it had been the first step in distancing himself from a life he wished he could forget. His father had thought nothing of selling Zephyr's mother's "favors" along with the other women who "worked" for him in the business that supplemented his less than stellar income from the family olive groves. And he cared nothing for the illegitimate son that had resulted from his own "sampling of the merchandise."

When Zephyr's mother had first left him at the orphanage so she could pursue a life away from his father's brothel, his innocent child self had been sure she would come back. He'd missed her and cried and prayed every day she would return. A few weeks later, she had. To visit. No matter how much that small boy had tearfully begged her to take him with her, she had once again left him behind.

It had taken him a few visits, but eventually, he'd realized he was no longer part of his mother's life. And she was no longer part of his. Which even a small boy, barely old enough to attend school, had been able to recognize as freedom from being a whore's son. An orphan, at least, had no past.

He'd learned to hide his. From everyone.

He would have stayed in the orphanage until he finished

school, but the monster whose blood tainted his own had decided an illegitimate son was better than no son at all. And Zephyr had had to leave. Now his best friend, Neo, had gone with him and they had made their own lives on the streets of Athens until lying about their ages to join a cargo ship's crew.

The move Neo considered their first step toward a new life, the life they now enjoyed. But Zephyr knew better. His journey had begun long before.

The simple truth was, as hardened as Neo appeared to be, inside—where it mattered—Zephyr was stone-cold marble in comparison.

CHAPTER ONE

"WHEN are we going to drop the bombs?"

Piper Madison's head snapped up at the question asked in a small boy's high-pitched tone. The dark-haired moppet, who could not be more than five, looked at the male flight attendant with earnest interest.

Glowing with embarrassed humor, his mother laughed softly. "He hasn't quite got the hang of not all planes being geared to war. His grandfather took him to an aeronautical museum and he fell in love with the B-52 bomber."

She turned to her son and explained for what was clearly not the first time that they were on a passenger plane going to visit Grandma and Grandpa. The little boy looked unconvinced until the first-class cabin flight attendant added his agreement to the mother's. Small shoulders drooped in disappointment and Piper had to stifle a chuckle.

There had been a time not so many years ago that her fondest hopes included being in that exasperated mother's place. Those dreams had died along with her marriage and she had accepted that. She had. Yet as much as she wished they didn't, those old hopes still caused a small pang in the region of her heart in moments like this.

But dreams of children definitely had no chance of resurrection in her current situation.

Trying to let the low-level background hum created by the

plane's engines soothe nerves already stretched taut, Piper leaned back in her seat and looked away from the domestic tableau.

It didn't work. Despite her best efforts, her heart rate increased as anticipation of her arrival in Athens thrummed through her. She couldn't stop herself looking out the window, her eyes eagerly seeking evidence of the airport.

For hours it had been nothing but a blanket of cloud with the occasional break where the peaks of the Alps crept through. It had been a while since she spotted the last peak and she knew they were almost to their Athens destination. Less than an hour from seeing *him*. Zephyr Nikos. Her current boss and part-time bed partner.

She was more than a little keen to see the man and the place of his birth. Besides, who didn't want to visit paradise?

For that's where they were ultimately headed, a small Greek island that at one time had been the vacation home of a fabulously wealthy Greek family. Not so flush now, the patriarch had sold the island to Stamos & Nikos Enterprises. Zephyr and his partner, Neo Stamos, planned to develop it as an all-inclusive spa resort. And she'd been given the interior design contract for the entire facility, with a budget large enough to bring in whatever kind of help she needed to see it to completion.

She was beyond excited about being brought in at the ground level on such an expansive project. It would be an amazing coup for her business, but satisfying personally on a creative level as well. Even so, her current heightened sense of anticipation was predominantly for the man who waited for her there.

She had spent the last six weeks missing Zephyr with an ache that scared her when she let herself think about it. She should not be so emotionally dependent on a man who was only *sort of* her lover.

She bit her lip on a sigh.

They were involved sexually, but not romantically. They weren't anything as simple as casual sex partners. That would be too easy. She'd know exactly how to handle her one-sided emotional entanglement then. But they were friends, too. Good friends. The kind of friends that hung out at least once a week before the sex benefits started and that increased to multiple times a week when they were in the same city.

To complicate things even more, he was also her boss.

Again…sort of. His company had hired her personal design firm for several projects over the past two-plus years, though this new development was by far the biggest and most far-reaching for her. He would be her boss in actual fact if she'd let him, too.

He'd offered her a staff job with salary and benefits she'd had a hard time turning down, but Piper had no desire to work for someone else. Not again. Not after losing both her husband and her job in one fell swoop only six months before she took on her first project with Zephyr's company.

She'd vowed then that she would not allow herself to ever be that vulnerable to upheaval again.

She'd thought marrying Arthur Bellingham would give her the stability she craved, among other things—like that family she'd dreamed about. It had turned out just the opposite, though. Art had shredded her emotions before tearing her life apart piece by piece until all she had left was her talent and her determination. She would never be in that place again.

Not even for Zephyr. Not that the sexy Greek real estate tycoon was offering her marriage, or even commitment. He'd offered her a salaried job. That was all.

If she wanted more, she certainly wasn't saying so. Up until the past weeks' long separation, she hadn't even admitted it to herself. Telling him wasn't in the cards she planned to play. Not when doing so would spell the immediate end to this whole friends-who-are-sexually-intimate situation.

And maybe their friendship as well.

Zephyr waited for Piper near the luggage carousel. He hadn't seen her in six weeks. She had been on a job in the

Midwest and he'd known if he didn't offer her the Greek job, he probably wouldn't see her again for another two months, or more.

Not that she wasn't the best interior designer for the job, but this project was bigger than anything she'd taken on before. He knew she could do it, though. And it wasn't as if he needed to explain his choice to anyone. That was one of the benefits to being the boss. The only person who might have something to say about it, and only because they were both working together on this development for the first time in years, was his best friend and business partner, Neo Stamos.

However, the man was knee-deep in wedding preparations right now. Cass might not want a big production, but Neo wanted their small wedding to be perfect in every way. Hell, Zephyr was surprised his friend hadn't insisted on designing and building a venue just for the event.

A group of newly arrived travelers surged toward the luggage carousel, bringing Zephyr's thoughts firmly to the present. He scanned the crowd for Piper's beautiful blond head. There she was, her attention caught by a small boy talking animatedly to his mother. The signature blue skirt-suit Piper wore highlighted her curves deliciously, while managing a claim to elegance. Yet, he doubted it was a designer label.

Piper's business was still operating on too fine a line for her to splurge on clothes, or even an apartment much bigger than a closet. He'd offered her a job that would have made it possible for her to live at a higher standard, but she'd turned him down. Twice. Damn, the woman was stubborn. And independent.

He wondered if she would turn down a shopping spree in Athens's fashion district?

She looked up and their gazes met. Eyes the color of a robin's egg filled with warmth and pleasure as they landed on him, her bow-shaped lips curved in a gorgeous smile. That look struck him like a blow to the chest.

He felt a grin take over his mouth without his permission,

a more honest smile than anything that usually masked his features. Not that he had to hide that he was pleased to see her. They'd hit it off when he hired her to update the main offices for Stamos & Nikos Enterprises a little over two years ago. Their friendship had only grown since. The addition of phenomenal sex to their relationship had only improved the situation as far as he was concerned.

In fact, Piper had been the reason Zephyr had encouraged Neo so strongly to develop interests outside their company, and to pursue his friendship with Cassandra Baker, the famous recluse master pianist. That had worked out better for Neo than Zephyr could have imagined. And Zephyr was happy for him. He really was.

However, it boggled his mind, to tell the truth. *Neo in love.* Zephyr shook his head. Sex and friendship were one thing, love something else altogether.

Piper's delicate brows drew together in a frown and she gave him a questioning look.

"It's nothing," he mouthed.

When she reached him, he pulled her into a tight hug. Her soft curves felt so good against him, the low-level arousal he'd experienced since waking that morning and realizing he would be seeing Piper today went critical. Just that fast.

Damn.

"I guess you *really* missed me." She leaned back, a sensual chuckle purring from her throat, her eyes glinting with teasing humor.

Chagrin washed over him. He wasn't some untried adolescent. Nevertheless, he laughed and admitted, "Yes."

"When is our first meeting with the architect?"

"The day after tomorrow."

"But you told me I needed to be here today."

"You needed a break."

"Building a new business is always consuming."

He shrugged because he couldn't disagree. For the first ten

years when he and Neo had been building their fortune, they had worked weekends and long hours during the week and hadn't taken so much as an afternoon off. Things had gotten a little better after that, though they were both too much of overachievers to develop much of a life outside their company.

After meeting Piper, Zephyr had started leaving the office around six instead of eight, but he still wasn't great about taking time off. However, Piper had sounded exhausted the last time they'd spoken on the phone, and he'd determined she would take a break, one way or another.

"Agreed, but I did not think you would begrudge an extra couple of days in Athens."

Her eyes lit up. "You mean I actually get to do some sight-seeing before submersing myself in the job?"

"Exactly. I'd hoped you'd consider the next couple of days as information-gathering time as well as our time on the island. We want the resort to fit into the island's ambiance, but also reflect Greek culture."

"Ambiance? I thought it was a private island. Empty."

"The family leased out land for a small fishing village and a few farms for local produce, as well as having their own fruit orchards and olive groves."

"Oh, that's perfect for what you are wanting to do."

"I thought so." But he enjoyed how in-tune with his vision she was.

"I'm glad I'll have time to really get to know the area then. I like to try and make my designs reflect the local setting's positive attributes."

"I know and I'm sure you've done a lot of research on Greek culture already." Heck, she'd researched it when they'd first met, telling him she wanted to understand him and Neo better as clients. He didn't know how much it had helped her, considering he and Neo had left Greece behind so many years ago. But there was no denying Piper *got him* in a way no one else did. And her design updates in their offices had been perfect. "Nothing can replace experiencing an environment in person though."

Unconsciously nestling her body into his, she smiled, clearly pleased. "True, but I didn't know I'd have the luxury to do so with this job."

He just grinned and shrugged.

She laughed. "Don't fool yourself into believing I'm not aware you have your own agenda here. One that includes judicious amounts of time between the sheets. You're a manipulator, you know that?"

She knew him well. "Is this a bad thing?"

"In this case?" She shook her head, her bright blue eyes going heavy-lidded. "No. Definitely no."

That's what he appreciated so much about her. Piper Madison was a gem among women, his very own polished diamond that did not require the setting of a relationship to shine. Unlike Neo's less worldly Cass, Piper had no illusions of love and romance. She enjoyed his body as he found pleasure in hers. No morass of untidy emotions to navigate, which was a very good thing.

Because unlike Neo, Zephyr had no love to give. "Let's get your case and we'll head to the hotel. It is a spa-resort."

"Scoping out the competition, are we?"

"Naturally." He gave in to the desire that had been riding him since her arrival and kissed her. And then he kissed her again for good measure. She tasted as sweet and arousing as always.

Eyes glowing with pleasure, she said, "Only, situated in the city, it can't hope to offer what we, I mean Stamos and Nikos Enterprises, will."

"There would be no point in developing a new property if we couldn't bring something to the table no one else has already offered."

Her azure gaze slid to his lips and stayed there for several seconds, and then she blinked at him with unfocused eyes before seeming to remember what he'd said and smiling wryly. "Always the overachiever."

"And you are not?"

"Hey, there's more than one reason you and I are such good friends."

"More than this, you mean." He rubbed himself against her subtly.

She gasped and stepped back. "You are dangerous." Letting her gaze drop to what he hoped his suit jacket hid from others' gazes, she winked. "I think getting to the hotel is a definite necessity."

"Are you tired?" he asked, tongue in cheek. "Need a lie down?"

"Get my case, Zephyr." She gave him a look that said she knew exactly what kind of lie down he had in mind and she wasn't necessarily averse.

"Gladly, *agapimenos*."

"Don't start in with the Greek endearments unless you want spontaneous combustion right here," she warned.

"But I like living on the edge."

She gave a significant look to the baggage rolling by on the carousel.

He turned smartly and started looking for the zebra-print luggage he had bought her after she complained about how her black suitcase looked like everyone else's in the airport. She'd laughed at the loud black-and-white print on the cases, but she used it.

She'd only brought one midsize case and her carry-on, so they were out of the airport and in the car he'd rented for the week a few minutes later.

"Mmm…nice. Definitely a step up from the Mercedes," she said, rubbing the leather upholstery in the fire-engine-red Ferrari convertible.

"Don't knock my car. It has heated seats and those come in handy in Seattle's colder winters. And a convertible would hardly be practical in such a wet city." But he was glad she liked the Ferrari. He'd wanted to spoil her a little, since she was always so determined not to spoil herself.

"There is that." She brushed her hand along the ceiling. "Are you going to lower the soft-top?"

"Of course." He pressed a button and the roof slowly disappeared.

Once the process had completed, he put the powerful car into gear and backed out of his VIP parking spot. With well-practiced movements in cutthroat driving, he maneuvered them through Athens toward their hotel. He swerved around a taxi that had stopped in a no-parking zone and then accelerated through a light turning red.

She put her head back and laughed out loud. "Oh, I like this. We really have two days for you and me to play, and nothing else?"

"We do."

"Thank you, Zephyr." She brushed a hand down his thigh.

Pleasure at both the touch and the gratitude he heard in her voice filled him. With an independent woman like Piper, it had been a risk to schedule vacation time for her without her knowledge. Even if he called it locale research. He was glad the risk had paid off. "What are friends for?"

"Is that all we are? Just friends?" she asked, not sounding particularly concerned.

So, he didn't go into masculine panic mode. "In my world there isn't anything *just* about being a true friend."

"I understand that. All of my so-called friends dumped me when I walked out on Art. I didn't realize they were only interested in spending time with me if I came as part of a power couple."

"Even though he cheated on you?" Zephyr asked in disgust.

"Art wasn't the only one who believed that hoary old refrain he was so good at spouting."

"Which one is that?"

"All men cheat," she clarified.

"We don't."

"The jury is still out on that one, but I was not about to stay married to a man who believed infidelity was as inevitable as the tide."

"You know I think you made the right choice divorcing that louse." At least her family had finally come around to that conclusion as well, even if her former friends had not.

"Me, too. But unfortunately, *that louse* runs one of the most successful design houses in New York."

"Hence your move to Seattle."

"Exactly. There just wasn't room enough in The Big Apple for both his ego and my career." She smiled sadly.

The bastard she'd been married to had done his best to blackball her in the design community. Zephyr had returned the favor over the past two years and Très Bon no longer held its prestigious top position status. Arthur Bellingham's word might send ripples out in the city, but Zephyr Nikos sent out waves big enough to drown in the international community.

The bastard who had done his best to ruin Piper's life was on the slippery slope of business decline already. Art would only find himself in deep, murky waters when he got to the bottom, too.

Zephyr had never told Piper, of course. She hadn't been exposed to his ruthless streak and he saw no reason to change that.

"Well, I am glad you came to Seattle," he said.

"Again, me, too." She tugged off her jacket, revealing the silky singlet she wore beneath it, and the fact she *wasn't* wearing a bra. "I certainly made a better circle of friends."

"Oh, I am round now?" he asked, practically choking on his lust as her hardened nipples created shoals in the slinky fabric of her top.

He forcibly snapped his attention back to Athens's typically snarled traffic, lest he cause an accident or do a poor job avoiding one. He could hardly do what he was fantasizing to her body from a hospital bed.

Having her in peril of the same didn't even bear thinking of.

"Don't be smart." She tapped his leg, having the opposite effect to the one he was sure she meant it to. "I have other friends."

"Name one."

"Brandi."

"She is your assistant."

"I have friends," Piper insisted stubbornly. "There's a reason I'm not available every night to keep you entertained."

Which wasn't something he actually liked, so he let the subject drop.

Usually, Piper noticed every tiny detail of her surroundings, always looking for ways to improve her own sense of design and aesthetics. However, she barely noticed the earth tones and ultramodern, simplistic design features of the luxury spa Zephyr had chosen for their stay as he led her through the oversized lobby to the bank of elevators on the far side.

She was too busy soaking in his every feature, her senses starved for the sight, taste and feel of him.

The past month and a half had been harder than any separation they'd had to date. For her anyway. Maybe for Zephyr, too, if the number of calls and texts she'd gotten from him was anything to go on. They'd had prolonged times apart before, but not since they started having sex regularly six months ago. Still, it wasn't as if they were a couple. They were friends, who were also casual sex partners. At least that's what she'd been telling herself since the first time they'd passed that intimate boundary nine months ago.

That first time, she'd thought it would be a one-off, something to get the sexual tension that had been growing between them out of the way of their friendship. She'd been wrong.

They hadn't gotten physical again until three months later, but connected sexually several times a week since then. When he made it clear, again, that he did not see the sex as anything more than physical compatibility for stress release, she'd told herself she wasn't ready for a committed relationship, either, so that was just fine with her. Art had done a real number on her ability to trust and she had a business to build. She didn't have a place in her life for a full-time relationship.

The only problem was: she wasn't sure she believed her own rhetoric any longer. Her natural optimism was doing its best to overcome her painfully learnt lesson on the ways of men. *The fact she was having such a complicated internal monologue on the matter was telling in itself,* she thought with an internal sigh.

She'd been careful not to ask for promises Zephyr might break, or make commitments she wasn't ready for.

But she'd come to realize over the past six weeks—while subsisting on phone calls, texts, instant messaging and e-mail—that emotions didn't abide by agreements, verbal or otherwise. That refusing to make a vow didn't stop her heart from craving the security that promise implied. Nor did it stop her from living like she'd made her own promises.

She'd missed Zephyr more than she'd thought possible and wanted nothing more right now than to wrap herself up in him and soak in his essence.

He seemed to want the same thing. He hadn't stopped touching her since they left the airport. He'd laid his hand over hers between gear changes in the car and he'd kept his arm around her waist all the way to the room.

He opened the door with a flourish. "Here we are."

The suite reflected the minimalist décor from downstairs, but its spaciousness spoke of the ultimate in luxury. "This place is bigger than my apartment."

"My closet is bigger than your flat," he said, sounding unimpressed.

She grimaced at the truth of his words, but the curve of

her lips morphed into a smile from the heat burning in his brown eyes.

From the feel of his arousal when he'd first hugged and kissed her hello, and the sexual need intensifying his features then and now, she expected to be taken against the door with a minimum of foreplay.

But that didn't happen. He set her cases aside and then lifted her right into his arms, high against his chest, in a move that made her feel cherished rather than just wanted.

She quickly banished that thought even as her gasp of surprise escaped her. "Going he-man on me?"

"Spoiling you more like."

"Oh, really? I could get used to this," she teased.

He didn't bother with a reply, but didn't look too fazed at the prospect. So not good for the odd blips of emotion that had been pestering her lately. But that was one thing she could say about Zephyr Nikos, whether it be in his role as friend, boss or bed partner, the man did not stint on his generosity.

Despite his obvious desire, rather than showing mass amounts of impatience, he laid her gently on the big bed and seemed determined to reacquaint himself with every facet of her body. He drove her crazy with reticence while pumping her for information on her time away from him.

After he asked yet another question about her experience in the Midwest decorating the interior for a new office building, she laughed. "We spoke every day, Zephyr. I can't think of anything I didn't already tell you."

The gorgeous tycoon actually looked like he might be blushing, his dark eyes reflecting chagrin. "I was just curious."

"You know what I do on a job. I've done it for Stamos and Nikos Enterprises often enough."

"Did you like the Midwest better than Seattle?" he asked with what she thought was entirely mistimed curiosity.

"Are you kidding?"

His expression said clearly he wasn't.

"I love Seattle. The energy in the city is amazing." And he was there.

"That's good to know."

Suddenly, all his questions started to make sense. "You heard."

CHAPTER TWO

ZEPHYR tried to look innocent.

"How? Who told you?"

"Does it matter? Information is more lucrative than platinum in my business."

"Did you seriously think Pearson Property Developments could offer me a better situation than your company already has done?"

"Moncy isn't your only consideration, it isn't even your main one, or you would have accepted my job offer by now."

It was true. She would make a lot more money working for him as an employee whose overheads were absorbed by the company rather than as a fledgling design business that sucked up the vast majority of the not-insubstantial fees charged to her clients.

"So, you thought I might like the Midwest enough to take Pearson's job offer?" She couldn't imagine it and disbelief colored her voice.

"They didn't just offer you a job."

"No, they also offered a contract for several projects they have in the pipeline over the next two years." While still leaving her an independent operator, the offer would provide the kind of security most up-and-coming designers dreamed about.

If living in a landlocked state without a single authentic

Vietnamese or Thai restaurant was what she wanted. It wasn't. She was too fond of the diversified and active culture of Seattle.

"I've gotten too spoiled to big-city living. The only Thai restaurant I found was run by a man named Arnie who thinks a good curry comes with corn-on-the-cob."

Zephyr shuddered. "So, you are not taking the contract."

"Doing so would have made it impossible to do this property. I wasn't willing to give up a chance at decorating a specialty resort in paradise for re-creating my first design in a series of cookie-cutter office buildings."

One of the things she and Art had disagreed on, besides the whole issue of marital fidelity, was her need to create, not merely re-create. For Art, the bottom line was always money. While Piper craved security, she needed the chance to stretch her artistic muscles just as much.

"I'm glad."

She smiled. "Good."

"I'm equally pleased you are here with me now." For a man like Zephyr, that was quite an admission.

It deserved rewarding, at the very least reciprocating honesty. Emotion she was doing her best to suppress colored her single-word answer. "Ditto."

He made a sexy sound, very much like a growl, before pulling her to him for a scorching kiss. Finally.

She'd missed him; she'd missed this so much. Being touched. Being held. She'd gotten very spoiled to seeing him so frequently.

She threw herself into the kiss without the least resistance. She adored his lovemaking, but she could do this for hours.

And from the way his lips moved against hers, so could he.

She felt herself being lifted and then she was straddling his thighs, her skirt rucked up around her hips. The mattress was firm enough to support his sitting up easily. What brand was it? She couldn't help wondering.

And then all work-related thoughts disappeared as her

brain focused on the only thing that mattered right now, the sensation of being held and kissed by the most amazing man she'd ever met.

His mouth fit over hers perfectly. And he tasted like her idea of heaven. He deepened the kiss, but with no sense of urgency, telling her silently that they had all the time in the world. He was the only man she'd ever known who treated kissing like an end unto itself.

The kiss broke for a moment, their lips sliding apart in a natural movement. He caressed her cheek and temple with his lips.

She smiled, warmed clear through and pleased by the fact he hadn't just missed sex with her. He seemed to have missed their connection almost as much as she had.

"I'm surprised you're not tearing my clothes off after six weeks going without," she whispered, the hushed quiet around them feeling almost sacred.

Then a chilling thought took her. Maybe he hadn't gone without. Maybe that's why he was so relaxed. They'd never made the commitment toward monogamy. He could very well have found someone else back in Seattle.

"I kept myself busy at work. With Neo cutting back his hours to spend more time with Cass, there's a lot of reorganization of responsibilities going on." He gave her gentle baby kisses all over face and neck between words. "Even if you had been in Seattle, I would barely have seen you over the past six weeks."

Which implied he hadn't been with anyone else, either.

"I didn't realize it was that bad." He'd mentioned something to that effect, but she'd thought he was just trying to make her feel better.

She should have known better. For all his apparent affability, Zephyr Nikos was an almost brutally honest man. He'd warned her early in their association that he didn't do "sensitive" and he hoped she could handle candor, even when it meant criticism. He'd been referring to their work association, but she'd gotten the impression he was that way on a personal level as well.

Then, after they'd become friends, she'd gotten proof of her impression. So, why did she keep looking for evidence to the contrary now that they were involved more intimately? On a physical level anyway.

He pulled his head back and met her eyes with a sardonic expression. "Neo is a force of nature. We've had to restructure our head office entirely, promoting several people into positions of greater authority while hiring others and training them to take over the new vacancies."

"With you picking up the slack."

The signs of exhaustion were there and she couldn't believe it had taken her this long to notice. Her delight in being in his company again was her only excuse. Dark shadows under Zephyr's eyes, his vitality muted—she wasn't the only one who needed a couple of days without work.

"It is worth it to see him so happy." There was something in Zephyr's tone. Not quite envy, not exactly sadness, but definite sincerity.

It confused her.

"I can't imagine Neo in love," was all she said, though.

"You've only met him a few times."

"And he's always the same. Intense. Focused. Almost dour." There was no almost about it, but she didn't want to offend Zephyr by calling his best friend and business partner an emotionless robot.

"Cass makes him laugh." The strange tone was there again and no more comprehensible to Piper.

Regardless, she could not picture Neo Stamos laughing. "He really *must* be in love."

"Yes."

She might not be able to interpret that tone, but Piper did know something about it bothered her. She scooted up his lap so the silk panties covering her were directly over the hard bulge behind his zipper.

Whatever was going on in Zephyr's head, his desire for her had not abated by even a centimeter.

He needed to relax and forget about Stamos & Nikos Enterprises for a while. She knew just how to help him do that.

She leaned forward and spoke against his lips. "No more talking, Zephyr."

"You have something better to do with my lips?" Every word brushed his lips provocatively against hers.

"Absolutely." She drew out the syllables, making each one a minicaress leading up to when she pressed their mouths together with serious intent.

He let her control the kiss for several tantalizing minutes she knew would not last. Allowing her tongue to tease his, he kept his hands locked onto her hips while she tunneled her fingers through his gorgeous dark hair. She rocked against him, bringing them both moan-producing pleasure.

One of the things she most adored about making love with this man was how totally into it he got. And how much he liked when she did the same. He never made her feel like a freak for enjoying sex. Art had often made cutting comments about her behavior in bed, reining in her abandon. And then he'd had the temerity to say that all men cheated because they couldn't get what they needed from one woman. But especially their wives.

Bull. Art hadn't been willing to take what Piper had been prepared to give. Zephyr, on the other hand, never made her feel dirty for getting lost in the physical. Her passion did not intimidate or disgust him. Not on any level.

Because his passion was just as deep and consuming. He didn't posture or pretend. He wasn't a man driven by appearances, like her ex-husband.

Zephyr did not worry about wrinkling or staining his clothes when their desires got in the way of a neat and tidy disrobing. Like now. It was clear from the way he touched and responded to her that he wasn't thinking about anything but the pleasure between them, the way their bodies pressed and writhed together in primal need.

It wasn't in the predatory nature of her tycoon to remain passive for long. And she waited with adrenaline-fueled anticipation for him to make his move.

He did not disappoint her, erupting from his sitting position to spin them around and lay her against the bed once more. He came down over her, his body heat and the strength of his bulging muscles surrounding her with his solid presence. A frisson of atavistic pleasure rolled straight down her spine directly to her feminine core.

She would never tell him, but she loved when her *über*-sophisticated lover went caveman on her. His big body rubbed against hers; his hands were everywhere. But then so were hers. He touched her through her clothes, then shoved her silk top up her torso with a growling wound deep in his chest. Masculine fingers caressed her stomach, circling her belly button before moving up to gently mold her unfettered breasts and pluck at her nipples.

Urgent sounds of need slipped from her mouth to his. Her body rocked upward of its own volition, sharp talons of sexual hunger piercing her and making her muscles tense and strain.

If he didn't claim her body with his soon, she was going to lose her mind. Or take over. Somehow.

One of his hands slid between them, then the pad of his thumb was exactly where she needed it to be, caressing her swollen clitoris right through the silk of her panties.

The pleasure built at light speed and she felt her climax taking her over before she'd even gotten a chance to start really aching for it. Of course, she'd been hungry for his brand of loving since the last night they spent together six weeks ago.

His voracious kiss swallowed her scream of undeniable

pleasure. It went on and on and on and on in an unending cascade of bliss that drained all coherent thought from her mind.

Then the caressing finger moved away and she floated on a haze of satiation. It was temporary, because she knew he wasn't finished, or even close to it.

The sound of a condom wrapper tearing filtered through her consciousness, but her eyes wouldn't focus. Everything was blurred by the mind-numbing pleasure she had just experienced.

It was her fragile panties tearing away from her body that got her attention, though. The look of near animalistic carnality hardening his features made her insides clench in wanton hunger. He pressed against her slick opening with his latex-covered shaft.

And then he was inside her, his long and thick erection filling her like no other man could.

He looked down at her, his dark eyes practically black with desire. "Okay?"

She answered with a tilt of her pelvis, taking him in as deep as he would go. The feel of his blunt head pushing inexorably against her cervix sparked another orgasm, this one deep inside, an intense contraction of her womb that tilted between pain and pleasure.

Though she didn't think she'd done anything to reveal the shock of internal delight, his openly feral gaze gleamed with satisfaction.

And then he started moving, setting a rhythm that both demanded her participation and coaxed it from her with jolt after jolt of electric pleasure.

They moved together with an urgency that would not be denied. It was only minutes before he was tearing his lips from her and roaring out his release.

Shockingly, her body contracted around him in a third muted climax sparked by the final swelling of his hardness pressing against her G-spot with inflexible pressure.

He said a four-letter word.

"I prefer the term *making love*." She grinned tiredly, her entire body boneless from the overwhelming cataclysm that had been their joining.

He barked out a laugh and shook his head. "That was incredible."

"That's one word for it." She looked down their bodies. They were both practically dressed. Clothes unzipped and moved out of the way only as much as absolutely necessary to make their copulating possible. "Earthshaking is another."

"That's two words."

"And two more words for you—still dressed."

His gaze traveled the path hers had and he took in their still dressed condition with widening eyes. "Unbelievable."

He sounded as shocked as she felt, which struck her as unbelievably funny and she started laughing. Soon his laughter joined hers and he had to grab the condom before rolling off her as their humor continued unabated for long minutes.

He stood up and disposed of the condom before yanking off slacks that looked like they belonged on the jumble heap. "I wonder what the dry cleaner is going to think of that."

"Do you really care?"

"No." He finished undressing and then started working on her clothes. "Your panties are goners, but I think the dry cleaner can save your skirt."

"You could have the decency to sound at least a little apologetic about that."

"Why? What is a single pair of panties in comparison to the pleasure we both just enjoyed?"

Too true, but it wouldn't do for her to say so. "They were my favorite pair."

"Oh, really?" He gave her his patented doubtful frown that had sent more than one negotiator toppling toward defeat. "I don't recall seeing them before. Ever. And I think I have more than a nodding acquaintance with the delectable bits of fabric you choose to cover your own even more enticing bits."

"Charmer." Then she gave him a fake pout. "I bought them new for today."

"So how could they be your favorites?"

"They were my *new* favorites."

"Well, they're rubbish now." And really? He didn't sound even sort of bothered by that.

Which she liked. A lot. Still, she wasn't ready to cede the game completely. "I thought you'd like them."

"I did. Couldn't you tell?"

She laughed, feeling joyous and free. "I'm only going to forgive you because I had multiple orgasms."

"Three of them. In a very short period," he added with well-deserved smugness. "It makes me wonder what I can do with the rest of the night."

What he did was make love to her until she passed out from exhaustion sometime around dawn…after no less than three more orgasms.

They slept in, waking at the tail end of the morning to share a decadent brunch. Then he took her to the Acropolis. She'd watched a travel video about the temple ruins found there, but nothing prepared her for how it felt actually standing where many claimed the modern constructs of Western Civilization had been born. Maybe not everyone reacted like she did, but she felt a sense of profundity that she could not shake.

She could not help staring at the Parthenon in absolute awe.

When she told Zephyr about it, he did not laugh at her like Art would have done.

Zephyr only nodded, his expression serious. "This is not just a pile of ingeniously put-together stone. We are standing on history. You cannot dismiss something like that."

"That's why your developments are so special, isn't it?"

"Because I recognize history when I see it?" he asked with underlying amusement.

She reached out and took his hand. She could not help

herself. She needed to touch this incredible man. "Because you recognize the unique flavor of wherever you are and rather than try to change it, you seek to enhance it."

Very few developers could make that claim, and none as successful as Stamos & Nikos Enterprises.

"Neo and I learned early to see the good in wherever we were." He laced their fingers together, giving her a look that implied he wasn't just talking about property development.

"Even the orphanage?" she asked softly.

"I admit I saw more good there than Neo did."

"I'm not surprised."

He shrugged.

"That's a pretty nice talent to have. I wish I'd had it as a child like you did." She might have found moving around as much as her family had done easier than she had. "Heck, I wouldn't mind having it now."

"Don't play down your strengths. That was one of the first characteristics I admired in you."

"Seriously?"

"Definitely. When you look at a property, you do not see what is, but what could be."

"That's not the same thing."

"No, but it comes from the same attitude."

"Then why was I such a miserable kid?" She felt like an idiot asking that. She'd been a grown-up for a long time. The little girl that found changing homes and schools every couple of years so traumatizing was long gone.

"It wasn't an inability to find the good in each new situation that your father's military career led you to that made you so unhappy. It was the fact you found so much to love and enjoy in each new place and that got ripped from you with every new reassignment."

Feeling light-headed, and not from the panoramic view of Athens, she swallowed after developeing a suddenly dry throat. Because Zephyr was exactly right. Every time she had found the place she wanted to occupy in her new world, she had been ripped away from it.

But still. "Lots of kids grow up the way I did."

"That doesn't make it any easier on each one that does it. There were more than two dozen other children in the orphanage my mother abandoned me to. That reality did not make my own situation any easier to accept when she left me behind."

"Your mother *abandoned you* to the orphanage?"

Zephyr walked to a viewpoint that overlooked Hadrian's Arch. He still had hold of Piper's hand, so she came with him. Feeling like the only connection he had with the present was their entwined fingers, he could not believe he had shared that information with Piper. He'd never even talked about it to Neo. Yet, he knew he was going to tell Piper the truth now.

Maybe not all, but at least some. He just didn't understand why.

"How old were you?" she asked, after several moments of somber quiet between them.

"Four, almost five." He looked down at her to gauge his tenderhearted lover's reaction.

She did not disappoint him. Her pretty blue eyes glazed over in shock. "I thought you were a baby, or something."

"No. My mother was a prostitute." Again, a sense of utter unreality that he should be telling Piper these things assailed him. "One of her clients fell in love with her and wanted to marry her, but he didn't want a living reminder of the life she'd led before they met."

As an adult man, he could almost understand that. Not forgive, but understand. As a child who had adored his mother, the only bright constant in his short life, the one he had relied on entirely for acceptance and love, he hadn't been so wise. Neither his child's mind, nor the heart he'd later encased in impenetrable stone, had been able to comprehend his mother's actions, or even her husband's attitude.

The man had been kind enough to the small boy the few

times they met before he decided to buy Leda's freedom from her *procurer*, Zephyr's father.

"But you were *her child*!" Piper's obvious shock nearly ripped her hand from his grasp.

He tightened his grip, unwilling to let her go. "My mother visited. Once a month, but I learned to wish she wouldn't."

"Because she never took you with her when she left."

"No." No matter how he'd begged at first.

"When was the last time you spoke to her?"

"Last month." But he hadn't seen her since he'd run away from the orphanage with Neo, this time by *Zephyr's* choice.

Piper stared up at him, her eyes swimming with emotion, her mouth opening and closing, but no sound coming out.

He took pity on her clear inability to fathom this state of affairs. "I contacted her after I made my first million. She was glad to hear from me."

"You sound like that surprised you."

"It did. Even though I was now wealthy, there was no guarantee she would want the reminder of her past."

"You thought money was all you had to give her."

Naturally. He'd never met a woman who didn't appreciate financial gifts, his mother setting that precedent early for his young mind. "Why would I believe anything else?"

"She was glad you were safe, though, wasn't she? I bet she cried that first time you called her."

That time and almost every one since. "You are right." Not that he understood why.

If his disappearance was such a hardship on his mother, surely she would not have dumped him at the orphanage in the first place? Nevertheless, she had not abandoned him entirely.

"She paid the orphanage to care for me." He had discovered that when he made his first donation to the home long before he amassed his first million.

It was the reason he had contacted her later. Without the knowledge she had attempted to provide for him in some way, he did not think he ever would have. But nothing could have altered the path he had taken with his father.

"Are we going to see her while we are here?" Piper's voice dripped with the emotion clouding her expression.

"No."

"Of course, I'm sorry." From looking on the verge of tears, Piper went to embarrassment in a single breath. "There's no reason to take your friend to visit your mother."

"It's not that. She would like you." How could she not? Piper was a very likable woman. "However, I have no intention of seeing my mother."

"What? Why not? Surely we have time. Even if she lives on one of the islands. We can skip the sightseeing."

"She lives in Athens. I bought her a house in Kifissia." The distance between that district and the one he had been born in was measured in more than kilometers, though.

Piper's brow furrowed. "According to the guidebook in our suite, that's the elite part of town."

"Is that what it said?"

"Well, as good as."

"The book is right. The wealthy have inhabited Kifissia for generations."

"And you bought your mother a house there."

He shrugged. What did Piper want him to say? He had wanted to give his mother a physical break from the past.

"Yet you are not going to visit her."

"No," he confirmed.

"But…"

"I have not seen her in more than twenty years, Piper."

"But you said you spoke last month." The confusion on Piper's face was adorable.

He kissed her. Not passionately, but he could not resist the innocent incomprehension covering her features.

"It was her birthday. So, I spoke to her."

"You call her once a year, on her birthday?" Piper guessed.

"Yes." The year after he first reconnected with Leda, he had made the mistake of asking what she would like for her birthday.

He'd become too ingrained in American customs. And he'd wanted the excuse to give her something nice, something to show her and the man she had married that Zephyr wasn't such a dead loss after all. He wasn't a lame puppy to be abandoned.

But his mother hadn't asked for a designer handbag, or a new television. She'd only wanted one thing. For Zephyr to call her once a year on her birthday, so she could know he was doing all right. She could follow his success in the papers now, but he still made that call.

Once a year.

"Does she call you?"

"I have asked her not to, unless there is a problem with my brother or sister." Keeping his mother at a distance was necessary and he could not change that.

"You have a brother and sister?"

He had expected some kind of criticism for his coldness toward his mother, but Piper hadn't focused on a situation he could not change. She'd zeroed in on the one reality *he* found truly important. His sister and brother.

"They are half siblings, but I feel a responsibility toward them nonetheless."

"How old are they?"

"Iola is twenty-nine. She is married to a good man and has three children of her own."

Six years younger than him, his sister had been born a year and a half after he went into the home.

His mother had missed her visit with him that month and the one after. He'd thought she'd finally grown tired of coming to see him and wasn't coming back. But she'd returned and she'd had a beautiful baby with her when she did.

"Have you met the children?"

"Yes, Iola insisted."

"You sound like you don't understand why."

"I'm the bastard child her mother gave birth to when living a life they would all rather forget happened. My sister doesn't even remember meeting me. She was too young the last time I saw her."

"Your mother brought her to visit?"

"Yes."

"That was cruel."

He shrugged. To his way of thinking, it had been much more cruel when his mother stopped bringing Iola. Some might have thought he would be jealous of the baby, but Zephyr had adored Iola from the very beginning. He had been heartbroken when his mother's husband had insisted Leda stop bringing his sister to visit when she was two.

But just like when he had begged to be taken with her, his mother turned deaf ears to his pleas to see the little girl he had allowed himself to love.

"I thought she was the most amazing being ever. I was in awe of her."

"What did she think of you?"

"I don't know. Her father did not want her to wonder about me, so my mother stopped bringing her on the visits when she was old enough to begin remembering them. My mother only brought my brother a handful of times as an infant for the same reason."

"Clearly, they *don't* want to forget you. Not if your sister insisted you meet her children."

"I take care of them." And even his stony heart could be moved by the little ones who called him Uncle Zee.

"You think that's the only reason they want you in their lives?"

"Why else?"

"Maybe for the same reason I'd want you in my life even if I didn't work with you." How could he be so unaware of his own true worth? she wondered.

"Would you?"

"Yes."

He didn't believe her, but he appreciated the sentiment.

"Does your brother-in-law work for you?" Piper asked.

"How did you know?"

"You said you take care of them. Does your brother work for you as well?"

"No. He's academically brilliant. He's finishing his doctoral thesis in physics right now."

"Let me guess, you've paid for his education."

"Naturally."

She threw her arms around him and kissed him, far more exuberantly than he had kissed her just a moment ago. "You are an amazing man, Zephyr Nikos."

He shook his head, but he was no idiot. He kissed her back and enjoyed the moment while it lasted, all the while wondering what in the hell was wrong with him that he had shared so much with Piper.

Maybe this friends-who-shared-sexual-intimacy wasn't such a good idea after all. He couldn't give her love and this openness was bound to give her the wrong impression.

CHAPTER THREE

HE TOOK her to the Plaka after she'd soaked in all the history she could from the Acropolis ruins. That, and the fact that visiting hours were over. He could have arranged for special dispensation but wanted to take her shopping in the ancient marketplace.

It was a tourist's paradise and Piper in tourist mode was completely charming. It also put them back on the kind of solid ground he understood. They found a shop that made authentic reproductions of ancient Greek jewelry and he bought her a necklace that would not have looked out of place on the neck of a senator's wife.

Piper had balked at the cost, but he had stood firm. If he wanted to buy her a souvenir of their time in Athens, he would.

He could afford to spoil her and she deserved to be spoiled. Especially after the way that bastard of an ex-husband had treated her. Zephyr would not pretend to give her love as Art had, but he could afford to give her gifts. And he would.

Later that night, on the terrace of an exclusive restaurant, Piper found herself enjoying the understated, elegant décor that managed to still convey the flavor of Athens. Like most Greek restaurants, the majority of the seating was outside. However, this restaurant did not have the crowded, noisy ambiance of the cafés in the Plaka.

As much as she had enjoyed the historic shopping district

closed off to automobile traffic, she appreciated the relative quiet of their current setting. Very much.

"Is this a favorite haunt of yours when you are in the country?"

"It is actually." Zephyr's brows furrowed. "How did you know?"

"I don't imagine the staff know most American businessmen by name, no matter how rich and powerful."

Looking oh so sexy in a light Armani sweater and body-hugging designer jeans, his lips quirked in his signature wry smile. "Point."

She was glad to see his smile. He'd seemed to draw back emotionally after opening up to her on the Acropolis. It was as if he regretted sharing so much about his past and needed to bring their focus firmly back to the present.

She could understand that. Zephyr was not a guy to wallow in emotion. Heck, he wasn't a guy to feel emotion a lot of the time, as far as she could see. But she'd realized something as they shopped in the Plaka—she felt plenty toward Zephyr. In fact, she was drowning in emotion for him and that emotion only had one name. Love.

"Thank you for sharing this place with me." She brushed her fingers over the gorgeous necklace he'd bought her earlier that day. "Thank you for everything."

The stones were warm from her body, but her heart was even warmer. He had insisted a kiss would make the purchase fully worthwhile. Since her kisses were free, she'd thought nothing of giving him one. Right there, in front of the proprietor, who had grinned and said something in Greek that made Zephyr chuckle.

Piper wasn't just feeling spoiled, she was feeling cherished and that was dangerous, she knew.

"It is my pleasure."

"You say that a lot." She smiled up at him.

"And it is true. You are an easy companion, Piper."

"I'm glad you think so. I don't hate your company, either."

"That is a relief. I would not like to think you'd been giving me pity sex all this time."

She couldn't help laughing at that bit of ridiculousness. "Right. Pity sex. I don't see it." Or feel it. No woman would pity this man. Desire him? Yes. Crave his kisses? Definitely. Hunger for his touch? Without doubt.

But pity? Nope. No way.

"I'm relieved to hear it."

She felt heat climb her cheeks and she shook her head. "Stop teasing me and eat your appetizer."

Surprisingly, her tycoon listened and did exactly that.

They were halfway through the appetizer when she asked something she'd been curious about for a while. "Are you going to be Neo's best man in the wedding?"

"Naturally."

"Are you looking forward to it?" she teased, sure he would grimace and give a negative.

But he smiled instead and said quite decisively, "Yes."

"You are?" She had not expected that.

"Of course. I worried that Neo had forgotten his dreams of home and family under the pressure of building our empire. When we first left Greece, that was all he'd talk about, how he was going to make something of himself and then make a proper family. He stopped talking about it maybe two years after we settled in Seattle."

"But you didn't want him to forget it entirely?" Wow, that was not an ambition she could picture Zephyr encouraging.

"No. He deserves a family, a home that is more than a place to live."

"Those are some pretty traditional sentiments for a self-admitted playboy."

"What can I say? I am a traditional guy."

That made her laugh. "I don't think so."

"What? Just because I am not married does not mean I never desire to enter the state." He didn't look like he was kidding.

But she couldn't get past the feeling he had to be pulling her leg. Zephyr was the original no-commitment guy. He'd made that clear from the very beginning of their sexual relationship. So much so, that she had assumed the first time had been a one-off.

He'd shocked her by coming back for more when they worked together on the next project, and continuing to see her in Seattle after that. But he'd been smart to give her the time to accept the change in their relationship, so she was ready to accept the new "friends with benefits" nature of it.

"You look flummoxed."

"I feel a little flummoxed," she admitted.

"I do not know why. It is the American dream, not just the Greek one, is it not? One day, I will find the right woman." He gave a self-deprecating smile that gave her butterflies. "Hell, I may even fall in love as Neo has done."

Those words felt like an arrow to her heart, because they implied he had not found that woman, therefore that woman could not be her. After finally coming to terms with her own feelings, that was a double blow to her heart. Her hand went to her necklace again, this time gaining no sense of comfort from the feel of the precious metal and stones. You had to love someone to cherish them.

So, what did that make this gift and all the other gifts he'd given her?

Unfortunately, after hearing his story earlier she feared she knew. This was Zephyr's relationship currency. Gifts and money. Not love. Not for the mother who had hurt him and not for Piper, either.

"You don't seem like the home-and-hearth type, Zephyr," she couldn't resist saying. "You live in the ultimate bachelor pad and you've dated far and wide. And deep and long besides."

Besides which he saw his relationships with his mother and siblings as monetary transactions.

"As was Neo before he met Cass. Me? I am as desirous of making my mark on the world in that way as any other man."

"You're serious?" The words were just a formality, though. There could be no doubt from his tone or his expression.

He was dead serious.

"Why wouldn't I be? Regardless of what I just said, I do not anticipate falling in love like Neo, but one day I *will* marry and procreate. Why build an empire if I have no intention of leaving it to someone?"

She didn't mention his nieces and nephew. Clearly, that wasn't what he meant. Zephyr wanted his *own* family. "But you don't think you will ever fall in love?"

"No."

That made more sense, even if it hurt enough to make it difficult to breathe.

"But…"

"But what? You loved your ex-husband, yes?"

She grimaced. "Yes."

"And did that bring you happiness?"

"No, but that doesn't mean I don't think love can happen, or make me happy when it does."

"Perhaps it will happen for you again one day."

"Maybe it will." It already had—with him—and his revelations on the Acropolis had only cemented that fact.

However, she could see it wasn't a truth he would be pleased if she shared. No matter how much that situation hurt her, she could not change it. She suddenly realized she was very likely to pay the price for another woman's actions. Actions that were decades old, but had not lost the power to hurt or mold Zephyr's actions.

But Zephyr's heart was not available to her and might never be.

His lips twisted in distaste. "Love is a messy emotion."

"No question, but it's good, too." Surely he could see that, especially now that Neo was so happily in that state?

"You don't regret loving Art?" Zephyr asked with calculated cool.

"No. I regret that he was a cheater and a liar and that his love was more words than substance."

"How is that different from regretting loving him?"

"My love was a good thing."

"That ended up causing you pain," he observed wryly.

She couldn't deny it. Loving Art had nearly destroyed her on every level. And loving Zephyr didn't look like it was going to be a much better prospect. At least she knew where she stood with him, though.

That was something, wasn't it?

Zephyr gave one of those self-deprecating smiles he used when negotiating and it made her stomach clench to have him use it on her. "Look, I'm not trying to be the Scrooge of happily ever after, but you and I both know someone loving you is no guarantee they won't betray you."

"That doesn't mean you shouldn't open yourself to love at all." She tried to keep the desperation his attitude evoked out of her voice. It wasn't his fault she'd been dumb enough to fall in love with the wrong man. Again.

"It works for me."

And she couldn't fault him for his attitude. Now that she knew his mother had abandoned him to build a better life for herself, Piper couldn't help understanding Zephyr's distrust of love.

"But Neo loves Cassandra and vice-versa. Or so you said."

"Cassandra is one woman in a million."

The pain those words caused took Piper by surprise, making her heart cramp and her whole chest cavity hurt. Because they implied she was *not* such a woman. Who was she kidding? Certainly not herself. This whole conversation put Zephyr's attitude toward her in stark relief.

He didn't love her. Not even a little. He didn't anticipate loving her, either. Not ever. Which was really not what she wanted to hear. The pain coursing through her mocked all the promises she'd made to herself after walking away from Art. She wouldn't lose her livelihood when she and Zephyr's sexual relationship ended, but she wasn't sure her heart would survive, even if her business did.

Piper was head over heels in love with a man who did not believe in the concept for himself, and moreover he looked forward to marrying one day. Only Zephyr clearly did not intend that woman to be her. Not when he so blithely told her maybe *she* would find love again one day.

He'd reneged on his own words of maybe finding love and she felt like retracting hers as well. Was the prospect of love worth the possibility of this pain again?

She remembered the last time she had felt this awful inability to breathe. It had been when she realized once and for all that Art did not love her and never had. And once again, for her pride's sake and maybe even for Zephyr's sake, she had to hide the devastation going on inside her.

"I think you might be right," she said, trying not to choke on the words.

"About what?"

"I do a pretty sucky job deciding who to fall in love with."

"I couldn't agree more."

She laughed, but felt no humor. "Thanks."

"I've no interest in talking about Art Bellingham anymore."

"Trust me, this whole conversation is leaving me cold."

His eyes narrowed, but he smiled. One of his "armor smiles" again and she wanted to be sick. "So, tell me what you want to do tomorrow."

She needed to do a better job of hiding her emotions. Starting now. "I'm a museum freak. I'd really like to see the National Archaeological Museum, the Acropolis Museum and maybe the Benaki Museum."

"That's quite a list considering you did not plan to sightsee on this trip."

"I spent the time you were in the shower pouring over the guidebook in our hotel suite."

"Ah. So, tomorrow is to be a gluttony of museums."

"If you'd rather do something else, I can find my own way to the museums."

His brow quirked at this suggestion. "There is nothing I would rather do than spend the time with you. I grew up in this city. I have seen it all."

She couldn't see him visiting the Acropolis when he was living on the streets, but she didn't say anything. It was taking all her wherewithal to tamp down emotions she had not fully acknowledged before today, feelings that would be unwelcome to their intended recipient and would cause her nothing but aching heartbreak.

"As long as we are planning our schedule, what would you like to do the day after tomorrow?"

"I thought we were flying out to the island."

"I've got a helicopter booked for late afternoon. I wanted to maximize your off time."

"You spoil me." And he did. He might not love her, but he was her friend and he cared enough to want her to be rested and happy. "This isn't supposed to be a vacation."

"Yes, in fact, these days are intended as exactly that. Surprise to you though they were."

"But the day after tomorrow was supposed to be work." She wasn't sure which would be worse, spending more time sightseeing or being stuck in close proximity with him on a private island paradise.

"So, I changed the schedule a little."

"Whatever you want."

He frowned. "I want you to enjoy yourself."

"I am in Greece, what is not to enjoy?"

"Then you will approve of a visit to Sounion and the temple ruins for Trident there?" he asked.

"Sure, that would be fine."

"Would you prefer to do something else?"

"No, not at all." It really didn't matter. She needed to come to terms with her own inner revelations and his as well. The setting for doing that hardly mattered.

"Then, Trident's Temple it is."

She nodded. "Thank you."

"Think nothing of it. I knew it had to bother you to be visiting Greece and only see a small barely developed island the whole time you were here. You've got far too curious and adventurous a nature to be content with that."

"You know me well." On the surface anyway.

He'd be shocked out of his Gucci leather loafers to discover she was in love with him. And not in a good way.

That night, their lovemaking was slow and intense. Zephyr unwrapped her like a fragile gift of immeasurable value, and she tried to take it at face value, unable to deal with the pain of dwelling on emotions she could not change. On either of their parts.

They did not join until he had reacquainted himself with every inch of her skin. But his behavior was so at odds with his implication at dinner—that she was not a special woman in his life—that as wonderful as it was, a curious sense of dissonance flavored their intimacy for Piper.

Afterward, silent tears of confused emotions tracked down her cheeks in the dark. She fell asleep wishing she'd remained blind to her feelings, and if not hers at least his.

Piper woke the next morning experiencing yet another set of contradictory feelings. As always, when she woke in Zephyr's arms, she felt safe, cared for, cherished even. Only this morning, that sense of rightness fought with her new knowledge. The absolute certainty that Zephyr did not love her, the possibility that he never would and the probability that he would eventually walk away. At least from their sexual intimacy.

She hadn't meant to fall in love, but she'd done it anyway. And looking back, she didn't see how she could have stopped herself. Zephyr was all that she could desire in both a friend and a lover.

They shared many of the same interests. That's how their friendship had started. She'd discovered he shared her love of European football. They watched the matches, rooting for opposite teams and yelling at the field officials in equal measure. Later, she'd learned he also found museums and art galleries as fascinating as she did, as well as being passionately interested in world politics just as she was.

He was more than a good friend, he was the best. He didn't just enjoy the same interests she did, he cared about her and watched over her. He'd helped her build her business by recommending her to other developers, he'd even taken care of her once when she had the flu. He'd done his utmost to provide her a miniholiday and make it special. And he'd succeeded.

He treated her like a queen, never dismissing her intelligence or condescending to her. She snuggled into his strong arms, sensual pleasure running up her spine as he brushed his leg across her thigh in his sleep. And he made love to her like the world's most accomplished gigolo. She could not forget that important little fact.

Imagining what Zephyr would think of being compared to a sexual mercenary, she had to smile. Rather than take offense, the arrogant tycoon would probably preen. His sexual prowess was a source of pride for him. If only he was as open to love as he was to making love, she would not be in such a quandary.

Unhappy with her thoughts and the conclusions she felt drawn to because of them, she lay beside him, watching his gorgeous face in repose.

A dark lock of his hair fell over his forehead, doing nothing to make him look less intimidating, even in sleep. She'd always heard even the most ruthless men looked younger and more vulnerable in their sleep, but not Zephyr. Although he was unconscious to the world, he still did not relax completely. He appeared ready to wake and jump into the crowded moments of his day at any moment.

Had he learned that type of subconscious awareness living with his mother in the seedy underworld of Athens, in the orphanage or on the streets, where he had fought for a chance at a worthwhile life? After their discussion at the Acropolis, aspects of his personality that had always intrigued her made more sense.

When she had first met Zephyr, she had believed he was a charming, rather laid-back businessman. Watching him in action at work, she had soon learned differently. While Zephyr appeared to be relaxed, even borderline indolent, he kept meticulous track of every aspect of his developments.

He had a knack for keeping even the most artistic temperament on track and on schedule. There was a certain element of ruthlessness she'd seen under the surface that never quite broke through his "let's cooperate and get this job done" businessman's façade. It only showed in a quick comment here, a directed instruction there, all delivered with that game-face smile she'd hated having directed at her during dinner the night before.

But when Zephyr Nikos spoke, everyone listened. *Everyone*. He was brilliant. He was wealthy. He was a true force to be reckoned with. Honestly? She wasn't sure what he was doing with her, a woman struggling to build an interior design firm in Seattle after her ex-husband shredded her reputation in New York.

He might be fantastic for her, but she wasn't really in his league, which only made their friendship that much more precious and their pseudo-lovers relationship that much more difficult to understand from his point of view.

Falling in love with him might have been inevitable, but getting involved sexually had not. She'd had a choice and she'd made it believing she could handle the limitations of what he was offering. She'd been mistaken. Spectacularly so.

How could she have been so stupid? She really did pick badly when it came to choosing men to love.

First, there had been Art, who had seemed like the perfect source of stability, but who had in fact destroyed her security. Then, there was Zephyr, who seemed so charming and open on the surface, but who was actually more closed off than any man she had ever known.

He only lost control in one setting that she knew of—and she knew him as well as anyone, besides maybe Neo Stamos. Zephyr lost control when they made love.

He had from the very beginning, which was why she'd been so sure their intimacy would end up a one-off. He'd looked positively shell-shocked after that first time, his usually perfectly groomed hair askew, and his big body glistening with sweat. She'd been so turned on by his overall state of dishabille; she had initiated another round of lovemaking.

He'd acquiesced soon enough, but the next morning, she'd woken alone and they hadn't mentioned the sex in any shape or form the next time they spoke. They'd been at the tail end of another job together when the sexual tension thrumming between them blew up into another bout of no-holds-barred sex.

And Piper realized now, that was when she had started really falling for the billionaire tycoon. No matter what she'd told herself at the time about commitment-free sex with a friend. She'd been allowed to see a side of Zephyr Nikos that he showed to no one else. Doing so had captured and enthralled her.

Even more so when he had admitted what she had already suspected to be true after his reaction to their first time—that he was not the same with other women. Unfortunately, Piper had allowed herself to build emotional ties on that flimsy pretext, while ominously lying to herself about what was going on in her own heart the whole time.

But was the pretext so flimsy?

Despite what his words the night before had implied, she

was special to him. They were friends and he had few enough of those, no matter how he liked to tease Neo to the contrary. Piper and Zephyr's sexual relationship had already lasted longer than any other one he'd had as well. And she already knew it drew out a side in Zephyr he did not regularly let loose.

So, in all three of those instances, she was not business as usual for the tycoon. Add that to the fact he was vacationing for the first time since she'd known him, *with her and for her benefit*, and it all added up to something special. Right?

Or was she grasping at straws as she had done with Art, not wanting to believe he was being unfaithful until confronted by irrefutable evidence?

One thing she knew, she wasn't going to lie to herself any longer. She loved Zephyr. Irrevocably and unequivocally. More than she'd ever loved Art, and she suspected more than she could ever love another person. But if Zephyr could not, or *would not*, love her, then she needed to stop this thing between them before she had no hope of coming out of it with a healable heart.

The thought of letting Zephyr go hurt so badly, an involuntary whimper slipped past her lips. He didn't wake up, but his arms tightened around her, only exacerbating the pain.

Because if she walked away from him, there would be no one there to comfort her.

And that led to her final decision. She wasn't going to waste what might well be her last days with Zephyr as even a pseudo-lover grieving a loss that had not come yet. She would squeeze every bit of joy out of their time together in Greece that she could.

Zephyr woke to the wonderfully pleasant experience of Piper giving him a massage. He was on his stomach, his arms relaxed above his head and his legs stretched out under the light covering of a sheet. She sat on his upper thighs, having an effect on him that he doubted she was going for.

Or maybe not. Piper was the most open and adventurous lover he'd ever had.

It bothered him that her moving him around had not woken him. His ability to incorporate her touch into his dreams showed how deeply he trusted her. As did the secrets of his past he'd shared with her the day before.

He'd never been tempted to tell that story to another woman, and no other lover had been allowed to sleep in his bed, much less wake him with a massage. He'd thought he'd been so clever in pursuing a sexual relationship without strings with the only woman he had ever considered a true friend. Now, he realized that kind of thing led to intimacies he did not crave.

He had to get his relationship with Piper back onto an even keel, or end at least the sexual side of it. Friendship and sex. Nothing more, and certainly nothing so deep it led to true confessions. He'd started at the Plaka, the day before, buying her gifts and clamping down on that dangerous urge to *talk*.

She'd done him a favor waking him with the massage. It would lead to sex and that was something he could handle. He didn't open his mouth to blurt out things better left unsaid when it was busy pleasuring her.

"Mmm..." He stretched under her kneading fingers, rubbing his cheek against the bottom sheet, taking in the scent of their lovemaking from the night before.

Call him earthy, but he loved that smell and often put off their morning shower so he could enjoy it.

"Like that?" Her voice was husky as if she was getting as much out of this as he was.

"Very much. Are you sure you've never gone to massage therapy school?"

"It's one of my many natural talents." Humor laced that sweetly husky voice.

"I admit, I am grateful for this particular talent."

"As you should be. So, I'm the only person in your life with this particular talent?"

"I've never asked Neo if he likes to give massages."

Soft laughter tinkled above him. "I'm having a hard time imagining that conversation."

"You're not the only one."

"There are no other women in your life who know how to relax your muscles like this? I find that hard to believe."

Was she fishing? He'd never asked her if she slept with other men, but he knew she didn't. He didn't make it a habit to sleep with more than one woman at a time, either. It led to messy complications, and he didn't do messy. Though he was rarely with a woman long enough for it to become an issue, he still followed his own rules. His longest liaisons could be measured in months, not years.

"There are no other women in my life, at least none that I would allow in my bed," he amended smartly.

After all, he had as many women working for him as men. Well, maybe not quite as many, but close. There weren't a lot of female construction workers as a percentage overall, especially in countries outside the United States.

She stilled above him. "I'm your only…"

Her words trailed off as if she didn't know how to term herself, and he could not help her. She wasn't a girlfriend per se. She was a friend with whom he shared his body and bed. But it became obvious that she was definitely fishing.

He didn't mind giving her the truth. "I haven't had sex with another woman since the second time we made love."

The first time had scared him shitless and he wasn't afraid to admit it. To himself. But then he'd realized that he was just more physically attracted to Piper than he had been to other women. Add in their friendship and the sex was mind-blowing. He'd decided to enjoy it as long as it lasted.

Because sex never did. Experience had taught him that. Just as it had taught him that while love might be transitory, and family couldn't necessarily be counted on, a true friend stuck with you through the years. He'd learned that from Neo.

Long after the sexual elements to their relationship were over, Zephyr had every expectation that he and Piper would continue to be friends.

"I've never asked for promises of fidelity." She'd gone back to massaging the pleasantly loosening muscles of his lower back.

"And I've never offered them." Because thanks to her ex, she would not believe them. "But if you are asking, I am telling you I don't have sex with other women right now."

"Because of me?"

"Because I have a rule about not having multiple sex partners at the same time," he explained.

"Serial monogamy?"

"Yes. I never make promises, you know that, but while I am having sex with one woman, I do not seek out release elsewhere."

"So, you haven't been with anyone else but me since we started sleeping together."

"Not since the second time, when I knew we would continue to have sex." He'd had a one-night stand after the first time he and Piper had gotten together, when he'd hoped to make their explosive sex a single shot. The hookup had only confirmed that mediocre sex was no substitute for what he had with her right now.

"The first time?"

"Wasn't planned and I wasn't sure we should repeat it."

"But you decided we should?" she asked softly.

"As did you."

"Yes."

"Once I realized you and I were going to have a prolonged sexual association, I stopped looking for that from anyone else." He looked down at her seriously.

"Even when we went weeks between getting together?"

"I don't break my own rules, Piper." He was no oversexed adolescent who could not go a few nights, or weeks, without.

It wasn't always easy, especially when they spoke on the phone and his body reacted with the predictability of Pavlov's dog, but a real man knew how to keep his zipper in the up position. Zephyr was nothing like his father.

Not one damn thing.

"Right." She snorted a laugh.

Pleasure from the massage tried to melt Zephyr's brain along with his muscular tension. "Yes, *right*," he affirmed with emphasis.

But he doubted she believed him, which was why he'd never made promises of fidelity during their temporary sexual relationship. Arthur Bellingham deserved so much more than the small comeuppance Zephyr had engineered for him.

CHAPTER FOUR

"WHAT about you?" he asked, deciding he wanted confirmation of what his instincts told him to be true. "Do you seek sexual release elsewhere when we cannot connect?"

"No." That was decisive enough.

"You made no promises, either," he reminded her.

"No, I didn't, but you're something special. No other man could live up."

"Nice to know." Call him arrogant, but *he* had no trouble believing *her*.

Her hands moved down to his buttocks, digging with her knuckles into his rock-hard glutes.

"Damn." He sighed. "That feels so good."

"I'm enjoying it as much as you are."

"I doubt that." Though he liked hearing it.

"Touching you is always a pleasure." The husky tenor was back in her voice.

Delicious. "Is this touching going to turn sexual?" he could not help hinting.

She scooted down his legs and her fingertips slid between them to caress the back of his balls. "Maybe."

The minx.

He was already hard, but the pressure grew more urgent as her soft touches on his scrotum continued. "You're on dangerous ground there, *pethi mou*."

"Am I?" She was no longer sitting on him, but her knees were still on either side of his.

He took that as an invitation and flipped onto his back, his breath expelling in a hard gust at the sight of her naked body above him. "You are so damn beautiful."

"You're prejudiced."

"You think so, *glyka mou*? I think you could have made millions as a model."

She smiled and shook her head. "Did you just call me sweet?"

"My sweet. You're learning Greek."

"Just that one."

Good. He wasn't sure he wanted her to know he often called her *his woman*. It might sound like he meant something more than he did, but even if their sex wasn't based in some foolish romantic commitment, he was a possessive guy. It was just the way he was made and sometimes, the words *yineka mou* slipped out. She was his, for now. Maybe he should be more circumspect. Now that she was learning what his Greek endearments meant.

His aching hard-on felt ready to explode, distracting him. He gave her his best cajoling look. "Ride me?"

Her stunning blue gaze went dark with passion as he'd known it would. "Do we have time?"

"Always." They were not on a tight schedule, even if she wanted to visit more museums in one day than he usually saw in a year.

She didn't require any more convincing, but moved into position above his bobbing erection. "You look ready to burst."

"I feel it," he choked out gutturally from between clenched teeth as her slick feminine flesh brushed against him.

She went to reach for a condom and he stayed her with a hand between her perfectly shaped breasts. "Neither of us has been with anyone else in almost two years. I've had two clean bills of health over that time."

He knew she'd tested every six months for a couple of years

after finding out Art was such a damn tomcat and wasn't surprised when she said, "Me, too."

"Then, let's go bare." She used the patch for birth control, so they didn't need to worry about making a baby neither of them were ready for.

"Yes," she breathed out, lowering her body so his hard length slid inside her moist channel.

He said that word that she always chided him for and had to fight the urge to surge upward with every ounce of self-control he had earned in his thirty-five years of life. She rewarded his restraint by dropping down and engulfing his entire length in her humid heat. Damn, massaging him *had* excited her.

She was slick with arousal and her inner muscles clenched at him in undeniable need. They moved together like animals mating and yet, not. Their supreme awareness of each other could be no less than human. Their gazes locked and never broke once during the wild ride.

The sensation of their bare skin moving together threw him into a convulsive climax, but he didn't have to worry. She was right there with him, her head thrown back, her pleasure falling from her lips in a keening cry that tingled at the base of his spine.

This moment in time was perfection.

Zephyr surprised himself by enjoying their gluttonous day of museum-viewing. While he liked museums, he wouldn't normally have planned an entire day around visiting as many as he could get to. However, Piper's enthusiasm and fascination was catching. That was the only excuse he could make for how interested he was, even in exhibits that he had seen before as a child on group trips with the other children from the home.

He'd refused to use the term *orphan* because he hadn't been one. He'd had both a mother and a father, even if neither had been willing to make him an important part of their life.

"This just goes to show that we repeat ourselves creatively. This would be considered 'modern art' by current art critics. If it hadn't been dated as being more than four thousand years old."

They were standing in front of an early Cycladic statue that did indeed look like something he might see in a gallery dedicated to modern artists. "It seems odd the statues would be so lacking in intricate detail when the pottery has such complicated patterns on it."

"I'm sure someone hundreds of years from now will find it strange that our houses are built like cookie-cutter images of one another, but we are so particular about what goes inside them."

He turned to her, laying a hand on her waist and not questioning the urge to do so. "You think so?"

"That, or they'll postulate we only ate on plastic because plastic dishes are the only ones that survive that long." Her azure eyes glittered with humor.

"We had stoneware in the home and you're right. It didn't last long."

"My mom bought those unbreakable dishes, but nothing could prevent us kids losing them. The small square bowls made too good a shovel in a pinch."

"I can just imagine you as a small child."

"I was a terror."

"But shy with strangers," he guessed.

"Yep. Teachers never believed my mom about me until I'd organized my first boycott of the cafeteria's no-name catsup. That stuff was nasty. Or had a petition going to reinstate outdoor school when budget cuts threatened that right of passage. It didn't usually happen until my second year in school anyway." She sounded altogether proud of herself.

"I see, you lulled the authority figures around you into complacency and then you sprang."

"That's about it."

He laughed. "I have no problem seeing that."

"Neither did my mother. School administrators were not so insightful." Her eyes twinkled mischeviously. "Until after the fact."

"I shudder to think what your children will be like." Her daughters would be stubborn, her sons protective and both would be intelligent.

She gave him a strange look followed by a negligent shrug that wasn't. Negligent. At least it didn't seem so to him, but he didn't ask her about it because she was already headed to the next display.

She stopped in front of a male kouros statue. "Nice to see Greek men haven't changed in all these millennia."

"I think I'm flattered." The statue had seriously developed abs and thighs that could crack an opponent's back in a wrestling match, ancient or modern. However, the genitals were nothing to write home about. "I hope you are not comparing certain aspects of my anatomy to his understated representation."

She gave him a mocking little smile that made him want to do something that would turn that smile into a grin. "I read somewhere that the aspect of a statue's form was deliberately underrepresented so the focus could be on the aesthetic rather than the sexual."

"That, or the only men willing to be used as artists' models had teeny weenies."

Piper burst out laughing as he'd expected her to, drawing the attention of those around them. While most of it was indulgent, one serious-looking elderly man glared. And a young woman sent daggers Piper's way, but he didn't know if that was for her laughter or the fact she was so clearly with him.

The woman had given him an encouraging once-over when he and Piper had first arrived at the National Museum, but he had ignored her.

Once again, he turned his back on her and smiled down at

his beautiful companion. "That is not something you have to worry about in my bed, no?"

"You, Zephyr Nikos, are a braggart. And a bad, bad man." The laughter still laced her voice and he wanted to kiss its flavor from her lips, but he refrained.

Stealing a kiss at the Acropolis, he could get away with. But he'd get more than one glare at such a public display of affection in the National Museum. Greece was not America, or even England for that matter, when it came to love affairs being conducted in public. It was generally a far more conservative country.

That had never bothered him before, but he wanted to kiss his *yineka*. However, he refused to embarrass her.

He would make up for it and then some when they returned to their room later.

The next morning, Piper tried to gather her thoughts as hot water pelted down over her during her solitary shower. The day before, they'd both admitted to fidelity and agreed to stop using condoms. She'd wanted the illusion of deeper intimacy for what she was coming to accept would have to be their last tryst and had readily agreed.

Only later had she begun to wonder if those were the actions of a man who would never love her? At first, she'd discounted his assertion he hadn't been with another woman since the second time they'd made love, but as the day wore on she'd asked herself why. And she hadn't liked the answer. She would not let Art have that much control of her present, regardless of how his betrayal had hurt.

But even believing in Zephyr's faithfulness, what did that mean? Was he capable of loving her? So many things pointed to a yes answer, even as his self-admissions denied the possibility.

Their time at the museums had been almost magical, full of laughter and subtle marks of affection between them. The little touches had added up and by the time they returned to their hotel to get ready for dinner, Zephyr had overcome her with a storm of desire. They'd missed their reservations and had a local café deliver dinner to their room.

Zephyr had been right when asked. For enough money, any restaurant *would* deliver food to a hungry couple. Even a couple who had refused to leave their hotel room while sating a different hunger than that of the stomach.

How could she end their sexual liaison without ending their friendship? Did she have enough strength of will to be his friend without falling back into his bed? And even if she did, would maintaining their friendship be the best thing for her emotional well-being? How was she going to get over him if she continued to see him?

But how could she stop seeing him without totally shattering what was left of her heart?

This morning had only added to her already roiling thoughts and emotions. They'd once again made love and it had been so profound, she'd been a breath away from blurting out her love for him.

She'd needed some time to get her emotions back under control and insisted Zephyr take one of his military-length showers. Alone. He often bragged about the quick grooming habits he'd learned on the ship he'd worked when leaving Greece and she wasn't above playing to that pride. She'd used the excuse that they needed to get going if they were going to make it to the seaside village that was home to Trident's temple ruins in time to actually see them.

Clearly indulging her, he'd agreed. And she'd gotten a few precious and necessary minutes to herself, both while he showered and now while she did.

The only problem was, her emotions were just as raw now as they had been while she and Zephyr made love. She ached with the need to tell him of her feelings, but was afraid that they would be an unwelcome burden. And she couldn't squash the hope that maybe if he just realized it was safe to love her, that she wouldn't betray him as others had in the past, he might let his heart out of its self-imposed prison.

Carefully, she swiped soapy hands over her birth control patch. Or rather where the patch was supposed to be.

No. No, no, no, no.

It was there. It had to be. She craned her neck over her shoulder to look down at her right hip, but saw nothing except smooth skin. She looked over the other side, praying she'd forgotten that she'd used a different hip this time. But no flesh-colored square resided there, either.

Where was it? She wasn't due to replace the weekly dose of birth control until the day after tomorrow and she wasn't scheduled to be without until a full week after that.

Oh, God. The prayer left her lips in desperation as she tried to remember the last time she'd checked the patch.

Having it there had become such second nature that she barely even noticed it anymore. She was always careful in the shower, never soaping the area directly. She'd lost one the first month she was using them, but she'd soon learned how to avoid corrupting the adhesive that held the hormone dispenser in place.

She forced her mind to bring up and scour images from the preceding days, but the last clear impression she had of her patch was during her shower in a Midwest hotel room the morning before catching her flight to Greece. No, she couldn't have lost it her first day in Athens.

It wouldn't have just fallen off. But the way she and Zephyr had touched that first time making love after their weeks-long separation had been rough, urgent and not at all careful of clothing, much less an adhesive square attached to her body. But if she'd lost it *then*, they had made love a number of times since without *any* form of protection.

Her breath choked in her throat at the very real possibility of what that could mean. No. She refused to believe God would be that cruel.

She felt like hyperventilating as she asked herself what to do now. How was she supposed to walk away from Zephyr if she was pregnant with his child? Would he believe that she had not done it on purpose? Losing the condoms had been his idea, but would he remember that when faced with the unexpected results?

She didn't want to tell him pregnancy was even a possibility. Doing so would only add stress between them when there was as much a chance she wasn't now carrying new life as that she was. Maybe even more so, considering how long she'd been on the patch.

However, if she didn't tell him, how would she explain the need to return to using condoms? Also, if she didn't, how would she ever be able to explain that level of dishonesty to herself? A lie of omission was still a lie, wasn't it?

She wanted Zephyr to believe it was safe to love her, that he could trust her with his deepest emotions and needs. How could she build that trust with him if she hid something this important from him? Wasn't it better to be honest and up-front about what was going on, rather than pretending everything was fine when it very much was not?

Hadn't Art done that to her? And before him, her parents? Who often waited until the last possible moment to warn her about the next move? They'd always justified this behavior by saying they had enough to deal with without her and her brother and sister having a month-long temper tantrum about leaving their friends behind. They gave just enough time for their children to say goodbye to their closest friends before uprooting them for her father's newest military assignment.

Certainty and something like a fatalistic dread settled inside her. Though maybe for the first time, she began to understand her parents' thinking; she wasn't about to play that kind of game with Zephyr.

She quickly finished her shower, dressed and pulled her hair into an easy ponytail, rather than styling it. She bypassed makeup and exited the en suite bathroom a good ten minutes ahead of schedule.

Zephyr was just closing the door behind their room-service delivery. He turned to her with a sexy smile. "Breakfast is served."

"Perfect." Should she tell him now, or wait until later?

"You look a little shaken," he said with a frown of concern. "Did you see a spider in the shower, or something?"

"Please. I'm not even a little arachnophobic." But *shaken* described nicely how she felt.

"That's good to know."

"Yes, well, um…"

He stopped uncovering dishes and stared at her, his concern obviously amping up a notch. "You're starting to worry me."

"That might be wise. To be worried, I mean. Though, honestly, they say it takes positively months to get pregnant after you stop using birth control usually." Oh, man, she was making a cake of this, a very messy one. "There's no reason to assume tragic consequences now."

"What are you talking about?" He stopped, going absolutely still. "Did you say *pregnant*? You're on the birth control patch."

"Yes, I would be, if it was actually there, I mean. If I had it on."

"Of course it's on. You *never* forget it." He was starting to look a little shaken himself.

"I didn't forget it this time, but it's not there."

"Not there?" Six feet three inches of solid muscle went boneless and he dropped to sit on the chair behind him. Hard. "Your…my…you…I…"

"You sound as coherent as I felt when I first realized it was gone." Truth was, she wasn't feeling that much better right now.

He stared off into space for several seconds and then shook his head. "I don't remember seeing it." He leaned on the table with his elbows, his head in his hands. "I don't remember seeing it, but I wasn't looking, either."

"Since that first time day before yesterday?"

"I wouldn't have noticed anything then. But no, not since." He looked at her with an expression she'd never seen on the big tycoon's face. Fear coupled with guilt. Severe guilt. "*I never even noticed.* Can you forgive me?"

Okay, that was not expected. She'd anticipated anger, blame, even horror, but not an obviously genuine guilt-fueled apology.

She crossed the room and dropped to her knees in front of him, putting her hands on his thighs. "It's not your fault. I didn't notice it was gone, either. We were, um…busy, in the shower yesterday and I'm just so used to it being there, I never even thought to check."

"But you checked today."'

"More like I noticed when I went to wash that area more carefully."

"I cannot believe I did not pay closer attention. And then I asked you to stop using condoms." His voice dripped with agonized culpability.

Okay, so she definitely did not have to worry about him blaming her, but she didn't want him feeling guilty, or like an idiot. Even if she did. "We're both adults. We *both* didn't realize. The patch was my responsibility."

"That is like saying that remembering to use a condom was my purview alone and I know you did not see it that way."

"It's not the same thing."

"Of course it is. Besides, sharing the blame does no good and makes no difference to the child we may have created."

"There's no reason to assume I'm pregnant." That was one leap of faith she did not want to make right now. "I told you, many women take months to get pregnant after they stop using the patch."

"You also called possible pregnancy a tragedy." He didn't look very happy about that. At all. "You would not consider termination?"

"What? No, definitely not. That would never be an option for me."

He looked relieved, but no happier. "Still, you consider the possible consequences *tragic*."

"I didn't mean that. Not really. I'm frightened of what this would mean for me, for us, if I were pregnant," she admitted, emotion choking her.

"I am neither of my parents. You understand?" He said something in Greek she had no hope of understanding, then gave her a look she wouldn't want to see across a boardroom or in a dark alley for that matter. *"I will not abandon my child."*

That was one thing she would never have worried about, even if he hadn't said it. Then a way of getting him off this line of enquiry came to her. "I would never expect you to, but could we please stop talking like pregnancy is a foregone conclusion?"

"And you?" he asked, clearly ignoring her plea.

She tried not to be offended he had even asked. In his mind, he had good reason for doing so. Irrefutable experience. But still, the question hurt. "I'm not your mother. I don't have to give my child up in order to leave a soul-destroying life behind."

"How long since your last period?"

"What, are you an expert on menstrual cycles?" she challenged.

"No."

"I'm not, either." She blew out a frustrated breath. "But I do know somewhere in the middle of your cycle is the most likely time for pregnancy to occur."

"And?"

She winced, wishing she could say something else. "I'm pretty much smack-dab there right now."

"Even so, as you say, many women do not fall pregnant quickly after being on birth control for a prolonged period. How long have you been on the patch?"

"I started taking it with Art and never went off, even though

I was celibate until that first time with you. I liked the way it balanced my monthly hormone cycle."

"That is a significant amount of time."

"Yes."

"So, the chances you are pregnant are diminished?"

"So I've been led to believe." She looked at him worriedly. "But diminished is not nonexistent."

"No."

"Are you very angry?"

"Angry? No. Well, maybe a smidge with myself. I feel like an idiot for not keeping more attentive track, especially when we stopped using condoms."

"But you are not angry at the prospect of carrying my child?"

"No." Oh, heck. She might as well go for broke. She was feeling reckless and tired of hiding feelings that were so strong they left little room for anything else. "I can't imagine anyone I would rather have as the father of my child."

Shock froze his features for several long seconds. "You do not mean that."

"I don't lie."

"No, you don't. No more than I."

That was something she still had to work on believing, but she wasn't going to tell him that. Because *Zephyr* had never done anything to earn her mistrust.

"I guess a billionaire real-estate tycoon would make an admirable choice as father for your child," he said in his second full-scale departure from tact.

She *just* managed to stop herself clouting him. "This is more of that, *they want me in their life for what I can buy for them garbage*, isn't it? I don't look at you as a meal ticket, Zee."

And he'd better get that through his head right now, or they were going to have more problems between them than an unanticipated possible pregnancy.

He jolted. "You have never called me that before."

Sometimes, he focused on the least important things.

"I've heard Neo do so." But he was right. For some reason, believing she might be pregnant with Zephyr's child made her feel more comfortable with the casual intimacy.

"Yes."

"If you don't like it, I won't do it again," she offered.

"I do not mind."

"Fine. Um, we need to make a plan."

"You need to eat breakfast." Again with the non sequitur, but maybe that was okay. For now.

She needed some time to think if nothing else. "So do you."

"Then let us eat." And incredibly, they managed to do that without any further discussion of possible consequences of the lack of birth control.

They were halfway to Sounion before he mentioned the morning's disturbing revelations again.

"So, a plan," he said as they drove down the coastal highway.

"We should, um, probably go back to using condoms until we know if I'm pregnant." She had realized during her personal ruminations that was as far as she wanted to go with contingency arrangements at present. Her mind simply refused to wrap around the prospect of a child. Their baby. Growing inside her body.

Yesterday, she'd been thinking she had to tell him goodbye once and for all and now she was faced with the prospect of never being able to do so, even if they stopped making love.

"Yes."

"I don't want to put another patch on, just in case, even though it is not likely, but we should definitely use condoms." She shook her head at herself. She didn't want to risk hurting a baby that probably didn't even exist.

"You've mentioned that point several times."

"Have I?"

"Yes."

"I'm sorry," she apologized distractedly.

"Are you that disturbed by the idea of being pregnant with my child?"

"We've already covered this ground."

"Then by the prospect of being pregnant at all?" He slid a sidelong glance at her before looking back at the road.

"I'm building a business. Having a baby will change a lot of things, including how much time I can spend on work." It was the only concern she was willing to voice right this second. She'd been on an emotional thrill ride since discovering the loss of her patch. Fear competed with hope and illicit joy at the prospect in equal measure.

"And this worries you?"

"A little," she admitted. "I'm willing to rearrange my priorities though. Any child of mine will not pay for the choices of its parents."

"As you felt you paid for yours." He saw immediately her determination to give her child everything she felt she'd missed out on.

"To an extent, but even more so, as you paid for yours."

"I cannot disagree there." He smiled grimly.

"I'm not asking you to."

"That is good."

"I hate this," she cried out on an explosive breath.

"What?"

"How stilted we are with each other. We were closer than we'd ever been and now this."

"We are friends," he said, frowning. "You being pregnant with my child will not change that."

"We are more than friends, Zee. At least give me that much." So, maybe she did want to deal with something besides the condom issue.

"What do you mean?"

"Don't play dumb. It's unbecoming, not to mention lacking in credibility."

"I am not playing at anything." He sounded offended, his

voice sliding into that zone she'd come to recognize as his anger. The chill-factor was definitely in evidence.

"I'm sorry." She stared out the window, blinking back tears she couldn't even name the exact reason for. "I don't mean to patronize you."

"Thank you."

"Somewhere along the way, we stopped being merely friends with benefits. I mean, for me anyway."

"You prefer the term *lovers*?" he asked.

"That would be a start." Not everything she wanted, but a definite beginning.

"But lovers are never permanent in my life." Worry crept back into his voice, letting her know this was a genuine concern on his part.

"Make me the exception."

"I do not know if I can do that." He sighed. "Though if you are pregnant, neither of us will have a choice."

The next-to-last thing she wanted was to be in his life by default. The last thing was to bc out of his life completely, which said what about her plans to walk away from what they had before she got even more hurt? "I don't want it to be that way."

"What we want is not always what we get."

She thought of the many times she'd had to move away from friends and activities that meant something to her. Then she remembered how helpless she had felt in the face of her ex-husband's unrepentant and repeated infidelity. "That's only too true."

He took a deep breath and let it out with a big smile somewhere between appearing genuine and his game face. "So, let us forget for today that you might be pregnant with my child."

"And on the verge of losing my dreams? Okay, I can do that."

His jaw went taut, but he let her flippancy go. "Good. We will go to Sounion and play tourists and then catch the helicopter there as planned and fly to the island early this evening."

"Will we make love tonight?"

"Did you want to make an appointment?" he teased.

"I just want to know that you haven't already decided you are bored with me."

"How can you even suggest that?"

"You're the one who said…you know what, never mind. Let's just focus on the present. Not the past. Not the future and definitely not the possibility we've started on that dynasty of yours earlier than expected." Not to mention with a woman he hadn't considered in the running for mother of his children a mere forty-eight hours ago.

"Right."

And somehow, they managed it. Though she had to give most of the credit to Zephyr. Every time she started to worry, he seemed to know…and knew exactly how to stop it.

CHAPTER FIVE

FROM the air, the view of Zephyr and Neo's newest acquisition was incredible. Piper had no problem imagining this small Greek island as an oasis for the resort's guests. Unlike many of the rocky islands that dotted the sea off the coastline of mainland Greece, this landscape was covered with lush grasses and green trees. There was a large olive grove and what looked like a citrus orchard.

They flew over the fishing village, traditional white houses with red roofs showing where the year-round residents lived. The boats that bobbed in the water, moored to the long dock, looked picturesque in their simplicity. No fancy trawlers here.

A tan circle painted with white directional lines about two hundred yards from a large villa set atop a cliff overlooking the sea had to be their landing destination. Piper shouldn't have been surprised that a family who at one time had the wherewithal to own an island had installed a helipad on it. Only, she was. She would have expected a landing strip for small planes and said as much to Zephyr on the walk to the villa.

A young man who introduced himself as the housekeeper's grandson insisted on carrying their luggage in a yard cart.

"The patriarch preferred travel by sea, but his children insisted on faster transportation to the mainland," Zephyr replied in response to her comment. "As to why it was a helicopter over a jet, I could not say. I think he balked at the excavation necessary for a flat runway long enough to service a jet."

"We'll be doing that excavation, won't we? I mean guests are going to want to be able to fly in."

The young man leading the way with his cart looked back at her, his expression troubled.

Zephyr did not seem to notice, but he shook his head in negation. "The focus of the spa resort is going to be total relaxation. It will start with a luxury yacht ride from the mainland."

"I bet you'll stick with helicopters." But she would have enjoyed a decadent ride on a yacht.

Zephyr shrugged. "I am not a prospective guest."

"Maybe you should be."

"Perhaps you should as well. We can attend the grand opening week together," he said as he reached out to open the front door, only to have it swing inward before he touched it.

An elderly Greek woman welcomed them inside before shooting rapid-fire instructions at her grandson, who took his cart around to the side of the villa.

"The young, they forget the proprieties," she said in perfect English, if accented charmingly. She shook her head. "Maybe that one *should* be a fisherman."

"There will be many jobs for those willing to work both building the resort and working there after it is completed."

"You will give first chance to locals?" the old woman asked with obvious hope.

"Yes," Zephyr said decisively. "We do not want the year-round residents to feel disconnected to the resort. Their participation in the venture is essential."

Her lined visage wreathed with a smile, the housekeeper led them into an oversized sitting room with a truly impressive view. The wall facing the sea had such large windows it felt like it was made of glass.

"Would you like refreshments?" she asked.

"Your former employer rhapsodized about the fresh lemonade made from local fruit."

Appearing pleased by the request, the housekeeper nodded. "I will send a girl with a tray."

"Thank you. Has Mr. Tilieu been told of our arrival?" Zephyr asked.

"He has, though how anyone could miss the sound of a landing helicopter, I do not know."

Piper stifled a grin, while Zephyr obviously bit back a smile.

"I take it you prefer to travel by boat?" Piper asked.

"I prefer not to travel at all, but how others can stand to ride in those noisy things is a mystery to me." The gray-haired woman waved her hands in dismissal.

"Sometimes needs must," Zephyr said wryly.

"As you say, Kyrie Nikos." Then she left.

He turned to Piper. "Beautiful, isn't it?"

"Absolutely gorgeous." She didn't even try to resist the lure of huge picture windows. "I could spend hours just looking out these windows."

He came to stand beside her, close but not touching. "It is mesmerizing. The sunset will be spectacular."

"Will we be able to watch it?"

"If that is your desire."

"You've been very indulgent with me this trip." Though since sharing his past with her, he had maintained a distance even his charm could not hide. Their discovery this morning had not altered that distance, despite other small changes in his behavior.

"You deserve a little spoiling."

"I won't complain about you thinking so."

"Good." He shifted beside her and she could feel his regard transferring to her from the view. "Speaking of being spoiled, do you want to attend the opening week with me?"

"I have no doubt you'll be here for the grand opening, but I sincerely doubt it will be for the rest and relaxation the resort is going to offer."

"I will make sure you are still pampered," he assured her.

"What about you?"

"What about me?" he asked, not following.

"Don't you think you could do with a bit of pampering?"

"I will avail myself of the spa services."

"To check their quality standard, I bet."

"So?"

"So, you're something of a workaholic," she clarified.

"As are you."

"I love my business." But she wasn't really a workaholic. Once her business was established, she had every intention of cutting back her hours to make room for other things. "I never intended it to be everything in my life."

"Then why do you consider the prospect of parenting the dissolution of your dreams?"

Shocked at his interpretation of her earlier words, she jerked in startlement. "I didn't mean my business."

He didn't look like he believed her. "What did you mean, then?"

"It's not something I want to discuss right now." Really. Truly. It would do neither of them any good to hash over her old dream of building a life with a man who loved her, and the more recently acknowledged dream of having Zephyr be that loving man.

He opened his mouth to say something, but before he got a chance, a masculine voice from behind them said, "You've arrived. Finally."

They both turned to face an attractive black man.

Zephyr stepped forward with his hand out. "Ah, Jean-René. Good to see you."

He turned back to Piper. "*Pethi mou*, this is our architect, Jean-René Tilieu. Jean-René, this is Piper Madison, our designer."

Jean-René's smile was white-white and full of charm as he bent over Piper's extended hand, rather than shaking it. "An exceptional pleasure, mademoiselle."

"*Merci*. I'm really looking forward to working with you. I find your work both inspiring and impressive."

"Ah, you know the way to a man's heart is flattery, *non*?"

Zephyr stepped forward and put his arm around Piper's waist. "Piper does not flatter, she always speaks the truth."

Jean-René gave them a speculative look and then met her eyes, his expression serious. "Then I am doubly honored by your praise, mademoiselle."

"Piper, please."

"That is an interesting name, *n'est-ce pas*?"

"I was named for one of my father's mentors in the army," she informed him.

Zephyr looked down at her. "You never told me that."

"It's a bit embarrassing, to be named after a grizzled army master sergeant who chewed tobacco and shot pistols with equal enthusiasm."

"Piper is a feminine name, though, *non*? This master sergeant who chewed tobacco is a woman?" Jean-René asked.

Piper laughed. "No, *Pipes* is his nickname and I never asked how he got it."

"That's probably best," Zephyr said, humor lacing his tone.

She smiled up at him. "That's what I thought."

"Two great minds." Jean-René flashed that brilliant smile again. "Clearly this project is in sympathetic hands."

"Without a doubt. I've studied your work in depth and I've worked on enough developments with Zephyr to know that our approaches are going to dovetail nicely." Her only concern, and it was not strong, was how the Greek contractor would be to work with as he was a complete unknown to her.

"*Très bien*. Do you wish to discuss initial thoughts over dinner, or wait until tomorrow?" he asked Zephyr.

Zephyr turned his head so his and Piper's gazes met. "What do you think?"

Why was he asking her? Maybe this was about watching the sunset. "Is the dining room on this side of the house?"

"No, but we can eat in here," Zephyr replied.

"*Mais oui*, the view of the setting sun is *magnifique*. I saw the most glorious rays yesterday evening when I arrived."

"Then it is settled." She stepped away from both men and headed toward the stairs. "I'm happy to jump right in, as I'm sure you are both eager to do. Which room is mine?"

"I had the housekeeper put us in the master suite." This time Zephyr did not ask her opinion and his expression dared her to disagree.

Like she was going to argue. She *enjoyed* sleeping with him. "I'll see you upstairs, then."

She went in search of the master suite, assuming it wouldn't be difficult to find and she was right. The fact that she found a maid inside unpacking their cases was almost as big a clue as the giant four-poster bed that would have looked silly anywhere *but* a master bedroom.

It was covered with a cotton spread in eggshell-white, decorated with intricate stitching a single shade darker. Gauze curtains draped the bed, the large picture window and the French doors leading out onto the second-story balcony that wrapped around the house. The armoire, dresser and matching bedside tables were heavy wooden pieces, stained dark. It was easy to tell that this had been a man's room, but she still liked it. A lot.

Taking in the gorgeous view, she skimmed off the royal-blue shortwaisted jacket she'd donned over a paler blue sheath dress that morning. She tossed it over the back of one of the twin oversized armchairs. They faced a large stone fireplace that was laid for a fire.

Interesting. If the weather leant itself toward doing so, she would want to talk to Jean-René about incorporating fire-places in the main areas of the resort at least.

"Pardon me, but do you speak English?" she asked the maid, who was now sliding their cases under the huge bed and out of the way.

"Yes."

"Great, because my Greek is nonexistent."

The young woman smiled. "You are American, yes?"

"Yes. I took Spanish in school." It was the only language she knew she would find at any high school, no matter where her father had been stationed, so she could take it for the full four years. "Will it get cold enough in the evenings to light the fire?"

"Some, yes. Not so cold, but the fire, it is cozy."

"I see." Piper smiled. "Thank you."

"You are welcome."

"When did Mr. Nikos give instructions for us to share a room?" She felt ridiculous asking, but *needed* the answer for some reason.

The maid gave her an odd look, but didn't hesitate to answer. "I do not know. On Monday, the housekeeper, she tell me to ready the room for Kyrie Nikos and his guest."

So, he'd planned to share a room all along. This was not altogether shocking. They did not take pains to hide their sexual relationship, but he was not usually so blatant in a work setting. Before his revelations over dinner in Athens, she would have taken this as a good sign for the future of their relationship.

Now, it just added to her confusion about the man she loved.

Prior to this morning, he had not considered her in the role of mother to his children. He had also made it clear he did not anticipate ever entering into a permanent relationship with her. All bets were off if she was pregnant, though. That was something she had no doubts about.

If she was carrying his baby, he would insist on marriage. His assertion he was nothing like his parents hadn't been necessary for her to realize Zephyr Nikos would insist on being a major player in his child's life.

She just wasn't sure what *she* wanted to do about that.

Zephyr found Piper sitting on a cushioned wrought-iron lounger on the terrace outside their bedroom. "Tired, *pethi mou*?"

"What?" She looked up at him, eyes the same color as the sea they'd been gazing at vague. "No. I was just thinking, trying to work things out and getting more confused in the process."

"Would you like a sounding board?"

"Not this time."

He frowned; that was not the answer he wanted, he realized. "You like the house?"

"You know I do. But *house*? I don't think so. *Mansion* more like. How many bedrooms does this place have anyway?"

"Twelve, four of them large suites like this one."

"Then how can you tell this is the master?" she challenged him.

"How did you tell?"

"The maid was unpacking our cases."

"Really, that was it?" One eyebrow raised knowingly.

"You know it wasn't."

He nodded. "The bed."

"It couldn't be in any room but the master."

"Exactly." He moved to stand in front of her and put a hand out, which she automatically took. "I'm glad we aren't tearing it down." Sometimes, they had no choice but to destroy in order to build something new. Thankfully, that was not necessary this time.

"Is it going to be part of the resort?" Piper asked, not looking all that pleased at the prospect.

He tugged her to stand, then took her place in the chair and pulled her into his lap. "At first, I thought it would, but every time I come, I grow more attached to the place. Neo likes it as well. I think we may keep it for our personal use, but he'll have to find his own master-suite bed, I'm keeping this one."

"Really?"

"Why so surprised? We agreed the bed is perfect."

"That's not what I meant." She squirmed until she was comfortable against him, having a predictable effect on the blood-flow south of his waist. "I don't see either of you relaxing enough to get any use out of it."

"He's getting married. They will have children. This is a good place to bring them. The resort will only make it better. Cass likes to travel, but prefers private residence to hotels."

"That makes sense, considering."

"Yes." He tugged her to relax further against his chest. "And you, can you imagine staying here on the occasional holiday?"

She sighed, her head coming to rest against his shoulder. "Too easily. If I owned a property like this, I wouldn't relegate it to vacation home, though. I couldn't resist living here." The buried longing in her voice surprised him. "I don't know how the previous owners did."

"How would you run your business from here?"

"I thought daydreams didn't have to be practical."

"Indulge me." He wrapped his arms around her waist, enjoying this moment of relaxed closeness.

She was good for him, which was just the dangerous kind of thinking he needed to avoid before he started spilling secrets again. This was about learning what was going on in her complicated brain, not revealing more of his own thoughts. And he would remember that.

"Living here would be the ultimate indulgence, but in answer to your all too prosaic question, with high-speed Internet, a reliable telephone service and a color fax machine, I could run my business from anywhere."

"It would require a lot of travel." Especially if she continued to work full-time.

"I travel a lot now."

Didn't he know it? He understood her desire to live here, though. "I forget how much I enjoy the sunshine sometimes, but a few days in Greece and I'm spoiled to blue skies again."

"We can't claim our fair share of those in Seattle." She gave a rueful sigh.

He chuckled. "This is true. The first year Neo and I lived there, we thought the rain would never end."

"Seattle gets all four seasons."

"And all of them have rain."

"True," she said grudgingly. "But it's better than New York blizzards, trust me."

"Here, though, the weather is perfect." He and Neo had not left Greece because they wanted to get away from the sunshine.

"If you are partial to a warm climate."

"Which I am."

"Me, too." She sighed. "Maybe I should have relocated to Southern California, when I left New York."

"No, we would not have met."

"You might have been better off."

What? He did not think so. He maneuvered her so their gazes met, and saw that her azure eyes were troubled. He shook his head. "Are you trying to imply that our friendship has been a detriment to me in some way?"

"Well, it's not as if I'm the woman you envisioned as the mother of your future children." Her voice echoed with pain he would not have expected.

"I had not given any thought to who that might be." No serious contemplation anyway. He had thought of her in that role, before they started having sex. He admired her character and thought she would make an ideal mother and wife, except for that romantic streak even her rotten marriage had not cured her of.

"But you would not have considered me."

"You are right." At least that had been his final determination.

She turned her head away completely, but not before he saw sadness making her blue eyes shimmer dangerously.

Oh, no. Tears were not going to happen. He gently, but inexorably, tugged her face back around. "Not because I do not think you would be eminently suitable, but because I knew you would never consider a…what did you call my nebulous marriage plans? *A business merger.*"

"Why would it have to be a business transaction between the two of us?" she asked plaintively.

"How could it be anything else?"

"Love."

"Love?" Hadn't they already discussed this? "Whatever propensity to love I may have had once is gone. Even if it were not, love does not always last. Blood ties do not count for much, either."

"So, there is nothing left but business?"

"True friendship can endure," he admitted.

"Like your friendship with Neo."

"Yes."

"He's the only person in your life who has never let you down, isn't he?"

"On a personal level? Yes." He brushed her lips with his thumb. "Well, not actually. You have never let me down, either."

"Until this morning." Her lower lip trembled and she bit it.

"You did not let me down."

"How can you say that?" she asked.

"It is the truth. We are done assigning blame, remember?"

"I don't think I got the memo." She gave a pale version of her usual teasing smile, but at least she was no longer on the verge of tears.

He hoped. "We agreed this morning."

"That was not agreement, that was you saying it did no good."

"I am right."

"You have what can be an annoying tendency to think you are." But she nuzzled his neck and he was not too worried.

"What can I say? I usually am."

She pulled back and gave him a gloating glare. "Ah, so you admit to at least some small level of infallibility."

"Naturally."

"You're so darn arrogant." She shook her head in bemusement. "Why do I find that charming again?"

"You tell me."

"I plead the Fifth."

"We are in Greece," Zephyr pointed out, "not the U.S. The Fifth Amendment does not apply here."

"I bet the Greek constitution has some similar guarantee against having to testify against themselves for their citizens."

"We are getting off topic here."

"You're right." Piper gathered her thoughts. "Why, if you trust friendship so much, do you think a marriage based on it would fail?"

"I did not say I believed a marriage between us would fail utterly, but it *would* fail to make you happy." And ultimately, that had decided him against the prospect.

"Why? Would you plan to sleep around after?"

"No. I could give you fidelity." Of that, he had no doubts. "However, I could not give you something you've made clear is of equal importance to you." Long before their discussion of love at dinner the other night, he had known she was still waiting for her fairy-tale ending complete with love ever after and Prince Charming.

He was a former street rat, no prince, and love was not, and never would be, on his agenda.

"You're talking about love again, aren't you?"

"Yes. Can you honestly say you would have considered a marriage proposal without it?"

She bit her lip and looked away, shaking her head once in negation.

"As I thought."

"So, where does that leave us?"

"I do not know." If she was pregnant with his child, he would try to convince her to accept his proposal, regardless of her finer feelings.

He knew his inner ruthlessness would show itself and he could not even be sorry about that. If she carried his baby, neither of their dreams took precedence. They would do what was best for their child.

He would never allow a child of his to be anything but absolutely certain of its place in his life. Unlike both his mother and father, Zephyr Nikos would consider his role as parent the most important one he would ever hold.

He did not know how to be a father, but he and Neo had self-educated themselves in business and that had been an eminently successful endeavor. With the same work and dedication, he could learn how to be a dad as well. Unlike when he was a teenager, he did not have to rely on used books, and firsthand experience at ground level.

He could afford to consult the most eminent minds in the field of child development, read the best books on the subject and do whatever else was necessary to be the best parent possible.

Zephyr had never done things by halves and becoming a parent would be no exception.

"I don't want to take an over-the-counter pregnancy test," Piper said after several quiet moments of her head resting on his shoulder again.

"So, we will wait until we return to Seattle and make an appointment with your doctor. We are only scheduled to be here three days."

"They'll feel like an eternity."

He could not disagree.

The contractor arrived the next morning and between the four of them, they kept extremely busy laying the groundwork for preliminary plans to be drawn up. Jean-René flirted shamelessly with Piper, making her smile when that worried expression slid into her eyes.

Zephyr did not worry about the other man, knowing he adored his French wife and would never consider betraying her. Besides, Zephyr had made it patently clear that he and Piper were together.

On their last night, they climbed the stairs after a lively postdinner discussion over whether or not to place the main resort near the current villa, or nearer the accessible beach on the northern shore of the island. Piper was in favor of the beach, but the contractor liked the idea of taking advantage of already existing power and water access.

Jean-René had played devil's advocate, arguing both for and against each of the locations.

Zephyr had made the final decision, going with the beach-front scenario. Guests would appreciate the easy access to the ocean and while the view might not be quite as majestic, it was still magnificent. Besides, it would give him and Neo and their future families privacy when they were on the island.

"You know he reminds me a little of Art, only different," Piper said.

"The contractor?"

"Jean-René. He flirts. All the time, but there is no sexual heat behind it."

"And there was with Art."

"Yes. He accused me of being immaturely jealous, but after seeing Jean-René in action, I can say definitely that the intent behind the flirting makes all the difference."

"Yes, Jean-René is a Frenchman. He flirts with a ninety-year-old grandmother as warmly as he would a runway model."

Piper nodded. "It's all about making a woman smile, without making her feel like sexual prey."

"Art did not understand the difference?"

"How could he? Any woman even halfway attractive to him *was* sexual prey." The disgust that tinged Piper's tone was a definite improvement over the grief that used to lie so heavily on her when she talked about her ex.

"*I* do not flirt." Or rather, he only flirted with intent and since he and Piper had begun their liaison, there had been no other woman he wished to seduce.

She laughed and hugged him, right there on the stairs. "No, you don't."

He enjoyed the spontaneous embrace. While she never

drew away from his displays of affection, she had been more circumspect in offering her own since they reached the villa. He didn't know if that was because she blamed him for her possible pregnancy, though she'd said she didn't. Or maybe she was responding to his pulling away from talking about personal things.

He just did not see the need to discuss their future when they did not know whether they needed to take a pregnancy into account, or not. He'd also resisted talking any more about his past. It was over and done. They did not need to keep re-visiting it.

He followed her into the bedroom and closed the door behind them. "Are you ready to go back to Seattle tomorrow?"

Drawing aside the drape at the window, she did not answer for several seconds. "I don't know."

"It is hard to leave here." He began divesting himself of his clothes.

"But I want to know."

He did not ask what she wanted to know. There was only one thing causing worry lines between her elegant brows.

Part of him, a very large part if he were honest with himself, *wanted* her to be pregnant. Then he could be selfish and convince her to marry him despite the lack of love between them. It would be the best thing for the baby and he trusted her to make the needs of her child paramount.

He cupped her shoulder, caressing her nape with his thumb. "I have something more interesting to focus on than a dark vista."

She turned to face him, her expression soft and yearning. "Do you?"

"Can you doubt it?"

She just shook her head and waited. Waited for him to kiss her, to touch her, to show her that in this at least, they had perfection.

And that was exactly what he did.

* * *

Piper flew back to Seattle in Zephyr's private jet with him. When they landed, she learned that he had already made an appointment for the next morning with her doctor. She wasn't even a little surprised by his excessive efficiency. She was a bit startled by the fact that he'd gotten an appointment so quickly. She was never so lucky with her doctor's appointment keeper.

But then Zephyr Nikos moved entire ranges, not simply single mountains, when he wanted to.

He spent the night with Piper in her apartment. They didn't make love that night, but he held her close in the darkness protecting her dreams and making her feel safe.

"We'll call you tomorrow with the results," the nurse said after setting the vial with Piper's blood aside.

Piper stood up and put the chair they'd used for the blood draw back against the wall at the head of the exam table. "Thank you. Have the doctor call my cell phone, all right?"

"Of course. I don't think our office has ever successfully gotten hold of you on your house or business line."

"I travel a lot."

"It must be nice." The nurse put the vial in a small red carrier.

"It can be." When she'd first moved to Seattle, she'd loved the travel, but after she and Zephyr became friends, she missed him when she was away. Even before the sexual side to their relationship started. "It can be exhausting, too."

"Well, if this test comes back positive, you can count on being exhausted even more." The wry grimace on the usually friendly nurse's face could in no way be described as a smile.

What was she supposed to say to that? Thank you? She was sure the other woman thought her information necessary, if not welcome. Piper would rather focus on the upside of this pregnancy…just as soon as she figured it out. She got up and grabbed her bag. "Well, um…goodbye."

"See you soon."

Piper didn't know about that. She rarely visited her doctor between physicals. Of course, if she was pregnant, that would have to change, wouldn't it?

CHAPTER SIX

ZEPHYR was waiting for her when she came out. "How did it go?"

"A little prick, a bandage and we were done." It seemed like something awfully innocuous to find out something so momentous.

"They'll know tomorrow?"

"That's what the nurse said." Piper had tried to dissuade Zephyr from coming to the doctor's office with her.

It wasn't as if she was having a difficult procedure, or something. But he'd insisted and now, she was kind of glad.

He put his hand out to take hers and led her outside. It was one of Seattle's rare sunny days. Not so uncommon in the summer, but not something to be taken for granted, either.

"I'm glad I'm not alone, which makes me feel like a real wuss," she admitted.

"You are facing the possibility of a major life change. That cannot help but be disconcerting. You are no weakling."

She smiled up at him and squeezed his hand. "Well, I'm glad you're here." Even if she hadn't wanted it that way at first.

"I am glad to be here."

"Do you have to go into the office today?" she asked as they settled into his Mercedes.

"No, but I did promise to have dinner with Cass and Neo tonight."

"Oh, okay." She pasted a bright smile on her face. "If you

could just drop me at my apartment. I'll drive to the office from there."

Or close her shades, put in the Coco Chanel biography she'd been meaning to watch and eat that pint of triple chocolate decadence hiding in the back corner of her freezer. It wasn't as if she had to go to work. She was her own boss. If she wanted a day off to wallow in worry, she could take it.

"Dinner isn't until this evening, and I was hoping you would come with me."

"Oh."

"I have no intention of leaving you alone to dwell."

He knew her too well. "Who said anything about dwelling?"

"We have been friends for years."

"Are you implying that makes you a mind reader?"

"I only wish—" he smiled "—but I do know you."

"Yes, you do."

"So, dinner with Cass and Neo?"

"Sure." She bit her lip and looked out the window. "You know Cass and I have never actually met."

"I know. It is time."

"Because I might be pregnant."

"Because you are my close friend and so are they," he explained.

"So we should all know each other?"

"Naturally."

"Your arrogance is showing again," she teased.

"But remember, you find it charming."

"It's a good thing for you that I do."

"Do you need to work today?" he asked this time.

"I have a few small jobs I could work on finishing up before your project swallows all my time." But she really didn't want to deal with any of them.

"Is that what you want to do?"

"No."

"Well, then?"

"There's a pint of chocolate ice cream in my freezer with my name on it." Piper clung on to her original plans.

"Really? I was unaware your name was triple chocolate decadence."

"You've been snooping in my cold storage?" She tried to sound outraged, but only managed mildly amused.

"Business tycoons crave ice cream, too. Even Greek ones."

"You ate my triple chocolate decadence?" The outrage came through bright and clear this time.

"Of course not. I ate the single-serving cherries jubilee buried behind the vegetarian meals you never eat but buy to make yourself feel better about your food purchasing habits."

She ignored the jab about her sadly ignored healthier food options. "I like cherries jubilee."

"With a healthy dose of hot fudge perhaps."

"Okay, so, I'm a chocoholic. Is that a crime?"

"Not in Seattle, home to more chocolate-flavored coffees than most small countries." He sounded indulgent. She loved him in this mood.

"Oooh, an iced mocha latte sounds good." Could she have caffeine if she was pregnant? "Maybe decaffeinated."

"We'll go through a coffee-shop drive thru."

"Why not stop somewhere?" she asked.

"Because I indulged your museum obsession in Athens, today is your day to indulge mine."

"You want to go to museums?"

"I have other obsessions," he said as he pulled up next to a coffee shack.

"You do? Other than making money, I wasn't aware."

"Right. You are probably the only person in the world besides Neo that knows that for the lie it is." They both made their orders and then he gave her a significant look. "You are one of those obsessions."

"You're turning into quite the silver-tongued devil, you know that?"

"I have always been good with my mouth."

"That can certainly be taken more than one way."

"You should know."

She felt herself blushing, despite their history together. Nevertheless, she agreed. "I do."

The young barista cleared his throat. With a blush darker than hers burning on his cheeks, he handed Zephyr their drinks.

Zephyr pulled his car back out onto the road. "You are not my only interest, however."

"My feelings might be hurt if you hadn't downgraded whatever you're going to try to talk me into from an obsession, which I am, to an *interest*."

"I like fish."

"I had noticed." Her blue eyes queried where he was going with this. "You eat it more often than either steak or chicken."

"Not to eat. To watch."

"You want to go whale watching?" she guessed.

"Not today. I was thinking the aquarium." That was so not what she expected to hear.

"You want to go the Seattle Aquarium…but that's for children."

"*I* don't think so."

"Seriously…you've been?"

"Several times."

Wow…just wow. "No way."

"I go when I need a place to think. Watching the fish can be very soothing."

"Even with all those children around?"

"I like to see happy families."

Somewhere over the Atlantic, Zephyr had become convinced that Piper was indeed pregnant. Regardless of the statistical probability after her years on the birth control patch. Therefore, he needed to convince her that marriage to him was a good option for her future, even without the love.

He wouldn't give her love, but he realized he could give her more of himself. It went against his desire for self-protection, but he now considered his sharing of his past with her as a brilliant tactical move on his part. Piper needed to feel emotionally connected to people she cared about. He had seen the effect his sharing had had on her.

She'd drawn closer to him even as he'd attempted to backtrack to a shallower level of emotional intimacy. With his baby's future on the line, he could and would give Piper a stronger connection, despite the fact he had no intention of allowing himself to be vulnerable to romantic love, were he even capable of the emotion.

Going to the aquarium wasn't some big romantic thing, but it would allow Piper to glimpse a part of his life he did not share with others. It wasn't much, but his instincts told him that sharing this habit with her would work toward convincing her they could have a strong enough marriage to raise children in.

Piper enjoyed the aquarium more than she thought she would. A lot more, but what she found most intriguing was watching the way Zephyr watched the other people there. She was sure he had no idea just how much his expression revealed of the inner man. His mouth would tilt in a half smile every time a child made an enthusiastic noise to its mother or father.

He watched the antics of the little ones with an indulgent grin and looked with pure longing at more than one set of parents visiting the aquarium with their kids.

"You really enjoy being here, don't you?" she asked him in the glassed-in tunnel of exotic fish.

"Very much." He looked around them with a wistful expression that was there and gone in a blink. "Everyone here has normal lives."

"You assume."

"I assume." He smiled ruefully at her correction.

"You have a normal life. Now."

"Do I?"

"Yes, of course," she said.

"I'm a workaholic tycoon that spends most of his time making money and creating places for other people to enjoy the fruits of theirs."

"So, spend some time enjoying them yourself."

"Alone?"

"You aren't alone right now." If she didn't know better, she would think he was making his case for how much he needed his own family.

"No, I am not."

"Does that make you happy?" she couldn't help asking.

"Yes, I like being here, in one of my favorite places, *with you.*"

"It's special." Really, really special. And he was sharing it with her. She reached up and kissed the corner of his mouth. "Thank you."

They both stepped to the side as a young boy went racing by, his older brother right behind him and a woman even farther back calling for them to slow down.

Looking harried, but smiling, she rushed to catch up. "Sorry about that. They're both crazy for the otter exhibit."

Zephyr tilted his head. "No problem. You're lucky to have such active children."

"That's one way to look at it." But her grin as she sprinted after her children said she saw it the same.

"You really do want children, for more than just having someone to pass on your legacy of wealth." How could she have thought anything else?

He looked down at her, his dark eyes filled with a longing she was just beginning to understand ran soul deep for him. "Yes."

Lost to anyone else around them, she reached up to cup his cheek. "You'll make a wonderful father."

"That is my sincere hope."

* * *

Cass was wearing a beautiful bright dress when she opened Neo's apartment door to Zephyr and Piper later that evening.

She grinned at Zephyr and pulled him in for a hug. "Long time, no see, stranger. How was Greece?"

"Warm and beautiful."

"You mean you actually took time to notice. When Neo told me you were taking a minivacation before going to the island, I almost fainted, but I'm glad."

"Hey, I am not as bad as my business partner."

"Only a robot works as many hours and holidays as Neo did before we met, but he's well on his way to reformed now."

The complacency in Cass's voice made him smile. "I noticed."

Cass turned to Piper. "Please tell me you're taking on the job for Zee. He needs someone to."

"Don't answer that," Zephyr demanded, then said, "*Yineka mou*, this is my best friend's fiancée, Cassandra Baker, world-renowned pianist and composer. Cass, this is Piper Madison, brilliant designer and my very good friend."

Cass's brows rose to her hairline and Zephyr realized he had made a mistake using that particular endearment in front of her. No doubt Neo had long since told her the translation and the implications often associated with it. Implications he was becoming more and more comfortable with.

Cass took both of Piper's hands in hers and squeezed them. "So, it *is* your job."

"I'm beginning to think so, yes." Piper glanced at him out of the corner of her eye. "Good friends have an obligation to look out for each other."

"That's the argument Zee used when talking me into taking the piano lessons that changed my life," Neo said as he came into the entryway. "Shouldn't we all go into the living room? It's got more comfortable seating."

He gave Piper a smile that seemed to startle her, but she

returned the gesture and said, "Good to see you again, Neo."

Then Cass led Piper away by the hand while Neo hung back to give Zephyr a traditional Greek greeting. "It is good to have you back in Seattle."

"I miss the island already."

"I felt the same after leaving." Neo nodded. "It is a special place."

"Special enough to consider making it a more regular aspect of my life."

"You are serious?"

"What would you think of delegating another level of responsibility to our well-trained staff and moving our offices to the island villa?"

Neo's eyes widened in shock. "You *are* serious."

"Never more so."

"Something has happened."

Zephyr shrugged, but was feeling nothing like complacent. "I'm ready to make changes in my life."

"Do you have news to share with me?"

"Not yet."

"But there will be?" Neo pressed.

"Perhaps."

"You're going to have to do better than that."

Not yet. "Give me until tomorrow."

Neo didn't push. Cass would have. Zephyr could just be thankful his friend would not have a chance to bring it up to her while Zephyr and Piper were there.

They walked into the living room to find Cass and Piper ensconced on the sofa going through digital pictures of the trip to Greece on Piper's minitablet PC.

"I didn't realize you'd brought that," Zephyr said as he took the chair next to Piper's spot on the sofa.

Neo sat beside his fiancée.

"I thought they might be interested in your trip."

"Our trip."

She rolled her eyes. "Our trip."

"I'd really like to go to this art museum while we're there," Cass said to Neo.

He kissed her temple. "Then we will definitely add that to our agenda."

"You're going to Greece soon?" Piper asked.

Cass beamed. "For our honeymoon."

"I seem to remember reading that you'd been there in a tour when you were younger."

"Yes." Cass looked a little startled. "You read about me?"

Piper blushed, but smiled. "When Zephyr told me Neo was getting married, I was understandably curious about the woman who had managed to lead him to such a human endeavor."

Cass laughed out loud. "Wow, and you told me once that Zephyr was the only person that really knew you well."

"I've worked for Stamos and Nikos Enterprises a few times." Piper gave them a look rife with meaning. "I met Neo on a couple of the projects, though he wasn't coordinating them."

"And you found me inhuman?" Neo asked, contriving to sound offended.

"You were so intimidating that I sent up a prayer of thanks you were not the lead on the project I'd been hired for." She winked conspiratorially at Cass. "I thought Zephyr was so much more laid-back and would be a much easier man to work for."

"But you learned the truth?" Cass asked with a teasing glance to Zephyr.

"It took a bit, but I did."

Zephyr feigned shock. "So, you *don't* think I'm easy to work for?"

"I think anyone excellent at their job, who makes a minimum of mistakes, if none at all, and who understands how very seriously you take the success of each development, will find you a pussycat to work for."

"That's a lot of caveats," Neo said, laughing.

Cass raised her brows at her fiancé. "I thought she did an admirable job of being diplomatic."

"I'm not sure if that was a character assassination, or an endorsement," Zephyr admitted.

"See? Diplomatic," Cass teased.

"Zephyr, you are an amazing man, but just like Neo, you're just a little superhuman for the rest of us. You just hide your intensity behind your charm."

"Are you saying I am not charming?" Neo demanded.

Piper made a zipping motion over her sealed lips and they all burst out laughing.

Cass leaned against Neo and rubbed her head against his shoulder. "Don't worry, Superman, I like you just the way you are."

Seeing his friends like this usually gave Zephyr a twinge of useless envy, but tonight all he felt was a fleeting hope Piper was seeing it, too. And perhaps realizing a reformed Greek street kid wasn't such a bad horse to place her wager on.

"Arrogance and all?" Neo prompted Cass.

She smiled and patted his leg. "That's part of your charm."

Neo gave Piper a triumphant look. "See, I *do* have charm."

"I can attest to the arrogance part of it, anyway," Piper said with a cheeky grin. "You and Zephyr both have bigger than the average dose."

"Has he not told you that if it is justified, then we are talking about confidence here?" Neo asked.

"That's right," Zephyr agreed.

Both Cass and Piper simply laughed and shook their heads.

"Want to see the pictures?" Piper asked Neo.

"But of course. I would like evidence of Zee playing the tourist."

"Well, here he is haggling with the jeweler in the Plaka over a necklace." She clicked to one of the photos he had not known Piper had taken. It showed him in animated conversation with a short, square Greek about twenty years Zephyr's senior.

"I thought you weren't supposed to try to bargain inside actual shops," Cass asked. "I've been reading up on it."

Zephyr waved his hand in dismissal. A Greek boy who made his livelihood on the streets of Athens learned to bargain with the taxman, if that's what it took. "What could it hurt to try? I was buying an expensive piece. If he wanted to move it that day, he needed to offer me an incentive."

"And did he?" Cass asked.

Piper laughed out loud at that. "Do you really need to ask? Of course. No one in their right mind says no to billionaire tycoon Zephyr Nikos."

"Remember that tomorrow," Zephyr said under his breath.

But they all three heard him and gave him looks of inquiry in varying degrees.

He shrugged. "Show Cass the pictures of the view of Athens from the Acropolis."

"Never mind that," Cass said. "Do you know what he's talking about, Piper?"

Piper frowned at him. "I do and it's not something I'm comfortable discussing right now."

"Does it have anything to do with why Zephyr asked me about moving the head offices to the island villa?" Neo asked.

Zephyr winced and bit back a particularly virulent curse.

"You did what?" Piper demanded, shock blatant in every centimeter of her lovely face.

"What?" screeched Cass. She gave Neo a confused look. "You told me we had to wait to talk to him about it until we'd been married at least a year!"

"You and Cass have already discussed it?" Zephyr asked, taking his turn at being taken aback.

"We've discussed many options for the future. Cassandra wants to experience other parts of the world and I want her to have every opportunity for maximum happiness," Neo said with a shrug.

Now, *that* did not surprise him. With more trepidation than he had felt since leaving Greece for the unknown, Zephyr shifted his gaze to Piper to see how she was taking this discussion.

Her azure eyes were fixed on him with steady intensity. "You're going to pull out all the stops if that test comes back positive, aren't you?"

"Would you expect anything different?" He was ruthless, but not dishonest.

"I guess not. I was trying very hard not to think about it at all, though." Her voice was tinged with rueful inevitability.

He did not know if that was good, or bad. "I am sorry."

"For showing your hand early?"

"For making you think about it."

"What exactly is it we're thinking about?" Neo asked in a voice others had learned not to ignore.

Luckily for Zephyr, he wasn't other people and he had no trouble ignoring his best friend and business partner's demand.

Piper closed her eyes with every evidence of counting to ten and he thought she'd probably succeed in ignoring Neo, too.

But then Cass elbowed her nosy fiancé. "Leave them alone, Neo." Then she sighed. "Besides, it's obvious and not something Piper should be forced to discuss before she's certain one way, or the other."

"One way, or the other, what?" Neo actually sounded plaintive.

Zephyr could not remember the last time he had heard that particular tone from Neo, but it had been at least a decade, probably longer. He had no idea how Piper would react to it. He thanked God and the angels besides when she laughed.

"So, what's for dinner?" she asked.

Even Neo knew enough to allow the subject change to pass without incident.

The rest of the evening went well, considering. Cass kept Neo in line and Piper did her best to ignore any and all leading comments and questions.

But she didn't turn toward his door when they left Neo's penthouse. Instead, she headed for the elevator.

He put his hand on her shoulder as she pressed the button. "Where are you going?"

"Home." She sighed and looked back at him. "I need some time to myself, Zephyr."

Unexpectedly, the request hit him in that place permanently wounded when his mother left him in the orphanage and never took him home with her again.

Even so, he asked, "Are you sure? You seem to sleep well in my arms."

"I'm not sure I'm going to sleep at all." Unfortunately, she looked like the thing she needed most right then was a good night's rest.

In his bed, snuggled against him, damn it.

But clearly, she did not agree. She did not want or need him right then. Maybe not at all.

"An even better reason for you not to be alone."

She shook her head, a sad look passing over her face. "I'm sorry."

Pleading not to be left behind when someone was intent on leaving you did no good. That was a lesson he had learned even better than how to make money and at a much younger age. But it still took an inordinate amount of inner fortitude to drop his hand from her shoulder.

He stepped back. "You will call me when you get word?" He did not like asking. It reminded him of asking for his mother's consideration and getting excuses for why things could not be different.

"Yes, of course."

But she did not.

Zephyr forced himself to wait until after lunch to try calling her. Surely, the doctor would have contacted her by now. His call went straight to voice mail, though. He did not bother to leave a message.

An hour later, he called her home, but got her voice mail again. At the office, her assistant answered the phone. However, she informed him that Piper was not in and not expected today.

Neo walked into Zephyr's office later that afternoon, after Zephyr had called Piper yet again, only to get the too professional message on her voice mail box.

"You look like hell. What's going on?" Neo demanded.

Without having to consider it, Zephyr told him. Everything.

"You should have brought her to meet Cassandra and I before last night," was Neo's first reaction.

"Why?" Neo had never been particularly interested in socializing with Zephyr's other friends, unless it advanced their company's interest.

"You have been in a sexual relationship with Piper for months and friends for over two years. How did I not know this?" Neo asked, rather than answering.

"You knew we were friends."

"Not that good of friends." Neo shook his head. "She's the reason you told me sex with a friend was so good, isn't she?"

"Yes."

"Have you been with anyone else sexually since you began your relationship with Piper?"

"Do you really think that is any of your business?"

"Probably not, but answer anyway," Neo insisted.

"Once, before I realized the first time wasn't going to be a single shot."

"And that did not tell you anything?"

"What? I like intimacy with Piper. I am too busy with our company to expend energy on other women."

Neo's lips twisted in a mocking frown. "How long has your head been in the dark place?"

Zephyr remembered accusing Neo of having his head up

his ass once, in regard to Cass. Apparently this was payback. "It's not. We both knew what we had and what we did not have."

"And now?"

"And now she may be pregnant with my child."

"So, that changes everything?" Neo asked.

"Naturally."

"Why?"

"You can ask?" After the way they had both grown up, he would expect Neo to be the first to understand.

"You are not taking my point," Neo said with exasperation. "Don't you see that she is bound to think you are only wanting marriage because of the baby?"

"That *is* the only reason. I would not have considered it otherwise."

"Why the hell not?"

"She deserves better."

For the second time in less than twenty-four hours, Neo looked absolutely gobsmacked. "You *are* the best."

"You are prejudiced." But the belligerent certainty in his friend's voice was surprisingly nice to hear.

"I am your brother, Cass says so. That means I'm allowed."

Zephyr felt warmth he hadn't known in decades, but he didn't let it show on his face. He was no pushover despite these weird emotional twinges he was experiencing. "So, step outside your personal bias and look at this from Piper's perspective."

"I do not see the distinction here." Neo's eyes filled with something far too close to pity for Zephyr's comfort. "You're a good man, Zephyr."

"I did not say I wasn't." Merely that Piper deserved better than what he had to offer her.

"So, what is the problem?"

"She wants to be *in love* with her next husband," Zephyr explained grimly. "Like she was with Art."

"And you do not love her?"

"No."

"Bull."

Zephyr shook his head. "Love doesn't work for everybody." At least on that truth, he was one hundred percent convinced. And he was one of those people.

Neo sighed. "You're right, but giving up before you even try isn't like you."

"Sometimes trying is the stupidest thing of all to do."

"That does not sound like you."

"And you sound like a broken record," Zephyr retorted.

"So, say something that makes me understand this defeatist attitude of yours."

"She left last night."

"When you wanted her to stay." Neo knew him so well, he did not even have to make it a question.

"She said she was sorry." Just like his mother had done, over and over again—first when leaving him behind and then when she refused to bring his little sister back to visit.

In situations like this, sorry didn't mean anything.

"She also said she would call you, *ne*?"

"Yes."

"So, trust her to do it."

"When?" Zephyr snapped.

"When she is ready."

"You were not this complacent with Cass."

"I was in love with Cassandra." Neo's look challenged Zephyr.

Apparently, if he was not in love, he had no right to be worried, cautious or impatient. Like hell. "So, because I'm not playing the romantic hero, I have to wait and wonder if my lover carries my child?"

"You have to wait because she will call when she is ready and not before."

"I am well aware of that." And it was doing nothing for his mood, which he was sure was obvious, even to Neo.

Neo looked at him like he was a newly discovered species. "I still cannot believe you had a lover for almost a year and I did not know it."

"I did not consider her my lover."

An unholy light gleamed in Neo's eyes. "My friend, this just gets better and better. When did *that* change?"

"In Greece."

"That trip had a pretty big impact even before the missing birth control patch was discovered."

"If you say so."

"What I say does not matter. On the other hand, what you and Piper say is of utmost importance."

"She *said* she would call, and she has not," Zephyr all but growled.

"Be patient and believe in your friendship if you will believe in nothing else."

"I have no other option."

"Then make it work for you, that is what men like us do. We do not give up."

That was one truth Zephyr could not deny.

Neo left and Zephyr forced himself to get to work on the piles of urgent papers and messages stacked on top of his desk from his time out of the office. It was nine o'clock that night before he admitted temporary defeat and left his office.

Piper still had not called, though he had called her on the hour, every hour, since the afternoon.

Piper sat outside the Seattle Aquarium, watching children and adults come and go. Her hand rested against her lower abdomen. She didn't feel any different. Her body had not changed at all, but inside her womb a baby grew. Her baby. Zephyr's baby. Their child.

The wholly unexpected fulfillment of one of her dearest hopes.

She should have called right away and told him the news,

but she couldn't. She had to think and she couldn't do that around him right now.

She loved a man who had taken great pains to make sure she understood he would never love her. And that same man was going to ask her to marry him. She was sure of it.

Because she carried his child.

In a normal world, that would result in an immediate and outright refusal on her part. Before meeting and falling in love with Zephyr Nikos, she would never have even considered for one second marrying a man who did not profess to love her. But Zephyr's perspective was a unique one.

In his world, love guaranteed nothing but pain. He hadn't come out and said so, but his story about his past made that clear. He had loved his mother and she had abandoned him to an orphanage. He had loved both of his half siblings, but they had been taken from him.

Even if he did love Piper, he might never be able to admit it.

One of the questions that chased round and round in her brain was whether or not she could accept that and marry him anyway. She had no doubts about her ability to raise this child on her own. She was an educated woman with her own successful business. She wasn't a billionaire, but she wasn't a pauper, either.

Zephyr could be part of the baby's life without marrying her as well. But he couldn't be a full-time dad if they didn't live together. Even in the best shared custody arrangements, both parents were forced to take a less pervasive role in their child's life.

And Zephyr wasn't going to be content with the role of part-time dad. Just because she refused to marry him did not mean he would not one day marry. He didn't just want to be a father; he wanted a family. That had been obvious when they'd visited the aquarium together.

He wanted what he saw all around him, and she could not blame him.

Which led to the other question that chased the first one over and over again: could she bear to stand aside while he married another woman and built a whole family with her? Could she stand her own child only having half-time with his or her daddy while others that came later got him each and every day?

Unlike Zephyr, her time at the Seattle Aquarium was doing nothing to help her think of answers to those hard questions.

Zephyr let himself into his empty apartment, annoyed when he realized the cleaning service had left the lights on in the living room again. His power bill was not the issue; indiscriminate wasteful use of the planet's resources was.

It had been almost a week since Piper was supposed to have called him. She hadn't been in to work, at least according to her assistant, Brandi. He'd gone by Piper's apartment, but she hadn't answered the door. Her phone had to be off and he'd finally stopped calling, but each day that went by echoed feelings he thought he would never again have to experience.

The fear of being abandoned was a live thing inside of him, but he hid it, even from Neo. He couldn't stand the feeling of helplessness that grew with every hour she did not call. Had he lost his friend? Was she going to try to keep him from his child if she was indeed pregnant?

One thing he knew was that he might feel helpless, but he wasn't. If she carried his child, she was not going to keep it away from him like his brother and sister had been. He would be a part of this child's life, even if marrying its mother wasn't an option.

He would fight for custody. She could be the weekend parent, if she didn't want to marry him. She was still building her business, she'd said so herself. He could free more of his time to parent their child hands-on and any decent judge would see that.

Disgusted with the direction of his thoughts, he yanked off his already loosened tie as he strode into the living room. He stopped dead at the sight that greeted him.

Piper was curled on his sofa, under a quilt he had brought back from Greece many years ago. As if she could sense his presence, her eyelids fluttered and then opened.

She gazed up at him drowsily. "Hi."

"You said you would call."

"I couldn't. I had to think."

"So, you left me hanging for almost a week?"

She flinched at the ice in his voice, but he could not help that. "I decided it wasn't something we should discuss on the phone but, um…maybe I should have called and told you that."

"Yes, you should have. I have been worried. I went by your apartment. You did not answer the door."

"I wasn't there. I went to *my* favorite place to think after trying yours and getting nowhere."

"Where is that?" he demanded.

"The beach."

"You could not have let me know you went out of town?"

"If I had called you, you would have talked me into seeing you."

"Maybe because that was what we both needed." Frustrated anger laced his voice. "At the very least, you could have let me know that you were waiting here today."

"I should have," she acknowledged as she sat up and brushed her hair back off her face. The beach might be her favorite place to think, but it had brought her no peace and despite just waking from a nap, she looked like she hadn't been getting enough sleep. "I was just so tired and thought you would come up after work. I didn't realize you would work until bedtime."

"It is hardly that."

"Close enough."

"Damn it! Do not try to sidestep the issue. If I had known you were here, I would have left my office immediately." He took a deep breath and let it out slowly to prevent his volume from increasing. "I was worried. Do you understand that?" Did she care? "I called your cell over and over again."

She looked down so he could not see her eyes, and target the guilt he would see there. "I turned it off."

"I figured that out."

She nodded. She stood up and came to him, then tilted her head back so their gazes met. Emotions he did not understand swirled in her blue depths.

"Tell me," he demanded, his tone softer than he intended.

How could he help feeling compassion? She looked like hell.

"I'm sorry I didn't call. It was inconsiderate and selfish of me. I should have called, no matter how hard it would have been. I kept thinking and thinking, but I couldn't make sense of anything no matter which way I looked at it. When I finally got here today, it was past four. I really thought I'd take a short nap and you would be here. And then we could talk."

"Instead I worked late, trying to keep my mind off the fact you did not keep your promise to call." Almost a week ago, but he had already said that and she had acknowledged it.

She nodded. "This situation is scary, Zephyr."

"I agree, but I would think that two friends facing down fear together would work better than each trying deal with it on his or her own."

"I'm sure you're right." She looked away again. "I just...I knew you'd want to get married and I didn't know what I wanted to do about that."

"So, you *are* pregnant."

She met his gaze, hers suspiciously glossy. "Yes, we're either very unlucky or wildly fortunate, depending on how you want to look at it."

"How do *you* look at it?" he demanded.

"Wildly fortunate? How else? I'm thrilled to be having your baby even if this whole situation scares me to death." She looked ready to shake apart.

Damn it. He would have noticed how fragile she was earlier if he hadn't been working through his own turmoil. He did not want to tell her the plans he'd been making when he first arrived, but would she give him a choice?

Hoping to convince her of their best option yet, he pulled her into his arms, keeping their gazes connected even as their bodies pressed together in comfort. "What are you so frightened of?"

"A lot of things."

"What scares you the most?"

"That I'll agree to marry you, we'll do the deed and then you'll finally fall in love—*with someone else*."

That was at the top of her fear factor list? He couldn't have been more stunned if she said she was terrified of an alien invasion snatching their baby from her womb. "I am not going to fall in love with another woman."

"You can't be sure of that."

"Yes, I can. Trust me, Piper. It is not even a possibility." Of all the things he'd been considering over her week-long silence, that was not one of them.

"Do you think there is even a tiny chance that someday you might fall in love with me?" She buried her face against his chest and waited for his answer.

He wanted to lie; it would make things so much easier, but he could not. "If I was capable of falling in love, I already would have."

"You really believe that?"

"Absolutely."

Her head tilted back so he could see her glare. "Everyone is capable of love."

"That is debatable."

"Yes, I guess it is." She grimaced. "There are certainly people that make a great case for that point of view anyway. I never considered you one of them, however."

He could not help that. He shrugged. "What else scares you?"

"Oh, the usual, what will happen to my business, what if I lose the baby, what if I'm a terrible mother, am I going to turn into a whale, can I learn Greek?" Her litany of worries came out in a voice garbled by suppressed tears he did not know what to do about.

"You are going to marry me." Why else would she need to learn Greek?

"How can I do anything else? I've looked at this situation from every side until I'm sick with it. If I don't marry you, we'll have to share custody and I'm not naive enough to think you are going to settle for being a weekend dad. You'll fight for at least equal custody, if not majority custody."

He was shocked. She realized that. "I…"

"Don't try to deny it."

"I wasn't going to."

Her lips trembled, but she blinked away the incipient moisture in her troubled blue eyes. "Good. We can't build a marriage on lies."

"I agree."

"The custody issue wasn't even the most distressing."

"It was not?" What could have worried her more?

"No. It was the certainty that if I didn't marry you, one day you would marry someone else and build a whole family with them."

"The thought of me married to someone else bothers you?" he asked, just to clarify. She had left him without any sort of contact for almost a week after all.

"Of course it does. *I love you.*"

Something inside his chest stuttered. "You love me?"

"Yes."

"Like a friend." He attempted to qualify.

She wrapped her arms around his neck and shook her head, those terrifying tears of hers spilling over now. "No, not like a friend."

"You won't convince anyone you love me like a brother." Maybe there was some special kind of love women left for the father of their children.

She shook her head again, a mysterious smile flirting with

the edge of her lips, despite the sadness in her eyes. "Like the only man in my universe, like the other half of my heart, like the part of my soul that's been missing my whole life but I didn't know it."

He would have staggered if they hadn't been holding each other so tightly. "Is that how you loved Art?" He did not know why he asked except for as some form of penance, because one thing he *never* wanted to hear was that she had loved her ex like that.

"My feelings for Art weren't even a shadow of what is in my heart for you."

Could he believe that? And if he did, what difference did it make? His mother had loved him, too, but she'd walked away when a choice had to be made. "And yet, you did not call."

"Loving you doesn't make me perfect, or even perfectly unselfish. In fact, it makes me terribly self-focused because it makes me so vulnerable to being hurt by you. I *want* to marry you so I know you won't—*can't*—leave me." The tears were in her voice now. "I want to be with you for the rest of my life and I wanted to be pregnant so bad, it was an ache in my gut that wouldn't let me sleep at all the night before the doctor's office called. I spent the darkest hours of that night in a perfect agony of guilt and unable to change my desires one jot even because of it. Did you hear all those *I*'s and *me*'s?"

"You *wanted* to carry my child?" he asked, ignoring self-flagellating guilt.

"Yes, more than anything. Which probably makes you wonder if I lost my patch on purpose, but I swear to you that I didn't."

"Of course not, but why did you want to?"

"Have you been listening to me at all? I knew a baby would tie you to me. Not because I'm not capable of being a single mother, but because you would not want me to be. I'm really ashamed of feeling that way, but I can't change it. I never would have done it on purpose, but I won't pretend I don't feel *wildly fortunate*, either. Which probably should make *you* reconsider whether or not you should marry me."

"So, if you wanted it so bad, why stay away so long?"

"Because when I got what I thought I wanted, I pictured a lifetime of being married to a man who is not in love with me and it terrified me."

"You have been so unhappy these past months?"

"No."

"Then, why should you be unhappy as my wife?" he demanded. Didn't she see how illogical she was being?

"I'm hoping I won't be."

"I'll make sure of it." She was going to accuse him of arrogance again, but before she got a chance, he decided to offer his own truth. "I also wanted you to be pregnant and I am very glad you have decided to marry me."

He could not resist the expression his words brought to her face, he kissed her and they spent several minutes lost in a very pleasant joint effort to leave an indelible mark on the other's lips.

"Do you think our mutual selfishness negates itself?" she asked as if the answer really mattered to her.

"I think that as long as we are both pleased with the outcome, it does not matter."

"I think maybe you're right." She looked up at him through her lashes. "Can we make love now?"

"Is it safe for the baby?"

"Very."

"You asked?"

"Of course I did. I know what we're like together and we are going to be together a lot now."

He liked the sound of that, though a tiny voice inside warned him not to get too used to it as it could all be taken away. After all, she had cut herself off from him while making her decision, showing she did not *need* him even if she loved him. "You'll move in with me?"

"This weekend."

"We are not sleeping apart again meantime."

"No, but I need to work and won't have time to pack for the move until the weekend."

"I'll hire movers."

"I'll still need to be there to supervise."

He could not argue that. "Do you want a big wedding?"

"No." She gave him a nervous look complete with a bitten bottom lip. "I just want our families there."

"I don't have any family."

"Oh, yes you do. I know your secrets now. Besides Neo, who is your brother in everything but genetics, there is your mother, her husband and your half siblings, et al. And I want them at our wedding."

"Why?"

"Because someday, I think it's going to matter to you that they were there. Besides, it will hurt your sister's feelings if we don't invite her."

"Why do you think so?" Piper saw things so differently than he did; he didn't always understand what made her say the things she did.

"She insisted on you meeting her children, didn't she? She considers you her brother and she'd be devastated if she discovered you didn't feel the same."

"I do. For good, or ill, she is my sister."

"It's all to the good."

"So you say."

"I'm almost a mother. I'm practically an oracle now. It comes with the territory," she said, tongue firmly in cheek.

And he laughed like he was supposed to before sweeping her into his arms. Making love sounded better than talking about his family. "What you are now, is mine."

"You seem pretty pleased about that." She didn't sound too disappointed by the prospect herself.

"I am." He carried her down the hall to his…to *their* bedroom.

"Are we really moving to Greece?" she asked between baby kisses smattered along his jaw.

"The island would be a good place to raise children."

"Yes, but I'd marry you regardless."

"You said you wanted it."

"I do." She grabbed his face, making him look her in the eye. "This isn't a business transaction. I don't love your money, or what it can buy for me. I love you, Zephyr."

She said so, but she'd still left him and not called for almost a week. Maybe Zephyr did not understand love, but he did not think it should be so easy to hurt someone if you loved them. He wasn't about to dwell on that now though, no more than he'd spent time pining over his mother's defection once he'd learned he had to accept it. Piper had agreed to marry him, even though, technically, he had not asked.

That was all that mattered right now.

Without answering her assertion, Zephyr carried Piper into the bedroom and laid her on the bed oh, so carefully. She smiled up at him, but he put his finger up with the gesture to wait a minute.

He leaned over and grabbed the phone from beside the bed, then pressed two buttons.

"Memory" and "One" she would bet.

Someone picked up on the other end.

"Congratulate me. We are going to have a baby and Piper has agreed to marry me." He smiled down at her while speaking into the phone.

Excited words in a definite masculine tone came through the headset, though they were too muffled to understand.

"Yes. I'll call you with details tomorrow."

Neo said something else.

"I will," Zephyr replied. "*Kalinichta.*"

He hung up the phone.

"Neo?" she asked, just to be sure.

"Yes. He knew I was waiting for your phone call. He was concerned about me." And even on the verge of making love to her, Zephyr thought to call his friend and settle his mind.

Maybe he'd wanted to share his news, too.

"You're a special man, Zephyr Nikos. Is he happy for you?"

"For us both. He and Cass will take us out tomorrow to celebrate if you are willing."

"Of course. Though I'll have to work during the day. I've taken way more time off than I should have."

"Do you think Brandi will relocate to the island with Cerulean Designs?"

"I'd like to ask her, but I don't know if I can continue to pay her salary once I cut back on my client list." Piper decided to begin undressing and remind Zephyr why he'd carried her in here to begin with. "I don't want to work anywhere near full-time if I don't have to."

Chocolate-dark eyes ate her alive as she peeled off her comfort jeans and T-shirt. "I am very pleased to hear that. We will work something out regarding Brandi."

"You mean you're going to offer to pay her." She paused in the act of unhooking her bra.

He could try to deny it, but she knew him. And his expression said he was already busy trying to come up with a compelling reason for doing so, given enough time.

"Why did you name your company Cerulean Designs?" he asked in an obvious bid to change the subject.

"Nice feint, but don't think I've forgotten this discussion."

"You haven't forgotten we were about to make love, either, have you?"

"I'm not the one still completely dressed."

"I can fix that quickly enough."

CHAPTER SEVEN

"Do IT."

Zephyr kicked off his designer loafers with two audible thumps as they landed somewhere on the carpet.

"After everything went down with my ex, I didn't have a lot to smile about, much less laugh," Piper said, answering his previous question. "I was watching a gay romance movie when the guy planning the wedding started yelling at his fabric supplier. The wedding planner was incensed that the supplier didn't know what cerulean was, much less how to spell it. I realized I didn't know what cerulean was, either, and I was an interior designer. I learned later it was the same shade of blue as my eyes, which I thought was sort of prophetic. Anyway, I started laughing at the movie, really amused, for the first time in too long. I named my company Cerulean Designs to remind myself that no matter what was going on in my life, there was always a reason to laugh."

Zephyr stopped undressing and stared down at her. "That's a great story."

"It's a good memory. It doesn't hurt to have the everyday reminder that I don't know all there is to know about design, either."

"Keeping you humble and positive at the same time. That's a lot of mileage for one business name." He pulled off his unbuttoned shirt and suit jacket in one go.

"Your turn."

"I'm already undressing."

"I mean to answer a question."

"Oh, okay. What?"

"Why Stamos and Nikos Enterprises as opposed to the other way around?"

"It was nothing so meaning-driven," he said as he pushed his slacks and boxers down his legs with impatient speed.

"What was it?"

"We flipped a coin for it. Neo won the toss."

She was still laughing when he came down over her completely, deliciously, wonderfully naked, and kissed the joy right from her lips. It tasted good, better than good—it was perfect.

"So, it doesn't bother you that we're getting married so close to you and Neo?" Piper asked Cass the next day when the other woman called to congratulate her.

"Not at all. I think it's fantastic you two want to get married in Greece. As you know, we're going to be there on our honeymoon, anyway."

"Zephyr's flying my parents and sibs to Athens for the ceremony." She'd been happy when they had all promised to attend. Of course, a paid-for vacation to Greece was nothing to sneeze at. And didn't that make her sound as cynical about money as her groom-to-be?

"Neo said Zephyr's inviting his own family," Cass said, unaware of Piper's cynical thoughts. "Neither of us even knew he was still in touch with them."

"His relationship with his mom is pretty complicated." Zephyr had taken Neo out to lunch and told his best friend the truth of his past, so Piper didn't have to sidestep the issue, but she didn't want to get into it too deeply, either.

Cass whistled softly. "You can say that again. I'm not sure, but I think Neo might have been better off losing his mom to an overdose than to a better life. That had to do a real number of Zephyr's ability to trust."

To love, as well, but Piper wasn't getting into that. "Between our two families, there will be less than two dozen guests. You'll be okay with that, won't you?"

"I am." The satisfaction and shy pride in Cass's voice was a truly lovely sound. "My agoraphobia is so much better now. I'm not about to book a concert tour, but my new agent isn't pressing for one, either."

Piper laughed.

Then silence fell for several seconds. It wasn't an uncomfortable silence, but she felt like she wasn't supposed to break it.

"I wanted to offer to play at your wedding, if you'd like."

"Are you serious? I thought you didn't perform anymore."

"It's not a performance, it's a gift. I'm..." Cass's voice trailed off then she took an audible breath. "I'm working on a song for you both."

"As in composing us a song?" Piper asked in shocked awe.

"Um...yes. Is that all right?"

"That's fantastic. I don't know what to say. *Thank you* seems so inadequate."

"I'm really happy to do it. Zee helped Neo see what was important and stopped the stubborn idiot from breaking my heart."

"Zephyr did?" Piper asked in even more shock.

"Oh, yes. I think men are just smarter about other people's relationships than their own."

"Maybe not all men."

"But definitely our men," Cass said emphatically.

Piper wasn't sure she considered Zephyr hers even though they were getting married. "Is Neo smarter about others then?"

"He knew you were special to Zee the minute he told us he was bringing you to dinner. It took Zephyr considerably longer than a single comment to figure out you were special to him."

"I can't argue with that."

"Are things okay with you two?" Cass asked delicately.

"Better than. He may not love me, but he wants me and really wants me to be the mother of his children."

"*You* do love him, though."

"So much."

"That's good. I think Zee deserves lots of love and a very special woman like you. Maybe he'll learn to trust in love by living with it and the positive results of it on a daily basis."

Piper was certainly hoping that was the case. "Thank you. Ditto Neo about the love of a special woman, even though I've just recently become convinced he's human."

Cass's laugh was sweet and light. "Don't worry. He just figured that out himself recently."

"You're awfully good for him."

"And you're fabulous for Zee."

"I'll try to be," Piper promised.

"Just be you…that's all he seems to need."

And even without the love, Piper thought Cass just might be right.

She had to hope so, because losing Art had devastated her. Losing Zephyr would kill her.

The day sped by as Piper tried to catch up on her work while still coming to terms with the huge changes in her life. Little more than two weeks ago, she had just acknowledged the fact that she had fallen in love with a man who, while having sex with her, did not consider himself her lover. Now, she was pregnant with his baby, engaged to be married and moving in with him.

Love her or not, she trusted Zephyr to be faithful. Her billionaire tycoon was nothing like her ex.

If anything, she felt like she was the one luring Zephyr into marriage under false pretenses. Only she wasn't. She'd told him she loved him, so it was no secret she had to feel guilty about. Just because she was getting the deepest desire of her heart, or at least its twin, didn't mean she was taking advantage of anyone. Zephyr wanted to marry her; he wanted their baby as much as she did.

No matter how fortuitous this pregnancy was for her, giving Piper a chance at a lifetime with the most amazing man walking, she had not gotten this way on purpose. Zephyr knew it, too. He even felt responsible.

So why did she still feel as though she was pulling a fast one on him?

Maybe because she knew with absolute certainty that Zephyr would not be marrying her if she *wasn't* pregnant. And she wasn't offering to wait until the iffy first trimester was over, was she?

No.

On top of all that, he had offered her the option of moving to Greece and living on a private island. Was it any wonder she felt like she'd been dumped in a waking dream?

Merely accepting the fact that she was pregnant was hard enough. She didn't feel any different, but the blood test assured her that she would be soon. Her hand slid to her still flat stomach while she clicked the print function on the presentation she'd just finished.

Brandi had done a lot of the preliminary work and it had only been a matter of changing a few things before it was ready for presentation. Thank goodness. Piper's mind was scattered to the four winds.

But scattered or not, there was one thing she was sure of: they would be happy together. If she didn't believe that, she would not be moving in with him, much less marrying him. But she did believe it, deep in her bones. He was perfect for her, even if he had a mental block where love was concerned. And she was perfect for him.

No matter how much everything else scared her, she had to cling to that knowledge.

And right now she had to work.

Giving a final read-through to the design proposal for a

local private attorney's office space, she left her office and headed toward the shop floor in search of her assistant.

"Hello, Pip."

Piper's head snapped up at the male voice she had not heard since leaving New York.

Wearing a designer suit from last year's line and looking years older than the last time she'd seen her ex-husband, Art Bellingham stood not five feet in front of her.

"What are you doing here?" she blurted out, her usual professional persona deserting her completely.

"An old friend can't drop by to visit?" He tried the smirking half smile she used to find so sophisticated, but now just seemed cheesy.

"You are not an old friend."

"That hurts, Pip. We were friends once." Now he was laying on the charm.

It wasn't working, not even sort of. She shook her head, clearing the cobwebs old memories had spun so quickly the moment she heard that annoying old nickname, and then looked around for her assistant, Brandi. Watching Piper and Art with avid interest, her twenty-two-year-old assistant was standing near a display of sample drapery fabrics.

Piper held the design proposal out to her. "Put this in presentation format and get the color boards we made to go with it. You'll be presenting it to the client at tomorrow morning's meeting."

"You sure I'm ready for that, boss?" Brandi asked, her focus now completely on the designs in her hands.

"Yes." The younger woman had done supervised presentations with aplomb. She was ready to fly solo.

"Fab! I'll get right on this." She rushed toward their work corner.

That took care of one distraction.

"Is this a business or social call?" Piper asked Art, feeling more in control of herself.

"A little of both, Pip."

"My name is Piper. I hate that nickname. I always did." And he'd always insisted on using it.

"Hey, don't get all offended." He put his hands up in mock supplication. "It's not always easy letting go of the past."

She crossed her arms and gave him a look she had learned from Zephyr when he dealt with particularly irritating suppliers. "Funny, after the way you blackballed my name in the New York interior design industry, I had no problem leaving my past behind."

"Is that why you sicced your billion-dollar pit bull on me?" He frowned and shook his head, signs of his disappointment that had affected her at one time like an arrow to the heart.

Now she felt nothing but some amusement that he thought the guilt card could *ever* work between them again. "I don't know what you are talking about."

"I was hurt when you walked away from our marriage. I may have said some things that could be taken in a detrimental way," he said like he was sharing some big confidence, "but that's no reason for you to destroy a design firm that's been in my family for three generations. I thought better of you, Pip—*Piper*, I really did."

His guilt trip attempts were getting old fast. "I repeat…I do not know what you are talking about." She tapped her sandal-clad foot. "Start making sense, or take your smarmy self out of my shop."

"*Smarmy?* Piper, is that really how you see me?"

"That wounded look stopped working before our marriage did, and I don't think you want chapter and verse on how I see you, Art."

He looked startled for a moment and then sighed. "You may be right about that. Look, I understand you having some sour grapes toward me, I really do."

"That's big of you."

He frowned. "But not my company. You built a name for yourself with Très Bon."

Seriously? He was going to use *that* argument about this—whatever this was. "A name that you dirtied with your rotten, not to mention *untrue* slurs."

"I told you, I was smarting from our breakup. I exaggerated some things. I wasn't myself."

"You made stuff up with the creativity of a fiction writer."

He grimaced. "You may have a point."

She was so done with this conversation. "So, you're here to apologize?"

"If that's what it takes."

"To do what exactly?" Piper asked, still bewildered as to what her ex was talking about.

"To get me off Zephyr Nikos's most wanted list."

Now, that was unexpected. "*Zephyr?* What has he got to do with you, or Très Bon for that matter?" Très Bon was not the type of design firm Zephyr used on his projects. They lacked the innovative approach he considered a must.

"He's been blackballing my company in circles that have debilitating influence."

"You don't honestly believe I convinced him to blackball you?" Piper asked, deeply offended. "You know me better than that."

"I thought I did, but a man like that wouldn't go after me without motivation. I'm beneath his notice." And didn't it pain Art to admit it?

"If he's been slandering you, why haven't you filed a lawsuit?"

"Right, like the man would be stupid enough to say anything he could be held liable for in a court of law."

"That's the first thing you've said that makes any sense. Zephyr is a very busy man. Why would he take even a few minutes from his jam-packed schedule to besmirch your company's vaunted reputation?"

"Ask him! All I know is that Très Bon is on the verge of bankruptcy and it's all that bastard's fault."

"First, don't you ever insult Zephyr Nikos in my presence again. He's a hundred times the man you are, or could even hope to be. Second, if you're on the verge of bankruptcy, it has more to do with the way you run your business on the edge of overextension and always have done."

"His smear campaign has cost me business!" Art insisted.

"Campaign? Now I know you're lying. Zephyr simply would not waste that much time on you."

Zephyr enjoyed Piper's staunch defense, but it was time to step in. "For a man in my position, it only takes a comment here and there," he said as he walked around the personalized paint chip display that blocked his view of Piper and Art.

Piper's expression lit up as she unfolded her crossed arms and gave him a bright smile. "Hi, Zee. I didn't know you were stopping by."

"I got word Arthur Bellingham was in Seattle." He gave the other man a once-over, not impressed with what he saw. Piper had been married to this? "I had a feeling he'd come crying to you rather than be a man and face me himself."

"Be a man?" Art asked in outrage. "I've never even met you, Mr. Nikos. How would I get an appointment?"

"Did you try calling my secretary?"

Art checked as if the idea had not occurred. "No."

"She has instructions to put your call through."

"You've given your secretary instructions about Art?" Piper asked, clearly attempting to assimilate that knowledge with her heretofore stated belief Zephyr had nothing to do with the shift in Très Bon's reputation. *"You had some kind of travel alert set on him, too?"*

Zephyr shrugged, not as relaxed as he wanted to appear. "I am a thorough man."

"You're a petty tyrant, is what you are," Art said, blotchy color rising in his face.

The man was every bit the idiot Zephyr had thought him. "Calling me names isn't the best way to try to get on my good side."

"Once you've set a course of action, you don't change it. There is no getting on your good side," the dissipated-looking designer huffed.

"I almost have to respect your foresight in not trying the rational one-businessman-to-another approach."

"Once I realized you were the man behind the fall of my company's reputation in the international development community, I did my research. Words like *stubborn*, *highly intelligent*, *ruthless* and *deceptively charming* are used to describe you. *Reasonable* is not."

"But I am a reasonable man."

"You always have been with me," Piper agreed with a smile.

"Of course you would say that," Art sneered. "You two are obviously having an affair."

"We are engaged to be married," Zephyr said in dangerous tones the other man would do well not to ignore, "not having an affair."

"Well, congratulations." Sarcasm dripped from every syllable.

"Thank you." Zephyr did sardonic truth up there with the best of them. "That happy news aside, I did not express my less than favorable opinion of your unimaginative and overpriced design firm for Piper's sake."

"Right," Art said sarcastically.

"Had you not done your level best to destroy not only your marriage, but also any hope of ongoing friendship with Piper as well, she probably would never have left New York."

"That's true," Piper added with a look that could only be termed sentimental.

Zephyr smiled at her. "I'm glad you came to Seattle."

"Me, too."

Art made a disgusted sound. "And you're trying to say you did not destroy my company because of her."

"Only indirectly. I demand the best, isn't that right, *yineka mou*?"

Piper nodded, looking no less perplexed. "Yes."

"You are the best."

"Thank you." Her lovely blue eyes began to gleam with understanding.

"If I had gone with the recommendation of one of my colleagues based on things he had heard as a result of Arthur Bellingham's very real smear campaign against you in New York, I would not have hired you for that first job."

"But you didn't."

"No, I spoke to local clients you had worked with and visited properties you'd finished, but most importantly, I liked the proposal you gave me for my own project better than anyone else's," Zephyr disclosed.

"So, what was the problem?" Art demanded, showing a real lack of understanding his offense, even after Zephyr explained it.

"Your lies almost cost me the work of a fantastic designer."

"So, you decided to destroy my business?"

"Are you an idiot? I did not destroy your business. I merely helped you along in the process." But would Piper see it that way, as well?

"You utterly *ruthless* bastard!" Art rasped in a low voice.

He could not deny it. He was ruthless and he was a bastard. His only real concern was how his new fiancée responded to this particular truth. "At least I'm an honest one. Unlike your creative dealing with the truth, I never once said something about your firm that wasn't true. I *wouldn't* hire Très Bon for one of my properties. You *are* overextended financially and have been for years. Your designs *are* unimaginative. And *you do* have a reputation for finishing a project over budget and late."

Art sniffed superiorly, an effort that was completely wasted on his audience. "That has never bothered my clients in the past."

"You mean they tolerated your shoddy business practices in order to attach the name of Très Bon to their buildings."

"It was a name worth having before you set out to destroy it."

"Your uncle and grandfather ran a decent, if conservative design firm. You've been doing your best to destroy their work with bad business decisions since taking over ten years ago."

"Don't you care about the people that are going to be out of work when Très Bon folds?" the other man asked, appealing to Piper, rather than Zephyr.

But it was Zephyr who answered. "Did you care about Piper having to leave New York, her career in tatters?"

"She's just one person!"

Yes, definitely an idiot. "And you lied about her."

"I *knew* it was about Pip."

Zephyr winced at the name and looked at Piper. "Do you like that ridiculous nickname?"

"No. I already told him not use it, but as usual with Art, he didn't listen to me." She sounded mildly annoyed, but it was the lack of expression on her face that concerned Zephyr.

"If he had, his business might not be in trouble right now."

"She left, not me!"

Piper frowned at her ex, but no real anger shined in her eyes. "I left because you cheated on me and then fired me when I filed for divorce." There was no real heat in her words, just a weary-sounding truth.

Art's glare wasn't so insouciant. "You didn't used to be vindictive."

"I'm not vindictive now."

"Then get him to stop." Art contrived to sound desperate and pleading. He even said, "Please."

Zephyr barked out a laugh and she looked at him with a question in her eyes. "Your ex is quite the actor."

"Oh, I think he's every bit as despairing as he sounds and frankly, I understand why," Piper responded.

"You feel sorry for him?" Zephyr demanded incredulously, his worry ratcheting up a notch.

"I know what it's like to have your career ripped away by the careless words of someone else. I'd never wish that on even my worst enemy."

"I have no problem wishing it on him," Zephyr admitted in the spirit of complete honesty.

"Obviously." She did not sound particularly condemning, but nor did she sound approving.

He couldn't help morbidly wondering if their relationship was going to survive the revelation of the ruthless aspect to his nature. Though was it a revelation? She'd known his plans to fight for majority custody without him ever having to voice them.

Zephyr turned cold eyes onto the other man. "What did you hope to gain by coming here?"

Art looked like he was trying to decide how honest to be. Finally, shoulders slumped, he said, "Ideally Piper would convince you to say you'd been mistaken about my firm."

"I do not lie." And he sure as hell hoped she would not ask him to.

"I'd settle for you calling off the dogs." Like he had any room to negotiate.

That was the most the other man could ask from Zephyr, but the request came with an inherent error in thinking. "I have not set any dogs on you. I did not have to." It really had been just a comment here and there.

He certainly hadn't offered favors for passing the word along.

"So you've implied. Everything is my fault, according to you."

"That is how I see it."

"So, you aren't going to do anything to help me?" he asked Piper rather than Zephyr once again.

This time Zephyr let her answer.

"I don't know what I can do," she said.

"You could come back to work for Très Bon."

It was all Zephyr could do not to bark out a decisive, "Hell, no," but he respected and trusted Piper to get the point across on her own.

"Not in this lifetime." There wasn't even an ounce of maybe in her voice.

Art waved his hand, dismissing her denial. "Think about it, we can open up a West Coast office and you can head it up."

"I'm not even flirting with interested." Piper was no slouch at sarcasm herself.

"Then, I guess there's nothing to do but claim bankruptcy and lay off all of Très Bon's employees."

Zephyr's disgust meter reached red levels. "Don't be a melodramatic ass. A halfway decent management consultant could pull your company out of the red with a stringent reorganization and consolidation of resources."

"Not if you keep blacklisting us."

Zephyr flicked a look at Piper and then back to the other man. "In future, you tell the truth about Piper's talent and abilities and I'll do my best to avoid having to tell the truth about yours."

"I guess that's the best I'm going to get."

"I could suggest a consultant for your reorg." See him be reasonable.

"I'll find my own consultant and my own way out." Art turned on his heel, his former bravado pulled around him like a tacky suit, and left.

"Man, you guys are better than the soaps," Brandi said, a color board in each hand. "I just wanted to check these were the ones we planned for this design."

"Yes, those are the ones." Piper rubbed her forehead, fatigue clear on her features. She had not gotten enough sleep the night before to make up for her sleepless night away from him. "I'll be gone for the rest of the day. If you need to contact me, call my cell."

"Like always, boss. No worries." She went back to the work area.

Piper sighed. "She thinks she's Aussie and she's never even been out of the States."

"The idea of moving to Greece should appeal."

"If I asked her to, I'm sure it would."

That did not sound good. Something cold settled in his gut. "So, you are not planning to ask?"

"I've done all the discussing of my private life in my place of business I want to for today. Let's go."

He wasn't about to argue. If she was going to tell him she had changed her mind about marrying him, he would rather hear it somewhere he had a chance at changing her mind. Somewhere private.

When they got to her apartment, Zephyr had his emotional game face on. The one that showed nothing except humor when he wanted it to. Piper wasn't sure what made him draw into himself like that, but she wasn't going to let the visit from Art drive a wedge between them. If seeing her ex had done one thing, it had driven home to her how lucky she was to have a man like Zephyr in her life now.

His sense of justice was a little overdeveloped, but that was better than being a man who not only lied to others, but also to himself. Like Art.

Thinking how to best handle the emotionless vibes coming off her sexy fiancé, she sighed and stopped in front of her door. "We forgot something when you came into my shop earlier."

"What was that?" he asked with a weariness she did not understand.

"To kiss."

"You want me to kiss you?"

He really had to ask? "Yes."

"I can do that."

"It wouldn't say much for our upcoming nuptials if you couldn't," she sassed.

Morphing into a sensual predator before her eyes, he pushed her against the apartment door with his body, one hand on either side of her head. "You know what I've noticed lately?"

"No, what?" Was that breathless voice hers?

"You've got a real thing for getting the last word."

She would have answered that, but his lips were in the way.

CHAPTER EIGHT

AND very nicely, too. She loved this side of him and didn't really care what that said about her.

He didn't rush the kiss and neither did she. Of one accord, they broke apart to turn together to unlock and open the door. Once through, Zephyr made sure it was shut and locked again before leaning back against it with her in front of him.

His hold said one thing. Talking could wait. Everything but this intense pleasure between them *would* wait.

He leaned down and sucked up a pleasure mark on her neck while his hands skimmed down the front of her body, only to sweep up again, bringing the hem of her shirt along the way. His fingertips brushed against the smooth skin of her torso.

She writhed against his hard body, reveling in the feel of his erection pressing into her back. "Yes, Zee, touch me."

His hands cupped her breasts, squeezing lightly in nothing short of a tease.

"More, you know I want more." And he loved it when she told him so. She'd discovered that fact early in their relationship.

"Do you, *yineka mou*?"

"You know."

He kissed all around her ear and whispered, "Oh, yes, I do know."

His hands slid inside her bra to play with her nipples as he nibbled on the supersensitive spot behind her ear, laving shimmering nerve endings with his tongue.

She pressed back against him harder, her feminine center aching for the attention he was showing to the rest of her body.

Proving he was really adept at reading her mind, one of his hands moved down to undo her trousers. Her body knew what that meant and hot liquid gushed between her legs as her entire body thrummed with a new level of nascent desire. He pushed fabric down her hips without ceremony along with her panties. She stepped out of the pile of blue linens and silk, not caring that she still wore the high-heeled sandals she'd had died blue to match this particular outfit.

His rogue hand slid right over her mound and then long, knowing fingers were playing a symphony on her clitoris, drawing it into swollen sensitivity.

She arched toward the touch, a mewling sound that would have embarrassed her if she was not so turned on coming from her throat. He played her right through to a shocking, intense, early orgasm.

Only then did he start taking his own clothes off. It all got really hectic then and somehow she ended up leaning, with her hands on the back of the couch, her legs spread, and still wearing her heels.

He pushed his big sex into her now pulsing depths, eliciting moans and groans from her as well as unrestrained pleas for more, more and more.

So darn good. "How can it always get better?"

"I don't know. I don't care." He started a driving rhythm that would have sent her right over the back of the couch if he didn't have both arms around her.

One hand continued to toy with her breasts and stomach while the other kept up constant stimulation to her clitoris.

She was screaming with her second orgasm as he roared out his climax inside her, long, sweaty, strenuous minutes later.

Afterward, he cajoled her into the shower, where they washed each other with as much pleasure as making love. She adored the domestic intimacy of showering together. It was one of the things that said most clearly to her that they were a couple.

They were making dinner together in her small kitchen when he said, "I thought you were going to back out of marrying me."

So, that was what had him behaving strangely earlier. "For heaven's sake, why?"

"You have seen my ruthless side and what it can lead to."

"I always knew you could be ruthless, but I have to admit I have a hard time reconciling the man I've come to love with one who would set out destroy someone else's reputation." She leaned up to kiss his jaw.

He turned away, tension radiating in every inch of his six-foot, three-inch frame. "You never asked me about my father."

"You know who your biological father is?" she asked in shock. She'd just assumed his mother had not known which of her clients had sired her oldest son.

"Yes."

"Well, don't make a meal of it." She pulled him around to face her. "Tell me."

"If you talked to the other men of his class, they would tell you he was a respected olive grove owner from an honorable family who was lucky in his investments. Only he and his wife had luxurious tastes in living that could not be supported with his olive income. He made investments, but not of the respectable kind."

"What do you mean?"

"He invested in a stable of women, and yes, that is what he called them. He treated them as well as he would horses, I suppose. He provided for their physical needs, while expecting them to serve his customers. And him. My mother was his favorite. He was the only man allowed to copulate with her without using a condom."

"He kept her working for him, even after she had his son?" What a prince…*not.*

"He did not recognize me as such. Not until I was older and he realized his legitimate wife was never going to give him an heir for the family's grove. He came to the home with the intention of claiming me. He thought I would be grateful he wanted to 'adopt' me."

"What a morally corrupt, not to mention selfish, *slimeball.*" Her heart ached for the child Zephyr had been and for the man whose ability to trust and love had been so damaged.

"That's how I saw it. I had no intention of playing dutiful son to a man who treated my mother like a commodity and was content to leave me in an orphanage for years."

"That's when you and Neo ran away from the home, isn't it?"

"Yes. He'd had much looser restrictions on him while living with his mother, before she died. The home felt like a prison to him."

"So, you two took off together."

"And helped each other build lives as far from the ones we'd been born to as it was possible to get."

"You both succeeded admirably."

"Yes."

But she was still interested in what had made him go tense. "So, you brought your dad up for a reason right now."

"You are right." He sighed and tried looking away again.

She wouldn't let him. "Tell me."

"When I was in a position to do so, I made sure the truth of his *investments* was brought to light."

Ah, that made sense. "That ruthless side of yours showing itself."

"Yes."

"Did he go to jail?"

"*Ohi*…no, he had money. He paid his way out of trouble, but he couldn't pay his respectable wife to stay with him. In a true twist of irony, he ended up married to one of his prostitutes and she's given him two children. Both daughters. She rules the home every bit as *ruthlessly* as he used to rule his 'stable.'" He stopped, his body going rigid, an expression of horror crossing his features. "We are not inviting them to the wedding. The girls are too young to know who or what I am and I have no interest in recognizing that pimp as my father."

She shuddered. "Don't worry, I wouldn't even consider it."

Relief showed on his face. "So."

"So?"

He looked at her like he couldn't quite figure out what was going on in her head. Since that was usually her role, she got an inappropriate little thrill from seeing the shoe on the other foot for a change.

"I am a very ruthless guy." He made it sound like that was some big revelation.

"It's a little disturbing," she said, unable to resist the urge to tease a little.

"Disturbing enough to make you question your decision to marry me?"

She refused to treat this like a serious question. "That depends."

"On what?"

"On whether there are any other people you feel the need to 'tell the truth' about." She fluttered her eyelashes at him, making it clear that she was joking.

He, however, looked as serious as a heart attack. "No."

"I was joking, Zee. I'm not really worried about it. Nothing I learned today changed in any way how I feel about you." She spelled it out for him because he seemed to need that.

"You do not think I am like my father?"

"What?" She grabbed his shoulders and tried to shake him. It didn't work, him being the buff stud that he was, but he got the idea. "How could you ask that? You are nothing like that user."

"But he is ruthless about getting what he wants."

"And you are ruthless in standing for the truth. That can be overwhelming at times and a great burden to bear at others, but it's as far from the man who exploits the weakness of others to provide for his own ill-gotten luxuries as the life you now live is to the one you were born to." She needed him to see that.

"I did not want him punished for what he did to me, but I wanted his world to see him for who he was and how he took advantage of others."

"I know."

"He destroyed too many lives."

"And I bet he was never sorry he did so. He and Art have more in common than you and him."

"Too bad they are not related."

"Yes, it is. Art's family are decent, nice people. I have no idea how he turned out so selfish and blind to his own faults."

"My mother did not want to give me up. Even when I was a small boy, I understood that. She felt she had no choice. She did not want me to be raised in a whorehouse."

"So, she chose the lesser of two evils, and paid the rest of her life for having to do so."

"I think you are right." He looked like he was having a revelation.

"It's that mother-to-be oracle thing again," she teased.

He smiled and then went serious again. "That is why you want to invite her to the wedding. You think it is time she stopped paying."

"I think it is time you both stopped paying for things that cannot be changed."

"I will call her tomorrow."

"Thank you."

Zephyr stared at his computer monitor. It displayed his latest project spreadsheet, but all he saw was an image from the past—his mother's face one of the many times she told him she loved him before leaving him at the home. He could see something in that mental picture that he had never let himself acknowledge before, the terrible pain in eyes so like his own.

His burned and he blinked rapidly.

"At Last" by Etta James started playing in that tinny way that ring tones did, bringing him firmly into the present.

He grabbed his cell phone and pressed the talk button without looking at the screen. "Hello, *pethi mou*."

What he lacked in sentiment, Piper made up for. She'd programmed the song into his phone as her personal ring tone after agreeing to marry him. She was going to go all gooey-eyed over the wedding ring set he had ordered to be over-nighted from Tiffany's. He'd had their names and the date they met engraved on the inside. It was such a little thing, but it would be special to her.

"How did it go?" Piper asked without preamble.

"She cried."

"You're not surprised."

"No." Not after Piper had warned him to expect it. "We agreed to meet for dinner on a day before the wedding, as you suggested." Piper had thought him seeing his mother for the first time in more than two decades at his wedding might be too much drama.

He'd agreed for his mother's sake. If he thought he might be grateful for it, too, he wasn't saying.

"Great. Are we meeting at a restaurant?"

"No, she asked us to come to her home," he replied.

"And you agreed?"

"Yes."

Piper was quiet for a second and then asked, "Will her husband be there?"

"Yes." He might as well get it all out at once. "He's coming to the wedding as well."

Absolute silence met that bombshell.

"He wanted to talk to me, too."

"What did he want to say?"

"That he was very, very, *very* sorry. That he was wrong to make my mother let me go. He said he wanted to tell me before, but he could not until I was ready to talk to him. He cried, too."

"I've heard Greek men do that sometimes."

"Not expatriates."

"Of course not." There was a teasing note in her voice, but he did not call her on it.

"I heard the story of how my sister and brother learned of my existence."

"Really?" The sound of Brandi asking a question in the background came over the phone. Piper covered the mouthpiece and he could hear the muffled sound of her answer before she said, "I thought it was odd your mother told them after not allowing you to see them once they were old enough to remember you."

"You never considered I might have told them?"

"No."

"Even with my ruthless streak?"

"Like I told you, it's a good kind of ruthlessness."

"You have a great deal of faith in me."

"Yes, I do."

His heart contracted at her words, but he ignored the strange sensation and said, "Iola found my mother crying over a pile of old photos. They were of me. My sister convinced our mother to spill the whole story."

"She must be pretty persuasive."

"She is very stubborn."

"Like her brother, hmm?"

"Perhaps."

Piper laughed. "There is no *perhaps* about it."

"You are treading on thin ice here."

"I like to live dangerously." Her smile carried in the sound of her voice.

"I can tell."

"How old was she when your sister found out about you?"

"Twelve. She was furious with her father. She called him

a monster and refused to speak to him at all for an entire year after finding out about me."

"Wow, she might even be *more* stubborn than you."

"You think?" He had always enjoyed the fact that to Piper, he was just a guy she could joke with, not someone she was too in awe of to treat like a human.

"I'll have to consider it."

"She never told me about all that once I contacted them. She let me believe my mother told her of her own volition, which in a way, she had. Iola did not want me to hate our mother."

"She also respected the distance you maintained. It's pretty obvious she felt you had the right to set the terms for your relationships with your family."

"Yes." And he had always appreciated that.

"Are you okay?"

"Naturally." A simple conversation with his mother and her husband wasn't about to disconcert him. Although, maybe there hadn't been anything simple about that phone call.

"You are the most amazing man, do you know that?" The warm approval in Piper's voice washed over him.

"You've said something to that effect before."

"Well, I mean it even more now," she assured him.

"You are good for my ego, even if I do not understand why you are so impressed."

"It took a lot to forgive your mom and her husband."

"I forgave them a long time ago." A man could not afford to expend the energy to maintain anger and hatred when he was building a new life for himself. "I simply did not trust them to be a positive part of my life. You have convinced me to give them a chance."

"I love you, Zephyr."

"Thank you."

She laughed. "You are welcome. I still say it takes a big man to overlook the sins of the past and forge new relationships in the present."

"I am glad you think so." He liked looking heroic in her eyes.

"So, our families are all going to be there. Tell me you got the church booked."

"Since we were flexible what day of the week we would be married, it was no problem. My secretary is booking your family's flights even as we speak. They will all arrive over the weekend, which will give them time to take in some sights before our wedding blessing on Thursday evening. We will fly over to Greece with Neo and Cass on the company jet after their wedding on Sunday."

"I'm still having trouble taking in the fact we'll be married in just over two weeks. In Greece, just like I dreamed."

"It is what you wanted." And what he had wanted for himself as well.

"So you made it happen."

"If a little unorthodox in my methods."

They had discovered that having the actual wedding in Greece required a lot of paperwork that would extend the date for their ceremony further out than they wanted. Neo had suggested a civil ceremony in Seattle followed by a blessing in Greece, for their families to attend. When Piper agreed, Zephyr had insisted on coordinating both events immediately.

"I kind of like it this way. The legal ceremony is private, just for us, and our families get to share in the communal blessing."

"As long as you are content so am I," Zephyr responded.

"Just keep saying stuff like that."

She was always so positive and it had only gotten better since they decided to get married. A man could be forgiven for being impressed with his own acumen in choosing such a woman to marry.

"How goes the great search for a dress?"

"Splendidly, thank you. I found the absolutely most perfect one ever online. The designer is shipping it to a downtown bridal shop in case any alterations are needed."

"Good."

"It's going to cost more than the GNP of a small country." He could tell she was striving to feel guilty and failing miserably. She must *really* love the dress.

"I do not care." He wanted everything perfect for her and he was only grateful she did not want a huge event that would require months of planning. Months in which she could change her mind about marrying him.

Or, God forbid, lose the baby and destroy his chances of getting her to marry him at all.

"So you said." She sighed happily. "Thank you."

"You are welcome."

"Are you sure we aren't rushing?"

Something clenched in his gut. "Are you having second thoughts?"

"No! Not at all."

Okay, so that was good. "Have you changed your mind about walking down the aisle with a noticeable bump?"

"Definitely not."

"Then we are not rushing things, we are simply being expedient."

"Right. Um, Art called a little bit ago."

Was that what had prompted her uncertainty? If so, was it because old feelings for her ex had resurfaced, or was it because seeing him made her question her decision-making skills when it came to marriage? "What did he want?"

"It finally sank in what you said about us getting married."

"He is not invited." Forgiving his family was one thing, her ex was a bridge too far.

"He wasn't angling for an invitation, well not entirely."

"That man has no shame." And even less business sense.

"And you don't even know the main reason he called."

But it wasn't hard to figure out. "Let me guess. He wanted a loan?"

"Yes! How could he?"

"For a man like him? Very easily."

Piper made a sound of disgust that transferred more than adequately over the cell phone. "I suppose so, but there was a time, and I find this really hard to accept now without considering myself an idiot, only I loved that man—or at least the man I believed him to be."

"He has feet of clay."

"His whole body is clay, if you ask me."

Okay, so definitely not resurrected tender feelings. Zephyr could afford to be generous. "Do you want me to bail his company out?"

"Would you, if I did?" she asked, sounding more curious than anything.

"Yes."

"You didn't even hesitate."

"I want you to be happy."

"Even if I wanted you to do it, giving Art a loan would just be throwing good money after bad. Most of his best designers have left the firm because of creative or financial difficulties. I suggested moving to smaller offices when I still worked at the firm, but he liked the 'grand' impression the space made on clients, the illusion that the firm was bigger than it was. He's still paying rent on prime New York commercial real estate much bigger than he needs."

"He doesn't want to acknowledge his poor choices and the effect they've had on his company."

"He never did. As for all the employees that would be out of work, I made a few phone calls. Along with learning his best designers had left Très Bon, I discovered he's mostly been staffing with temporary interns since the year after I left. He always was more about appearances than substance."

"So, no loan?"

"No loan," Piper confirmed.

"I am sorry."

"So am I, for the people who do rely on Très Bon for their

livelihood and for his uncle, who is still living. Old Mr. Bellingham has to watch his company fall apart, but then he could have stepped back into the picture at any time. He gave acting control to Art, but never signed over his ownership of the company."

"So, your ex is *not* an issue between us."

"I told you he wasn't."

"You had feelings for him a long time after the divorce," he reminded her.

"You're right, but I got over him. With your help."

He didn't have to ask himself why that knowledge was so satisfying. "Where are we sleeping tonight?"

"My place. The movers are going to be there in the morning to pack me up."

"I look forward to sharing the same home." And for the first time, his penthouse apartment would be a home with her living there.

The move went smoothly and Piper was surprised at how easily her things integrated into Zephyr's apartment. It helped that he gave her carte blanche on the décor and over what furniture stayed and what had to go.

That could have made her feel like he didn't care how their home together took shape, but he noticed every change. And commented on it in some positive way. He'd just got through telling her how he liked the way her curtain scarves brought a splash of color to that side of the living room.

"Why are you staring at me like that?" he demanded.

"Like what?"

His eyes narrowed and she wondered if he'd say it. She knew what was in her eyes right now: love, adoration and even a bit of hero worship.

He was so perfect for her.

"Like I am the perfect man." Ah, he got it.

"Why wouldn't I?"

"No one is perfect, Piper."

"True, but then you don't have to be perfect for me to love you. You just have to be *perfect for me*. And you are."

He looked unconvinced, but he did not argue. "Did your dress arrive?"

"Yes."

"Who is the designer?"

"I'm not telling." His curiosity was cute, but if she told him that, he would be *so* offended. "You'll have to wait until our wedding blessing in Greece before you get to see me in all my glory."

"You aren't going to wear it for the civil ceremony?"

"Nope." She enjoyed teasing him about it. Who would have thought Zephyr Nikos would be so naff that he wanted to know what her wedding dress looked like? And he said he wasn't sentimental.

Right.

"I suppose you'll wear one of your work outfits to the courthouse, it being a weekday morning."

"I suppose you'll see when you get there." She adjusted the angle of the silk and bamboo screen she'd put in the corner.

"I don't plan to wear a blindfold on the way there."

"And I don't plan to spend the night in our apartment on Thursday."

That got his attention, and not in the fun way. "What? Why not?"

"Tradition."

"But…" He let his voice trail off, thought for a second and then gave her an immovable look. "Fine, but that tradition only gets one airing, do not think you are going to sleep anywhere but in our bed every night thereafter."

"Duly noted."

"I mean it, even the night before the wedding blessing in Greece."

She laughed. "Fine, but I'm leaving our bed early in the

morning and you're not going to see me until I walk down the aisle of the church again later that day."

"That is acceptable."

"I'm glad you approve." She sashayed over to him and wound her arms around his neck. "I know we're in a rush but I want to observe all the traditions that are important to you and me."

He pulled her in close. "No problem, just remember, no doubling up on traditions because we're having two ceremonies."

"But some traditions are worth doing twice, like the part where the officiant says, 'You may kiss the bride.' And I think having two wedding nights could be earthshaking. I even bought two different sets of sexy lingerie." She gave him her best fake disinterested look. "I suppose I could take one of them back."

Over her dead body.

"Let's not get hasty."

"So, you think—"

"That two wedding nights are worth two wedding ceremonies and all that entails."

She grinned up at him triumphantly.

"Except the sleeping apart thing. That's a one-time event."

"Agreed." It wouldn't be the same after the civil ceremony anyway.

Her family and his might not know they were already legally wed when they arrived in Greece, but she would.

"So, where are you going the night before our ceremony?"

"Cass invited me to stay with her and Neo. We're taking the limo to the courthouse. Neo is driving you."

"You've got it all planned, do you?"

"Any objections?"

"I could do without a night alone in an empty bed."

"You'll survive just fine." She gave him a small peck on the lips.

He returned it with interest before saying, "So you say. I probably won't sweep a wink."

"You'd better. I expect a wedding night to remember." As if he could give her anything but.

"*Every* night we spend together is one to remember."

"You know, for a man who staunchly denies any sense of romance, you do mushy awfully well."

CHAPTER NINE

"THE truth is not sentimental." Zephyr tried to look offended, but he was obviously pleased. Even if he didn't want to be.

"Whatever you say. I'm just glad I'm getting such a romantic guy to spend the rest of my life with."

Now, he was looking worried. "I don't do hearts and flowers, Piper. You know me better than that."

"Sometimes, I think I know you better than you know yourself." She could tell right away she shouldn't have said that aloud.

If Zephyr were a dog, his hackles would be at full attention. For a billionaire tycoon, he did a pretty fair imitation. "Like you knew Art?"

She understood where the question came from, but it still hurt. "I thought I knew my ex, but it turned out I only saw the man he wanted me to, until his whole facade came crashing down."

And she felt pretty gullible acknowledging that, but seeing Art again in person had made her realize just how much of who she thought he was had been a result of her imagination and his acting ability.

"You say you love me, but you have made me into some kind of superhero in your mind. What happens when you see me for the man I really am, unsentimental, ruthless tycoon and all?"

"First of all, I do see you for who you are, Zephyr Nikos." No matter how naive she had been with her ex, she hated that

Zephyr thought her judgment regarding him could be skewed. It was not the same at all. It wasn't. "We were friends before we were lovers," she reminded him. "I've seen you in every aspect of life from your most impatient day on the job to the moment when you realized your mom didn't give you up without immense regret."

"So?"

Sheesh, did he really think stuff like that didn't matter? But then not loving her, maybe it didn't to him. "So, I know you can be ruthless, but I also know you aren't obsessed with revenge. If you were, you would have done something to your mother's husband, but you never did. You bought them a house, put his children through school. You never did a single thing to hurt him. You're just not *that* ruthless."

"But I am."

"Oh, really?"

"You are being deliberately obtuse."

She pulled away from him, crossed her arms and glared. "No, that would be you."

"Is this our first fight?" he asked, as if the concept amused him.

She was not laughing. "No. We argued before." He was too fond of getting his own way for even their friendship to have been all smooth sailing.

And maybe so was she.

"Not since we got engaged." He tugged her toward the couch.

She put up token resistance, but grudgingly allowed herself to be maneuvered into a spot beside him. She refused to sit on his lap, however, and kept her arms crossed. "Considering how recent that is, that's not saying much."

"You said first of all."

"So?"

"That implies you have more to say on the subject. You might as well get it all out now."

Her first reaction was to accuse him of fishing, but then she realized this whole discussion might have taken the turn it did because he needed reassurance. And no way would Mr. Arrogant Alpha think to simply ask for it.

If Zephyr needed reassurance, she was happy to give it to him. Even if he was being more than a little annoying, but it was odd how she had told him she loved him and he was the one needing proof.

She was the one marrying a man who had told her he could not love her, and she had no fears she was not doing the right thing for her. Almost no fears. All right. Fine. *No fears she was willing to give voice to*. But what woman in her situation wouldn't be at least a little nervous?

"Maybe you aren't sentimental by nature, but you are just sappy enough for me, all right? You may not see yourself as romantic, but the way you are with me, the things you say and do, are all I ever wanted in that department. Art *pretended* to be the kind of man I could love. You are that man. You don't pretend to be anything. In fact, you are almost brutally honest at times."

"And that does not give you pause?" His tone doubted her sanity.

She did her best not to take offense. "No. Trust comes hard for me now. Knowing just how unwilling you are to lie, even when a lie would serve you well, is a great comfort to me. I *know* I can trust you, and I didn't think I'd ever be able to say that to a man I loved again."

"What is love without trust?"

"I don't know." Why didn't he ask her something easy like what the meaning of life was, or something? "I'm not a philosopher. I never pretended to be. All I know is that I do love you. I do trust you because of who you are. And nothing is going to change the way I see you. So, you might as well get used to it."

"I suppose I don't have much choice."

"Not if you still want to marry me."

"That is never up for discussion."

"Good."

"Can we progress to the makeup sex now?" he asked with a leer that should have irritated her.

But it just made her laugh. She uncrossed her arms. "I think maybe we can."

They were soaking in a bubble bath after a tender session of lovemaking that had wrung every ounce of emotion and pleasure from her.

"I thought makeup sex was supposed to be all hot, sweaty and urgent."

"We have that without the lively discussions beforehand."

"True."

"Besides, I do not like to fit the stereotypes."

"No worries there. You are very much your own man, Zephyr."

"And you are a very special woman, Piper Madison."

"Be careful, you're sliding into sentimentality there."

"Then perhaps this is the ideal moment to do this."

"This?"

But he was leaning over the side of the oversized tub, reaching for something, and did not answer. When he straightened, there was a dark blue ring box with a white satin bow around it in his hand. There was no mistaking the signature look. He'd been shopping at Tiffany.

"Zephyr?" she asked in a voice that would not come out above a whisper in her suddenly dry throat.

He looked directly into her eyes, his espresso gaze both serious and warm. "Piper Madison, would you do me the honor of becoming my wife?"

He went blurry as happy tears filled her eyes and made her vision watery. "You know I will."

He took a gorgeous diamond-and-platinum engagement ring from the box and slid it onto her finger. "Every woman deserves a proposal before marrying."

"Thank you," she said in a choked voice.

"I knew you were going to go gooey on me."

She laughed. "That's me. Gooey."

"And incredibly sweet."

She swiped the water from her eyes. "I do love you."

"Wait until you see what I had done to the wedding rings." She grabbed for the box but he held it above his head. "No, no, no…not until the ceremony."

"You're just getting me back for my wedding gown."

"You yourself said I am not obsessed with revenge. I am merely revering tradition."

"You are revering a chance to keep me in suspense."

He shrugged. "Maybe."

"*You…*" She launched herself at him.

He tossed the box before accepting her weight as he wrapped his arms around her.

With frequent looks toward the street, Zephyr paced the landing at the top of the courthouse steps. He tugged at the neck on the white dress shirt he wore with the ring in his pocket. His gaze skimmed toward the building.

Neo lounged against the wall and watched him with a smirk.

Zephyr glared over at his closest friend. "You just wait. Come Sunday at the front of the church, *you* won't be so complacent."

"No, but I won't make a prat of myself pacing all over the sanctuary, either."

"I'm expending excess energy."

"And what do you call looking at your watch every thirty seconds? Checking the time?"

"They were supposed to be here five minutes ago."

"Are you seriously worried Piper isn't going to show up?"

"She wouldn't even let me text her last night." She'd said she wanted to observe the full tradition and he had indulged her.

He was an idiot.

Neo rolled his eyes. "Man, you have got it bad."

Zephyr refused to answer that silliness. "What I have is six minutes past the hour on my watch."

"And a bride arriving."

Zephyr spun around and sure enough, the limo was pulling up in front of the courthouse. An unreasonable amount of relief washed over him for the amount of time she was actually late, but she had left him once, if only for a week. And Zephyr knew better than most how easy it was to leave behind someone you professed to love.

The driver double-parked and turned on his flashers. Zephyr sprinted down the steps to open the door before the driver got around the car to do it.

Cass came out first, wearing a bright pink suit and a huge grin. "Happy wedding day, Zee."

"Thanks."

She stepped past Zephyr as he looked at his bride. And Piper looked like a bride.

She was wearing a short veil and a white cocktail-length dress with layers and layers of chiffon in the full skirt. Her blue eyes sparkled with a happiness he never wanted to see dimmed.

She put her hand out to him. "Help a girl out?"

Something went *twang* in his chest as he tugged her out of the limo and straight into his arms. Then, with a flip of her veil, he claimed her lips in a kiss he could no more have stopped than he could stop his own heartbeat.

The sound of honking horns and wolf whistles finally broke through to his consciousness and he reluctantly pulled back.

"I thought the kiss was supposed to come after the ceremony?" Cass teased.

Neo laughed. "We expatriate Greek tycoons do things our own way."

Piper looked up at Zephyr with passion glazed eyes. "I like the way you do things."

"Good. I have become set in my ways."

"You're a traditionalist with a twist." She sighed happily. "I like it."

"I like what you are wearing." She was right he was a traditionalist. He was more than a little pleased she had taken the effort to look like a bride for their legal ceremony. And such a beautiful bride.

She gave him a mischievous smile. "Wait until you see what I've got on under it."

He swore. "Do not say things like that."

"Why not?" she asked, all innocence.

"I do not fancy getting married with an erection in my pants." But he wasn't sure it was going anywhere, even if she refrained from all further naughty comments. He found the bridal look unbearably sexy on her.

"I can do that to you?" she asked teasingly.

"You know you can." Too damn easily.

"I'll try to be good."

"Not too good," he couldn't help saying as they headed up the steps arm in arm.

The ceremony was short and to the point. All the pomp and circumstance was being reserved for the church blessing in Greece.

So, the sense of profundity choking Zephyr as he signed the marriage certificate was totally unnecessary. However, it did not go away even as he handed the pen to Piper. Her hand trembled as she signed her own name and he didn't feel quite as foolish. This was a life-altering moment, after all.

They were now legally man and wife. She was his as no one had been since the day he walked through the children's home's doors.

He pulled her to him. "Is it time for the kiss now?"

"Yes, I do believe it is."

He tilted his head down and she met him halfway. Their lips met and clung in a kiss of promise.

He pulled his head back. "Mine."

"Yes, my personal caveman, I am yours. And you are mine." Her soft smile said she didn't mind his Neanderthal moments, but there was an emotion lurking in her azure eyes he did not understand. It was almost as if despite all her assurances to the contrary, linking her life to his frightened her on some level.

"Are you two sure you and Neo aren't blood brothers?" Cass asked with laughter. "You've got so many of the same primitive tendencies."

"We are brothers in every way that counts," Neo said with certainty.

Zephyr nodded his agreement.

"I guess that makes us sisters-in-law," Piper said to Cass with a happy smile.

Cass looked down at her own engagement ring with a satisfied grin. "Come Sunday we will be."

"I'm looking forward to it."

"Me, too."

"Right now, I'm looking forward to a champagne brunch back at the penthouse," Neo said. "My housekeeper has promised a repast fit for the superrich tycoons we are."

But it wasn't the penthouse they ended up in. Neo's housekeeper, Dora, was waiting for them in the lobby of the Nikos and Stamos Enterprises building, along with what looked like the majority of their employees. Big banners that read Congratulations Zephyr and Piper, and Congratulations Neo and Cassandra, hung on either side of the reception area. Black-clad waitstaff walked between groups of Stamos & Nikos Enterprises employees with black trays of food and silver trays of champagne.

Zephyr and Neo's personal assistants were standing together in front of the reception area. "Congratulations!" they said in unison.

"Ms. Parks, you planned this?" Cass asked in shock.

"With the help of Mr. Nikos's personal assistant and Mr.

Stamos's housekeeper, yes." The office automaton actually managed a smile for them all.

Dora rushed up and hugged first Neo and then Zephyr. "We wanted to do something to let you all know how pleased your employees are that you have both found personal happiness."

Cass hugged the housekeeper back and kissed her cheek. "Thank you. This is really special."

The older woman patted Cass's arm. "And you only stay as long as you are comfortable. Everyone understands. You are among friends here."

Several people who had gotten to know Piper when she worked on his projects came up to tell her how happy they were she'd finally made an honest man out of Zephyr. It was unreal. To hear them tell it, plenty of people realized there was something between them.

Of course, the sexual tension between them before they made love the first time had gotten pretty thick. And he hadn't made much effort to hide their intimate relationship afterward.

Neo took good-natured umbrage because he *hadn't* realized, though.

Zephyr just put his arm possessively around Piper's waist and enjoyed himself.

He received more good wishes at the surprise reception than he had over the entire course of his life. There were even gifts—appliances and the usual suspects in wedding presents as well as donations in all their names to area shelters that catered to families with children and to the foster care system.

"It's so perfect," Piper said in a tear-choked voice.

"I have always said we hire the best," Neo said smugly.

"Without doubt," Zephyr agreed.

The employees within earshot smiled, some laughed, and some even returned the compliment.

By the time he led Piper into their apartment a few hours later, an unfamiliar warmth suffused Zephyr's being.

"That was so nice of them," she said as she kicked off her wedding-white shoes.

"Neo was as surprised as I was."

"You had no idea they were planning anything?"

"None at all."

"Cass was shocked Neo's PA was in on it. She thought Ms. Parks hated her."

"I've often wondered if Ms. Parks is even human, but hate Cass? Who could? She's almost as sweet as you."

"You're being sappy again." Piper removed the short veil and tossed it toward the sofa. "I like it."

"And I like the idea of finding out what is underneath your wedding gown."

"Dress…it's a wedding dress. My wedding gown is ten times fancier. I feel like a modern-day royal in it."

"What was the name of the gown's designer again?"

"I didn't tell you and I'm not about to." She walked right into his arms. "I know you'd try to look it up on the designer's Web site."

"Smart, too." He cuddled her close. "Is it any wonder I wanted you for the mother of my children?"

"It's a good thing I got pregnant unexpectedly then, isn't it? You weren't going to do a thing about it." There was something in her tone he could not quite place.

"You know why."

"Yes, but I think we're both getting the long end of the stick on this marriage."

The relief he felt when she said that was all out of proportion.

"Even though I don't…" He didn't finish the thought, curiously unwilling to speak the words denying his love aloud.

So much for his vaunted honesty.

She shook her head, putting her hand up as if she would stop the words from coming out. "Don't say it. Not today. Not right now. I *do* and that's all that matters this minute."

It was not that easy. He knew it, but he could not deny her. "I need you." That had to be enough.

"Yes." With a flirtatious smile that masked something deeper, she put her hands behind her back. "More than you've ever wanted any other woman." Then he heard the sound of a zipper lowering.

His entire being took notice of that tantalizing sound. "In every way, you are unique in my life." That truth was one he could give her without apology.

"That is enough," she said as if she'd read his mind earlier.

"Is it?"

"Yes," she said fiercely. "Isn't it?" she almost demanded.

He nodded, unable to do anything but agree. "Yes. Enough. We arc good together."

She did a little shimmy with her torso and her dress loosened. "We are *great* together." The white chiffon slid forward and down her arms. As it fell, it revealed the top of a baby-blue corselet that pushed her delicious breasts into mouthwatering prominence.

"Amazing."

"Together?"

"In every way."

She smiled that enigmatic smile women had been using on men since time immemorial and shifted her body just so. Air whooshed out of his lungs as the dress fell in a puddle of demure white chiffon at her feet, uncovering the rest of her scandalous unmentionables. The strapless corselet stopped just shy of her hips, leaving the tiny blue satin triangle of the thong she wore below it completely exposed. Her sheer stockings were held up midthigh with matching garters.

She turned in a slow circle, giving him a delectable view of her bare backside framed by the thin strings of her thong, tied together in a perfect little bow right in the center. Looking back over her shoulder, she winked and blew him a provoking kiss.

"You're an agent provocateur."

She gave that perfect peach of a bottom a little wiggle. "I try."

Once she was again facing him, she struck a pose that would have made a 1940s film vamp proud. "You like?"

"I—" His voice broke off in an embarrassing sound he refused to call a squeak. He cleared his throat. "I *adore*. *Yineka mou*, you are my favorite fantasy come to life."

"You've got a thing for pregnant women in sexy lingerie?"

"I've got a *thing* for you looking like a perfectly wrapped gift just waiting to be opened."

"You do seem to enjoy unwrapping me."

"I would have to be insane not to."

She sighed happily and licked her lips in what he would swear was an unconscious motion, despite her obvious attempt to provoke, and that just made the action all the more maddening. "I'm not a supermodel, Zee, but you have a way of making me feel like I could be."

Then that made them even, as she had a way of making him feel like a superhero. He put his hands out to her. "Come here."

She shook her head, the curls she'd put in her silky blond hair swaying against her shoulders. "Not yet."

"Why not?"

"You are wearing too many clothes."

"And you don't want to unwrap me?" he teased.

"Another time."

"You want me to undress for you."

"You know I do."

He did. If he had a tendency to unwrap her like a gift, she made no bones about the fact she got a lot of pleasure out of watching him undress.

He didn't have to do anything corny, like try to emulate a male stripper. Simply removing his clothes in his regular, methodical way could get her color up and turn her breathing erratic.

So, that was what he did. First, slipping out of his jacket and letting it lie where it fell on the floor. His tie came next, then the dress shirt that felt as constricting as a straightjacket.

He toed his shoes and socks off, then his slacks slid down his hips with a single shake before he stepped out of them. There was already a dark wet spot on the front of the black briefs that barely contained his erection, but he did not remove them.

They'd played this game before.

He put his arms out, offering himself for her pleasure. "How's this?"

"You're still wearing one last bit." A knowing smile teased her bow-shaped lips. She liked that last barrier to full disclosure.

"It's less than you."

She put her hand against her chin as if she was thinking that over. Then she shrugged and bent forward, giving him a tempting view of her breasts pressed so provocatively against the top of the corselet.

She stopped with her hands on one of her garters and looked up at him, sensual invitation glowing brightly in her azure eyes. "Did you want to do this?"

Hc did, oh, yes, he did. Without answering, he crossed the distance between them and then dropped to his knees in front of her. Gently, he brushed her hands away. "Mine."

"Yes, my caveman. Unwrap your very personal wedding pressie."

He slid the garter down her leg, caressing her shapely limb through the soft stocking as he did so. He did the other leg before returning to the original stocking to roll it down her thigh, over her calf and slip it off her perfectly shaped foot. "So beautiful."

"Thank you." Her voice was as hushed as his had been.

He removed her last stocking and then caressed up and down her legs. "Your skin is silkier than the stockings."

"Can't talk," she stuttered out as her knees tried to buckle.

He wrapped an arm around her waist to help her stand. "Is that bone in your corset?"

She'd worn this type of thing before and he'd loved it, but the stiffened fabric had never had anything unyielding sewn in its lining to give it form like the sexy number she had on right now.

"Metal. They're metal stays," she managed to say between panting breaths.

He wrapped his hands around her corseted waist, unexpectedly turned on even more by how it felt. "We're courting danger here. If I come in my briefs, blame your too-tempting self."

"You like the lingerie that much?"

"For the first time, I'm tempted to leave your sexy bits on while making love to you." There had been times he had not had the patience to get undressed, but he had never before wanted to keep an article of clothing on her while coupling their bodies.

"Whatever you want."

And damn if that didn't excite him even more.

"But this has to go," he said as he tugged the tie on the back of her thong and pulled the now useless triangle of silk away from her body.

He didn't wait for her to demand equal treatment before removing his own briefs, careful not to catch himself on the dark fabric stretched to capacity. Piper teased him about being oversized, but he thought he was just the right proportion for the tight heat that waited for him between her legs.

She reached out and caressed his length in one long stroke. They both shuddered at the contact. "Want you," she whispered wantonly. "Want this." She squeezed.

He groaned in preorgasmic pleasure. "You need to stop if you want that inside of you before it explodes like a Roman candle."

"More like Mount Vesuvius and I know you, you won't go soft. Not when you're like this."

"You're trying to kill me with pleasure."

She laughed, but the sound stuttered as he returned the favor, sliding his fingers between the wet folds of her sex. He tested the moisture and heat of her vaginal opening, pushing his middle finger far inside her and pressing right against the G-spot he'd spent a good long time acquainting himself with on previous occasions of intimacy.

"Oh, yes, Zee, right there."

He brushed his thumb right over the swollen nub of her pleasure and she squirmed and squealed. "Right *there*, *ne*?"

"Is this where the Greek endearments start?" she gasped out.

"They never stopped, *yineka mou*."

"What does that one mean? Cass seems to like it a lot."

"If you can think about Cass right now, I'm doing something wrong," he mock-growled.

Piper rode his hand with jerky movements. "Just tell me."

"My woman. Literally, now, *my wife*."

"You've always been more possessive than you wanted to admit."

"It's my Mediterranean blood."

She wrapped her arms around his neck, leaning up for a kiss that he didn't hesitate to give her. After several seconds spent in that pleasant pastime, she nuzzled his neck. "Make love to me, *husband*."

CHAPTER TEN

LEAVING their wedding finery in piles on the floor, he swept her into his arms and carried her into the bedroom with long, rapid strides. Once there, he changed his mind about using the bed and detoured to the armchair in the corner.

He sat down and then maneuvered her so she straddled his thighs.

She looked at him with passion-glazed eyes as she rubbed her wet, swollen nether lips against his achingly hard length. "Mmm…"

"Put your hands on the arms of the chair and don't let go," he instructed.

"But—"

"You said anything I wanted."

A sensual little laugh from her sent shivers of sensation through him. "I did."

When her hands were where he wanted them, he pushed up on her hips until she was spread open for him and completely accessible to his touch, but unable to pleasure herself without his cooperation. The fact she allowed him to control their lovemaking like this had his heart rate in the stratosphere and his sex harder than steel.

Her trust awed him, but all he wanted was to give her the maximum amount of pleasure possible. He began with her face, first trailing his fingertips along her cheekbones, jawline and then her lips. "Gorgeous."

She smiled, her lips parted on short panting breaths.

He kissed her, not deeply, just to let her know how much he loved that pretty curve of her mouth. Then he traced over where his fingertips had touched with his lips, then the barely there scrape of his teeth and finally laving each sensitized bit of flesh with the tip of his tongue.

He moved to her neck, caressing every susceptible spot on her nape, shoulders, upper back and chest he had spent so many hours discovering over the past months. She shivered as his fingertips skated over a particularly vulnerable spot between her shoulder blades.

"You play my body better than Cass plays the piano," Piper said on a low moan.

"I am obsessed."

"I believe you." She moaned again as his thumbs slid down inside the corselet and swept back and forth over her turgid nipples.

He kept up the caress, until they were such hard points they felt like pebbles against the pads of his thumbs. "Did it excite you to wear this under your demure little wedding dress?" he growled.

"You know it did." She loved wearing sexy things just for him, things no one else could see or know about but that he would discover when they were alone together.

"I remember the first time you left your panties off during the workday."

"You went ape-crazy when you realized that night in the hotel room."

He had and she'd laughed at him, at both his shock and his excitement, but not meanly. Only in pleasure of a secret shared, a bit of joke for his amusement.

This delectable outfit outdid the panty-free escapade by leaps and bounds.

She moaned and nodded as his mouth found that spot where her shoulder and neck joined that turned her into mush. "I was ready to make love long before the surprise reception was over."

"How did I get so lucky to end up with such a naughty woman?" he wondered out loud.

"I was never like this before." Her breath hitched as he gently bit down on the spot he enjoyed tormenting so much.

He lifted his head and looked at her. "No, this side of you is all mine."

"You're so possessive." She took a deep breath, clearly trying to gain control on her rampaging emotions. "Are you sure you don't have any dragons in your ancestry?"

"No mythical creatures, but maybe a conqueror or two. I am Greek." He had continued the caress of her nipples and breasts with his thumbs. It was enough stimulation to arouse, but not enough to satisfy and he knew it.

"You are incredible. Now, please…just…*please*, stop teasing me."

"I am not teasing you." No, he had every intention of following through on the promise of his touch. "I am driving you to the same frenzy of need roiling inside me."

"I'm already there."

"No, but you will be soon."

He arched up with his hips and used the steel rod between his legs to caress her intimate flesh.

She arched and cried out as his head brushed right over her swollen clitoris. "I want you inside me!"

"Soon." Before she had a chance to complain, he grabbed her corselet-covered waist and shifted her so the opening to her body was poised directly where it needed to be. He brought her down and surged up all in one movement, which elicited a scream of pure pleasure from her and a matching agonized groan from him.

Her restraint broke and she started rocking against him

with pure intent. He met her thrust for thrust until they climaxed together, their bodies caught in the rigor mortis of *la petite mort* for long seconds of bliss so complete, his vision went dark at the edges.

She collapsed against his chest, breathing so hard he got a little worried. He immediately started working on the ties of the corselet, getting it off of her faster than he was sure she'd managed to get into it.

The red marks where it had pressed into her skin were sexy, but he shook his head. "No more corselets or corsets, either, not until after the baby is born."

She fluttered her hand at him, so sated her eyes were mere slits of presleeping exhaustion. "Whatever."

"Thank you. You give the best gifts."

"I try," she slurred against his chest.

She was sleeping by the time he carried her to the bed and tucked her between the sheets, wrapping her securely in his arms.

Piper woke the next morning with a not-so-pleasant feeling of nausea. She groaned and swallowed convulsively as the sensation grew acute when she tried to sit up. She fell back on the bed, but that didn't help. Neither did Zephyr's big arm landing over her middle.

"Ugh…get off, Zee."

"Huh?" He sat straight up in bed, giving her a look of intense inquiry. The man was almost inhuman sometimes. "What is the matter?"

"The baby is finally making itself felt."

He frowned. "You look pale. Are you okay?" His brain seemed to catch up with his mouth and he asked, "What do you mean?"

"Morning nausea."

His expression cleared instantly and he jumped out of the bed with entirely too much energy. "I read about that. There are several recommendations, but the most popular is flat ginger ale and soda crackers. I've got some in the kitchen on standby."

"You've got flattened ginger ale on hand in the kitchen?" she asked, for the moment her incredulity winning over the morning sickness.

"Of course. It's Canada Dry, so there's actually ginger in the beverage. That's what is supposed to help. I've got the necessary inventory for the other suggestions as well, but let's try the crackers and pop first."

"Fine."

He was gone less than a minute before returning with a small package of saltines and a glass of amber liquid. "Take small sips and eat at least five crackers slowly before trying to sit up again."

She did and was thrilled when her next attempt to get out of bed was met with a much more mild form of queasiness. "It helped."

"Good. Now that you'll be sleeping with me every night, I can make sure you have what you need in the morning to keep from feeling too ill."

She smiled at his reiteration that there would be no more nights spent apart. "You've gotten spoiled to having me available for your nightlong cuddle." For a man who had never had a serious relationship, he was a professional cuddler.

"And I can watch over you."

"Right. This minute, you can watch me take a shower, or join me for one. Your choice."

She wasn't the least surprised when he was right behind her stepping into the decadently spacious glassed-in cubicle.

They spent the day enjoying their newly married status and packing for Greece. Everything was rosy until Zephyr had the realization that morning sickness might translate to airsickness. He paced their living room before dinner, reiterating his litany of worries and hinting that maybe they should change their plans.

That was not going to happen.

"I never get nauseated while flying," she tried to assure him.

"But now you have morning sickness."

"Which appears to be limited to mornings, for which I am very grateful."

"I'm thankful for that as well, but we cannot be sure—"

"And we can't prevent it happening by worrying about it, either."

"We should never have planned this wedding blessing in Greece."

Oh, he did not just go there. "You told me that you always expected to get married in Greece, no matter who you ended up married to." And she wasn't letting him lose that dream. Full stop. Period.

"Well, yes."

"And you know it is something I want, too. It just feels right, Zee. Besides, no way are we cancelling our plans now. Half my family is already there and your mom is dying to see you for the first time in decades."

"But—"

"I'm going to be fine. I promise." Man, if he was this bad now, what was he going to be like in the delivery room?

He'd probably demand the good drugs early. Which, come to think of it, was not such a bad thing.

"You cannot promise such a thing."

"I can. You'll be with me, so I know I'll be fine."

"I do not share your confidence."

"That's too bad, but we are not postponing the wedding blessing until I have to waddle down the aisle with a watermelon for a belly."

"Fine, but we will take a supply of soda crackers and flat ginger ale."

"Good idea. A Valium might be a good idea as well."

He stared at her in shocked disapproval. "You cannot take a Valium. It might hurt the baby."

"I wasn't thinking of the antianxiety meds *for me*."

* * *

The next morning was a repeat of the one before it, with the exception that after settling her tummy, Piper and Zephyr got ready to attend Neo and Cass's wedding.

It was a beautiful ceremony in one of Seattle's most traditional cathedral-style churches. Cassandra was a gorgeous bride in a gown with a long train and Neo looked exceedingly handsome in his tailored tuxedo. Zephyr stood up for Neo and one of Cass's first musical protégées acted as her attendant. Neo had invited his housekeeper and doctor. Cass had invited her new agent and a couple of her other former students. Other than Piper, there were no other guests at the formal wedding.

Unless you counted Cass's online friends, who were watching via the live feed from the camera placed on a tripod with a view of the aisle and altar.

Afterward, they all attended an intimate champagne brunch in a private room at one of Seattle's finest restaurants. Piper drank sparkling grape juice and enjoyed herself immensely.

Cass was so incredibly happy, so obviously in love and so very clearly certain of Neo's love that it brought tears to Piper's eyes. Neo didn't leave his bride's side for even a moment between the ceremony and when they left for his penthouse several hours later.

The next day, they were just as sweet. Neo held his brand-new wife's hand in their seats side-by-side on the company jet, while they waited to take off for Greece.

Since Zephyr had Piper's hand firmly clasped in his, she couldn't even work up a little emotional jealousy at the other woman's good fortune in being so obviously loved.

Zephyr might not love her, but if there was a difference in the way he treated her from the way Neo treated Cass, Piper could not see it. Maybe one day, that lack of love would show itself in ways that would hurt, but it wasn't now and Piper wasn't some drama queen who borrowed trouble from what might happen.

* * *

"You're pregnant, aren't you?"

Piper didn't even try to respond to her mother's question immediately. It was her first time alone with her parents since meeting up at the swank hotel Zephyr's secretary had arranged as their home base for the week of the wedding.

They were supposed to be relaxing together in the living area of Piper and Zephyr's palatial suite while Zephyr took a conference call in their bedroom. Afterward, they were going to have dinner together since the following night, Zephyr and Piper would not be available because they would be dining in his mother's home.

"It's not exactly a secret, Piper," her dad said when she didn't answer right away. "Why else would a billionaire marry you on such short noticc?"

"Because he wants to?" she asked, feeling a little piqued her dad would put it that way.

"Does he love you, honey?" her mom asked.

"I love him, very much."

"That's what I thought. Did you get pregnant on purpose? Nothing good ever comes of machinations like that." Her mother sounded like a Victorian matron, not a modern woman with a daughter who was not only well past the age of making her own choices, but also already married and divorced.

"I did not," she replied hotly, seeing no reason to pretend she wasn't offended. "I would never do something like that and you should know me well enough to realize that."

Her mom frowned. "It was a legitimate question."

"No, it wasn't. And what is this, the Spanish Inquisition? I thought you were happy for me. That's how you sounded on the phone. Why all the questions now?"

Her dad made a point of looking around the luxurious suite and then back at Piper. She wasn't sure what that was supposed to signify, maybe more of the whole "what would a billionaire see in you except his baby" thing?

"I'm worried about you, baby." Her mom gave her that look that all mothers knew and all daughters cringed from.

"Don't be." She could not believe this. The church ceremony was in less than forty-eight hours and her parents were pulling some kind of skewed intervention. "Zee is really good to me."

"But is he good for you?" her dad asked in that old military officer-in-charge voice she'd dreaded since she was a child.

"Of course he is. How can you ask that?"

Her mom reached out and squeezed Piper's shoulder. "Money isn't everything."

"You think I am marrying him for his money? *Did you even meet him?*"

"Of course we met him. You introduced us."

"I was being sarcastic, Mom. I just can't believe you think money is the only thing Zephyr has to offer me. Or if it was, that I'd be interested. I've been taking care of myself for a long time. I've built a successful business after having my career trashed. I haven't gone through a string of loser boyfriends since Art. There's just been Zephyr and he's the most amazing man I've ever known."

How could they not see that?

"He's larger than life, that's for sure." Her mom's words agreed with Piper, but her tone was another story. "I'm just not sure that kind of man makes for a secure home."

"Oh, you mean as opposed to a husband whose career requires uprooting yourself and your children every couple of years?" Who was her mother to question Piper's choices based on that criteria, on any?

He dad got all blustery. "There's no reason to get snippy, missy. I was serving my country and well you knew it."

"Well, Zephyr serves me."

"What the hell is that supposed to mean?" her dad demanded.

"He does everything in his power to make me happy." Wasn't that obvious? It was to her. "He takes care of me, but he lets me take care of him, too. He doesn't play lord of the manor with me, but I know I can rely on him when I need him to be there for me."

"But he doesn't love you," her mother guessed in a gentle voice filled with pity.

Wow, was it a parent's job to rip their child's heart out? If it was, Piper wasn't taking that one on when this baby grew up. "Why would you say that?" she demanded in a tone far from friendly.

"Because you didn't say he did. You would have by now if it was true." The pity was still there in her mom's grey eyes.

Piper hated it. She didn't need anyone's pity. She'd chosen this marriage and she didn't regret it. She almost told them about the civil ceremony to shut them up, but she wasn't sure even that would do it. "I have what I need from him."

"You need his heart."

"That's my business."

"You're our daughter," her dad asserted. "Your happiness is our business."

"Zephyr does make me happy. Can't you see that?"

"Your dad and I think you should consider waiting to get married. At least until you get through your first trimester. I miscarried twice. What will you do if that happens to you? What happens to your marriage if the reason for that marriage doesn't come to full term?"

"That is not a scenario I am willing to discuss." She'd thought about it and decided that they would have to deal with that tragedy just like any other couple. She wasn't marrying him for the baby's sake and she didn't think he would dump her for the lack of it, either. He wanted children and one day; God willing in nine months, they would start that part of their family.

"I didn't raise you to hide from the hard stuff, Piper." Her dad's frown was softened by the very real love and concern in his eyes.

That's what she had to cling to, the knowledge that her parents loved her and were only concerned about her. They weren't trying to hurt her. "I'm not hiding."

"She's merely choosing to focus on the positive." Zephyr's voice filled Piper with relief, even as she was mortified at the thought he had overheard even part of this discussion with her parents.

Her father stood up to face Zephyr. "That's all well and good, but maybe you can answer what happens if my daughter doesn't have your baby?"

"We would deal with that tragedy like any other couple."

She couldn't help smiling at his words, which were so like her thoughts. They really were on the same wavelength.

"Some of those couples split up under the weight of the grief and *those* men and women have the benefit of love on both sides."

"I don't know about other people, but I don't give up in the face of adversity and neither does your daughter. You, of all people, should be intimately aware of that fact. She survived leaving friends and familiarity behind time and again in her childhood and a disaster of a first marriage as an adult." He put his arm out to her. "Piper isn't going to give up on our marriage, no matter what we have to face together."

She practically flew off the sofa to land against his side, the relief she felt in the shelter of his presence nearly physical. His words created another welcome layer of protection against her parents' fears and her own secret ones.

He put his arm around her waist and looked down at her as if they were the only two people in the room, as if her opinion was the only one that mattered. "You said nothing would change your feelings for me."

"It won't."

"Well, nothing will change the fact that I want you to be the mother of my children and the woman at my side, including the far-reaching possibility you will not carry this baby to term."

"Then we're golden." She smiled even as tears burned at the back of her eyes.

He set his espresso gaze on each of her parents in turn. "If that's not good enough for you, I am sorry, but I will not give your daughter up. Not now, not ever."

That was a statement of long-term intent if she'd ever heard one.

"We're not suggesting you give her up. Merely that you hold off on the wedding for a while." Piper's mom gave Zephyr her *let's be reasonable* look. "Surely, you can be a father to your child without being married to its mother."

"I can be a better father and helpmate to your daughter if we are married." Zephyr wasn't budging and she didn't think his attitude would be any different if they hadn't already been through a civil ceremony.

Piper was certain that if this discussion had come a week ago, he would have responded the same way. Unlike her parents, who were giving a very different attitude in person than they had when she called to tell them her news.

"I just don't understand," she said. "You didn't say anything about not wanting me to get married when we talked on the phone."

"This isn't something you say over a telephone line." Her mom met her eyes, willing Piper to understand.

She didn't. Not one little bit. "And you wouldn't have gotten a free trip to Greece out of it, either."

"Piper!" her mother admonished.

Her dad just frowned at her with that disappointed expression he reserved for misbehaving troops and his children.

Zephyr shook his head. "She didn't mean that." But he didn't sound disappointed in her.

He understood her parents were really hurting her and right, wrong or indifferent, she'd lashed out. "Of course I didn't. I'm sorry, but this is my time to celebrate and you're diminishing it for me."

"That is not our intention. We just want what is best for you." Her mom sounded as sincere as Piper had.

Zephyr gave her parents a considering look. "Tell me something, did you suggest she wait to marry Arthur Bellingham?"

"No," her mother answered as if she'd been forced to.

"We thought he was perfect for her," Piper's father admitted.

"That is why you are so determined to make her reconsider her decision now, isn't it? You didn't protect her from pain once and now you are going overboard to do so."

Piper had not considered that possibility. "Is that true?"

Her mom's eyes filled with tears. "We just don't want your heart broken again."

"Everyone faces pain in life, but we can't stop taking chances because of it. I trust Zee to be the husband I need. If I'm wrong, I'll deal with the fallout. What I need from you right now is not advice, but support. Can you give that to me?"

"Yes, of course," her dad said even as her mother bit her lip in worry.

But they both hugged her and apologized for hurting her feelings, if not for doubting Zephyr.

Surprisingly, dinner was relaxed and pleasant. It was as if, once having voiced their concerns, her parents gave themselves permission to simply enjoy the celebration of their daughter's second marriage. She appreciated that and did her best not to hold the discussion in her and Zephyr's suite against them.

Thankfully, her siblings' reactions were not nearly so complicated. They were thrilled for her and Zephyr, and let them both know it. They also readily admitted they thought it was beyond lovely they got a free vacation out of attending their baby sister's wedding.

Dinner with Zephyr's mother and her family was every bit as emotional as the afternoon before had been, but in a completely different way. Leda was ecstatic that her son was willing to build a relationship with her. She, too, guessed Piper was pregnant, but treated it completely as the reason for rejoicing that it was. She made it clear she was very happy Zephyr had found Piper to spend the rest of his life with and that she was looking forward to another grandchild to spoil.

His siblings were even more pleased than Piper's, his sister going so far as to offer herself as a resource for a first-time mom.

"That went well," Piper said as she dropped onto the sofa in their suite's living area after returning from the house in Kifissia.

"*Ne*...yes." Zephyr joined her on the couch, tugging her into his body and practically across his lap.

"You're such a cuddler."

"I like holding you."

"That works well for me as I like being snuggled, a lot."

"We are perfect complements to each other." He sounded very satisfied by that observation.

"We are." Even if the love only went one direction, he acted like he loved her, and in the end, wasn't it actions that mattered the most?

"Your parents are wrong," he said with absolute certainty. "This marriage is not a bad thing for either of us."

She leaned up and kissed the corner of his mouth, loving that she had the freedom to do so. "I know. And considering the fact we're already married, that's a good thing."

"Would you have listened more closely to their advice if we hadn't already gotten legally wed?"

"Seriously? You're asking me that?"

"I am."

She tilted her head to one side, considering him, and decided the time had come for a little full disclosure. "I am perfectly aware that there is a significant risk the first trimester."

"So?"

"So, I considered hashing that all out, but I didn't want to wait to marry you until we were sure. It would have felt too much like we were only getting married because I'm pregnant and while I believe that is the reason you first considered marriage, I also believe that you wouldn't tie my life to yours if you didn't want to on a level beyond that. I'm not saying you love me, but I do believe you need me." She cupped his face with both her hands. "And I *want* to be married to you."

"You are saying that you would have wanted to marry me regardless of whether or not you carried my child. The baby was a necessary catalyst to get over *my* reticence."

"Exactly." When he didn't say anything, she asked, "How do you feel about that?"

"I am surprised. Even though you said you loved me, I thought you were marrying me mostly because you are pregnant."

"Nope. I love you, and for me, that sort of goes hand in hand with me wanting to spend the rest of my life with you."

"Does it?"

She dropped her hands from his face, letting them rest against his chest, feeling his heartbeat under one palm. "Yes."

"What does it mean when a man wants to marry a woman more than he wants anything else in his life?"

Was he implying that was how he had felt? "What are you saying, Zephyr?" She couldn't afford to make assumptions about something this important.

"If your parents had convinced you to pull away from me, I would have begged you to reconsider."

"I would *never* push you away."

"That is good to hear because my experience with begging not to be left behind has not been so successful."

Suddenly, she heard exactly what he was saying and her heart filled with an aching, all-consuming love while her eyes filled with tears. "You will never have to beg me not to leave you, Zephyr. Never. I promise. I would give up anything in my life before I would give you up. My business. My reputation. My family. My friends. Anything."

"You mean that."

"Yes."

"I, too, would give up anything to be with you." There was such truth and feeling in his words, she could not breathe. "I love you, Piper."

"You don't mean that." But he did.

She could see it in every line of his face, in the dark depths of his eyes, and hear it in every word that spilled from his lips. Yet even as one part of her was doing cartwheels because he loved her, another was questioning it, doubting this happiness could truly be hers.

"Have I ever lied to you?"

"No, but you said—"

"I would have begged you to stay."

"I'm pregnant with your child."

"A wonderful bonus to be sure, but *you* are the prize, Piper Nikos. I thought my emotions had been encased in stone, but your joy in life, your inner and outer beauty, your love, they are the diamond drill bits needed to break through."

Tears slid hotly down her cheeks, but she did not rub them away. "You're getting poetic."

"Neo says that happens when you fall in love."

"I can't imagine it with him."

"You don't need to. I am the only Greek tycoon you need to be concerned with. Ever."

She wanted to laugh, but her throat was too thick with her joyful tears. "You're certainly the only man, Greek or otherwise, that I love."

"And you are the only woman I love, have ever loved or ever will love with all my heart." He kissed her, sealing the words between them like a vow.

When the kiss ended, he held her close, his hands caressing her like he was giving himself proof that she really was there. "I am sorry it took me so long to realize what I felt for you was love. I do not know how long it might have taken if

I had not overheard your parents trying to talk you out of being with me."

"You mean that conversation actually had something positive come from it?"

"If you consider me realizing I would beg you to stay if I had to and then subsequently coming to terms with what that willingness meant, then yes."

"I guess I can forgive them completely now."

He laughed and so did she.

"I can't wait to tell them you love me."

"I want to do it."

"Okay." She kissed him softly. "But tell me again, first."

And he did. Over and over, until every tiny shadow in her heart was filled with the light of their love.

Zephyr stood at the front of the church, Neo at his side, just as he had been for every life-altering moment since they met in the orphanage in Athens.

"Nervous?" Neo asked.

"Not at all. My love will walk down the aisle in just the right time."

"Did you say your *love*?"

"Ne."

"I knew you'd get your head out of your ass."

Their quiet laughter faded as the organ music heralded his bride's entrance into the sanctuary. Her mother stood and the rest of the guests—their combined families—followed suit. He knew they watched her trek up the aisle like he did, but he could not tear his gaze away from Piper for confirmation.

Her blond hair was piled on top her head in a complicated pile of curls he could not wait to muss. She wasn't wearing a veil this time, just a tiara and a radiant, glorious smile for everyone in the church to see. Her sleeveless gown whispered as one layer of taffeta moved against the other while she walked down the aisle alone.

He had not known that was her plan, but he felt the rightness of it. She offered herself to him, heart, body and soul.

The shimmering beadwork and gathered skirt with the long train on her dress *was* worthy of a modern-day royal.

"She looks like a princess," Neo observed, reflecting Zephyr's thoughts with satisfaction.

Just as Zephyr had felt contentment at Cass's beauty on his brother-by-choice's behalf.

"She is the queen of my heart."

"And you are the king of hers."

"Superman. She thinks I'm a superhero."

Neo laughed, but Zephyr ignored the quiet chuckles as Piper stopped in front of him.

He put his hand out. She took it and they turned to face the priest for a blessing on the marriage that bound the love that had made both their lives complete.

EPILOGUE

PIPER sat on a lounger on the balcony off the master bedroom of the island villa, holding her week-old baby son. He slept in the crook of her arm, oblivious to the heated discussion between his daddy and uncle about whether an American or Greek university would be the best choice for his education.

"Won't they be flabbergasted if little Erastos turns out to be an artist and wants to study at the Sorbonne?" Cass asked with laughter.

"Flabbergasted maybe, but not disappointed. Zephyr will be proud of his son, no matter what path he chooses to follow."

"And Neo? Do you think he will be proud of his child, even if he or she wants to do something flighty like play the piano or something?" Cass asked meaningfully.

"You're pregnant?" Piper demanded with joy.

The other woman had been trying since she and Neo had married, but up to now, the couple had no success. They'd been discussing visiting a fertility specialist.

Cass positively beamed. "I am."

Zephyr stopped arguing midrant and then slapped Neo on the shoulder. "You didn't tell me, you dog!"

"With any luck, we will have a daughter and she will fall as hard for your son as these special women have for us."

Zephyr looked over at Piper, his expression so filled with love it almost hurt to see it. "I can't imagine a better future for my son."

THE GREEK TYCOON'S ACHILLES HEEL

BY
LUCY GORDON

Lucy Gordon cut her writing teeth on magazine journalism, interviewing many of the world's most interesting men, including Warren Beatty, Charlton Heston and Sir Roger Moore. She also camped out with lions in Africa, and had many other unusual experiences which have often provided the background for her books. Several years ago, while staying in Venice, she met a Venetian who proposed in two days. They have been married ever since. Naturally this has affected her writing, where romantic Italian men tend to feature strongly.

Two of her books have won the Romance Writers of America RITA® Award. You can visit her website at www.lucy-gordon.com.

PROLOGUE

THE lights of the Las Vegas Strip gleamed and glittered up into the night sky. Down below, the hotels and casinos rioted with life and money but the Palace Athena outshone them all.

In the six months since its opening it had gained a reputation for being more lavish than its competitors, and today it had put the seal on its success by hosting the wedding of the beautiful, glamorous film star, Estelle Radnor.

The owner of the Palace, no fool, had gained the prestige of staging her wedding by offering everything for free, and the gorgeous Estelle, also no fool where money was concerned, whatever might be said of her taste in men, had seized the offer.

The wedding party finished up in the casino, where the bride was photographed throwing dice, embracing her groom, throwing more dice, slipping an arm around the shoulders of a thin, nondescript young girl, then throwing more dice. The owner watched it all with satisfaction, before turning to a young man who stood regarding the performance sardonically.

'Achilles, my friend—'

'I've told you before, don't call me that.'

'But your name has brought me such good luck. Your excellent advice on how to make this place convincingly Greek—'

'None of which you've taken.'

'Well, my customers *believe* it's Greek and that's what matters.'

'Of course, appearance is everything and what else counts?' the young man murmured.

'You're gloomy tonight. Is it the wedding? Do you envy them?'

'Achilles' turned on him with swift ferocity. 'Don't talk nonsense!' he snapped. 'All I feel is boredom and disgust.'

'Have things gone badly for you?'

A shrug. 'I've lost a million. Before the night's out I'll probably lose another. So what?'

'Come and join the party.'

'I haven't been invited.'

'You think they're going to turn away the son of the wealthiest man in Greece?'

'They're not going to get the chance. Leave me and get back to your guests.'

He strolled away, a lean, isolated figure, followed by two pairs of eyes, one belonging to the man he'd just left, the other to the awkward-looking teenager the bride had earlier embraced. Keeping close to the wall, so as not to be noticed, she slipped away and took the elevator to the fifty-second floor, where she could observe the Strip.

Here, both the walls and the roof were thick glass, allowing visitors to look out in safety. Outside ran a ledge which she guessed was there for workmen and window cleaners, but inaccessible to customers unless they knew the code to tap into the lock.

She was staring down, transfixed, when a slight noise made her turn and see the young man from downstairs. Moving quietly into the shadows, she watched, unnoticed, as he came to stand nearby, gazing down a thousand feet at the dazzling, distant world beneath.

Up here there were only a few lamps, so that customers could look out through the glass. She had a curious view of his face, lit from below by a glow that shifted and changed colour. His features were lean and clean-cut, their slight sharpness emphasised by the angle. It was the face of a very young man, little more than a boy, yet it held a weariness—even a despair—that suggested a crushing burden.

Then he did something that terrified her, reaching out to the code box and tapping in a number, making a pane of glass slide back so that there was nothing but air between him and a thousand foot drop. Petra's sharp gasp made him turn his head.

'What are you doing there?' he snapped. 'Are you spying on me?'

'Of course not. Come back in, please,' she begged. 'Don't do it.'

He stepped back into comparative safety, but remained near the gap.

'What the hell do you mean, "don't do it"?' he snapped. 'I wasn't going to *do* anything. I wanted some air.'

'But it's dangerous. You could fall by accident.'

'I know what I'm doing. Go away and let me be.'

'No,' she said defiantly. 'I have as much right to take the air as you. Is it nice out there?'

'What?'

Moving so fast that she took him by surprise, she slipped past him and out onto the ledge. At once the wind attacked her so that she had to reach out and found him grasping her.

'You stupid woman!' he shouted. 'I'm not the only one who can have an accident. Do you want to die?'

'Do you?'

'Come inside.'

He yanked her back in, stopping short in surprise when he saw her face.

'Didn't I see you downstairs?'

'Yes, I was in the Zeus Room,' she said, naming the casino. 'I like watching people. That place is very cleverly named.'

'You know what Zeus means, then?' he asked, drawing her away to where they could sit down.

'He was the King of the Greek gods,' she said, 'looking down on the world from his home on the top of Mount Olympus, master of all he surveyed. That must be how the gamblers feel when they start playing, but the poor idiots soon learn differently. Did you lose much?'

He shrugged. 'A million. I stopped counting after a while. What are you doing in a casino, anyway? You can't be more than fifteen.'

'I'm seventeen and I'm...one of the bridal party.'

'That's right,' he said, seeming not to notice the way she'd checked herself at the last moment. 'I saw her embracing you for the camera. Are you a bridesmaid?'

She regarded him cynically. 'Do I look like a bridesmaid?' she demanded, indicating her attire, which was clearly expensive but not glamorous.

'Well—'

'I don't really belong in front of the cameras, not with that lot.'

She spoke with a wry lack of self-pity that was attractive. Looking at her more closely, he saw that she wore no make-up, her hair was cut efficiently short, and she'd made no attempt to enhance her appearance.

'And your name is—?' he queried.

'Petra. And you're Achilles. No?' The last word was a response to his scowl.

'My name is Lysandros Demetriou. My mother wanted to call me Achilles, but my father thought she was being sentimental. In the end they compromised, and Achilles became my second name.'

'But that man downstairs called you by it.'

'It's important to him that I'm Greek because this place is built on the idea of Greekness.'

To his delight she gave a cheeky giggle. 'They're all potty.'

They took stock of each other. He was as handsome as she'd first sensed, with clean cut features, deep set eyes and an air of pride that came with a lifetime of having his own way. But there was also a darkness and a brooding intensity that seemed strange in this background. Young men in Las Vegas hunted in packs, savouring every experience. This one hid away, treasuring his solitude as though the world was an enemy. And something had driven him to take the air in a place full of danger.

'Demetriou Shipbuilding?' she asked.

'That's the one.'

'The most powerful firm in Greece.' She said it as though reciting a lesson. 'What they don't want isn't worth having. What they don't acquire today they'll acquire tomorrow. If anyone dares to refuse them, they wait in the shadows until the right moment to pounce.'

He grunted. 'Something like that.'

'Or maybe you'll just turn the Furies onto them?'

She meant the three Greek goddesses of wrath and vengeance, with hair made of snakes and eyes that dripped blood, who hounded their victims without mercy.

'Do you have to be melodramatic?' he demanded.

'In this "pretend" Greek place I can't help it. Anyway, why aren't you in Athens grinding your enemies to dust?'

'I've done with all that,' he said harshly. 'They can get on without me.'

'Ah, this is the bit where you sulk.'

'What?'

'During the Trojan war Achilles was in love with this girl. She actually came from the other side, and was his prisoner, but they made him give her back, so he withdrew from the battle and sulked in his tent. But in the end he came out and started fighting again. Only he ended up dead. As you could have done on that ledge.'

'I told you I wasn't planning to die, although frankly it doesn't seem important one way or the other. I'll take what comes.'

'Did she do something very cruel?' Petra asked gently.

In the dim light she could barely see the look he turned on her, but she sensed that it was terrible. His eyes were harsh and cold in the gloom, warning her that she'd trespassed on sacred ground.

'Stop now!' howled the Furies. 'Run for your life before he strikes you dead.'

But that wasn't her way.

'She?' he asked in a voice that warned her.

She laid a gentle hand on his arm, whispering, 'I'm sorry. Shouldn't I have said that?'

He rose sharply and strode back to the gap in the glass wall and stood gazing out into the night. She followed cautiously.

'She made me trust her,' he whispered.

'But sometimes it's right to trust.'

'No,' he insisted. 'Nobody is ever as good as you think they are, and sooner or later the truth is always there. The more you trust someone, the worse it is when they betray you. Better to have no illusions, and be strong.'

'But that would be terrible, never to believe in anything, never to love or hope, never be really happy—'

'Never to be wretched,' he said harshly.

'Never to be alive,' she said with gentle urgency. 'It would be a living death, can't you see that? You'd escape suffering, but you'd also lose everything that makes life worth living.'

'Not everything. There's power. You'd gain that if you did without the other things. They're only weaknesses.'

'No,' she said, almost violently. 'You mustn't give in to that way of thinking or you'll ruin your life.'

'And what do you know about it?' he demanded, angry now. 'You're a child. Has anyone ever made you want to smash things and keep on smashing until nothing is left alive—including yourself?'

'But what do you gain by destroying yourself inside?' she demanded.

'I'll tell you what you gain. You don't become—like this.' He jabbed a finger at his heart.

She didn't have to ask what he meant. Young as he was, he lived on the edge of disaster, and it would take very little to push him over. That was why he dared to stand here, defying the fates to do their worst.

Pity and terror almost overwhelmed her. Part of her wanted to run for her life, get far, far away from this creature who might become a monster if something didn't intervene. But the other part wanted to stay and be the one to rescue him.

Suddenly, without warning, he did the thing that decided her, something terrible and wonderful in the same moment. Lowering his head, he let it fall against her shoulder, raised it, dropped it again, and again and again. It was like watching a man bang his head against a brick wall, hopelessly, robotically.

Appalled, she threw her arms around him and clutched a restraining hand over his head, forcing him to be still. His despair seemed to reach out to her, imploring her comfort, saying that only she could give it to him. To be needed so desperately was a new experience for her and, even in the midst of her dismay, she knew a kind of delight.

Over his shoulder she could see the drop, with nothing to protect him from it. Nothing but herself. She gripped him tight, silently offering him all she could. He didn't resist, but now his head rested on her shoulder as though the strength had drained out of him.

When she drew back to see his face the bitter anguish had gone, leaving it sad and resigned, as though he'd found a kind of peace, albeit a bleak and despairing peace.

At last Lysandros gave her a faint smile, feeling deep within him a desire to protect her as she had tried to protect him. There was still good in the world. It was here in this girl, too innocent to understand the danger she ran just by being here with him. In the end she would be sullied and spoiled like the rest.

But not tonight. He wouldn't allow it.

He tapped a number into the code pad and the glass panel closed.

'Let's go,' he said, leading her away from the roof and down into the hotel.

Outside her door he said, 'Go inside, go to bed, don't open this door to anyone.'

'What are you going to do?'

'I'm going to lose a lot more money. After that—I'm going to do some thinking.'

He hadn't meant to say the last words.

'Goodnight, Achilles.'

'Goodnight.'

He hadn't intended what he did next either, but on impulse he leaned down and kissed her mouth gently.

'Go in,' he said. 'And lock your door.'

She nodded and slipped inside. After a moment he heard the key turn.

He returned to the tables, resigned to further losses, but mysteriously his luck turned. In an hour he'd recovered every penny. In another hour he'd doubled it.

So that was who she was, a good luck charm, sent to cast her spell and change his fortunes. He only hoped he'd also done something for her, but he would probably never know. They would never meet again.

He was wrong. They did meet again.

But not for fifteen years.

CHAPTER ONE

THE Villa Demetriou stood on the outskirts of Athens on raised ground, from which the family had always been able to survey the domain they considered theirs. Until now the only thing that could rival them had been the Parthenon, the great classical temple built more than two thousand years before, high on the Acropolis, far away across the city and just visible.

Recently a new rival had sprung up, a fake Parthenon, created by Homer Lukas, the one man in Greece who would have ventured to challenge either the Demetriou family or the ancient gods who protected the true temple. But Homer was in love, and naturally wished to impress his bride on their wedding day.

On that spring morning Lysandros Demetriou stood in the doorway of his villa, looking out across Athens, irritated by having to waste his time at a wedding when he had so many really important things to deal with.

A sound behind him made him turn to see the entrance of Stavros, an old friend of his late father, who lived just outside the city. He was white-haired and far too thin, the result of a lifetime of self-indulgence.

'I'm on my way to the wedding,' he said. 'I called in to see if you fancied a lift.'

'Thank you, that would be useful,' Lysandros said coolly. 'If I arrive early it won't give too much offence if I leave early.'

Stavros gave a crack of laughter. 'You're not sentimental about weddings.'

'It's not a wedding, it's an exhibition,' he said sardonically. 'Homer Lukas has acquired a film star wife and is flaunting her to the world. The world will offer him good wishes and call him names behind his back. My own wish for him is that Estelle Radnor will make a fool of him. With any luck, she will.

'Why did she have to come to Athens to get married, anyway? Why not make do with a false Greek setting, like that other time?'

'Because the name of Homer Lukas is synonymous with Greek shipbuilding,' Stavros said, adding quickly, 'after yourself, of course.'

For years the companies of Demctriou and Lukas had stood head and shoulders above all others in Greece, or even in the world, some reverently claimed.

They were opponents, foes, even outright enemies, but enemies who presented a civilised veneer to outsiders because it was profitable to do so.

'I suppose it might be a real love-match,' Stavros observed cynically.

Lysandros raised his eyebrows. 'A real—? How many times has she been married? Six, seven?'

'You should know. Weren't you a guest at one of the previous weddings, years ago?'

'Not a guest. I just happened to be in the Las Vegas hotel where it was held and watched some of the shenanigans from a safe distance. And I returned to Greece the next day.'

'Yes, I remember that. Your father was very puzzled—pleased, but puzzled. Apparently you'd told him you wanted nothing more to do with the business now or ever again. You vanished for two years, but suddenly, out of the blue, you just walked in the door and said you were ready to go to work. He was even afraid you wouldn't be up to it after…well…'

He fell silent, alarmed by the grim look that had come over Lysandros's face.

'Quite,' he said in a quiet voice that was more frightening than a shout. 'Well, it's a long time ago. The past is over.'

'Yes, and your father said that all his fears were groundless because when you returned you were different, a tiger who terrified everyone. He was so proud.'

'Well, let's hope I terrify Homer Lukas. Otherwise I'm losing my touch.'

'Perhaps you should be scared,' Stavros said. 'Such threats he's been uttering since you recently bilked him and his son of billions. *Stole* billions, according to him.'

'I didn't steal anything, I merely offered the client a better deal,' Lysandros said indifferently.

'But it was at the last minute,' Stavros recalled. 'Apparently they were all assembled to sign the contracts, and the client had actually lifted the pen when his phone rang and it was you, giving him some information that you could only have acquired "by disgraceful means".'

'Not as disgraceful as all that,' Lysandros observed with a shrug. 'I've done worse, I'm glad to say.'

'And that was that,' Stavros resumed. 'The man put the pen down, cancelled the deal and walked out straight into your car, waiting outside. Rumour says Homer promised the gods on Olympus splendid offerings if only they would punish you.'

'But I've remained unpunished, so perhaps the gods weren't listening. They say he even uttered a curse over my wedding invitation. I hope he did.'

'You're really not taking anyone with you?'

Lysandros made a non-committal reply. He attended many weddings as a duty, sometimes with companions but never with one woman. It would interest the press too much, and send out misleading signals to the lady herself, which could cause him serious inconvenience.

'Right, let's get going,' Stavros said.

'I'm afraid I'll have to catch you up later,' Lysandros excused himself.

'But you just said you'd go with me—'

'Yes, but I've suddenly remembered something I must do first. Goodbye.'

There was a finality in the last word that Stavros dared not challenge.

His car was waiting downstairs. In the back sat his wife, who'd refused to come in with him on the grounds that she hated the desolate house that seemed to suit Lysandros so perfectly.

'How can he bear to live in that vast, silent place with no family and only servants for company?' she'd demanded more than once. 'It makes me shiver. And that's not the only thing about Lysandros that makes me shiver.'

In that, she knew she was not alone. Most of Athens would have agreed. Now, when Stavros had described the conversation, she said, 'Why did he change his mind about coming with us?'

'My fault. I stupidly mentioned the past, and he froze. It's almost eerie the way he's blotted that time out as though it never happened, yet it drives everything he does. Look at what happened just now. One minute he was fine, the next he couldn't get rid of me fast enough.'

'I wonder why he's really going to leave early.'

'He'll probably pass the time with a floozy.'

'If you mean—' she said a name, 'she's hardly a floozy. Her husband's one of the most influential men on the—'

'Which makes her a high class floozy, and she's keeping

her distance now because her husband has put his foot down. Rumours reached him.'

'He probably knew all the time,' his wife said cynically. 'There are men in this city who don't mind their women sleeping with Lysandros.'

Stavros nodded. 'Yes, but I gather she became too "emotional", started expecting too much, so he dropped the husband a hint to rein her in if he knew what was good for him.'

'Surely even Lysandros wouldn't be so cruel, so cold-blooded—'

'That's exactly what he is, and in our hearts we all know it,' Stavros said flatly.

'I wonder about *his* heart,' she mused.

'He doesn't have one, which is why he keeps people at a distance.'

As the car turned out of the gate Stavros couldn't resist looking back to the house. Lysandros stood there at the window, watching the world with a brooding air, as though it was his personal property and he had yet to decide how to manage it.

He remained there until the car had vanished through the gates, then turned back into the room, trying to clear his mind. The conversation had disturbed him and that must be quickly remedied. Luckily an urgent call came through from his manager at the port of Piraeus, to say that they were threatened with union trouble. Lysandros gave him a series of curt orders and promised to be there the next day.

Today he would attend Homer Lukas's wedding as an honoured guest. He would shake his rival's hand, show honour to the bride, and the watching crowds would sigh with disappointment not to see them at each other's throats, personally as well as professionally.

Now, more than ever, his father's advice rang in his head. *'Never, never let them know what you're thinking.'*

He'd learned that lesson well and, with its aid, he would spend today with a smile on his face, concealing the hatred that consumed him.

At last it was time for his chauffeur to take him to the Lukas estate. Soon he could see Homer's 'Parthenon', in which the wedding was to take place, and it loomed up high, proclaiming the residence of a wealthy and influential man.

A fake, he thought grimly. No more authentic than the other 'Greek setting' in Las Vegas.

His thoughts went back to a time that felt like another world and through his mind danced the girl on the roof, skinny, ordinary, yet with an outspoken innocence that had both exasperated and charmed him. And at the last moment, when she'd opened her arms to him, offering a comfort he'd found nowhere else in the world and he'd almost—

He slammed his mind shut. It was the only way to deal with weakness.

He wondered how she'd come to be one of the wedding party; probably the daughter of one of Estelle Radnor's numerous secretaries.

She might be here today, but it was probably better not to meet again after so long. Time was never kind. The years would have turned her into a dull wife with several children and a faithless husband. Where once she had sparkled, now she would probably seethe.

Nor had he himself been improved by time, he knew. A heaviness had settled over him, different from the raging grief that had possessed him in those days. That had been a matter of the heart and he'd dealt with it suitably, setting it aside, focusing on his head, where all sensible action took place.

He'd done what was right and wise, yet he had an uneasy feeling that if he met her now she would look right through him—and disapprove.

At last they arrived. As he got out of his car and looked around he had to admit that Homer had spent money to great effect. The great temple to the goddess Athena had been re-created much as the original must have looked when it was new. The building was about seventy metres by thirty, the roof held aloft by elegant columns. Marvellous statues abounded, but the greatest of all was the forty-foot statue of Athena, which had mysteriously developed the face of Estelle Radnor.

He grimaced, wondering how long it would be before he could decently depart.

But, before he could start his social duties, his cellphone shrilled. It was a text message.

I'm sorry about what I said. I was upset. You seemed to be pulling away when we'd been growing so close. Please call me.

It was signed only with an initial. He immediately texted back.

No need to be sorry. You were right to break it off. Forgive me for upsetting you.

Hopefully that would be an end to it, but after a moment another text came through.

I don't want to break off. I really didn't mean all those things. Will I see you at the wedding? We could talk there.

This time it was signed with her name. He responded.

We always knew it couldn't last. We can't talk. I don't wish to subject you to gossip.

The answer came in seconds.

I don't care about gossip. I love you.

Madness seemed to have come over her, for now she'd stepped up the intensity, signing *your own forever*, followed by her name. His response was brief.

Please accept my good wishes for the future. Make sure you delete texts from your phone. Goodbye.

After that he switched off. In every way. To silence a

machine was easy. It was the switching off of the heart and mind that took skill, but it was one he'd acquired with practice, sharpening it to perfection until he would have guaranteed it against every female in the world.

Except perhaps one.

But he would never meet her again.

Unless he was very unlucky.

Or very lucky.

'You look *gorgeous*!'

Petra Radnor laughed aside the fervent compliment from Nikator Lukas.

'Thank you, brother dear,' she said.

'Don't call me that. I'm not your brother.'

'You will be in a couple of hours, when your father has married my mother.'

'Stepbrother at most. We won't be related by blood and I can yearn after you if I want to.'

'No, I think you'll be the brother I've always wanted. My *kid* brother.'

'Kid, nothing! I'm older than you.'

It was true. He was thirty-seven to her thirty-two, but there was something about him that suggested a kid; not just the boyish lines of his face but a lingering immaturity that would probably be there all his life.

Petra liked him well enough, except for his black moods that seemed to come from nowhere, although they also vanished quickly.

He admired her extravagantly, and she justified his admiration. The gaunt figure of her teen years had blossomed, although she would always be naturally slender.

She was attractive but not beautiful, certainly not as the word was understood among her mother's film-land friends.

She had a vivid personality that gleamed from her eyes and a humour that was never long suppressed. But the true effect was often discovered only after she'd departed, when she lingered in the mind.

To divert Nikator's attention, she turned the conversation to Debra, the starlet who would be his official companion.

'You two look wonderful together,' she said. 'Everyone will say what a lucky man you are.'

'I'd rather go with you,' he sighed.

'Oh, stop it! After all the trouble Estelle took to fix you up with her, you should be grateful.'

'Debra's gorgeous,' he conceded. 'At least Demetriou won't have anything to match her.'

'Demetriou? Do you mean Lysandros Demetriou?' Petra asked, suddenly concentrating on a button. '*The* Lysandros Demetriou?'

'There's no need to say it like that, as though he was important,' Nikator said at once.

'He certainly seems to be. Didn't he—?'

'Never mind that. He probably won't have a woman on his arm.'

'I've heard he has quite a reputation with women.'

'True. But he never takes them out in public. Too much hassle, I guess. To him they're disposable. I'll tell you this, half the women who come here today will have been in his bed.'

'You really hate him, don't you?' she asked curiously.

'Years ago he was involved with a girl from this family, but he ill-treated her.'

'How?'

'I don't know the details. Nobody does.'

'Then maybe she ill-treated him,' Petra suggested. 'And he reacted badly because he was disillusioned.'

He glared at her. 'Why would you think that?'

'I don't know,' she said, suddenly confused. A voice had whispered mysteriously in her mind, but she couldn't quite make out the words. It came from long ago, and haunted her across the years. If only—

She tried to listen but now there was only silence.

'She fled, and later we heard that she was dead,' Nikator continued. 'It was years ago, but he knew how to put the knife in, even then. Be warned. When he knows you're connected with this family he'll try to seduce you, just to show us that he can do it.'

'Seduce?' she echoed with hilarity. 'What do you think I am—some helpless maiden? After all this time around the film industry I've learned to be safely cynical, I promise you. I've even been known to do a bit of "seducing" myself.'

His eyes gleamed and he reached out hopeful hands. 'Ah, in that case—'

'Be off,' she told him firmly. 'It's time you left to collect Debra.'

He dashed away, much to her relief. There were aspects of Nikki that were worrying, but that must wait. This was supposed to be a happy day.

She checked her camera. There would be an army of professional photographers here today, but Estelle, as she always called her mother, had asked her to take some intimate family pictures.

She took one last look in the mirror, then frowned at what she saw. As Nikator had said, she looked gorgeous, but what might be right for other women wasn't right for Estelle Radnor's daughter. This was the bride's big day, and she alone must occupy the spotlight.

'Something a little more restrained, I think,' Petra murmured.

She found a darker dress, plainer, more puritanical. Then she swept her luxuriant hair back into a bun and studied herself again.

'That's better. Nobody will look at me now.'

She'd grown up making these adjustments to her mother's ego. It was no longer a big deal. She was fond of Estelle, but the centre of her life was elsewhere.

The bride had already moved into the great mansion, and now occupied the suite belonging to the mistress of the house. Petra hurried along to say a last encouraging word before it was time to start.

That was when things went wrong.

Estelle screamed when she saw her daughter.

'Darling, what are you thinking of to dress like that? You look like a Victorian governess.'

Petra, who was used to her mother's way of putting things, didn't take offence. She knew by now that it was pointless.

'I thought I'd keep it plain,' she said. 'You're the one they'll be looking at. And you look absolutely wonderful. You'll be the most beautiful bride ever.'

'But people know you're *my* daughter,' Estella moaned. 'If you go out there looking middle-aged, what will they say about *me*?'

'Perhaps you could pretend I'm not your daughter,' Petra said with wry good humour.

'It's too late for that. They already know. You've got to look young and innocent or they'll wonder how old *I* am. Really, darling, you might try to do *me* credit.'

'I'm sorry. Shall I go and change?'

'Yes, do it quickly. And take your hair down.'

'All right, I'll change. Have a wonderful day.'

She kissed her mother and felt herself embraced as warmly as though there'd never been an argument. Which, in a sense, was true. Having got her own way, Estelle had forgotten it had ever happened.

As she left the room Petra was smiling, thinking it lucky

that she had a sense of humour. Thirty-two years as Estelle Radnor's daughter had had certain advantages, but they had also demanded reserves of patience.

Back in her room, she reversed the changes, donning the elegantly simple blue silk dress she'd worn before and brushing her hair free so that it fell gloriously about her shoulders. Then she went out into the grounds where the crowds were gathering and plunged into introductions. She smiled and said the right things, but part of her attention was elsewhere, scanning the men to see if Lysandros Demetriou had arrived.

The hour they had spent together, long ago, now felt like a dream, but he'd always held her interest. She'd followed his career as far as she could, gathering the sparse details of his life that seeped out. He was unmarried and, since his father's death had made him the boss of Demetriou Shipbuilding, he lived alone. That was all the world was allowed to know.

Occasionally she saw a photograph that she could just identify as the man she'd met in Las Vegas. These days his face looked fearsome, but now another face came into her mind, a naïve, disillusioned young lover, tortured out of his mind, crying, 'She made me trust her,' as though that was the worst crime in the world.

The recent pictures showed a man on whom harshness had settled early. It was hard to realise that he was the same person who'd clung to her on that high roof, seeking refuge, not from the physical danger he'd freely courted, but from the demons that howled in his head.

What had become of that need and despair? Had he yielded to the desire to destroy everything, including his own heart?

What would he say to her if they met now?

Petra was no green girl. Nor was she a prude. In the years since then she'd been married, divorced, and enjoyed male company to the full. But that encounter, short but searingly intense, lived in her mind, her heart and her senses. The awareness of an overwhelming presence was with her still, and so was the disappointment she'd felt when he'd parted from her with only the lightest touch of the lips.

Now the thought of meeting Lysandros Demetriou again gave her a frisson of pleasurable curiosity and excitement. But strangely there was also a touch of nervousness. He'd loomed so large in her imagination that she feared lest the reality disappoint her.

Then she saw him.

She was standing on the slope, watching the advancing crowd, and even among so many it was easy to discern him. It wasn't just that he was taller than most men; it was the same intense quality that had struck her so forcefully the first time, and which now seemed to sing over the distance.

The pictures hadn't done him justice, she realised. The boy had grown into a handsome man whose stern features, full of pride and aloofness, would have drawn eyes anywhere. In Las Vegas she'd seen him mostly in poor light. Now she could make out that his eyes were dark and deep-set, as though even there he was holding part of himself back.

Nikator had said no woman would be with him, and that was true. Lysandros Demetriou walked alone. Even in that milling crowd he gave the impression that nobody could get anywhere near him. Occasionally someone tried to claim his attention. He replied briefly and passed on.

The photographer in Petra smiled. Here was a man whose picture would be worth taking, and if that displeased him at first he would surely forgive her, for the sake of their old acquaintance.

She took a picture, then another. Smiling, she began to walk down until she was only a few feet in front of him. He glanced up, noticed the camera and scowled.

'Put that away,' he said.

'But—'

'And get out of my sight.'

Before she could speak again he'd passed on. Petra was left alone, her smile fading as she realised that he'd looked right through her without a hint of recognition.

There was nothing to do but move on with the crowd and take her place in the temple. She tried to shrug and reason with herself. So he hadn't recognised her! So what? It had been years ago and she'd changed a lot.

But, she thought wryly, she could dismiss any fantasies about memories reaching over time. Instead, it might be the chance to have a little fun.

Yes, fun would be good. Fun would punish him!

The music started as the bride made her entrance, magnificently attired in fawn satin, looking nowhere near fifty, her true age.

Petra joined the other photographers, and forgot everything except what she was meant to be doing. It was an ability that had carried her through some difficult times in her life.

Lysandros was seated in the front row. He frowned at her as if trying to work something out, then turned his attention to the ceremony.

The vows were spoken in Greek. The bride had learned her part well, but there was just one moment when she hesitated. Quickly, Petra moved beside her, murmured something in Greek and stepped back. Lysandros, watching, frowned again.

Then the bride and groom were moving slowly away, smiling at the crowd, two wealthy, powerful people, revelling in having acquired each other. Everyone began to leave the temple.

'Lysandros, my friend, how good to see you.'

He turned and saw Nikator advancing on him, arms outstretched as though welcoming a long-lost friend. Assuming a smile, he returned the greeting. With a flourish Nikator introduced his companion, Debra Farley. Lysandros acted suitably impressed. This continued until everyone felt that enough time had elapsed, and then the couple moved on.

Lysandros took a long breath of relief at having got that out of the way.

A slight choke made him turn and see the young woman with the luscious fair hair. She was laughing as though he'd just performed for her entertainment, and he was suddenly gripped by a rising tension, neither pleasure nor pain but a mysterious combination of both, as though the world had shifted on its axis and nothing would ever be the same again.

CHAPTER TWO

'YOU did that very convincingly,' Petra said. 'You should get an Oscar.'

She'd spoken in Greek and he replied in the same language.

'I wasn't as convincing as all that if you saw through me.'

'Oh, I automatically disbelieve everyone,' she said in a teasing voice. 'It saves a lot of time.'

He gave a polite smile. 'How wise. You're used to this kind of event, then? Do you work for Homer?' He indicated her camera.

'No, I've only recently met him.'

'What do you think of him?'

'I've never seen a man so in love.' She shook her head, as if suggesting that this passed all understanding.

'Yes, it's a pity,' he said.

'What do you mean?'

'You don't think the bride's in love with him, surely? To her, he's a decoration to flaunt in her buttonhole, in addition to the diamonds he's showered on her. The best of her career is over so she scoops him up to put on her mantel-piece. It almost makes me feel sorry for him, and I never thought I'd say that.'

'But that means someone has brought him low at last,' she

pointed out. 'You should be grateful to her. Think how much easier you'll find it to defeat him in future.'

She was regarding him with her head on one side and an air of detached amusement, as though he was an interesting specimen laid out for her entertainment. A sudden frisson went through him. He didn't understand why, and yet—

'I think I can manage that without help,' he observed.

'Now, there's a thought,' she said, apparently much struck. 'Have you noticed how weddings bring out the worst in people? I'm sure you aren't usually as cynical and grumpy as now.'

This was sheer impertinence, but instead of brushing her aside he felt an unusual inclination to spar with her.

'Certainly not,' he said. 'I'm usually worse.'

'Impossible.'

'Anyone who knows me will tell you that this is my "sweetness and light" mood.'

'I don't believe it. Instinct tells me that you're a softie at heart. People cry on your shoulder, children flock to you, those in trouble turn to you first.'

'I've done nothing to deserve that,' he assured her fervently.

The crowd was swirling around them, forcing them to move aside. As they left the temple, Lysandros observed, 'I'm surprised Homer settled for an imitation Parthenon.'

'Oh, he wanted the original,' she agreed, 'but between you and me—' she lowered her voice dramatically '—it didn't quite measure up to his standards, and he felt he could do better. So he built this to show them how it ought to have been done.'

Before he could stop himself he gave a crack of laughter and several people stared at the sight of this famously dour man actually enjoying a joke. A society journalist passing by stared, then made a hasty note.

She responded to his laughter with more of her own. He led her to where the drinks were being served and presented her with a glass of champagne, feeling that, just for once, it was good to be light-hearted. She had the power of making tension vanish, even if only briefly.

The tables for the wedding feast were outside in the sun. The guests were taking their places, preparing for the moment when the newly married couple would appear.

'I'll be back in a moment,' she said.

'Just a minute. You haven't told me who you are.'

She glanced back, regarding him with a curious smile. 'No, I haven't, have I? Perhaps I thought there would be no need. I'll see you later.'

Briefly she raised her champagne glass to him before hurrying away.

'You're a sly devil,' said a deep voice behind him.

A large bearded man stood there and with pleasure Lysandros recognised an old ally.

'Georgios,' he exclaimed. 'I might have known you'd be where there was the best food.'

'The best food, the best wine, the best women. Well, you've found that for yourself.' He indicated the young woman's retreating figure.

'She's charming,' Lysandros said with a slight reserve. He didn't choose to discuss her.

'Oh, don't worry, I'll back off. I don't aspire to Estelle Radnor's daughter.'

Lysandros tensed. 'What are you talking about?'

'I don't blame you for wanting to keep her to yourself. She's a peach.'

'You said Estelle Radnor's daughter.'

'Didn't she tell you who she was?'

'No,' Lysandros said, tight-lipped. 'She didn't.'

He moved away in Petra's direction, appalled at the trap into which he'd fallen so easily. His comments about her mother had left him at a disadvantage, something not to be tolerated. She could have warned him and she hadn't, which meant she was laughing at him.

And most men would have been beguiled by her merriment, her way of looking askance, as though that was how she saw the whole world, slightly lopsided, and all the more fun for that.

Fun. He barely knew the word, but something told him she knew it, loved it, even judged by it. And she was doubtless judging him now. His face hardened.

It was too late to catch her; she'd reached the top table where the bride and groom would sit. Now there would be no chance for a while.

A steward showed him to his place, also at the top table but just around the corner at right angles to her—close enough to see her perfectly, but not talk.

She was absorbed in chatting to her companion. Suddenly she laughed, throwing back her head and letting her amusement soar up into the blue sky. It was as though sunshine had burst out all over the world. Unwillingly he conceded that she would be enchanting, if—*if* he'd been in a mood to be enchanted. Fortunately, he was more in control than that.

Then she looked up and caught his eye. Clearly she knew that her little trick had been rumbled, for her teasing gaze said, *Fooled you!*

He sent back a silent message of his own. *Wait, that's all. Just wait!*

She looked forward to it. Her smile told him that, causing a stirring deep within him that he had to conceal by fiercely blanking his face. People sitting close by drew back a little, wondering who had offended him.

There was a distant cheer and applause broke out as Mr and Mrs Homer Lukas made their grand entrance.

He was in his sixties, grey-haired and heavily built with an air of natural command. But as he and his bride swept into place it suited him to bend his head over her hand, kissing it devotedly. She seemed about to faint with joy at his tribute, or perhaps at the five million dollar diamond on her finger.

The young woman who'd dared to tease Lysandros joined in the applause, and kissed her mother as Estelle sat down. The crowd settled to the meal.

Of course he should never have mistaken her for an employee. Her air of being at home in this company ought to have warned him. And when she moved in to take close-up photographs both bride and groom posed at her command.

Then she posed with the happy couple while a professional photographer took the shots. At this point Nikator butted in.

'We must have some of us together,' Lysandros could just hear him cry. 'Brother and sister.'

Having claimed a brother's privilege, he snaked an arm about her waist and drew her close. She played up, but Lysandros spotted a fleeting look of exasperation on her face, and she freed herself as soon as possible, handing him back to Debra Farley like a nurse ridding herself of a pesky child.

Not that he could blame Nikator for his preference. In that glamorous company this creature stood out, with her effortless simplicity and an air of naturalness that the others had lost long ago. Her dress was light blue silk, sleeveless, figure-hugging, without ornament. It was practically a proclamation, as though she were saying, *I need no decoration. I, myself, am enough.*

No doubt about that.

As the party began to break up he made his way over to her. She was waiting for him with an air of teasing expectancy.

'I suppose that'll teach me to be more careful next time,' he said wryly.

'You were a little incautious, weren't you?'

'You thought it was a big joke not to tell me who you were while I said those things about your mother.'

'I didn't force you to say them. What's the matter with you? Can't you take a joke?'

'No,' he said flatly. 'I don't find it funny at all.'

She frowned a little, as though confronting an alien species. 'Do you find anything funny—ever?'

'No. It's safer that way.'

Her humour vanished. 'You poor soul.'

She sounded as though she meant it, and the hint of sympathy took him aback. It was so long since anyone had dared to pity him, or at least dared to show it. Not since another time—another world—long ago…

An incredible suspicion briefly troubled his mind. He ordered it gone and it obeyed, but reluctantly.

'If you feel I insulted your mother, I apologise,' he said stiffly.

'Actually, it's me you insulted.'

'I don't see how.'

She looked into his face with a mixture of incredulity, indignation, but mostly amusement.

'You really don't, do you?' she asked. 'All this time and you still haven't—you *really* haven't—? Well, let me tell you, when you meet a lady for the second time, it's considered polite to remember the first time.'

'For the second—? Have we ever—have we—?'

And then the suspicion wouldn't be banished any longer. He *knew*.

'It was you,' he said slowly. 'On the roof—in Las Vegas—'

'Boy, I really lived in your memory, didn't I?'

'But—you're different—not the same person.'

'I should hope not, after all this time. I'm the same in some ways, not others. You're different too, but you're easier to spot.

I was longing for you to recognise me, but you didn't.' She sighed theatrically. 'Hey ho! What a disappointment!'

'You didn't care if I recognised you or not,' he said flatly.

'Well, maybe just a little.'

An orchestra was getting into place and the dancing area was being cleared, so that they had to move to the side.

He was possessed by a strange feeling, of having wandered into an alien world where nothing was quite as it looked. She had sprung out of the past, landing in his path, challenging him with memories and fears.

'Even now I can't believe that it's you,' he said. 'Your hair's different—it was cut very short—'

'Functional,' she said at once. 'I was surrounded by film people making the best of themselves, so I made the least of myself as an act of adolescent defiance.'

'Was that all you could think of?'

'Consider my problem,' she said with an expansive gesture. 'The average teenager goes wild, indulges herself with wine, late nights, lovers—but everyone around me was doing that. I'd never have been noticed. So I cut my hair as badly as possible, bought cheap clothes, studied my school books and had early nights. Heavens, was I virtuous! Boring but virtuous.'

'And what happened?' he asked, fascinated.

She chuckled. 'My mother started to get very worried about my "strange behaviour". It took her a while to accept the fact that I was heading for the academic life.'

'Doing what?'

'I've made my career out of ancient Greece. I write books, I give lectures. I pretend to know a lot more than I actually do—'

'Like most of them,' he couldn't resist saying.

'Like most of them,' she agreed at once.

'Is your mother reconciled?'

'Oh, yes, she's terribly impressed now. She came to one of my lectures and afterwards she said, "Darling that was wonderful! *I didn't understand a word.*" That's her yardstick, bless her. And in the end it was me who introduced her to Homer.' She looked around. 'So you could say I'm to blame for all this.'

It was time for the dancing. Homer and Estelle took the floor, gliding about in each other's arms until the photographers had all had their fill.

'Aren't you taking any pictures?' he asked.

'No, mine's just the personal family stuff. What they're doing now is for the public.'

Nikator waved as he danced past with Debra in his arms. Petra sighed.

'He may be in his late thirties but he's just a silly kid at heart. What it'll be like when he takes over the firm I can't—' She broke off guiltily, her hand over her mouth. 'I didn't say that.'

'Don't worry. You didn't say anything the whole world doesn't already know. It's interesting that you're learning already.'

There was a sardonic edge to his voice, and she didn't have to ask what he meant. The two great families of Greek shipbuilding survived by getting the edge on each other, and inevitably that included spying. The kind of casual comment that others could risk might be dangerous.

The dance ended and another one began. Debra vanished in the arms of a powerful producer, and Nikator made his way in Petra's direction.

'Oh, heavens, dance with me!' she breathed, seizing Lysandros and drawing him onto the floor.

'What are you—?' Somehow he found his arms around her.

'Yes, I know, in polite society I'm supposed to wait for you to ask me,' she muttered, 'but this isn't polite society, it's a goldfish bowl.'

He felt she couldn't have put it better.

'But your fears may be misplaced,' he pointed out. 'With you being so boring and virtuous he probably wasn't going to ask you at all.'

'He has peculiar tastes.' She added hurriedly, 'And I didn't say that, either.'

She was like quicksilver in his arms, twisting and turning against him, leading him on so that he moved in perfect time with her and had to fight an impulse to tighten his grip, draw her against his body and let things happen as they would. Not here. Not now. Not yet.

Petra read him fairly accurately, and something thrilled in her blood.

'Don't you like dancing?' she asked after a while.

'This isn't dancing. It's swimming around that goldfish bowl.'

'True. But we annoyed Nikator, which is something gained.'

She was right. Nikator's expression was that of a child whose toys had been snatched away. Then Lysandros forgot everything except Petra. Her face was close to his and the smile in her eyes reached him directly.

'What will you do after this?' he asked.

'Stay here for a few days, or weeks. It's a chance for me to do some research. Homer has great contacts. There's a museum vault that's never opened for anyone, but he's fixing it for me.'

He glanced down at the slender, sensual body moving in his arms, at the charming face that seemed to smile more naturally than any other expression, and the blue eyes with their mysterious, tantalising depths, and he knew a sense of outrage. What was this woman doing in museums, investigating the dead, when everything in her spoke of life? She belonged not in tombs but in sunlight, not turning dusty pages but caressing a man's face and pressing her naked body against his.

The mere thought of her nakedness made him draw a sharp breath. The dress fitted her closely enough to give him a good idea of her contours, but it only tempted him to want more. He controlled his thoughts by force.

'Is visiting museums really your idea of being lucky?' he asked slowly.

'I'm going to see things that other scholars have been struggling to see for years. I'll be ahead of the game.'

'But isn't there anything else you want to do?' he asked.

'You mean, what's a woman doing worrying her little head about such things? Women are made for pleasure; serious matters should be left to men.'

Since this came dangerously near to his actual thoughts he was left floundering for a moment. He wished she hadn't used the word 'pleasure'. It was a distraction he could do without.

'I didn't mean it like that,' he managed to say at last, 'but when life offers you so many more avenues—'

'Like Nikator? Yes, I could throw myself into his arms, or anything else he wanted me to throw myself into—careful!'

'Sorry,' he said hastily, loosing his fingers, which he'd tightened against her instinctively.

'Where was I? Ah, yes, exploring avenues.'

'Forget Nikator,' he snapped. 'He's not an avenue, he's a dead end.'

'Yes, I'd managed to work that out for myself. I'm not seventeen any more. I'm thirty-two, in my dotage.'

In her dotage, he thought ironically, with skin like soft peach, hair like silk and eyes that teased, inviting him just so far and warning him against going any further. But she was right about one thing. She was no child. She'd been around long enough to discover a good deal about men, and he had an uneasy feeling that she could read more about him than he wanted her—or anyone—to know.

'If you're fishing for compliments you picked the wrong man,' he said.

'Oh, sure, I'd never come to you for sweet nothings, or for anything except—yes, that would be something—' She hesitated, as though trying to phrase it carefully. 'Something you could give me better than any other man,' she whispered at last.

He struggled not to say the words, but they came out anyway. 'And what's that?'

'Good financial advice,' she declared. 'Aha! There, I did it.'

'Did what?'

'I made you laugh.'

'I'm not laughing,' he said through twitching lips.

'You would be if you weren't trying so hard not to. I bet myself I could make you laugh. Be nice. Give me my little victory.'

'I'm never nice. But I'll let you have it this once.'

'Only this once?' she asked, raising her eyebrows.

'I prefer to claim victory for myself.'

'I could take that as a challenge.'

Then there was silence as their bodies moved in perfect time, and she thought that yes, he was a challenge, and what a challenge he would be; so different from the easy-going men with whom she'd mostly spent her life. There was a darkness about him that he made little attempt to hide, and which tempted her, although she knew she was probably crazy.

'Do your challenges usually work out as you plan?' he asked.

'Oh, yes,' she assured him. 'I won't settle for anything less than my own way.'

'I'm exactly the same. What a terrible battle looms ahead.'

'True,' she said. 'I'm trembling in fear of you.'

He didn't speak, but a slow smile overtook his face—the smile of a man who didn't believe her and was planning a clever move.

Petra had a strange feeling that the other women on the dance floor were staring at her. Most of them had slept with Lysandros, she'd been warned, and suddenly she knew it was true. Their eyes were feverish, full of memories, hot, sweet and glorious, followed by anguish. Mentally they raked her, undressed her, trying to imagine whether she would please him.

And that was really unnerving because she was trying to decide the same thing.

They spoke to her, those nameless women, telling her that he was a lover of phenomenal energy, who could last all night, untiring, driving her on to heights she'd never reached before, heights she wanted to discover.

There was one woman in particular whose greedy gaze caught her attention. Something about the extravagantly dressed, petulant creature made Petra wonder if this was the most recent of Lysandros's conquests—and his rejections. Her eyes were like the others, but a thousand times more bitter, more murderous.

Then Lysandros turned her in the dance, faster and faster, taking her to a distant place where there was only the whirling movement that shut out the rest of the world. She gave herself up to it completely, wanting nothing else.

Would she too lie in his arms in a fever of passion? And would she end up like the others, yearning wretchedly from a distance?

But something told her that their path together wouldn't be as simple as that.

Suddenly they were interrupted by a shout from a few yards off. Everyone stopped dancing and backed away, revealing the bride and groom locked in a passionate embrace. As befitted a glamorous couple, the kiss went on and on as the crowd cheered and applauded. Then some of the others began to embrace. More and more followed suit until it seemed as though the whole place was filled with lingering kisses.

Lysandros stood motionless, his arm still around her waist, the other hand holding hers. The space between them remained barely a centimetre. It would take only the slightest movement for him to cover that last tiny distance and lay his lips on hers. She looked up at him, her heart beating.

'What a performance!' he exclaimed, looking around and speaking in disapproving tones. 'I won't insult you by subjecting you to it.'

He released her, stepping back and giving her no choice but to do the same.

'Thank you,' she said formally. 'It's delightful to meet a man with a sense of propriety.'

She could have hit him.

'I'm afraid I must be going,' he said. 'I've neglected my affairs for too long. It's been a pleasure meeting you again.'

'And you,' she said crisply.

He inclined his head courteously, and in a moment he was gone.

Thunderstruck, she watched him, barely believing what had happened, and so suddenly. He was as deep in desire as herself. All her instincts told her that beyond a shadow of doubt. Yet he'd denied that desire, fought it, overcome it, *because that was what he had decided to do.*

This was a man of steely will, which he would impose no matter what the cost to himself or anyone else. He'd left her without even a glance back. It was like a blow in the stomach.

'Don't worry. Just be patient.'

Petra looked up to see the woman who'd caught her attention while they'd danced. Now she recalled seeing her arrive at the wedding with one of the city's most wealthy and powerful men. She was regarding Petra with a mixture of contempt and pity.

'I couldn't help watching you—and Lysandros,' she said,

moving nearer. 'It's his way, you see. He'll come just so close, and then withdraw to consider the matter. When he's decided that he can fit you in with his other commitments he'll return and take his pleasure at his own time and his own convenience.'

'If I agree,' Petra managed to say.

The woman gave a cold, tinkly laugh.

'Don't be absurd, of course you'll agree. It's written all over you. He could walk back right this minute and you'd agree.'

'I guess you know what you're talking about,' Petra said softly.

'Oh, yes, I know. I've been there. I know what's going through your head because it went through mine. "Who does he think he is to imagine he can just walk back and I'll yield to him on command?" But then he looks at you as if you're the only woman in the world, and you do yield on his command. And it'll be wonderful—for a while. In his arms, in his bed, you'll discover a universe you never knew existed.

'But one day you'll wake up and find yourself back on earth. It will be cold because he's gone. He's done with you. You no longer exist. You'll weep and refuse to believe it, but he won't answer the phone, so after a while you'll have to believe it.'

She began to turn away, but paused long enough to say over her shoulder, 'You think you'll be different, but with him no woman is ever different. Goodbye.'

CHAPTER THREE

THE party went on into the evening. Lights came on throughout the false Parthenon, music wafted up into the sky, assignations were made, profitable deals were settled. Petra accompanied Estelle into the house to help her change into her travelling clothes.

The honeymoon was to be spent on board the *Silver Lady*, Homer's yacht, refurbished for the occasion and currently moored in the port of Piraeus, about five miles away. Two cars bearing luggage and personal servants had already gone on ahead. There remained only the limousine to convey the bride and groom.

'Are you all right?' Estelle asked, glancing at her daughter's face.

'Of course,' Petra said brightly.

'You look as if you were brooding about something.'

In fact she'd been brooding about the stranger's words.

'When he's decided that he can fit you in with his other commitments he'll return and take his pleasure at his own time and his own convenience.'

That was not going to happen, she resolved. If he returned tonight he would find her missing.

'Do you mind if I come to the port to see you off?' she asked suddenly.

'Darling, that would be lovely. But I thought you'd be planning a wild night out.'

'Not me. I don't have your energy.'

In the car on the way to the port they drank champagne. Once on board, Homer showed her around the stately edifice with vast pride, finishing in the great bedroom with the bed big enough for six, covered with gold satin embroidered cushions.

'Now we must find a husband for you,' he declared expansively.

'No, thank you,' Petra hurried to say. 'My one experience of marriage didn't leave me with any desire to try again.'

Before he could reply, her cellphone rang and she answered.

'I'm afraid my manners left something to be desired,' said a man's voice. 'Perhaps I can make amends by taking you to dinner?'

For a moment she floundered. She had her speech of rejection ready prepared but no words would come.

'I'm not sure—'

'My car's just outside the house.'

'But I'm not there. I'm in Piraeus.'

'It won't take you long to return. I'll be waiting.'

He hung up.

'Cheek!' she exploded. 'He just takes it for granted I'll do what he wants.' Seeing them frowning, she added, 'Lysandros Demetriou. He wants to take me to dinner, and I wasn't given much chance to say no.'

'That sounds like him,' Homer said approvingly. 'When he wants something he doesn't waste time.'

'But it's no way to treat a lady,' Estelle said indignantly.

He grinned and kissed her. 'You didn't seem to mind.'

As they were escorting her off the yacht Petra suddenly had a thought.

'How did he know my cellphone number? I didn't give it to him.'

'He probably paid someone in my household to find out,' Homer said as though it was a matter of course. 'Goodbye, my dear.'

She hurried down the gangplank and into the car. On the journey back to Athens she tried to sort out her thoughts. She was angry, but mostly with herself. So many good resolutions ground to dust because of a certain tone in his voice.

On impulse she took out her phone and dialled the number of Karpos, an Athens contact, an ex-journalist whom she knew to be reliable. When he heard what she wanted he drew a sharp breath.

'Everyone's afraid of him,' he said, speaking quickly. 'In fact they're so afraid that they won't even admit their fear, in case he gets to hear and complains that they've made him look bad.'

'That's paranoid.'

'Sure, but it's the effect he has. Nobody is allowed to see inside his head or his heart—if he has one. Opinion is divided about that.'

'But wasn't there someone, a long time ago—? From the other family?'

'Right. Her name was Brigitta, but I didn't tell you that. She died in circumstances nobody has ever been able to discover. The press were warned off by threats, which is why you'll never see it mentioned now.'

'You mean threats of legal action?'

'There are all kinds of threats,' Karpos said mysteriously. 'One man started asking questions. The next thing he knew, all his debts were called in. He was on the verge of ruin, but it was explained to him that if he "behaved himself" in future, matters could be put right. Of course he gave the promise, turned over all his notes, and everything was miraculously settled.'

'Did anything bad happen to him afterwards?'

'No, he left journalism and went into business. He's very successful, but if you say the name Demetriou, he leaves the room quickly. Anything you know, you have to pretend not to know, like the little apartment he has in Athens, or Priam House in Corfu.'

'Priam House?' she said, startled. 'I've heard of that. People have been trying to explore the cellar for years—there's something there, but nobody's allowed in. Do you mean it's his?'

'So they say. But don't let on that you know about it. In fact, don't tell him you've spoken to me, please.'

She promised and hung up. Sitting there, silent and thoughtful, she knew she was getting into deep water. But deep water had never scared her.

She also knew that there was another aspect to this, something that couldn't be denied.

After fifteen years, she and Lysandros Demetriou had unfinished business.

He'd said he would be waiting for her and, sure enough, he was there by the gate to Homer's estate. As her car slowed he pulled open the door, took her hand and drew her out.

'I won't be long,' she said. 'I just have to go inside and—'

'No. You're fine as you are. Let's go.'

'I was going to change my dress—'

'You don't need to. You're beautiful. You know that, so why are we arguing?'

There was something about this blunt speech that affected her more than a smooth compliment would ever have done. He had no party manners. He said exactly what he thought, and he thought she was beautiful. She felt a smile grow inside her until it possessed her completely.

'You know what?' she said. 'You're right. Why are we arguing?' She indicated for her chauffeur to go on without her and got into Lysandros's car.

She wondered where he would take her, possibly a sophisticated restaurant, but he surprised her by driving out into the countryside for a few miles and stopping at a small restaurant, where he led her to an outside table. Here they were close to the coast and in the distance she could just make out the sea, shimmering beneath the moon.

'This is lovely,' she said. 'It's so peaceful after all the crowds today.'

'That's how I feel too,' he said. 'Normally I only come here alone.'

The food was simple, traditional Greek cooking, just as she liked it. While he concentrated on the order Petra had the chance to consider him, trying to reconcile his reputation as a ruthless tyrant with the suffering boy she'd met years ago.

That boy had been vulnerable and still able to show it, to the extent of telling a total stranger that a betrayal of trust had broken his heart. Now he was a man who inspired fear, who would deny having a heart, who would probably jeer at the idea of trust.

What had really happened all those years ago? And could it ever be put right for him?

She thought again of dancing with him, the other women with their envious, lustful glances as they relived hours spent in bed with that tall, strong body, yielding ecstatically to skills they'd found in no other man.

'Are you all right?' Lysandros asked suddenly.

'Yes—why do you ask?'

'You drew a sharp breath, as though you were in pain.'

'No, I'm not in pain,' she hurried to say.

Unless, she thought, you included the pain of wanting something you'd be wiser not to want. She pretended to search her bag. When she glanced up she found him regarding her with a look of wonder.

'Fifteen years,' he said. 'So much has happened and we've changed, and yet in another way we're still the same people. I would have known you anywhere.'

She smiled. 'But you didn't recognise me.'

'Only on the surface. Inside, there was a part of me that knew you. I never thought we'd meet again, and yet somehow I was always certain that we would.'

She nodded. 'Me too. If we'd waited another fifteen years—or fifty—I'd still have been sure that we would one day talk again before we died.'

The last words seemed to reach right inside him. To talk again before they died. That was it. He knew that normally his own thoughts would have struck him as fanciful. He was a strong man, practical, impatient of anything that he couldn't pin down. Yet what he said was true. She'd been an unseen presence in his life ever since that night.

He wondered how he could tell her this. She'd inspired him with the will to talk freely, but that wasn't enough. He didn't know how.

The food arrived, feta and tomato slices, simple and delicious.

'Mmm,' she said blissfully.

He ate little, spending most of his time watching her.

'Why were you up there?' he asked at last. 'Why not downstairs, enjoying the wedding?'

'I guess I'm a natural cynic.' She smiled. 'My grandfather used to say that I approached life with an attitude of, *Oh, yeah?* And it's true. I think it was already there that night in Las Vegas, and it's got worse since. Given the madhouse I've always lived in, it could hardly be any other way.'

'How do you feel about the madhouse?'

'I enjoy it, as long as I'm not asked to get too deeply involved in it or take it seriously.'

'You've never wanted to be a film actress yourself?'

'Good grief, no! One raving lunatic in the family is enough.'

'Does your mother know you talk like that?'

'Of course. She actually said it first, and we're agreed. She's a sweetie and I adore her, but she lives on the Planet Zog.'

'How old is she really?'

'As old as she needs to be at any one moment. She was seventeen when she had me. My father didn't want any responsibility, so he just dumped her, and she struggled alone for a while. Believe me, anyone who just sees her as a film star should see the back streets of London where we lived in those years.

'Then my father's parents got in touch to say that he'd just died in a road accident. They hadn't even known we existed until he admitted it on his deathbed. They were Greek, with strong ideas about family, and I was all the family they had left. Luckily, they were nice people and we all got on well. They looked after me while Estelle built her career. My grandfather was a scholar who'd originally come to England to run a course in Greek at university. At first I didn't even go to school because he reckoned he could teach me better, and he was right.'

'So you grew up as the one with common sense?'

'Well, one of us had to have some,' she chuckled.

'How did you manage with all those stepfathers?'

'They were OK. Mostly they were lovelorn and a bit dopey, so I had a hard job keeping a straight face.'

'What about the one in Las Vegas?'

'Let's see, he was the—no, that was the other one—or was he? Oh, never mind. They're all the same, anyway. I think he was an aspiring actor who thought Estelle could help his ambitions. When she finally saw through him she tossed him out. She was in love with someone else by then.'

'You're very cool about it all. Doesn't all this "eternal love" affect you?'

'Eternal love?' She seemed to consider this. 'Would that be eternal love as in he tried to take every penny she had, or as in he haunted the set, throwing a fit whenever she had a love scene, or as in—?'

'All right, I get the picture. Evidently the male sex doesn't impress you.'

'However did you guess?'

'But what about your own experience? There must have been one or two brave enough to defy the rockets you fire at them?'

Her lips twitched. 'Of course. I don't look at them unless they're brave enough to do that.'

'That's the first of your requirements, is it? Courage?'

'Among other things. But even that's overrated. The man I married was a professional sportsman, a skier who could do the most death-defying stuff. The trouble was, it was all he could do, so in the end he was boring too.'

'You're married?' he asked slowly.

'Not any more,' she said in a tone of such devout thankfulness that he was forced to smile.

'What happened? Was it very soon after our meeting?'

'No, I went to college and studied hard. It was the same college where my grandfather had been a professor, and it was wonderful because people couldn't care less that I was a film star's daughter, but they were impressed that I was his granddaughter. I had to do him credit. I studied to improve my knowledge of the Greek language, learned the history, passed exams. We were going to come here and explore together, but then he and my grandmother both died. It's not the same without him. I so much wanted to make him proud of me.'

She hesitated, while a shadow crossed her face, making him lean forward.

'What is it?' he asked gently.

'Oh—nothing.'

'Tell me,' he persisted, still gentle.

'I was just remembering how much I loved them and they loved me. They needed me, because I was all that was left to them after their son died. They liked Estelle, but she wasn't part of them as I was.'

'Wasn't your mother jealous of your closeness to them?'

Petra shook her head. 'She's a loving mother, in her way, but I've never been vital to her as I was to them.'

'How sad,' he said slowly.

'Not really. As long as you have someone who needs you, you can cope with the others who don't.'

At that moment all the others who hadn't needed her seemed to be there in the shadows, starting with Estelle, always surrounded by people whose job it was to minister to her—hairdressers, make-up artists, lawyers, psychologists, professional comfort-givers, lovers, husbands. Whatever she wanted, there was always someone paid to provide it.

She was sweet-tempered and had showered her daughter with a genuine, if slightly theatrical affection, but when a heavy cold had forced Petra to miss one of her weddings—Fourth? Fifth?—she'd shrugged, said, "Never mind" and merely saved her an extra large piece of cake.

Petra had soon understood. She was loved, but she wasn't essential. She'd tried to take it lightly, saying that it didn't matter, because she'd found that this was one way to cope. Eventually it had become the way she coped with the whole of life.

But it had mattered. There, always at the back of her mind, had been the little sadness, part of her on the lookout for someone to whom she was vitally necessary. Her. Not the money and glamour with which her mother's life surrounded her, but *her*.

And perhaps that was why a young man's agony and desperation had pierced her heart on a roof in Las Vegas fifteen years ago.

'But your grandparents died,' Lysandros said. 'Who do you have now?'

She pulled herself together. 'Are you kidding? My life is crowded with people. It's like living with a flock of geese.'

'Including your mother's husbands?'

'Well, she didn't bother to marry them all. She said there wasn't enough time.'

'Boyfriends?' he asked carefully.

'Some. But half of them were simply trying to get close to my mother, which didn't do my self-confidence any good. I learnt to keep my feelings to myself until I'd sized them up.' She gave a soft chuckle. 'I got a reputation for being frigid.'

They were mad, he thought. No woman who was frigid had that warmth and resonance in her voice, or that glow on her skin.

'And then I met Derek,' she recalled. 'Estelle was making a film with a winter sports background and he was one of the advisors. He was so handsome, I fell for him hook, line and sinker. I thought it had happened at last. We were happy enough for a couple of years, but then—' she shrugged '—I guess he got bored with me.'

'*He* got bored with *you?*' he asked with an involuntary emphasis.

She chuckled as though her husband's betrayal was the funniest thing that had ever happened to her. He was becoming familiar with that defensive note in her laughter. It touched an echo in himself.

'I don't think I was ever the attraction,' she said. 'He needed money and he thought Estelle Radnor's daughter would have plenty. Anyway, he started sleeping around, I lost my temper and I think it scared him a little.'

'You? A temper?'

'Most people think I don't have one because I only lose it once in a blue moon. Now and then I really let fly. I try not to because what's the point? But it's there, and it can make me say things I wish I hadn't. Anyway, that was five years ago. It's all over. Why are you smiling?'

When had anyone last asked him that? When had anyone had cause to? How often did he smile?

'I didn't know I was smiling,' he said hastily.

'You looked like you'd seen some private joke. Come on. Share.'

Private joke! If his board of directors, his bank manager, his underlings heard that they'd think she was delusional.

But the smile was there, growing larger, happier, being drawn forth by her teasing demand.

'Tell me,' she said. 'What did I say that was so funny?'

'It's not—it's just the way you said "It's all over", as though you'd airbrushed the entire male sex out of your life.'

'Or out of the universe,' she agreed. 'Best thing for them.'

'For them, or for you?'

'Definitely for me. Men no longer exist. Now my world is this country, my work, my investigations.'

'But the ancient Greeks had members of the male sex,' he pointed out. 'Unfortunate, but true.'

'Yes, but I can afford to be tolerant about them. They helped start my career. I wrote a book about Greek heroes just before I left university, and actually got it published. Later I was asked to revise it into a less academic version, for schools, and the royalties have been nice. So I feel fairly charitable about the legendary Greek men.'

'Especially since they're safely dead?'

'You're getting the idea.'

'Let's eat,' he said hastily.

The waiter produced chicken and onion pie, washed down with sparkling wine, and for a while there was no more talking. Watching her eat, relishing every mouthful, he wondered about her assertion that men no longer existed for her. With any other woman he would have said it was a front, a pretence to fool the world while she carried on a life of sensual indulgence. But this woman was different. She inhabited her own universe, one he'd never encountered before.

'So that's how you came to know so much that night in Las Vegas,' he said at last. 'You gave me a shock, lecturing me about Achilles.'

She gave a rueful laugh. 'Lecturing. That just about says it all. I'm afraid I do, and people get fed up. I can't blame them. I remember I made you very cross.'

'I wasn't thrilled to be told I was sulking,' he admitted, 'but I was only twenty-three. And besides—'

'And besides, you were very unhappy, weren't you?' she asked. 'Because of *her*.'

He shrugged. 'I don't remember.'

Her gentle eyes said that she didn't believe him.

'She made you trust her, but then you found you couldn't trust her,' she encouraged. 'You don't forget something like that.'

'Would you like some more wine?' he asked politely.

So he wasn't ready to tell her the things she yearned to know, about the catastrophe that had smashed his life. She let it go, knowing that hurrying him would be fatal.

'So your grandfather taught you Greek,' he said, clearly determined to change the subject.

'Inside me, I feel as much Greek as English. He made sure of that.'

'That's how you knew about Achilles? I thought you'd been learning about him at school.'

'Much more than that. I read about him in Homer's *Iliad*, how he was a hero of the Trojan war. I thought that story was so romantic. There was Helen, the most beautiful woman in the world, and all those men fighting over her. She's married to Menelaus but she falls in love with Paris, who takes her to Troy. But Menelaus won't give up and the Greek troops besiege Troy for ten years, trying to get her back.

'And there were all those handsome Greek heroes, especially Achilles,' she went on, giving him a cheeky smile. 'What made your mother admire Achilles rather than any of the others?'

'She came from Corfu where, as you probably know, his influence is very strong. Her own mother used to take her to the Achilleion Palace, although that was chiefly because she was fascinated by Sisi.'

Petra nodded. 'Sisi' had been Elizabeth of Bavaria, a romantic heroine of the nineteenth century, and reputedly the loveliest woman of her day. Her beauty had caused Franz Joseph, the young Emperor of Austria, to fall madly in love with her and sweep her into marriage when she was only sixteen.

But the marriage had faltered. For years she'd roamed the world, isolated, wandering from place to place, until she'd bought a palace on the island of Corfu.

The greatest tragedy of her life was the death of her son Rudolph, at Mayerling, in an apparent suicide pact with his mistress. A year later Sisi had begun to transform the Palace into a tribute to Achilles, but soon she too was dead, at the hands of an assassin. The Palace had subsequently been sold and turned into a museum, dedicated to honouring Achilles.

'The bravest and the most handsome of them all, yet hiding a secret weakness,' Petra mused.

She was referring to the legend of Achilles' mother, who'd sought to protect her baby son by dipping him in the River Styx, that ran between earth and the underworld. Where the waters of the Styx touched they were held to make a man immortal. But she'd held him by the heel, leaving him mortal in the one place where the waters had not touched him. Down the centuries that story resonated so that the term 'Achilles heel' still meant the place where a strong person was unexpectedly vulnerable.

Of all the statues in the Achilleon, the most notable was the one showing him on the ground, vainly trying to pull the arrow from his heel as his life ebbed away.

'In the end it was the thing that killed him,' Lysandros said. 'His weakness wasn't so well-hidden after all. His assassin knew exactly where to aim an arrow, and to cover the tip with poison so that it would be fatal.'

'Nobody is as safe as they believe they are,' she mused.

'My father's motto was—never let anyone know what you're thinking. That's the real weakness.'

'But that's not true,' she said. 'Sometimes you're stronger because other people understand you.'

His voice hardened. 'I disagree. The wise man trusts nobody with his thoughts.'

'Not even me?' she asked softly.

She could tell the question disconcerted him, but his defences were too firmly riveted in place to come down easily.

'If there was one person I could trust—I think it would be you, because of the past. But I am what I am.' He gave a self-mocking smile. 'I don't think even you can change me.'

She regarded him gently before venturing to touch his hand.

'Beware people you think you can trust?' she whispered.

'Did I say that?' he asked quickly.

'Something like it. In Las Vegas, you came to the edge of saying a lot more.'

'I was in a bad way that night. I don't know what I said.'

A silence came down over him. He stared into his glass,

and she guessed that he was shocked at himself for having relented so far. Now he would retreat again behind walls of caution and suspicion.

Was there any way to get through to this man's damaged heart? she wondered. And, if she tried, might she not do him more harm than good?

CHAPTER FOUR

'I'M SORRY,' Lysandros said quietly. 'This is me; it's who and what I am.'

'You don't let anyone in, do you?' Petra said.

He shook his head with an air of finality. Suddenly then he said, 'But I will tell you one thing. It may only be a coincidence, but it's strange. After I'd taken you back to your room I returned to the tables and suddenly started winning back everything I'd lost. I just couldn't lose, and somehow that was connected with you, as though you'd turned me into a winner. Why are you smiling?'

'You, being superstitious. If I'd said all that you'd make some snooty masculine comment about women having overly vivid imaginations.'

'Yes, I probably would,' he admitted. 'But perhaps you just exercise a more powerful brand of magic.'

'Magic?'

'Don't tell me you've studied the Greek legends without discovering magic?'

'Yes,' she conceded, 'you meet it in the most unexpected places, and the hard part is knowing how to tell it from wishful thinking.'

She spoke the last words so softly that he barely heard

them, but they were enough to give him a strange sensation, part pleasure, part pain, part alarm.

'Wishful thinking,' he echoed slowly. 'The most dangerous thing on earth.'

'Or the most valuable,' she countered quickly. 'All the great ideas started life as wishful thinking. Wasn't there an ancestor of yours who thought, *I wish I could build a boat*? So he built one, then another one, and here you are.'

'You're a very clever woman.' He smiled. 'You can turn anything around, just by the light you throw on it. The light doesn't just illuminate; it transforms all the things that might have served as a warning.'

'But perhaps they should be transformed,' she pointed out. 'Some people become suspicious so quickly that they need to come off-guard and enjoy a bit of wishful thinking.'

'I said you were clever. Talking like that, you almost con vince me. Just as you convinced me back then. Maybe it really is magic. Perhaps you have a brand of magic denied to all other women.'

There was a noise behind him, reminding him that they were in a public place. Reluctantly he released her hand, assuming a calm demeanour, although with an effort.

A small buzz came from his inner pocket. He drew out his phone and grimaced at the text message he found there.

'Damn! I was planning to go to Piraeus tomorrow in any case, but now I think I'd better go tonight. I'll be away for a few days.'

Petra drew a long breath, keeping her face averted. Until then she'd told herself that she wasn't quite sure how she wanted the evening to end, but now she had to be honest with herself. An evening spent talking, beginning to open their hearts, should have led to a night in each other's arms, expressing their closeness in another way. And only now that it was being denied to her did she face how badly she wanted to make love with him.

'Will you be here when I get back?' he asked.

'Yes, I'm staying for a while.'

'I'll call you.'

'We'd better go,' she agreed. 'You have to be on your way.'

'I'm sorry—'

'Don't be,' she said cheerfully. 'It's been a long day. I was fighting to stay awake.'

She wondered if he would actually believe that.

When they reached the Lukas villa the great gates swung open for them, almost as though someone had been watching for their arrival. At the house he opened the car door and came up the steps with her. She looked up at him, curious about his next move.

'Do you remember that night?' he asked gently. 'You were such an innocent that I made you go to bed and saw you to the door.'

'And told me to lock it,' she recalled.

Neither of them mentioned the other thing he'd done, the kiss so soft that it had been barely a whisper against her lips—a kiss without passion, only gentle concern and tenderness. It had lingered with her long after that evening, through days and weeks, then through years. Since then she had known desire and love, but nothing had ever quite erased the memory of that moment. Looking at him now, she knew why, and when he bent his head she longed for it to be the same.

He didn't disappoint her. His lips lay against hers for the briefest possible time before retreating, almost as though he'd found something there that disconcerted him.

'Goodnight,' he said quietly.

He left her before she could react, going down to the car and driving away without looking back, moving fast, as though making his escape.

'Goodnight,' she whispered.

It was only when he was out of sight that she remembered she hadn't asked him how he'd known her phone number.

Petra soon found that her hours were full. Her reputation had gone before her, ensuring that several societies contacted her, asking her to join their excursions or talk to them. She accepted as many invitations as possible. They filled the hours that passed without a word from Lysandros.

One invitation that particularly attracted her came from The Cave Society, a collection of English enthusiasts who were set on exploring an island in the Aegean Sea, about twenty miles out. It was a mass of caves, some of which were reputed to contain precious historical relics.

Nikator was scathing about the idea, insisting that the legend had been rubbished years ago, but the idea of a day out in a boat attracted her.

'Mind you, the place I'd really like to see is Priam House, on Corfu,' she told him. 'Is it true that Lysandros owns it?'

He shrugged. 'I think so.'

She was mostly free of Nikator's company. He spent much time away from home, leaving her free to explore Homer's magnificent library. Sometimes she would take out a tiny photograph she kept in her bag and set it on the table to watch over her.

'Like you watched over me when you were alive, Grandpa,' she told the man in the picture, speaking in Greek.

He was elderly, with a thin, kindly face and a hesitant smile. When he was alive that smile had always been there for her.

He had told her about her father, which Estelle hadn't been able to do very fully. And he'd shown her pictures, revealing her own facial likeness to the young man whose life had been cut short.

But there had been another likeness.

'He had a hasty temper,' Grandpa had said sadly. 'He didn't

mean to be unkind, but he spoke first and thought afterwards.' He'd looked at her tenderly. 'And you're just the same.'

It was true. She was naturally easy-going, but without warning a flash of temper would come streaking out of the darkness, making her say things she afterwards regretted. She'd fought to overcome it and had succeeded in dampening it down to the point when few people ever detected its existence. But it was still there, ready to undermine her without warning.

In the final months of her marriage it had made her say things that would have made a reconciliation impossible, even if she'd wanted one. Right now it was probably a good thing that Lysandros wasn't there to hear the thoughts that were bouncing around like Furies in her brain, demanding expression.

One evening Nikator returned home suddenly and locked himself in his room, refusing to open to anyone, even Petra.

'Perhaps Debra will come to see him,' she suggested to Aminta, the housekeeper.

'No, she's gone back to America,' Aminta said hurriedly.

'I thought she was here until next week.'

'She had to leave suddenly. I should be getting on with my work.'

She scuttled away.

It might mean anything or nothing, Petra thought, and she would probably never know. But for a while Aminta avoided her.

Nikator finally emerged, with a slight swelling on his lips which he refused to discuss beyond saying he'd had a fall. Petra didn't feel like pursuing the subject, but she made a mental note to spend as much time out of the house as possible.

Since the evening of the wedding she'd seen Lysandros only once and that was by chance at a grand banquet given by the city authorities. He'd made his way over to her and said courteously that he hoped she was enjoying Athens. He'd mentioned contacting her again in the next few days, but made no specific plans.

He seemed to be alone. No lady had been invited to accompany him to this occasion, just as her own invitation had made no mention of a guest. She was left wondering at whose behest she had been invited.

After their evening together she had been in turmoil. Behind Lysandros's civilised veneer she sensed a man who was frighteningly alone, locked in a prison of isolation, seeking a way out, yet reluctant to take it. It didn't matter that their first meeting had been so long ago. It had left them both with the sense that they knew each other, and under its influence he'd begun the first tentative movements of reaching out to her. Yet he'd been able only to go so far, then no further. Try as he might, the prison bars had always slammed shut at the last moment.

Her heart ached for him. The pain he couldn't fight had affected her, and she would have rescued him if she could. But in the end it was his own nature that stood in the way, and she knew she could never get past that unless he allowed her.

At night she would relive the brief kiss that he'd given her. Any other man would have seized her in his arms and kissed her breathless, which, truth to tell, she'd half hoped he would do. Instead, he'd behaved with an almost Victorian propriety, caressing her lips in a way that called back that other time when he'd thought only of protecting her. And in doing so he'd touched her heart more than passion would ever do.

But there was passion, she knew that. She couldn't be so close to him without reading the promise of his tall, hard body, the easy movements, the power held in check, ready to be unleashed. Nor could she misunderstand the look in his eyes when they rested on her, thinking her unaware. Some day—and that day must come soon—she would break his control and tempt him beyond endurance.

But gradually her despondency gave way to annoyance. Now she could hear the strange woman at the wedding again, warning her that she was one of many and would yield as easily as the others.

'No way,' she muttered. 'If you think that, boy, have you got a shock coming!'

Briskly she informed the household that she would be away for few days, and was in her room packing a light bag when her phone rang and Lysandros's voice said, 'I'd like to see you this evening.'

She took a moment to stop herself exploding at his sheer cheek, and managed to say calmly, 'I'm about to leave for a few days.'

'Can it wait until tomorrow?'

'I'm afraid not. I'm really very busy. It's been a pleasure knowing you. Goodbye.' She hung up.

'Good for you,' Nikator said from the doorway. 'It's about time somebody told him.'

'It's kind of you to worry about me, Nikki, but I promise you there's no need. I'm in charge. I always have been. I always will be.'

The phone rang again.

'I know you're angry,' Lysandros said. 'But am I beyond forgiveness?'

'You misunderstand,' she said coolly. 'I'm not angry, merely busy. I'm a professional with work to do.'

'You mean I really am beyond forgiveness?'

'No, I—there's nothing to forgive.'

'I wish you'd tell me that to my face. I've been inconsiderate, but I didn't…that is…help me, Petra—please.'

It was as though he'd thrown a magic switch. His arrogance she could fight, but his plea for help reached out to touch her own need.

'I suppose I could rearrange my plans,' she said slowly.

'I'm waiting by the gate. Come as you are; that's all I ask.'

'I'm on my way.'

'You're mad,' Nikator said. 'You know that, don't you?'

She sighed. 'Yes, I guess so. But it can't be helped.'

She escaped his furious eyes as soon as she could. Now she could think of nothing but that Lysandros wanted her. The thought of seeing him again made her heart leap.

He was where he'd said he would be. He didn't kiss her or make any public show of affection, but his hand held hers tightly for a moment and he whispered, 'Thank you,' in a fervent voice that wiped out the days of frustrated waiting.

Darkness was falling as Lysandros took her into the heart of town, finally stopping at a small restaurant that spilled out onto the pavement. From here they could look up at the floodlit Parthenon, high on the Acropolis, dominating all of Athens.

The waiter appeared, politely enquiring if they were ready to visit the kitchen. Petra was familiar with this habit of allowing customers to see the food being prepared, and happily followed him in. Delicious aromas assailed them at once, and it took time to go around trying to make a choice. At last they settled on fried calamari followed by lamb fricassee and returned to the table.

For a while the food and wine occupied her. Sometimes she glanced up to find him watching her with an intense expression that told her all she wanted to know about the feelings he couldn't put into words. For her it was enough to know that he had those feelings. The words could wait.

At last he said politely, 'Have you been busy?'

'I've been doing a lot of reading in Homer's library. I've had some invitations to go on expeditions.'

'And you've accepted them?'

'Not all. How has your work been?'

'No different from usual. Problems to be overcome. I tried to keep busy because...because...' his voice changed abruptly '...when I was alone I thought of you.'

'You hid it very well,' she pointed out.

'You mean I didn't call you. I meant to a thousand times, but I always drew back. I think you know why.'

'I'm not sure I do.'

'You're not like other women. Not to me. With you it has to be all or nothing, and I—'

'You're not ready for "all",' she finished for him. Without warning her temper gave a sudden, disconcerting flare. 'That's fine, because neither am I. Are you suggesting that I was chasing you?'

'No, I didn't mean that,' he said hastily. 'I was just trying to apologise.'

'It's all right,' she said.

In fact it wasn't all right. Her contented mood of a moment ago had faded. The strain of the last few days was catching up with her, and she was becoming edgy. She'd wanted him and he'd as good as snubbed her.

Suddenly the evening was on the verge of collapse.

'Can I have a little more wine?' she asked, holding out her glass and smiling in a way that should have warned him.

He took the hint and abandoned the apology, making her feel instantly guilty. He was doing his best, but these were uncharted seas for him. It was she who held the advantage. Resolutely, she worked to lighten the atmosphere.

'Actually,' she said between sips, 'the most exciting thing that's happened to me is an invitation from The Cave Society.'

She told him about the letter. Like Nikator, he was sceptical.

'I'm not swallowing it hook, line and sinker,' she assured him. 'I'm too much of an old hand for that.'

'*Old* hand,' he murmured, regarding her appreciatively.

'Very old. In terms of my reputation, I'm ancient. This—' she pointed to her luxuriant golden mane '—is just dye to hide the fact that I'm white-haired. Any day now I'm going to start walking with a stick.'

'Will you stop talking nonsense?'

'Why?' she asked, genuinely puzzled. 'Nonsense is fun.'

'Yes, but—' He retired, defeated. It wasn't possible to say that the contrast between her words and the young, glorious reality was making him dizzy.

'Oh, all right,' she conceded, 'I don't think there's anything to be found in those caves. On the other hand, I'll usually go anywhere and do anything for a "find", so perhaps I should.'

'But what are you going to find that thousands of others have failed to find?'

'Of course they failed,' she teased, 'because they weren't me. Something is lying there, waiting for me to appear from the mists of time—knowing that the glory of the discovery belongs to me, and only me. Next thing you know, they'll put my statue up in the Parthenon.'

She caught sight of his face and burst out laughing.

'I'm sorry,' she choked, 'but if you could see your expression!'

'You were joking, weren't you?' he asked cautiously.

'Yes, I was joking.'

'I'm afraid I'm a bit—' He shrugged. 'It can be hard to tell.'

'Oh, you poor thing,' she said. 'I know you can laugh. I actually heard you, at the wedding reception, but somehow—'

'It's just—'

'I know,' she said. 'You think too great a sense of humour is a weakness, so you keep yours in protective custody, behind bolts and bars, only to be produced at certain times.'

Lysandros tried to speak, to make some light-hearted remark that would pass the matter off, but inwardly he felt himself retreating from her. Her words, though kindly meant, had been like a lamp shone into his soul, revealing secrets. Not to be tolerated.

'Are you ready for the next course?' he asked politely.

'Yes, please.'

It was definitely a snub, yet she was swept by tenderness and pity for him. He was like a man walking a path strewn with boulders, not knowing they were there until he fell and hurt himself.

And she had a sad feeling that she was the only person in the world who saw him like this, and therefore the only person able to help him.

If only she could, she thought with a qualm of self-doubt. She was still feeling her way tentatively. Suppose she persuaded him to trust her, then faltered and let him down, abandoning him again to mistrust and desolation? Suddenly that seemed like the greatest crime in the world.

As the waiter served them she became aware that a man and a woman were hovering close, trying to get a look at her. When she looked straight at them, they jumped.

'It *is* her,' the woman breathed. 'It *is* you, isn't it?' Then, pulling herself together, she said, 'You really are Petra Radnor?'

'Yes, I am.'

'I saw you on a talk show on television just before we left England, and I've read your books. Oh, this is *such* a thrill.'

There was nothing to do but be polite. Lysandros invited them to sit at the table. His manner was charming, and she wondered if he secretly welcomed the interruption.

'I'm just learning that Miss Radnor is a celebrity,' he said. 'Tell me about her.'

They plunged in, making Petra groan with embarrassment. They were Angela and George, they belonged to The Cave Society and had only just arrived in Athens.

'Our President told us that he'd written to you,' Angela bubbled. 'You will accept our invitation to come to the island, won't you? It would mean so much to us to have a real figure of authority.'

'Please,' Petra said hastily, 'I am not a figure of authority.'

'Oh, but you—'

It went on and on. Petra began to feel trapped. Vaguely she was aware that Lysandros's phone had rung. He answered and his face was instantly full of alarm.

'Of course,' he said sharply. 'We'll come at once.' He hung up. 'I'm afraid there's a crisis. That was my secretary to say I must return immediately, also Miss Radnor, whose presence is essential.'

With a gesture he summoned the waiter, paying not only for his meal and hers but whatever their guests had consumed.

'Good evening,' he said, rising to his feet and drawing her with him. 'It's been a pleasure meeting you.'

They made their escape, running until they were three streets away. Then, under the cover of darkness, he pulled her into his arms.

'Now!' he said.

CHAPTER FIVE

PLEASURE and relief went through her. She had wanted this so much, and now everything in her yearned towards him. Her mouth was ready for him but so was every inch of her body. As he grasped her, so she grasped him, caressing him with hands and lips.

'How did you arrange for the phone to ring?' she gasped.

'It didn't. I simply pressed a button that set the bell off, then I pretended to answer. I had to get you away from there, get you to myself.'

He kissed her again, and his kiss was everything she'd wanted since their meeting. Nothing else in her life had been like it. Nothing else ever would be. It was the kiss she'd secretly longed for since he'd cheated her with a half-kiss all those years ago.

'What have you done to me?' he growled. 'Why can't I stop you doing it?'

'You could if you really wanted to,' she whispered against his mouth. 'Why don't you…why don't you…?'

'Stop tormenting me—'

At that she laughed. Why should she make it easy for him?

'Siren—witch—'

But his lips caressed her even as they hurled names at her.

He was in the grip of a power stronger than himself, and that was just how she wanted him.

From far in the distance an unwelcome sound broke into her joy. It came closer and she realised that a crowd of youngsters had appeared at the end of the street, singing, dancing, chanting up into the sky. Then she recalled that this was European Music Night, when Athens was filled with public celebration.

The crowd passed them, offering good wishes to a couple so profitably engaged. Lysandros grasped her hand and began to run again, but there was no escape. Another crowd appeared from another side street, and another. Seeking an exit, they found themselves in an open square where a rock band was playing on a makeshift stage.

'Where can you get privacy in this place?' Lysandros roared.

'You can't,' Petra cried. She was laughing now, every nerve in her body thrumming with joy. 'There's no privacy; there's only music and laughter—and whatever else you want—'

'It's not funny,' he growled.

'But it is, it is—can't you see—? Oh, darling, please try to understand—please try—'

He relented and touched her face. 'Whatever you say.'

He wasn't quite sure what he meant by that, but he knew they'd come to a place where she was at home, sure-footed, able to lead without faltering. A wise man would accept that and, since he prided himself on his wisdom, he did the sensible thing and let her lead him into the dance.

All about them the other couples swung around, while the band hollered. He knew nothing except that he was looking down at her face and she was laughing, not with amusement but with joy and triumph, inviting him to share. Once, long ago, she'd taken his hand and led him through the tunnel to success. Now she could do it again, except that this success would be different, not a matter of money and crushing foes, but a joyous richness and light, streaming ahead, leading to new life, and whatever that life might bring.

'Let's go,' he cried.

'Where?' she called back in delight.

'Anywhere—wherever you want to take me.'

'Then come.'

She began to run, taking him with her, not knowing where she was heading or why; only knowing that she was with him and that was enough. Now the whole of Athens seemed to be flaming around them.

She stopped at last and they stood, gasping together, their chests heaving. From overhead came the sound of fireworks racing up into the black sky, exploding in an orgy of light, while down below the crowd cried out its pleasure.

'Phew!' she said.

He gave a sigh of agreement and she thumped him lightly.

'You shouldn't be out of breath. I thought you worked out every morning in the gym.'

He did exactly that, and was fully as fit as she expected, but in her company his breathlessness had another cause. He reached for her. Petra saw the firework colours flash across his face, and then his arms were tight about her and his mouth was on hers, teasing, provoking, demanding, imploring.

'Who are you?' he gasped. 'What are you doing in my life? Why can't I—?'

'Hush, it doesn't matter. Nothing matters but this. Kiss me—kiss me.'

She proceeded to show him what she meant, sensing the response go through him, delighting in her power over him and his over her. Soon they must reach the moment that had been inevitable since their meeting, and everything in her yearned towards it.

Lysandros felt as if he were awaking from a dream, or sinking into one. He wasn't sure which. Her plea of 'Kiss me' was entrancing, yet something deep inside him was drawing away. He tried to fight it. He wanted her, but so much that it alarmed him.

Impulse had made him call her tonight. Impulse had made him drag her away from their unwanted companions. Impulse—the thing he'd battled for years—was beginning to rule him.

A puppet dancing on the end of her chain. And she knew it.

'What is it?' she asked, feeling him draw away.

'This place is very public. We should get back to the table; I think I left something there.'

'And then?' she asked slowly, unwilling to believe the thought that was coming into her head.

'Then I think we should both—go home.'

She stared at him, trying to believe what he was doing, feeling the anger rise within her. He hadn't left anything behind and they both knew it. But he was telling her the magic was over. He'd banished it by an act of will, proving that his control was still strong, although he'd brought her to the edge of losing hers. It was a demonstration of power, and she was going to make him regret it.

'How dare you?' she said in a soft, furious voice. 'Who the hell do you think you are to despise me?'

'I don't—'

'Shut up. I have something to say and you're going to listen. I am not some desperate female who you can pick up and put down when it suits you. And don't pretend you don't know what I mean because you know exactly. They're all standing in line for you, aren't they? But not me.'

'I don't know who gave you such an idea,' he grated.

'Any woman you've ever known could have given it to me. Your reputation went before you.'

His own anger rose.

'I'll bet Nikator had something to say, but are you mad enough to listen to him? Don't tell me he fools you with that "little brother" act!'

'Why shouldn't I believe he's concerned about me?' she demanded.

'Oh, he's concerned all right, but not as a brother. The rumours about him are very interesting at the moment. Why do you think Debra Farley left Athens so suddenly? Because he went too far, wouldn't take no for an answer. Have a look at his face and see what she did to it when she was fighting him off. I gather it took a lot of money to get her to leave quietly.'

'I don't believe it,' she said, ignoring the whispers within her brain.

'I do not tell lies,' Lysandros snapped.

'No, but you can get things wrong. Even the great, infallible Lysandros Demetriou makes mistakes, and you've really made one about me. One minute you say you'll follow "anywhere I want to take you". The next moment it's time to go home. Do you really think I'll tamely accept that sort of behaviour?

'What am I supposed to do now, Lysandros? Sit by the phone, hoping you'll get in touch, like one of those Athens wives? When you called tonight I should have told you to go and jump in the lake—'

'But you didn't, so perhaps we—'

The words were like petrol on flames.

'Well, I'm doing it now,' she seethed. 'You have your work to do, I have mine, and there's no need for us to trouble each other further. Goodnight.'

Turning swiftly away before he could reach out, she hurried back through the streets to the little restaurant. George and Angela were still there, beaming at the sight of Petra.

'We just knew you'd come back,' Angela said. 'You will come to the cave, won't you?'

'Thank you, I look forward to it,' Petra said firmly. 'Why don't we discuss the details now?' She smiled at Lysandros with deadly intent. 'I'll get a taxi home. Don't let us keep you. I'm sure you're busy.'

'You're right,' he said in a forced voice. 'Goodnight. It's been a pleasure meeting you all.'

He inclined his head to them all and was gone. Nor did he look back, which Petra thought was just as well, or he would have seen a look of misery on her face that she wouldn't have admitted for all the world.

Lysandros awoke in a black depression. Now the magical sunshine that had flooded the path ahead had died, replaced by the prosaic everyday light of the city. She wasn't here, and it shamed him to remember how her presence had made him act.

'Wherever you want to take me.' Had he really said that?

He should be glad that she'd hurled the reminder at him, warning him of the danger into which he'd been sleepwalking, saving him in time.

In time?

He rose and went through the process of preparing for the day, moving like an automaton while his brain seethed.

She alarmed him. She mattered too much. Simply by being herself she could lure him out of the armoured cave where he lived, and where he had vowed to stay for the rest of his days.

For years women had come and gone in his life. He'd treated them well in a distant fashion, and seen them depart without regret. But this woman had broken the mould, and he knew that he must cut ties now or risk yielding to weakness, the thing he dreaded most in the world.

He went to his desk, meaning to write a polite letter, accepting her dismissal. That way he wouldn't have to hear her voice with its soft resonance, its memory of pleasure half experienced, still anticipated. He drew paper towards him and prepared to write.

But the pen seemed to have developed a life of its own, and refused to do his bidding. His brain shut down, denying him the necessary words.

This was her doing. She was like one of the sirens of legend, whose voices had lured sailors onto the rocks. How much had they known, those doomed men? Had they gone unknowingly to their death, or had they recognised the truth about the siren-song, yet still been drawn in, unable to help themselves? And when it had been too late, and they sank beneath the waves, had they cursed themselves for yielding, or had their suffering been worth it for the glimpse of heaven?

He would have given anything to know.

At last he gave up trying to write. It was she who had broken it off, and there was nothing more to be said. More business problems made another journey to the port essential, and for several days he had no time to think of anything else. On the journey back to Athens he was able to relax in the feeling of having regained command of his life.

Petra would have replaced him with another eager suitor, and that was best for both of them. He was even glad of it. So he told himself.

On the last mile home he switched on his car radio to hear the latest news. A commentator was describing a search taking place at sea, where a boat had been found overturned. Those aboard had been exploring a cave on an island in the gulf.

'One of those missing is known to be Petra Radnor, daughter of film star Estelle Radnor, who recently married—'

He pulled over sharply to the side of the road and sat in frozen stillness, listening.

She'd said she'd go anywhere and do anything for a 'find', but had she really wanted to go? Hadn't she tried to slide out of it, but then fallen back into the clutches of George and Angela only because of him?

If she hadn't been angry with me she wouldn't have gone on this trip. If she's dead, it's my doing—like last time—like last time—

At last life came back to his limbs. He swung the car round in the direction of the coast, driving as though all the devils in hell were after him.

Night was falling as he reached the sea and headed for the place where the boats were to be found. Outwardly he was calm but he couldn't stop the words thrumming in his head.

She's dead—she's dead—you had your chance and it's gone—again—

A crowd had gathered in the harbour, gazing out to the water and a boat that was heading towards them. Lysandros parked as close as he could and ran to where he could have a better view of the boat.

'They've rescued most of them,' said a man nearby. 'But I heard there was still someone they couldn't find.'

'Does anyone know who?' Lysandros asked sharply.

'Only that it was a woman. I doubt if they'll find her now.'

You killed her—you killed her!

He pressed against the rail, straining his eyes to see the boat coming through the darkness. In the bow stood a woman, huddled in a blanket, as though she'd been rescued from the water. Frantically he strained to see more, but her face was a blur. A passing light suggested that her hair might be light. It could be Petra—if only he could be sure.

His heart was thundering and he gripped the railing so

hard that his hands hurt. It must be her. She couldn't be dead, because if she were—

Shudders racked him.

Suddenly a shout went up, followed by a cheer. The boat was closer now and at last he could see the woman. It was Petra.

He stood there, holding the rail for support, taking deep breaths, trying to bring himself under control.

She would be here in a few moments. He must plan, be organised. A cellphone. That was it! She would have lost hers in the water, but she'd need one to call her mother. He could do that to please her.

Her eyes were searching the harbour until at last she began to wave. Full of joyful relief, Lysandros waved back, but then realised that she wasn't looking at him but at someone closer. Then he saw Nikator dart forward, reaching up to her. She leaned down, smiling and calling to him.

Lysandros stayed deadly still as the boat docked and the passengers streamed off seeking safety. Petra went straight into Nikator's arms and they hugged each other. Then Nikator took out his cellphone, handing it to her, saying things Lysandros couldn't hear, but could guess. Petra dialled, put the phone to her ear and cried, 'Estelle, darling, it's me, I'm safe.'

He didn't hear the rest. He backed hastily into the darkness before hurrying to find his car. Then he departed as quickly as he could.

She never saw him.

Aminta took charge of her as soon as she reached home, making her have a hot bath, eat well and go to bed.

'It was all over the news,' she told Petra. 'We were so worried. Whatever happened?'

'I don't really know. At first it just seemed like an ordinary storm, but suddenly the waves got higher and higher and we overturned. Did you say it was on the news?'

'Oh, yes, about how you were all drowning and they couldn't rescue everyone.'

'There's one woman they're still looking for,' Petra sighed.

She slept badly and awoke in a dark mood. Somewhere in the house she heard the phone ring, and a moment later Aminta brought it in to her.

'It's for you,' she said. 'A man.'

Eagerly she waited to hear Lysandros's voice, full of happiness that she was safe. But it was George, to tell her that the missing woman had been found safe and well. She talked politely for a while, but hung up with relief.

There was no call from Lysandros. The news programmes must have alerted him to her danger, yet the man who had kissed her with such fierce intensity had shown no interest in her fate.

She couldn't blame him after the way she'd ordered him out of her life, yet the hope had persisted that he cared enough to check that she was safe. Apparently not.

She'd been fooling herself. Such interest as he'd ever had in her had been superficial and was now over. He couldn't have said so more clearly.

Nikator was waiting for her when she went downstairs.

'You shouldn't have got up so soon,' he said. 'After what you've been through. Go back to bed and let me look after you.'

She smiled. It had been good to find him on the quay to take her home, and she was feeling friendly towards him. For the next few days he behaved perfectly, showing brotherly kindness without ever crossing the line. It was bliss to relax in his care. Now she was sure that the stories about him weren't true.

If only Lysandros would call her.

* * *

After several days with no sign from Petra, Lysandros called her cellphone, without success. It was still functioning, but it had been switched off. It remained off all the rest of that day, through the night and into the morning.

It made no sense. She could have switched to the answer service; instead, she'd blocked calls completely.

He refused to admit to a twinge of alarm. But at last he yielded and called the Lukas house, getting himself put through to Homer's secretary.

'I need to speak to Miss Radnor,' he said gruffly. 'Be so kind as to ask her to call me.'

'I'm sorry, sir, but Miss Radnor is no longer here. She and Mr Nikator left for England two days ago.'

Silence. When he could manage to speak normally, he said, 'Did she leave any address or contact number?'

'No, sir. She and Mr Nikator said that they didn't want to be disturbed by anyone, for a long time.'

'What happens in an emergency?'

'Mr Nikator said no emergency could matter beside—'

'I see. Thank you.' He hung up abruptly.

At the Lukas mansion the secretary looked around to where Nikator stood in the doorway.

'Did I do all right?' she asked.

'Perfect,' he told her. 'Just keep telling that story if there are any more calls.'

Lysandros sat motionless, his face hard and set.

She's gone—she's not coming back—

The words called to him out of the past, making him shudder.

She's gone—

It meant nothing. She had every right to leave. It was different from the other time.

You'll never see her again—never again—never again—

His fist slammed into the wall with such force that a picture fell to the ground and smashed. A door opened behind him.

'Get out,' he said without looking around.

The door closed hastily. He continued to sit there, staring—staring into the darkness, into the past.

At last he rose like a man in a dream and went up to his room, where he threw a few clothes into a bag. To his secretary he said, 'I'll be away for a few days. Call me on the cellphone if it's urgent. Otherwise, deal with it yourself.'

'Can I tell anyone where you are?'

'No.'

He headed for the airport and caught the next flight to the island of Corfu. To have used his private jet would have been to tell the world where he was going, and that was the last thing he wanted.

In Corfu he owned Priam House, a villa that had once belonged to his mother. It was his refuge, the place he came to be alone, even to the extent of having no servants. There he would find peace and isolation, the things he needed to save him from going mad.

The only disturbance might come from students and archaeologists, attracted by the villa's history. It had been built on the ruins of an ancient temple, and rumours abounded of valuable relics that might still be found.

Light was fading as the villa came into sight, silent and shuttered. He left the taxi while there was still a hundred yards to go, so that he might approach unnoticed.

He opened the gate noiselessly and walked around the side of the villa. All seemed quiet and relief flooded him. At last he let himself in at the back and went through the hall to the stairs. But before he could climb he saw something that made him freeze.

The door to the cellar was standing open.

It was no accident. The cellar led directly to the foundations and that door was always kept locked for reasons of safety. Only he had the key.

Rage swept through him at having his solitude destroyed. At that moment he could have done violence. But his fury was cold, enabling him to go down the stairs and approach his quarry noiselessly.

Someone was in the far corner of the cellar with only one small light that they were using to examine the stones, so that the person couldn't be seen.

'Stop right there,' he said harshly. 'You don't understand the danger you're in. I won't tolerate this. I allow nobody in here.'

He heard a gasp as the intruder made a sharp movement. The torch fell to the floor. His hand shot out in the darkness, found a body, seized it, grappled with it, brought it down.

'Now,' he gasped, 'you're going to be sorry you did this. Let's look at you.'

He reached over for the torch that lay on the flagstones and shone it directly into his enemy's face. Then he froze with shock.

'Petra!'

CHAPTER SIX

PETRA lay looking up at him, her eyes wide, her breath coming in short gasps. Hurriedly he got to his feet, drawing her up with him and holding her, for she was shaking.

'You,' he said, appalled. '*You!*'

'Yes, I'm afraid so.'

She swayed as she spoke and he tightened his grip lest she fall. Swiftly he picked her up and carried her out of the cellar and up the stairs to his room, where he laid her gently on the bed and sat beside her.

'Are you mad to do such a thing?' he demanded hoarsely. 'Have you any idea of the danger you were in?'

'Not real danger,' she said shakily.

'I threw you down onto stone slabs. The floor's uneven; you might have hit your head—I was in such a rage—'

'I'm sorry, I know I shouldn't—'

'The hell with that! You could have died. Do you understand that? *You could have died and then I—*' A violent shudder went through him.

'My dear,' she said gently, 'you're making too much of this. I'm a bit breathless from landing so hard, but nothing more.'

'You don't know that. I'm getting you a doctor—'

'You will not,' she said firmly. 'I don't need a doctor. I haven't broken anything, I'm not in pain and I didn't hit my head.'

He didn't reply but looked at her, haggard. She took his face between her hands. 'Don't look like that. It's all right.'

'It isn't,' he said desperately. 'Sometimes I lose control—and do things without thinking. It's so easy to do harm.'

She guessed he was really talking about something else and longed to draw the truth out of him, but instinct warned her to go carefully. He'd given her a clue to his fierce self-control, but she knew by now that he would clam up if she pressed him.

And the time was not right. For the moment she must comfort him and ease his mind.

'You didn't do me any harm,' she insisted.

'If I had I'd never forgive myself.'

'But why? I broke into your house. I'm little more than a common criminal. Why aren't you sending for the police?'

'Shut up!' he said, enfolding her in his arms.

He didn't try to kiss her, just sat holding her tightly against him, as if fearing that she might try to escape.

'That's nice,' she murmured. 'Just hold me.'

She felt his lips against her hair, felt the temptation that ran through him, but sensed wryly that he wasn't going to yield to it. He had something else on his mind.

'How badly bruised are you?' he asked.

'A few knocks, nothing much.'

'Let me see.'

He got to work, opening the buttons of her blouse, drawing it off her, removing her bra, but seemingly unaffected by the sight of her bare breasts.

'Lie down so that I can see your back,' he said.

Wondering, she did so, and lay there while he studied her.

'It's not so bad,' she said.

'I'll get a shirt for you to wear tonight.'

'No need. My things are next door. I've been here several days. Nobody saw me because of the shutters. I brought enough food to manage on and crept about. You see, I'm a really dishonest character.'

He groaned. 'And if something had happened to you? If you'd had a fall and been knocked out? You could have died without anyone knowing and lain here for days, weeks. Are you crazy, woman?'

She twisted around and sat up to face him.

'Yes, I think I am,' she agreed. 'I don't understand anything any more.'

He ground his teeth. 'Do I need to explain to you why the thought of your being in danger wrenches me apart? Are you insensitive as well as crazy and stupid?'

'My danger didn't bother you when I was on that boat that overturned.' A thought struck her. 'Unless you didn't know about it.'

'Of course I knew about it. I went to the harbour in case you needed me. I saw you arrive. After that, I knew you were all right.'

'You—?' she echoed slowly.

'The accident was on the news. Of course I went to see how you were. I saw you get off the boat, straight into Nikator's arms. I didn't want to disturb a touching reunion, so I went home.'

'You were there all the time?' she whispered.

'Where the hell would you expect me to be when you were in danger?' he raged. 'What do you think I am? Made of ice?'

Now she was glad of the understanding that was gradually coming to her, and which saved her from misjudging him. Without it she would have seen only his anger, entirely missing the fear and pain which tortured him more because he had no idea how to express them.

'No,' she said helplessly, holding out her arms to him. 'I'd never think that. Oh, I've been so stupid. I shouldn't have let you fool me.'

'What does that mean?' he asked, going into her arms.

'You hide from people. But I won't let you hide from me.'

He looked down at her naked breasts, just visible in the shadowy light. Slowly, he drew his fingertips down one until they reached the nipple, which was already proud and expectant.

'No more hiding,' he murmured.

'There's nowhere to hide from each other,' she said. 'There never was.'

'No, there never was.'

She began to work on his buttons but he forestalled her, undressing quickly, first his jacket, then his shirt. She leaned towards him so that her breasts touched his bare skin, and felt the tremors that possessed his body, guessed that he would have controlled them if he could, for he was still not yet ready to abandon himself. But that control was beyond him, she was delighted to see.

They removed the rest of their clothes, watching each other with brooding possessiveness, taking their time, for this mattered too much to be rushed. He was still fearful lest he hurt her, caressing her gently, almost tentatively, until the deep motion of her chest told him of her mounting impatience.

For too long she'd dreamed of this moment, and nothing was going to deprive her of it now. She kept her hands against his skin, moving them softly to tease him and make sure he continued with what he was doing.

His touch had made her nipples hard and peaked, so that when she leaned against him he drew a long, shaking breath at the impact.

'This is dangerous,' he whispered.

'Who for?' she challenged. 'Not me.'

'Does nothing scare you?'

'Nothing,' she assured him against his lips, 'nothing.'

She released him briefly to finish removing her clothes, and when he had done the same they returned to each other with new fervour. Now she had what she wanted—the sight of him naked and eager for her—and her blood raced at the thought of meeting his eagerness with her own.

His fingers on her skin made it flame with life.

'Yes—' she whispered. 'Yes—yes—I'm here—come here—'

He pressed her gently back against the pillows and began to caress her everywhere—her neck, her waist, her hips. He was taking his time, arousing her slowly, giving her every chance to think if this was really what she wanted. But thinking was the last thing she could do now. Everything in her was focused on one craving—to enjoy the physical release he could give her and discover if it fulfilled all the wild hopes she'd been building up. It would. It *must*.

She caressed him in return, wherever she could reach, frustrated by her limits. She wanted all of him, and even now that he was loving her in the way she most craved, it mysteriously wasn't enough.

Many times she'd wondered about him as a lover. She knew he could be cool, ironic, distant, but with flashes of intensity through which another, wholly different man could be glimpsed. She'd been intrigued by both men, wondering which of them would finally be tempted to her bed, but none of the pictures that came into her head satisfied her. They were incomplete. As a lover he would have yet another identity and she was eager to meet him.

When he finally moved over her she lay back with a sigh, waiting for him. And he was there, inside her, claiming her, completing and fulfilling her. She clasped her legs around him at once, wanting everything, and heard him give a soft growl, as though, by her gesture, she'd told him something he needed to know.

She gasped, rejoicing at the power in his hips as they released the desire that had overcome him, driving her own desire to new heights and making her thrust back at him, digging her fingers cruelly into his flesh.

'Yes—' she whispered. *'Yes!'*

To her delight he was smiling, as though her pleasure gladdened his heart. She'd known he would be a strong lover but her imagination had fallen short of the reality. He took her with power, never seeming to tire, bringing her to the brink several times before taking her over the edge so that his cry joined with hers as they fell together into a bottomless chasm.

For a long time she lay with her eyes closed, enfolded in the world where only pleasure and satisfaction existed. When she opened them again she found that he was lying with his head on her chest, breathing hard. He lifted it slowly and looked at her.

'Are you all right?' he whispered.

'Everything is fine,' she assured him.

Further words failed her. She knew that what had just happened had transformed her life, not merely because he was the most skilled lover she had ever known, but because her heart reached out to him in a way it had never done for any other man. He could possess her and give to her, but what he claimed in return was something she rejoiced to give. By taking from her, he completed her, and that was beyond all words.

He rose and looked at her. Surveying him in return, she smiled. He still wanted her.

Hooking her arm around his neck, she eased herself up, but then winced.

'Did I hurt you?' he demanded, aghast. 'I forgot—'

'So did I,' she promised him. 'I think I'll get in the shower and see what the rest of me looks like.'

He helped her off the bed, which she needed for her exertions seemed to have weakened her. Clinging to him, she went slowly into the bathroom, switching on the lights so that he could see her clearly for the first time, and turning her to look at her back. She heard him draw a sharp breath.

'Nasty,' he said. 'You must have landed on something sharp. I'm so sorry.'

'I can't feel anything,' she said shakily. 'I guess I have too many other things to feel.'

He started the shower and helped her to get under it, soaping her gently, then laving her with water and dabbing her dry. Then he carried her tenderly back to bed and went to fetch her things from the room where she had been camping.

'You wear cotton pyjamas?' he asked as her nightwear came into view.

'What were you expecting? Slinky lingerie? Not when I'm alone. These are practical.'

'I'll see what I can find us to eat,' he said. 'I may have to go out.'

'There's some food in the kitchen. I brought it with me.'

He made them coffee and sandwiches, tending her like a nanny.

'We ought to have talked before anything happened,' he said. 'I didn't want to hurt you.'

She smiled. 'That's easy to say, but I don't think we could have talked before. We had to get past a certain point.'

He nodded. 'But now it's going to be different. I'm going to look after you until you're better.' Tenderly he helped her into her pyjamas, and a thought seemed to strike him. 'How long have you been here?'

'Three days.'

'When did you get back from England?'

'I haven't been to England. What made you think I had?'

'When I found your phone turned off I called the house and spoke to someone who said you'd gone to England with

Nikator. There was a message that neither of you wanted to be disturbed—for quite a while.'

'And you believed that?' she demanded. 'What are you—dead in the head?'

'How could I not believe it? There was nothing to tell me any different. You'd vanished without a trace. Your phone was switched off.'

'I lost it in the water. I've got a new one.'

'How was I supposed to know? You might have gone with him.'

But he knew that wasn't the real reason for his credulity. Nikator's lie had touched a nerve, and that nerve led back to a lack of self-confidence so rare with him that he couldn't cope with it.

Petra was still indignant.

'It wasn't possible,' she fumed. 'It was never possible, and you should have known that.'

'How could I know it when you weren't there to tell me?' he asked reasonably. 'If I didn't think it through properly, maybe it's your fault.'

'Oh, right, fine. Blame me.'

'You left without a word.'

'*I* didn't say a word? What about you? I don't go pestering a man who's shown he doesn't want me.'

'Don't tell me what I want and don't want,' he said with a faint touch of the old ferocity.

'You were pushing me away, you know you were—'

'No, that's not what I—'

'Sending me different signals that I couldn't work out.'

He tore his hair. 'Maybe I couldn't work them out myself. You told me you'd finished with me—'

'I didn't actually say that—'

'The hell you didn't! Have you forgotten some of the

things you said? I haven't. I'll never forget them. I never wanted you to go away. And then—' he took a shuddering breath '—you could have died on that boat, and you might not have been on it if it weren't for me. I just had to know you were safe, but after that—well, you and he seemed so comfortable together.'

'Except that he took the chance to spread lies,' she seethed. 'I was actually beginning to think he might not be so bad after all. I'll strangle him.'

'Leave it for a while,' he soothed. 'Then we'll do it together. But until then you stay in bed until I say you can get up.'

'I'm not fragile,' she protested. 'I won't break.'

'That's my decision. You're going to be looked after.'

'Yes, sir,' she said meekly, through twitching lips.

He threw her a suspicious glance. She retaliated by saluting him.

'I understand, *sir*. I'll just keep quiet and obey, because I'm gonna be looked after whether I like it or not, *sir*!'

He smiled then. 'Oh, I think you might like it,' he said.

'Yes,' she said happily. 'I think I just might.'

That night she slept better than she'd done for weeks. It might be the effect of snuggling down in Lysandros's comfortable bed, waited on hand and foot and told to think of nothing but getting well. Or perhaps it was the blissful sensation of being beside him all night, ordered to, 'Wake me if you need anything.'

Or the moment when she half-awoke in the early hours to find him sitting by the window, and the way he hurried over, saying, 'What is it? What can I do for you?'

This man would astound those who only knew him in the boardroom. His tenderness was real, and so, to her delighted surprise, was his thoughtfulness. He visibly racked his brains to please her, and succeeded because it seemed to matter to him so much. She slipped back contentedly into sleep.

When she awoke the next morning he was gone and the house was silent. Had she misread him? Had he taken what he wanted, then abandoned her to make her suffer for invading his privacy? But, although that fitted with his reputation, she couldn't make herself believe it of the man who'd cared for her so gently last night.

'Aaaaah,' she gasped slowly, rubbing her back as she eased her way out onto the landing.

Downstairs, the front door opened, revealing him. As soon as he saw her at the top of the stairs he hurried up, demanding, 'What are you doing out of bed?'

'I had to get up for a few minutes,' she protested.

'Well, now you can go right back. Come along.'

But once inside the bedroom he pointed her to a chair, saying brusquely, 'Sit there while I remake the bed.'

Gladly she sat down, watching him pull the sheets straight, until finally he came to help her stand.

'I'm just a bit stiff,' she said, clinging to him gladly and wincing.

'You'll be less stiff when I've given you a good rub. I went out for food and I remembered a pharmacy where they sell a great liniment. Get undressed and lie down.'

She did so, lying on her front and gasping as the cool liniment touched her. But that soon changed to warmth as his hand moved here and there over her bruises.

'They seem more tender now than last night,' she mused.

'You should have rested at once,' he told her. 'It's my fault you didn't.'

'Yes,' she remembered, smiling. 'We did something else instead. It was worth it.'

'I'm glad you think so, but I'm not touching you again until you're better.'

'Aren't you touching me now?'

'This isn't the same thing,' he said firmly.

And it wasn't, she thought, frustrated. His fingers moved here and there, sometimes firm, sometimes soft, but tending her, not loving her. There was just one moment when he seemed on the edge of weakening, when his hand lingered over the swell of her behind, as though he was fighting temptation. But then he won the fight and his hand moved firmly on.

She sighed. It wasn't fair.

Later, in the kitchen, she watched as he made breakfast.

'They wouldn't believe it if they could see you now,' she teased.

He didn't need to ask who 'they' were.

'I'm trusting you not to tell them,' he said. 'If you breathe a word of this I'll say you're delusional.'

'Don't worry. This is one secret I'm going to keep to myself. You don't keep any servants here?'

'I have a cleaning lady who comes in sometimes, but I prefer to be alone. Most of the house is shut up, and I just use a couple of rooms.'

'What made you come here now?'

'I needed to think,' he said, regarding her significantly. 'Since we met…I don't know…everything should have been simple…'

'But it never has been,' she mused. 'I wonder if we can make things simple by wanting it.'

'No,' he said at once. 'But if you have to fight—why not? As long as you know what you're fighting for.'

'Or who you're fighting,' she pointed out.

'I don't think there's any doubt about who we'll be fighting,' he said.

'Each other. Yes, it makes it interesting, doesn't it? Exhausting but interesting.'

He laughed and she pounced on it. 'I love it when you laugh. That's when I can claim a victory.'

'You've had other victories that maybe you don't know about.' He added with a touch of self-mockery, 'Or maybe you do.'

'I think I'll leave you to guess about that.'

'It would be a mistake for me to underestimate you, wouldn't it?'

'Definitely.'

Briefly she thought, if only he were always like this, charming and open to her. But she smothered the thought at once. A man who was always charming was like a musician who could only play one note. Eventually it became tedious. Lysandros was fascinating because she never knew who he was going to be from one moment to the next. And nor did he know with her, which kept them both on alert. Could anything be more delightful?

'I'm sorry about last night,' he said.

'I'm not.'

'I mean I'm sorry I didn't wait until you were better.'

'Listen, if you'd had the self-control to wait I'd have taken it as a personal insult. And then I *would* have made you sorry.'

He gave her a curious look. 'I think you will one day, in any case,' he said.

'Perhaps we should both look forward to that.'

She rose, reaching out to take some plates to the sink, but he forestalled her. 'Leave it to me.'

'There's no need to fuss me like an invalid.' She laughed. 'I really can do things for myself.'

His reply was a look of sadness. 'All right,' he said after a moment.

'Lysandros, honestly—'

'I just wish you'd let me give you something—do things for you—'

Heart-stricken, she touched his face, blaming herself for being insensitive.

'I didn't want to be a nuisance,' she whispered. 'You have so many really important things to do.'

He put his arms right around her and drew her close against him.

'There's nothing more important than you,' he said simply.

Later she was to remember the way he'd held her and wonder at it. It hadn't been the embrace of a lover, more the clasp of a refugee clinging onto safety for dear life. He couldn't have told her more clearly that she'd brought something into his life that was more than passion—more life-enhancing while he had it, more soul-destroying if he lost it.

CHAPTER SEVEN

WHEN the washing-up was done Petra asked, 'What are we going to do today?'

'You're going to rest.'

'I think a little gentle exercise will be better for me. I could continue exploring the cellar—'

'No!' This time there was no doubt that he meant it. 'We can have a short outing, an hour on the beach, and lunch, then back here for you to rest.'

'Anything you say.'

Lysandros regarded her cynically.

There was a small car in the garage and he drove them the short distance to the shore, where they found a tiny beach, cut off from the main one and deserted.

'It's private,' Lysandros explained. 'It belongs to a friend of mine. Don't stretch out in this burning sun, not with your fair skin. Do you want to get ill?'

He led her to the rocks, where there was some shade and a small cave that she used for changing. Now she was glad she'd had the forethought to bring a bathing costume when she came to Corfu, meaning to enjoy some swimming while she investigated his house. No chance had occured, but now she changed gladly, longing to feel the sun on her skin, and emerged to find that he'd laid out a large towel for her to lie on. There was even a pillow, making it blissful to lie down, although she hadn't been awake long.

He'd brought some sun lotion to rub in, but was doubtful.

'You shouldn't have this as well as liniment,' he explained. 'We'll leave it for a while, but you stay in the shade. No, don't try to move the towel. Leave it where I put it.'

'Yes, sir. Three bags full, sir.'

He frowned. 'This is something I sometimes hear English people say, but I don't understand it.'

She explained that the words occurred in a nursery rhyme, but he only looked worried.

'You say it to make fun of someone?' he ventured.

'Only of myself,' she said tenderly. 'The mockery is aimed at me, and the way I'm tamely letting you give me orders.'

This genuinely puzzled him. 'But why shouldn't I—?'

'Hush.' She laid a finger over his lips. He immediately kissed it.

'It's for your own good,' he protested. 'To care for you.'

'I know. The joke is that part of me is as much of a sergeant major as you are. I give orders too. But I let you say, "Do this, do that" without kicking your shins as I would with any other man. It's like discovering that inside me is someone else that I've never met before.'

He nodded. 'Yes, that's how it is.'

To complete her protection he'd hired a large parasol. Now he put it up and made sure that she was well covered.

'What about you?' she said. 'You might catch the sun, unless I rub some of that lotion into you.'

Unlike her, he was dark and at less danger from sunburn, but the thought of caressing him under the guise of sun care was irresistible.

'You think I need it?' he asked.

'Definitely.'

He gave her a brief look and lay back beside her so that she could begin work on his chest. He said nothing for a while, just lay still while her fingers worked across his skin, curving to shape the muscles, enjoying herself.

'How did we get here?' he murmured.

'I don't know. We seem to have missed each other so many times. You'd come just so far towards me, then clam up. Everything would be fine between us, then you'd act as though I was an enemy you had to fight off. That night in Athens—'

'I know. I'm sorry about that. I hated myself at the time, but I couldn't stop. You were right to reject me.'

He wasn't fighting her any more and suddenly there was a vulnerable look on his face that she couldn't bear to see. He was powerful and belligerent, but this was her territory where her skills were greater than his, and it was dangerously easy to hurt him.

'We've never understood each other well,' she said gently. 'Perhaps now we have a chance to do that.'

His brow darkened. 'Are you sure you want to try? It might be better not to. I'm bad news. I hurt people. I don't mean to, but often I'm so cut off that I don't realise I'm doing it.'

'You wouldn't be trying to scare me, would you?'

'Warn you. I doubt I could scare you.'

'I'm glad you realise that.'

'So listen to me. Be wise and go now. I'm bad for you.'

'That's all right; I'll just retaliate in kind. When it comes to being bad, you are dealing with an expert.' He started to reply but she silenced him. 'No, I talk, you listen. I've heard what you have to say and I'm not impressed by it. I'm a match for you any day. If we fight, we fight, and you'll come off worst.'

'Oh, will I?' Now his interest was aroused.

'You'd better believe it,' she chuckled. 'Won't that be a new experience for you?'

'A man should be prepared for new experiences. That's how he gets strong and able to achieve victory every time.'

'Every time, hmm?'

'Every time,' he assured her.

'We'll put that to the test. Right now—' she drew back and got to her feet '—I'm going for a swim.'

She was off down the beach before he could get to his feet. By the time he caught her she'd reached the water and hurled herself in. He followed, keeping up with her as she swam out to sea, then getting ahead and stretching out his hands to her. She clasped them, looking up, laughing, rejoicing in the sunlight.

'Steady,' he said, supporting her as she leaned over backwards.

They swam for a while, but she was stiff and as soon as he saw her wince slightly he said, 'Now we're going ashore to have something to eat.'

As they walked up the beach she took the chance to study him. Last night she'd lain with this man, welcomed him inside her, felt a pleasure that only he had ever been able to give, but in the poor light she hadn't seen him properly. Now she looked her fill at his tall muscular body that might have belonged to an athlete instead of a businessman.

Certain moments from their lovemaking came back to her, making her tremble. How easily he'd driven her to new heights, how fierce was the craving he could make her feel, how inspired were the movements of his hands, knowing just where and how to touch her. If she could have had her way she would have pulled him down onto the sand right then. Instead, she promised herself that the wait would not be long.

They found a small restaurant by the sea, and sat where they could watch the waves.

'What happened with the boat?' he asked.

'I don't know really. The weather was fine at first. We went to several caves, didn't find anything. I should never have gone—'

'And you wouldn't have done but for me. If you'd died—'

'That's enough of that.' She stopped him firmly. 'I didn't die. End of story.'

'No,' he said softly. 'It's not the end of the story. We both know that.'

She nodded but said no more.

'After we quarrelled I was sure that we had nothing further to say to each other, but then I heard of your danger and—' he made an agitated gesture '—nothing's been the same since. When I saw you safe the world became bright again, but then there was Nikator. When I heard you'd gone away with him—'

'You should have known better than to believe it.'

'But how could I? You wouldn't believe me when I warned you about him and when I saw you together I thought you'd chosen him over me. I don't really know you at all, except that something here—' he touched his heart '—has always known you.'

'Yes, but that isn't going to make it easy,' she reflected. 'The path led in so many directions that it was confusing, and in the end we stumbled against each other by accident.'

'This meeting was hardly an accident,' he observed lightly. 'You broke into my house.'

'True. I committed a criminal act,' she said, smiling. 'I didn't actually want to. I had planned to ask you to let me explore, but then we quarrelled and—' She gave an eloquent shrug.

He nodded. 'Yes, when you've told a man to go and jump in the lake it would be hard to ask him a favour in the next breath.'

'I'm glad you understand my difficulty. And I couldn't just go tamely away without investigating, could I? Breaking and entering was my only option.'

'But how did you get in? My locks are the most up-to-date.'

Her smile told him that these were minor difficulties, made to be overcome.

'Estelle made a film about organised crime a few years back,' she recalled. 'One of the advisers was a locksmith. I learned a lot from him. He said there was no such thing as a lock that couldn't be picked, even a digital one.'

He regarded her cautiously, not sure whether to believe her. At last he ran a finger gently down her cheek, murmuring, 'So you wouldn't call yourself an honest woman?'

'Honest? Lysandros, haven't you understood yet? I'm a historian. We don't *do* honest, not if it gets in the way. If we want to investigate something, we just go ahead. We break in, we forge papers, we tell lies, we cheat, we do whatever is needed to find out what we need to know. Of course we sometimes get permission as a matter of convenience, but it's not important.'

He grinned. 'I see. And if the owner objects—?'

She regarded him from dancing eyes and leaned forward so that her breath brushed his face.

'Then the owner can take his silly objections and stuff them where the sun doesn't shine,' she murmured.

'I'm shocked.'

'No, you're not. I'll bet it's what you do yourself every day of the week.'

'And I would bet that you could teach me a few new tricks.'

'Any time you like,' she murmured against his lips.

'I was talking about business.'

'I wasn't. Let's go home.'

On the way he stopped off to buy food in quantity, and

Petra realised that he was stocking up for several days. She smiled. That suited her exactly.

The sun was setting as they entered the house and locked the world out. In the shadowy hall he took her into his arms for a long kiss. The feel of his mouth on hers was comforting and thrilling together. He was partly hers and she was going to make him completely hers, as she was already his.

He kissed her neck, moving his lips gently, then resting with his face against her, as though seeking refuge. She stroked his hair until he looked up, meeting her eyes, and together they climbed the stairs to the bedroom.

Last night they had claimed each other with frantic urgency. Tonight they could afford to take their time, confident in each other and their new knowledge of their hearts and what they shared.

At first he moved slowly, cautiously, and she loved him for his care for her. As every garment slipped away he touched her bare flesh as though doubtful that he could take the next step. She undressed him in the same way, eager to discover the body she'd admired on the beach that day.

It didn't disappoint her. He was hard and fit, reminding her of what she'd enjoyed once, making her tremble with the thought of what was to come.

He laid her on the bed and sat for a moment, watching her with possessive eyes.

'Let me look at you,' he whispered.

She was happy for him to do so, knowing that she would please him. A man who'd discovered unexpected treasure might have worn the look she saw on his face. She raised her arms over her head, revelling in flaunting her nakedness for him, knowing that it was worth flaunting.

At last he laid a gentle hand on one breast, relishing the movement as it rose and fell with her mounting desire, then leaning down to circle the nipple with his lips and begin a soft assault. She took a long shuddering breath and immediately arched against him.

'Yes,' she murmured, 'yes—'

'Hush, we don't have to rush.'

How could he say that? she wondered. Already his arousal was fierce and strong, making her reach out with eager exploring fingers. But he was in command of himself, with the power to take his time while he teased and incited her.

'You're a devil,' she whispered.

He didn't reply in words, but he raised his head long enough for his eyes to flash a humorous message, saying, clearer than words, that a devil was what he knew she wanted, and he was going to fulfil her desire.

He increased his devilment, turning up the tension as he got to work on the other breast, moving even more slowly now, making sure she was ready, but she was ahead of him, more than ready, eager and impatient.

'Now,' she breathed. *'Now!'*

He was over her before the words were out, finding the place that was clamouring for him, claiming it with a swift movement that sent her into a frenzy of pleasure.

This was unlike anything that had happened to her before. No man had ever filled her so completely, while still leaving her with a feeling of freedom. She thrust back against him, needing more of him, demanding everything, receiving it again and again.

When it was over she held him tightly, as though needing him for safety in this new world that had opened. But then she realised that there was no safety, for either of them. That was the glory of it.

He raised his head and there was a kind of bafflement in his eyes.

'You—' he said softly, 'you—'

'I know,' she whispered. 'It's the same with me.'

It was as though her words had touched a spring within him, releasing something that brought him peace. He laid his head down on her again, and in a moment he was asleep.

Petra didn't sleep at once. Instead, she lay savouring her joy and triumph, kissing him tenderly, silently promising him everything. Only gradually did she slip away into the happy darkness.

They spent most of the next day in bed, not making love, but cuddling, talking, then cuddling some more in a way that would have been impossible only a short time ago. His body, so perfectly formed and skilled for giving her sexual pleasure, was mysteriously also formed for things cosy, domestic and comforting. It was a mystery, and one she would enjoy solving later.

'I don't know what I'd have done if I'd lost you,' he murmured as they lay curled against each other. 'It felt like being in prison, except that somehow you had the key, and you could help me break out.'

'You kept coming to the edge of escape,' she remembered, 'but then you'd back off again and slam the door.'

'I lost my nerve,' he said with self-contempt. 'I wasn't sure if I could manage, so I'd retreat and lock the doors again. But I couldn't stay in there, knowing you were outside, calling to me that the world was a wonderful place. You saved me the first time; I knew you could save me again.'

'How did I save you?'

His only reply was a long silence, and she felt her heart sink. So often they'd come to the point where he might confide in her, but always his demons had driven him back. This time she'd hoped it might be different, that their loving had given him confidence in her. But it seemed not. Perhaps, after all, nothing had changed.

She'd almost given up hope when Lysandros said in a low voice, 'I never told you why I was in Las Vegas. The fact is

I'd quarrelled with my family. Suddenly it seemed hateful to me that we were always at war about so much. I wanted no more of it. I left home and went out to "live my own life", as I put it. But I got into bad ways. The night we met I'd been like that for two years, and I was headed for disaster if something didn't happen to save me. But something did. I met you.'

'And quarrelled with me,' she said with just a hint of teasing.

'We didn't quarrel,' he said quickly. 'Hell, yes, I suppose we came to the edge of it because I wasn't used to being told a truth I didn't want to hear—that dig about Achilles sulking in his tent.'

'But it wasn't a dig. I was just running over the legend in my usual thoughtless way.'

'I know. You may even have done me a favour.'

Another silence while he fought his inner battle.

'It's all right,' she said. 'Don't tell me anything you don't want to.'

'But I do want to,' he said slowly. 'If you only knew how much.'

She touched his hand again, and felt him squeeze her fingers gratefully.

'That remark got to me,' he said at last. 'I was twenty-three and…I guess, not very mature. I'd left my father to cope alone. You showed me the truth about myself. I did a lot of thinking, and next day I came home and told my father I was ready to take my place in the business. We became a partnership and when he died ten years ago I was able to take over. Thanks to you.'

'Should I be proud of my creation?'

'Do *you* think so?'

'Not entirely. You're not a happy man.'

He shrugged. 'Happiness isn't part of the bargain.'

'I wonder who you struck that bargain with,' she mused. 'Perhaps it was the Furies.'

'No, the Furies are my advance troops that I send into battle. This isn't about my feelings. I do my job. I keep people in work.'

'And so you benefit them. But what about you, yourself, the man?'

His eyes darkened and he seemed to stare into space. 'Sometimes,' he said at last, 'I've felt he hardly exists.'

She nodded. *'He's* an automaton that walks and talks and does what's necessary,' she said. 'But what about *you*?' She laid a soft hand over his heart. 'Somewhere in there, you must exist.'

'Perhaps it's better if I don't,' he said heavily.

'Better for whom? Not you. How can you live in the world and not be part of it?'

He grimaced. 'That's easier than you think. And safer.'

'Safer? You? The man who's supposed to be immortal?'

'*Supposed* to be—'

'Except for that one tiny place on the heel? Shame on you, Achilles. Do you want me to think you're afraid to take the risks that we less glorious mortals take every day?'

He drew a sharp breath and grasped her. 'Oh, you're good,' he said. 'You're clever, cunning, sharp; you know how to pierce a man's heart—'

'You have no heart,' she challenged him. 'At least, not one you care to listen to.'

'And if I listened to it, what do you think it would say to me—about you?'

'I can't tell you that. Only you can know.'

'It will speak in answer to your heart,' he riposted cunningly. 'If I knew what that was saying—'

'Can't you read it?' she whispered.

'Some of it. It laughs at me, almost like an enemy, and yet—'

'Friends laugh too. My heart is your friend, but perhaps an annoying friend. You'll have to be prepared for that.'

'I am, I promise you. Petra—Petra—say you want me.'

'If you haven't worked that out for yourself by now—'

His hands seemed to touch her everywhere at once.

'I hope that means what I think it means,' he growled. 'Because it's too late now.'

She put her arms around his neck. 'Whatever took you so long?'

When she awoke it was early morning and she was alone. Beside her the bed was empty, but the rumpled sheet and pillow showed where he had been. Touching the place, she found that it was still warm.

She sat up listening, but there was only silence. Slipping out of bed, she went to the door, but when she opened it she saw that there was no light on in the bathroom, and some instinct told her that he was in trouble.

She thought she could hear a faint sound from the far end of the corridor. Moving quietly, she followed it to the end, where it turned into another corridor. There she heard the sound again, and this time it sounded like soft footsteps, back and forth. She followed it to the end and waited a moment, her heart beating, before turning the corner.

A short flight of stairs rose before her. At the top stood Lysandros, by the window, looking out onto the world below. He turned, walked back and forth like a man seeing his way in unfamiliar territory, finally coming to a halt in front of a door.

She waited for him to enter the room. Perhaps she could follow him quietly, and so gain a clue to his trouble. But instead he remained motionless for what seemed like an age. Then he leaned against the door, his shoulders sagging in an attitude that suggested he was on the point of collapse. She was about to go to him, offering comfort, when he straightened up and turned around in her direction.

Hurriedly she retreated, and vanished before he could see her. She managed to reach the bedroom without being discovered and was huddled down with her back to him when he came in. She sensed him get in beside her and lean over her, apparently trying to check if she was asleep. She decided to chance it and opened her eyes.

'Hello,' she said, opening her arms to him.

Now, surely, he would come into them and tell her what had happened, because now they were close in hearts and minds and he didn't need to hide things from her.

But, instead, he drew back.

'I'm sorry if I disturbed you,' he said. 'I was just thinking of getting up.'

'You're going to get up now?' she asked slowly.

'Yes, I get stiff lying here all night, but you stay. I'll bring you some coffee later.'

He left the room quickly, leaving her wanting to scream out a protest.

No matter what happiness they seemed to share, beneath it was a torment that hounded him, and which he could not bring himself to share with her. Everything she'd longed for was an illusion. She was still shut out from his deepest heart. She buried her face, and the pillow was wet with her tears.

CHAPTER EIGHT

PETRA wondered how Lysandros would be when they met again at breakfast, whether he would show any awareness of what had happened. But he greeted her cheerfully, with a kiss on the cheek. They might have been any couple enjoying a few days vacation without a care in the world.

'Is there anything you'd like to do?' he asked.

'I'd love to go to Gastouri.'

She was referring to the tiny village where the Achilleion Palace had been built.

'Have you never been before?' he asked in surprise.

'Yes, but it was a hurried visit to get material. Now I'll have time to explore properly.'

And perhaps, she thought, it would help her cope with the sadness of being rejected again.

The village lay about seven miles to the south, built on a slope, with the Palace at the top, overlooking the sea. This was the place that the Empress Elizabeth had built to indulge her passion for the Greek hero, who seemed to have reached out to her over thousands of years. His courage, his complex character, his terrible fate, all were remembered here.

As soon as they entered the gates Petra was aware of the

atmosphere—powerful, vital, yet melancholy, much as Achilles himself must have been.

Just outside the house was the statue of the Empress herself, a tiny figure, looking down with a sad expression, as though all hope had left her.

'She used to annoy my father,' Lysandros said. 'He said she was a silly woman who couldn't pull herself together.'

'Charming.'

'When my mother brought me here he'd insist on coming too, and showing me the things *he* wanted me to remember, like this one.'

He led the way to a tall bronze statue showing Achilles as a magnificent young warrior, wearing a metal helmet mounted with a great feathered crest. On his lower legs was armour, embossed at the kneecaps with snarling lions.

From one arm hung a shield while the other hand held a spear. He stood on a sixteen-foot plinth, looming over all-comers, staring out into the distance.

'Disdainful,' Petra said thoughtfully. 'Standing so far above, he'd never notice ordinary mortals like us, coming and going down here.'

'Perhaps that's how Sisi liked to picture him,' Lysandros suggested with a touch of mischief.

'Sisi knew nothing about it,' Petra said at once. 'After her death the Palace was sold to a man, and *he* put this statue here.'

He grinned. 'I might have guessed you'd know that.'

'So that's who your father wanted you to be,' she reflected, straining her head back to look up high to Achilles' face.

'Nothing less would do for him. There's also the picture inside which he admired.'

The main hall was dominated by a great staircase, at the top of which was a gigantic painting depicting a man in a racing chariot, galloping at full speed, dragging the lifeless body of his enemy in the dirt behind.

'Achilles in triumph,' Petra said, 'parading his defeated enemy around the walls of Troy.'

'That was how a man ought to be,' Lysandros mused. 'Because if you didn't do it to them, they would do it to you. So I was raised being taught how to do it to them.'

'And do you?'

'Yes,' he replied simply. 'If I have to, otherwise I wouldn't survive, and nor would the people who work for me.'

'Parading lifeless bodies?' she queried.

'Not literally. My enemies are still walking about on earth, trying to destroy me. But if you've won, people have to know you've won, and the lengths you were prepared to go to. That way they learn the lesson.'

For a moment his face frightened her, not because it displayed harshness or cruelty, but because it displayed nothing at all. He was simply stating a fact. Victory had to be flaunted or it was less effective, and she could see that he didn't really understand why this troubled her.

They moved on through the building, looking at the friezes and murals, the paintings and statues all telling of another world, yet one that still reached out to touch this one. Lysandros might speak wryly of his mother's fascination with the legendary Achilles, yet even he felt the story's power over him.

Heroism was no longer simple as in those days, but he'd been born into a society that expected him to conquer his enemies and drag them behind his chariot wheels. The past laid its weight on him, almost expecting him to live two lives at once, and he knew it. Fight it as he might, there were times when the expectations almost crushed him.

If she'd doubted that, she had the proof when they moved

back into the garden and went to stand before the great statue depicting Achilles' last moments. He lay on the ground, trying to draw the arrow from his heel, although in his heart he knew it was hopeless. His head was raised to the heavens and on his face was a look of despair.

'He's resigned,' Lysandros said. 'He knows there's no escaping his destiny.'

'Then perhaps he shouldn't be so resigned,' Petra said at once. 'You should never accept bad luck as inevitable. That's just giving in.'

'How could he help it? He knew his fate was written on the day he was born. It was always there on his mind, the hidden vulnerability. Except that in the end it wasn't hidden, because someone had known all the time. None of us hide our weaknesses as well as we think we do.'

'But perhaps,' she began tentatively, 'if the other person was someone we didn't have to be afraid of, someone who wouldn't use it against us—'

'That would be paradise indeed,' Lysandros agreed. 'But how would you know, until it was too late?'

They strolled for a while in the grounds before he said, 'Is there any more you need to see here, or shall we go?'

On the way home his mood seemed to lighten. They had a cheerful supper, enlivened by an argument about a trivial point that he seemed unable to let go of, until he covered his eyes with his hands, in despair at himself.

'It doesn't matter, does it?' he groaned. 'I know it doesn't matter and yet—'

'You're a mess,' she said tenderly. 'You don't know how to deal with people—unless they're enemies. You deal with *them* well enough, but anyone else—you're left floundering. You know what you need?'

'What's that?'

'Me. To put you on a straight line and keep you there.'

'Where does this line lead?'

'Back to me, every time. So make up your mind to it; I'm taking charge.'

He regarded her for a moment, frowning, and she wondered if she'd pushed his dictatorial nature too far. But then the frown vanished, replaced by a tender smile.

'That's all right, then,' he said.

She smiled in a way that she could see he found mystifying. Good. That suited her perfectly.

Quickly she reached into her pocket, drew out a small notebook and pencil that never left her, then began counting on her fingers and making notes.

'What are you doing?' he demanded.

'Calculating. Do you know it's exactly eighteen hours and twenty-three minutes since you made love to me?' She sighed theatrically. 'I don't know. Some men are all talk.'

Before he could think of an answer, she rose and darted away.

'Hey, where are you going?'

'Where do you think?' she called back over her shoulder from halfway up the stairs.

He managed to pass her on the stairs and reach the bedroom first.

'Come here,' he said, yanking her close and holding her tightly, without gentleness. *'Come here.'*

It was less a kiss than an act of desperation. She knew that as soon as his lips touched hers, not tenderly but with a ferocity that mirrored her own. They had shared kisses before, but this was a step further. In the past she'd been struggling with her own reaction, and doubtful of his. But the previous two times they'd made love had told each of them something about the other, and where they were going together.

Now there were no doubts on either side, no room for

thoughts or even emotions. They wanted each other as a simple physical act, free of everything but the need for satisfaction.

His mouth seemed to burn hers while his tongue invaded her, demanding, asking no quarter and giving none. His urgency thrilled her for it matched her own, but she wouldn't let him know that just yet. She had another plan in mind.

'Mmm, just as I hoped,' she murmured.

He ground his teeth. 'You pulled my strings and I jumped, didn't I?'

''Fraid so. And you have another problem now.'

'Surprise me.'

'I'm a horrible person. In fact I'm just horrible enough to get up and walk away right now.'

His hands tightened on her in a grip of steel. *'Don't even think about it.'*

She began to laugh with delight, revelling in the ruthless determination with which he held her, threw her onto her back and invaded her like a conqueror. She was still laughing when her explosion of pleasure sent the world into a spin.

Afterwards he looked down at her, gasping and frenzied. 'You little—*it's not funny!*'

'But it is funny. Oh, my darling, you're so easily fooled.'

He began to move inside her again, slowly, making her wait but leaving her in no doubt that he had the strength and control to prolong the moment.

'Were you expecting this too?' he whispered.

'Not exactly expecting, but I was hoping—oh, yes, I was hoping you'd do just what you're doing now—and again—and again—oh, darling, *don't stop!*'

She ceased to be aware of time, losing track of how often he brought her to climax. It didn't matter. All that mattered was that he'd transported her to another world, while giving her the vital feeling that she too had transported him. Whatever happened to them happened together, and she cared about nothing else.

When he finally managed to speak it was with ironic humour.

'I did it again, didn't I? Danced to your tune. Is there any way I can get one step ahead of you?'

She seemed to consider this. 'Probably not. But I'd hate you to stop trying.'

Now it was his turn to laugh. She felt it against her before she heard it, and her soul rejoiced because it was through laughter that she could reach him.

The next few days were hazy. They spent much of the time out, wandering the island or lazing on the beach, their evenings indoors, talking with a freedom which once would have been impossible. They spent the nights in each other's arms.

She knew it couldn't last for ever. For now they were living in a world apart, where each of them could yield to the new personality the other could evoke. He could doff his harsh exterior, emerge from the prison cell where his heart normally lived, and let her see the side of him that was charming and outgoing.

But it was unreal. Such perfect happiness could never last unchallenged. Sooner or later she must face the part of him that remained hidden from her, or retire in defeat because he wouldn't allow her in.

She'd never told him of the night she'd followed him to the distant room. Once she slipped upstairs to try the door and, as she'd expected, found it locked. In her mind it came to symbolise the fact that she still hadn't gained entry into the deepest heart of him. Despite their happiness, she wondered if she ever would.

One night she awoke to find herself alone again. The door was open and from a distance she thought she could hear sounds. Quickly she scrambled out into the corridor and was just in time to see Lysandros turning the corner. He walked in a slow, dazed manner, as though he was sleepwalking.

When she reached the little staircase he was just standing at the top. He approached the door slowly, then, before her horrified eyes, he began to ram his head against it again and again, as though by seeking pain he could blot out unbearable memories.

Suddenly she was back on the roof all those years ago and he was in her arms, banging his head against her, seeking oblivion from misery too great to be borne. And she knew that fifteen years had changed nothing. In his heart he was the same young man now as then.

She would have run to him, but he stopped suddenly and turned, leaning back against the door. Through the window the moonlight fell on his face, showing her a depth of agony that shocked her.

He didn't move. His eyes were closed, his head pressed back against the door, his face raised as though something hovered in the darkness above him. As she watched, he lifted his hands and laid them over his face, pressing them close as though he could use them as a shield against the Furies that pursued him. But the Furies were inside him. There was no escape.

Wisdom told her to retreat and never let him know that she'd seen him like this, but she couldn't be wise now. He might try to reject her, but she must at least offer him her comfort.

She moved the rest of the way quickly and quietly, then reached up to draw his hands away. He started, gazing at her with haggard eyes that saw a stranger.

'It's all right; it's only me,' she whispered.

'What are you doing here?'

'I came because you need me—yes, you do,' she added quickly before he could speak. 'You think you don't need anyone, but you need me because I understand. I know things that no one else knows, because you shared them with me long ago.'

'You don't know the half of it,' he whispered.

'Then tell me. What's in that room, Lysandros? What draws you here? What do you see when you go inside?'

His reply startled her. 'I never go inside.'

'But…then why…?'

'I don't go in because I can't bear to. Each time I come here, hoping to find the courage to enter, but that never happens.' He gave a mirthless snort of laughter. 'Now you know. *I'm a coward.*'

'Don't—'

'I'm a coward because I can't face her again.'

'Is she in there?' Petra asked.

'She always will be. You think I'm mad? Well, perhaps. Let's see.'

He opened his hand, revealing the key, allowing her to take it and put it in the lock. Turning it slowly, she pushed on the door. It stuck as though protesting after being closed for so long, but then a nudge opened it and she stood on the threshold, holding her breath, wondering fearfully what she would find.

At first she could see very little. Outside the dawn was breaking, but the shutters were still closed and only thin slivers of light managed to creep in. By their faint glow she realised that this room had been designed as a celebration of love.

The walls were covered in paintings depicting gods, goddesses and various Greek legends. Incredibly, Petra thought she recognised some of them.

'These pictures are famous,' she murmured. 'Botticelli, Titian—'

'Don't worry, we didn't steal them,' Lysandros said. 'They're all copies. One of my mother's ancestors wanted to "make a figure" in the world. So he hired forgers to go all over Europe and copy the works of great artists—paintings, statues. You'll probably recognise the statues of Eros and Aphrodite as well.'

'The gods of love,' she whispered.

'His wife directed matters, and had this room turned into a kind of temple.'

'It's charming,' Petra said. 'Had they made a great love match?'

'No, he married the poor woman for her money, and this was her way of trying to deny it.'

'How sad.'

'Love often is sad when you get past the pretty lies and down to the ugly truth,' he said in a flat voice.

But now she scarcely heard him. Disturbing impressions were reaching her. Something was badly wrong, but she wasn't sure what. Then she drew closer to a statue of Eros, the little god of love, and a chill went through her.

'His face,' she murmured. 'I can't see, but surely—'

With a crash Lysandros threw open the shutters, filling the room with pale light. Petra drew a sharp, horrified breath.

Eros had no face. It looked as if it had been smashed off by a hammer. His wings, too, lay on the floor.

Now she could look around at the others and see that they were all damaged in a similar way. Every statue had been attacked, every painting defaced.

But the worst of all was what had happened to the bed. It had been designed as a four-poster but the posts too had been smashed, so that the great canopy had collapsed onto the bed, where it lay.

Someone had attacked this temple to love in a frenzy, and then left the devastation as it was, making no attempt to clear up. Now she could see the thick dust. It had been like this, untouched, for a long, long time. That was as terrible as the damage with its message of soul-destroying bitterness.

'You asked if she were in here,' Lysandros said. 'She's been here since the night I brought her to this house, to this room, and we made love. She'll always be here.'

'Was she here when—?'

'When I did this? When I took an axe and defaced the statues and the pictures, smashed the bed where we'd slept, wanting to wipe out every trace of what I'd once thought was love? No, she wasn't here. She'd gone. I didn't know where she was and after that—I didn't find her until she died, far away.'

He turned to the wrecked bed, gazing at it bleakly as though it held him transfixed. Shivers went through Petra as she realised that he'd spoken no more than the truth. His dead love was still present, and she always would be. She followed him through every step of his life, but she was always here, in this house, in this room, in his heart, in his nightmares.

'Come away,' she said. 'There's nothing here any more.'

It wasn't true. In this room was everything that was terrible, but she wouldn't admit that to him, lest her admission crush him further. She drew him to the door and locked it after them. She knew it would take more than a locked door to banish this ghost from his dark dreams, but she was determined to do it.

He's got me now, she told the lurking presence in her mind. *And I won't let you hurt him any more.*

She didn't speak to Lysandros again, just led him back to their bed and held him in her arms.

At last some life seemed to return to Lysandros and he roused himself to speak.

'Since we've been here together, I've found myself going more and more to that room, hoping that I could make myself enter and drive the ghost away.'

'Perhaps I can help you do that,' she suggested.

'Perhaps. I've resisted it too long.'

'Am I something you need to resist?' she whispered.

He took so long to reply that she thought he wasn't going to say anything, but at last he spoke as though the words were dragged out of him by pincers.

'From the first evening you have filled me with dread,' he said slowly. 'With dread—with fear. There! That's the truth. Despise me if you will.'

'I could never despise you,' she hastened to say. 'I just can't think of any reason why you should be afraid of me.'

'Not of you, but of the way you made me feel. In your presence my defences seemed to melt away. I felt it when we met at the wedding. When I discovered that you were the girl on the roof in Las Vegas I was glad, because it seemed to explain why I was drawn to you. We'd been practically childhood friends so naturally there was a bond. That's what I told myself.

'But then we danced, and I knew that the bond was something far more. I left the wedding early to escape you, but I called you later that day because I had to. Even then I couldn't stay away from you because you had an alarming power, one I shied away from because I'd never met it before and I knew I couldn't struggle against it.

'Do you remember the statue we saw in the Achilleion Palace? Not the first one where Achilles was in all his glory, but the second one, where he was on the ground, trying to remove the arrow, knowing that he couldn't? Did you see his face, upturned to the sky, begging help from the gods because he knew that this was stronger than him and only divine intervention could save him from its power?'

'But he was fighting death,' Petra reminded him. 'Do I represent death?'

He smiled faintly and shook his head.

'No, but you represent the defeat of everything I believed was necessary to keep me strong. The armour that kept me at a cautious distance from other people, the watchfulness that never let me relax, so that I was always ahead of the game and all the other players. In your presence, all of that vanished. I implored the gods to return my strength so that I could be as safe against you as I was against everyone else, but they didn't listen—possibly because they knew I didn't really mean it.

'Your power over me came from something I'd never considered before. It wasn't sex, although there was that too. Lord, how I wanted to sleep with you, possess you! It drove me half demented, but I could cope with that. It was something else, much more alarming.'

'I know,' she said. 'I could make you laugh. I've always loved doing that, not because it gave me power but because I hoped it might make you happy.'

'It did, but it also alarmed me because it meant I was vulnerable to you as to nobody else in the world, man or woman. So I departed again. This time I went away for days, but then I began to worry that you might have returned to England, and I discovered I didn't want that after all. I was acting like a man with no sense, wanting this, wanting the opposite, not knowing what I wanted—like a man in love, in fact. So I called you.'

'I was with Nikator,' she remembered. 'He guessed it was you and warned me against you.'

'He was right.'

'I know he was. I never doubted that for a moment. Do you think I care what that silly infant thinks, as long as you come back to me?'

'When I saw you again I knew I couldn't have stayed away any longer,' he said, 'but I also knew I'd come back to danger. I was no longer master of myself, and that control—that mastery—has been the object of my life. I understood even then that I couldn't have both it and you, but it's not until now—'

It was only now that he'd brought himself to face the final

decision, and for a moment she still wasn't sure which way it would go. There was some terrifying secret that haunted him, and everything would depend on what happened in the next few minutes.

Suddenly she was afraid.

CHAPTER NINE

AT LAST he began to speak.

'It started in my childhood with my mother's fantasies about Achilles and his hidden vulnerability. I understood the point about keeping your secrets to yourself, but in those days it was only theory, little more than a game. I was young, I had more money than was good for me, I felt I could rule the world. I fancied myself strong and armoured, but in truth I was wide open to a shrewd manipulator.'

'Is that what *she* was?' Petra asked.

'Yes, although it wasn't so much her as the men behind her. Her name was Brigitta. She was a great-niece of Homer, not that I knew that until later. We met by chance—or so I thought—on a skiing holiday. In fact she was an excellent skier, but she concealed that, just kept falling over, so I began to teach her and somehow we fell over a lot together.

'Then we abandoned skiing and went away to be by ourselves. I was in heaven. I didn't know any girl could be so lovely, so sweet, so honest—'

He drew a ragged breath and dropped his head down onto his chest. He was shaking, and she wondered with dismay if this was only memory. After all these years, did some part of his love still survive to torment him?

She reached out to touch him but stopped at the last minute and let her hand fall away. He didn't seem to notice.

After a while he began to speak again.

'Of course I was deceiving myself. It had all been a clever trap. She was thrown into my path on purpose so that I could make a fool of myself over her. Even when I discovered who she was I didn't have the wit to see the plot. I believed her when she said she'd concealed her background because she was truly in love with me and didn't want me to be suspicious. Can you imagine anything so stupid?'

'It's not stupid,' Petra protested. 'If you really loved her, of course you wanted to think well of her. And you must have been so young—'

'Twenty-one, and I thought I knew it all,' he said bitterly.

'How old was she?'

'Nineteen. So young; how could I possibly suspect her? Even when I found out she was using a false name, that she'd engineered our meeting—even then I believed that she was basically innocent. I *had* to believe it. She was the most beautiful thing that had ever happened to me.'

She could have wept for the boy he'd been then. To cling to his trust in the face of the evidence suggested a naïvety that nobody meeting him now would ever believe.

'What happened?' she asked.

'We planned to marry. Everyone went wild—the two foes putting their enmity aside to join forces and present a united front to the world. My father advised me to delay; he was uneasy. I wouldn't listen. We came here to be alone together and spent the summer living in this house. I wouldn't have thought that anyone could be as happy as I was in those weeks.'

His mouth twisted in a wry smile.

'And I'd have been right not to believe it. It was all an illusion, created by my own cowardly refusal to face the fact that she was a spy. She didn't learn much, but enough for the Lukas family to pip us to the post on a lucrative contract. It was obvious that the information must have come from her, and that she'd listened in to a telephone conversation I'd had and managed to see some papers. She denied it at first, but there was simply no other way. I turned on her.'

'Well, naturally, if you felt betrayed—'

'No, it was worse than that. I was cruel, brutal. I said such things—she begged my forgiveness, said she'd started as a spy but regretted it in the end because she came to love me truly.'

'Did you believe her?' Petra asked.

'I didn't dare. I sneered at her. If she truly regretted what she'd donc, why hadn't she warned me? She said she tried to back out but Nikator threatened to tell me everything. But he promised to let her off if she did one last job, so that's what she did.'

'But Nikator must have been little more than an child in those days,' Petra protested.

'He was twenty. Old enough to be vicious.'

'But could he have organised it? Would he have known enough?'

'No. There was another man, a distant cousin called Cronos, who hadn't been in the firm more than a couple of years and was still trying to make his mark. Apparently he was a nasty piece of work, and he and Nikator hit it off well, right from the start. People who knew them said they moved in the same slime. Cronos set it up and used Nikator as front man.'

'Cronos set it up?' she echoed. 'Not Homer?'

'No, to do him justice, he's a fairly decent man, a lot better than many in this business. Thc story is that after the whole thing exploded Homer tore a strip off Cronos and told him to get out if he knew what was good for him. At any rate Cronos vanished.

'Obviously, I don't know the details of any family rows, but my impression is that Homer was shocked by Nikator's behaviour. Being ruthless in business is one thing, but you don't involve innocent young girls. But Nikator had come down hard on Brigitta when she tried to get free. He bullied her into "one last effort", and she thought if she did that it would be over.'

'No way,' Petra said at once. 'Once he had a blackmail hold over her he'd never have let it go.'

'That's what I think too. She was in his power; I should have seen that and helped her. Instead, I turned on her. You can't imagine how cruelly I treated her.'

But she could, Petra thought. Raised with suspicion as his constant companion, thinking he'd found the love and trust that could make his life beautiful, he'd been plunged back into despair and it had almost destroyed him. He'd lashed out with all the vigour of a young man, and in the process he'd hurt the one person he still loved.

'I said such things,' he whispered. 'I can't tell you the things I said, or what they did to her—'

'She'd deceived you.'

'She was a child.'

'So were you,' she said firmly. 'Whatever happened to her, *they* were responsible, the people who manipulated her. Not you.'

'But I should have saved her from them,' he said bleakly. 'And I didn't. We had a terrible scene. I stormed out of the house, saying I hated the sight of her and when I returned she'd vanished. She left me a letter in which she said that she loved me and begged my forgiveness, but there was nothing to tell me where she'd gone.'

Petra made no sound, but her clasp on him tightened.

'I couldn't—wouldn't believe it at first,' he went on in a voice that was low and hoarse. 'I went through the house calling her name. I was sure she had to be hiding somewhere, waiting for a sign from me. I cried out that we would find our way somehow, our love was worth fighting for.'

And after each call he'd stood and listened in the silence. Petra could see it as clearly as if she'd walked the house with that devastated young man. She heard him cry, *'Brigitta!'* again and again, waited while he realised that there would be no answering call, and felt her heart break with his as the truth was forced on him.

And she saw something else that he would never speak of—the moment when the boy collapsed in sobs of despair.

'What did you do after that?' she asked, stroking his hair.

'I believed I could find her and still make it right. I set detectives on her trail. They were the best, but even they couldn't find her. She'd covered her tracks too well. I tried the few who remained of her family in another country, but they weren't close and she hadn't been in touch with them. I tried Nikator. There was just a chance that he knew something, but I'm convinced he didn't. I scared him so badly that he'd have told me if he could.

'In the end I faced facts. A woman who could escape so completely must have been very, very determined to get well away from me. But I didn't stop. Months passed, but I told them to keep looking because I couldn't face the prospect of never seeing or talking to her again. I had to ask her forgiveness, do what I could to make it right.

'At last I got a message from a man who said he thought he might have found her, but it was hard to be sure because she couldn't talk and just sat staring into space all the time. I went to see her and found—' He shuddered.

Petra didn't make the mistake of speaking. She simply sat with him in her arms, praying that her love would reach him and make it possible for him to confront the monster.

'I found her in a shabby room in a back street, miles away,' he managed to say at last. 'The door was locked. The last time anyone had gone in there she'd been so frightened that she'd locked it after them. I kicked it open and went in.

'She was sitting up on a bed in the corner, clutching something in her arms as though she had to protect it. She screamed at the sight of me and backed away as though I was an enemy. Maybe that's how I looked to her then. Or maybe she just didn't know me.'

Another silence, in which she felt his fingers tighten on her arm, release her and tighten again.

'At last all the fight seemed to go out of her. She sagged against the wall and I managed to get close and look at what she was holding.'

His grip was agonisingly tight. Petra closed her eyes, guessing what the bundle had been, and praying to be wrong.

'It was a dead baby,' Lysandros said at last.

'Oh, no,' Petra whispered, dropping her head so that her lips lay against his hair.

'It was premature. She'd hidden her pregnancy and had no proper medical attention, so she gave birth alone. Then she just sat clutching the child and not letting anyone near her. She'd been like that for days, shivering, starving, weeping.

'I begged her to calm down, told her it was me, that I loved her, I'd never harm her, but she told me to go away because she had to feed the baby. By that time he must have been dead for days. He was cold in her arms.

'The people who owned the house were decent and kindly, but they couldn't cope. I had her moved to hospital, ordered the best attention for her, said I'd pay for everything—whatever money could buy, I'd give her.' He said the last words with bitter self-condemnation.

'I went to see her every day in the hospital, always thinking that the care she was receiving would soon take effect, she would become herself again, and we could talk. But it didn't happen. As she became physically stronger her mind seemed to retreat further into a place where I couldn't follow, and I understood that she wanted it that way. But still I waited, hoping she'd recover and we could find each other again.

'Then she had a heart attack, apparently an adverse reaction to a drug she'd been given, but the doctors told me that she wasn't fighting for life. Her will had gone, and it was only a matter of time. I sat beside her, holding her hand, praying for her to awaken. When she did I told her that I loved her and begged her forgiveness.'

'Did she forgive you?' Petra asked quietly.

'I don't know. She only said one thing. By that time she'd accepted that the child was dead and she begged me to make sure he was buried with her. I gave her my word and, when the time came, I kept it. She's buried with our baby in her arms.'

'She must have recognised you to ask such a thing,' Petra said.

'I've told myself that a thousand times, but the truth is that she might have said it to anyone she thought had the power to ensure that it happened. I've tried to believe that she forgave me, but why should I? What right do I have after what I did? I terrified her into running away and hiding from the world when she desperately needed help.

'What kind of life did she have? The doctors told me she was severely undernourished, which had damaged the child, hence the premature birth—and death—of my son.'

'You have no doubt that—?'

'That he was mine? None. She must have been about a month pregnant when we parted. They were very tactful. They offered me a test, to be sure, but I refused. Such a test implied a doubt that dishonoured her. She was carrying my son when I abandoned her.'

'But you didn't throw her out,' Petra protested.

'No, I wanted her to stay here until I could arrange our breakup to look civilised in the eyes of the world,' he said savagely. 'And then, fool that I was, I was surprised when I came back and found her gone. Of course she fled. She looked into the future I'd mapped out and shuddered. I didn't throw her out, but I drove her out with coldness and cruelty.

'If I'd known—everything would have been different, but I made her feel that she had no choice but to run away from me. So there was nobody to help her when she knew about her condition. She faced everything alone, and they both died.

'I was with her to the last. She died in my arms, while I prayed for a word or a look to suggest that she knew me. But there was nothing. She'd gone beyond my reach and all I could do was hold her while she slipped away, never knowing that I was begging her forgiveness. I destroyed her life, I destroyed her last moment, I destroyed our child—'

'But it wasn't—'

'It's my fault—don't you understand? *I killed them, both of them.* I killed them as surely as if I'd—'

'No,' she said fiercely. 'You mustn't be so hard on yourself.'

'But I must,' he said bleakly. 'If I'm not hard on myself, who will be? How many times since then have I gone to her tomb and stood there, watching and waiting for something that's never going to happen?'

'Where is her tomb?'

'Here, in the garden. I had the ground consecrated and got the priest to come and bury them both at the dead of night. Then I covered the place so that nobody can find it by accident.

'Then I had to decide what to do with myself. I looked at what this kind of life had made of me, and I hated it. I told my father I was finished with it all, and took the next plane out of Greece, trying to escape what I'd done, what I'd turned into.

'When you and I met, I'd been on the run for two years.' He gave a brief bark of laughter. 'On the run. Like a criminal. That's how I felt. I went to Monte Carlo, to New York, Los Angeles, London, Las Vegas—anywhere I could live what they call "the high life", which is another way of saying I indulged myself in every despicable way. I drank too much, gambled too much, slept around too much, all because I was trying to escape myself. But at the end, there was always a menacing figure waiting for me at the end of the road. And it was me.

'Then, one night in Las Vegas—well, you know the rest. You showed me to myself in a light I couldn't bear, and I returned to Greece the next day.'

'It wasn't just me,' Petra said. 'You were ready to see things differently or I couldn't have had any effect.'

'Maybe. I don't know.' He gave her a faint smile. 'Part of me prefers to give you the credit—my good angel, who stopped me going even further astray the first time and now—'

'Now?' she asked cautiously.

'I'm not blind, Petra. I know about myself. I'm not a man anyone in their right mind could want to meet. I scare people, and that's been fine up to now. It suited me. But you showed me the truth then, and somehow you've done it again. For years I've sheltered deep inside myself because that way I felt safer. I keep people at a distance because if you don't let yourself need anyone, nobody can hurt you.

'But I can't keep you at a distance because you've been in there—' he touched his heart '—for a long time. I've never told anyone else what I've told you tonight, and I never will. Now you know all my secrets and I'm glad of it, for a burden is gone from me.'

He rested his face against her and she dropped her head, while her tears fell on him.

They slept for a while and awoke in each others' arms, to

find daylight flooding into the room. Anxiously, Petra looked at his face but was reassured. He was smiling, relaxed.

'No regrets?' she asked softly.

He shook his head. 'None with you. Never. Come with me.'

They dressed and he took her hand, leading her downstairs and out of the house.

She'd briefly glimpsed the garden from an upstairs window and seen that it was mainly a wilderness. Everything was overgrown, and now she thought she knew why.

He led her to a distant place under the trees and removed some branches and leaves. Beneath them was a stone in which were carved a few simple words and dates. He had hidden Brigitta and her child away from the world, protecting them as best he could. Without asking, Petra knew that nobody else had ever seen this place.

'So many times I've stood here and begged her forgiveness,' he said. 'What should I tell her about you?'

Her grandfather had once told her that no true Greek was ever completely free of the past. Now Lysandros, this modern man, at home in the harsh world of multibillion dollar business, spoke like an ancient Greek who felt the River Styx swirl around his feet and, beyond it, Hades, the other world, where souls still suffered and communicated with the living.

Could it be true? Was Brigitta there now, gazing at him across the waters, drawing him back, crying that he was hers alone and they should be together for all eternity?

No! She wouldn't allow it.

'You don't have to tell her anything about me,' she said. 'She knows that I love you, just as she does. And, because of that love, she forgives you. Don't forget that where she is now, she understands everything she didn't understand before and she wants your suffering to end.'

It touched her heart to see the relief that came into his face, as though anything said by herself could be trusted, however strange or outrageous it might sound to anyone else.

They walked slowly back into the house and upstairs. Now he kissed her softly, almost tentatively, letting her know that this was different from any other time. They had crossed a boundary of love and trust, and the way ahead was changed for ever.

'Mine,' he whispered, 'all mine.'

'Yours as long as you want me,' she whispered back.

'That will be for ever.'

'And are you mine?' she asked.

'I think I've been yours since the first moment. In my heart I always knew. It just took this long to admit it.'

They lay down, holding each other, touching gently, eager to explore yet unwilling to hurry. Taking their time was a tribute that they owed to each other and they paid it in full. He sought the places where her bruises had been worst, laying his lips over them in care and comfort.

'I'm fine now,' she said. 'You've looked after me so well.'

'And I always will,' he vowed.

His fingers played in a leisurely way over her breasts, first one, then the other, almost as if he were discovering them for the first time, wondering at their beauty. At last he laid his face against them and she felt his tongue, softly caressing. Tremors went through her. New life invaded her body.

She began to run her own hands over him, exploring and teasing him, rejoicing at the suppressed groan that came from him.

'You do your magic,' he breathed. 'Where does it come from? Are you one of the sirens?'

'Do you want me to be?'

'Only for me. No other man must hear that siren-song. And I must hear it for ever.'

She turned, pressing him gently onto his back and lying across him so that her peaked nipples brushed him lightly.

'But they did hear it for ever,' she said, inviting him further into the fantasy. 'Those doomed sailors knew it would be the last sound they ever heard. Did they follow it willingly?'

This was the question he'd asked himself many times but always in solitude. Now, in her arms, he knew the answer.

'Willingly,' he agreed, 'because at the last nothing else mattered. Nothing else—ever—but to follow that song wherever it led.'

She smiled down at him. 'An adventurous man,' she mused. 'That's what I like. I'm going to take you to such places—where no one's ever been before—'

'Wherever it leads,' he murmured. 'As long as it leads us together.'

When he turned again to bring her beneath him she went gladly, opening for him in warmth and welcome, feeling herself become complete, and then complete again as they climaxed together.

'No,' she begged as it ended. 'Don't leave me.'

'I shall never leave you,' he said, changing her meaning. 'My body will never leave you and nor will my heart. I'm yours. Do you understand that? Yours for always.'

'My darling—'

'I wish I could find the words to tell you what it means to me to have found someone I need never doubt. It's more than happiness. It's like being set free.'

'Dearest, be careful,' she said worriedly. 'I'm human, not perfect.'

'Rubbish, you *are* perfect,' he said, laughing.

'I'll never knowingly betray you, but I might make some silly human mistake. Please, please don't think me better than I am, in case you end up thinking me worse than I am.'

'It wouldn't be possible to think you better than you are,' he said. 'You are perfect. You are honest and true, and divinely inspired to be the one person on earth who can keep me safe and happy.'

There was no middle way with this man, she realised. It was all or nothing, with no reservations. The heartfelt simplicity with which he placed himself and his fate in her hands made her want to weep. And silently she prayed that he might never be disappointed in her, for she knew it would destroy him.

CHAPTER TEN

LYSANDROS awoke in the darkness to find Petra watching him.

'What is it?' he asked. 'Something on your mind? Tell me.' When she still hesitated he sat up and slipped an arm around her. 'Tell me,' he repeated. 'You've always wanted me to talk, but how often do you confide in me?'

When she didn't answer he said, 'It has to work each way, you know. If you don't honour me with your confidence, what am I to think?'

'All right, I will,' she said slowly.

'But it's hard, isn't it?'

'Yes, because I've never really explained it before. There was nobody to explain to. You asked me if I was yours. In fact I'm yours more than you know.'

He thought for a moment. 'You mean something special by that, don't you?'

'Yes. There are things I couldn't tell you because they might have been a burden on you.'

'You? A burden? That isn't possible.'

'If you knew how much I depend on you, you might find it a weight.'

'Now you're humouring me. Isn't it me clinging to you because I find in you what I can find in nobody else?'

'I hope you do, but it's mutual and I couldn't admit that before. But, since we've found each other, maybe I can.'

He touched her chin, turning it gently towards him so that he could regard her intently. Now she had all his attention. Something in her voice told him this was vital.

'You're the first person I've ever really mattered to,' she said simply.

'Your mother—'

'Estelle's a darling but I've never figured high on her list of priorities. She'd have loved a pet cat just as much. She's always been dashing off here and there, leaving me with other people, and I didn't mind because the other people were my grandparents and I loved them. But that was pure luck. If we hadn't been lucky enough to have found them, I sometimes wonder what she'd have done.

'My grandparents loved me, but each came first with the other. That's as it should be, but when she died I knew he wouldn't be long following.'

'There must have been men who wanted you,' he observed.

'Well, they wanted something. Maybe it was me, maybe it was what I brought with me—money, a glamorous background. It left me rather cynical, and I kind of hoisted the cynicism into place as a defence, rather like Achilles kept his shield at the ready.'

He nodded. 'And when you do that, there are always some people who only see the shield.'

'Yes, you know about that, don't you?' She gave a wry smile. 'We're not so different, you and I. Your defence is glaring at people, mine is laughter and pretending never to mind about anything.'

'I had begun to understand that,' he said. 'But I didn't really see behind it until now. Your shield is more skilful than mine.'

'Nobody sees behind it unless I show them. But I can show you because of what you give me.'

'I need you more than any man has ever needed a woman since the dawn of time,' he said slowly.

'You need me as nobody else ever has or ever will, and that's the greatest gift in the world. Nobody has ever given it to me before, and I don't want it from anyone else. You've made me complete. I was afraid I'd go through life without ever having that feeling.'

He laid his forehead against her.

'And I was afraid you'd find me too demanding,' he said.

'You could never be demanding enough,' she assured him. 'The more you demand, the more you fulfil me. You've given me life, as though my real self had only just been born. I don't think you really understand that yet, but you will, my love. It will take time.'

'And we have all the time in the world,' he said, taking her into his arms.

Now their lovemaking was different, infused with the knowledge of each other's heart that they had just discovered. To Petra it was more like a wedding night than the real one she'd known years ago.

At some time in the dawn he murmured, 'There's a story of how, after Achilles' death, he was honoured as a great lord among the other dead souls. But he longed only to be alive and said he would rather return to live on earth as a servant than stay among the dead as a lord. I never understood that story until now.'

'You mean,' she mused, 'that if I were to treat you like a servant, that would be fine as long as you were with me?'

He considered. 'Can I think about that some more?'

He felt her shaking against him and joined in her laughter. She watched him with delight and saw an answering delight in his eyes. He touched her face and spoke softly.

'Love me,' he said in a voice that almost pleaded. 'Love me.'

She knew a surge of joy and reached out to caress him, draw him back into her arms and show him that he belonged there. They made love slowly, yet with a subtle intensity that said more than a million words.

It was much later that it occurred to her that he'd said not, *Make love to me*, but 'Love me.' And only when it was too late did she understand the distinction.

Next day he swept her out into the car and drove down to the shore.

'But not the same as last time,' he said. 'This is a fishing village—at least it was when this island still had a thriving fishing industry. Now they cater for tourists who are interested in fishing. It's time you met my friends.'

His friends turned out to be a family of one-time fishermen, who greeted Lysandros like a long-lost brother and drew Petra into the warmth.

There seemed to be dozens of them. She lost track of the husbands, wives, sons, daughters, cousins, nieces and nephews. She only knew that they all smiled and treated Lysandros as one of the family.

'My mother brought me here for a holiday when I was a kid,' he explained. 'I ran off to go exploring, got lost and the family rescued me. We've been the best of friends ever since.'

She guessed that they'd been well rewarded. The fishing boat on which they now ran tourist expeditions was top of the range. But it was hard to be cynical about these people and when Kyros, the patriarch, said that the nicest thing about Lysandros was not his generosity but the days when he could find time to visit she felt inclined to believe it.

He seemed to size her up, finally deciding that he could trust her with further confidences.

'One day, years ago,' he told her, 'we found him wandering alone on the beach. We hadn't known that he was coming here. He hadn't let us know, or come to the house. Later he said he'd meant to visit us but he arrived in the early morning when the beach was deserted and he thought he'd take a walk. He walked there for hours. A friend saw him and told us. I went down there and walked with him for a while, but he wouldn't come home with me.

'Then my sons took over and they walked with him all night, up and down, up and down, the length of the beach. He was like a machine, talking only in grunts. At last he began to slow down and we managed to persuade him to come with us. We put him to bed and he slept for two days.'

'Did he ever tell you what made him like that?' Petra asked.

'I don't think he knew a lot about it. He just seemed to have been lost in another world, one he couldn't remember or didn't want to remember. We didn't press him. He was our friend, in trouble, and that's all we needed to know. We did suggest that he should see a doctor, but he said we had been his doctors and he wanted no other. I've never seen him like that again so perhaps we were able to make him a little better. I hope so, anyway. He's such a nice guy.'

It was obvious that he knew nothing of the reality of Lysandros's life. The well-known name Demetriou told him that this was a businessman, rich enough to buy them the boat, but they had no conception of the full extent of his fortune and power.

And that was why they mattered to him so much, Petra realised. They were the close-knit, loving, knockabout family he'd never had and would have loved to have. To them he was 'a nice guy', a little removed by his money, but not enough to stop him being one of them.

Unlike virtually everyone else, they neither feared him nor

showed exaggerated respect, which was a relief to him. Instead, they ribbed him mercilessly, yelled cheerful insults, challenged him to races along the sand and rioted when they beat him.

The girls cast soulful eyes at his handsome face and powerful, elegant movements, but their husbands and boyfriends pulled them firmly aside, glaring possessively, daring Lysandros to try to take advantage, forgiving when he didn't.

How different from the Athens husbands who would pimp their wives into his bed in exchange for a contract. No wonder Lysandros loved coming here. It was his only contact with normal life, and the sight of him relishing it was as much a revelation as anything she'd learned in the last few days. He even helped Kyros's wife, Eudora, with the cooking.

Later Eudora whispered in her ear, 'You're the only woman he's ever brought here. That's why everyone's looking at you. Don't tell him I told you.'

She gave a satisfied nod, as though she personally had brought about the miracle, and scurried away.

Afterwards they went out in the boat. Dressed in a swimsuit, Petra sat in the prow, wondering if life could get any better than this.

She drew a deep contented breath, looking up at the sky, then around her at the sea and the horizon. There, a little distance away in the boat, were Lysandros and Kyros chatting casually, laughing in the easy way of friends.

Then she blinked, uncertain whether she'd seen what she thought she'd seen.

Was she going mad, or had Kyros cocked his head significantly in her direction, mouthing the words, 'Is she—the one?'

And had Lysandros nodded?

I'm fantasising, she told herself hastily. *I can't have read Kyros's lips at this distance. Can I?*

But when she looked again they were both regarding her

with interest. To save her blushes she dived overboard and Lysandros joined her.

'Careful, it's deep out here,' he said, holding out his hands to steady her.

She took them and he trod water, drawing her closer, closer against his bare chest, until he could slip his arms right around her, kissing her while treading water madly. Behind them they could hear cheers and yells from the boat.

When they climbed back on board Kyros hinted slyly that there was a cabin below if they wished. More cheers and yells while his wife told him to behave himself and he silenced her with a kiss. It was that sort of day.

Returning home, they ate their fill before going out into the village square where there was dancing. Lysandros could dance as well as any of them. The girls knew it and queued up for their turn. Petra was untroubled. She had all the male attention she could possibly want, and she was enjoying the sight of him unselfconscious and actually seeming happy.

He saw her watching him and waved before being drawn back into the dance by three young females at once, while their menfolk looked on wryly. At the end he blew each of them a kiss before holding out his hands to Petra and drawing her onto the floor.

'Dance with me,' he murmured. 'And save me from getting my throat cut.'

He was showing her off in public, but why? To make a point to the others, or simply because he was more than a little tipsy? Joyfully she decided that she didn't care. This was the man nature had meant him to be before the demons got their destructive hands on him, and if it was the last thing she did she would open the door that led back to that world and lead him through it.

'We ought to be going,' he gasped at last. 'The trouble is, that wine Kyros serves is…well…' He sat down suddenly.

'And everyone else is as woozy as you,' she said. 'Even me.'

'I'm not.' The young man who spoke was the eldest son of the house, wore a priest's garb and was stone cold sober. 'I'll drive you home.'

'And I'll pay for your taxi back,' Lysandros said sleepily. 'Done.'

On the way home they sat in the back, with his head on her shoulder, his eyes closed. As the car came to a halt the priest looked back and grinned.

'I've never seen him let go like that before,' he said. 'I congratulate you.'

She didn't ask what he meant. She didn't need to. Her spirits were soaring.

Lysandros awoke long enough to hand over a bundle of notes. 'That'll pay for the taxi. Anything over, put it in the collection box.'

The priest's eyes popped as he saw the amount.

'But do you know how much you've given—?'

'Goodnight!' Lysandros was halfway up the path.

She undressed him while he lay back and let her do all the work.

'You think you're a sultan being attended by the harem,' she observed as she finished.

He opened one eye. 'It seemed only fair to show you that I can behave as badly as any other man who dances with a dozen women, gets smashed out of his mind and lets his wife wait on him. Goodnight.'

He rolled over and went to sleep on his front, leaving her with the view of the most perfectly shaped male behind she'd ever seen, and wondering if he knew he'd called her his wife.

He slept late next morning, unusual for him. She rose and

made coffee, returning to find him leaning back against the pillow, one arm behind his head and a wicked look in his eyes. Nor was the wickedness confined to his eyes. A glance at the rest of him told her that he was ready to make up for the deficiencies of the night before.

But she decided not to indulge him at once. They drank coffee sedately, although the look in his eyes was far from sedate. She showed no sign of noticing this, but after a while she slipped off her flimsy silk nightdress and began to find small jobs to do about the room, knowing that they gave him a perfect view of her from various angles.

'Do you have to do that?' he asked in a strained voice.

'Well, I thought one of us should do some tidying up,' she said innocently.

'Come here!'

Wasting no further time, she raced to the bed and took him in her arms.

'Just let me love you,' she said.

'As long as you do love me,' he said heavily.

'I do. I always will.'

He would have spoken again but she silenced him by laying her mouth against his, taking his attention so that at first he didn't notice her softly wandering hands until the excitement building with her caresses overtook him totally and he drew a long shuddering breath.

'I have ruthless ways of making my wishes known,' she whispered against his mouth.

'I believe you,' he groaned.

'You think you know me, but you haven't begun to discover what I'm capable of.'

'Why don't you—show me?'

She let her fingers explore a little further, reaching the

place between his legs where his response was rapidly growing out of control. 'Like that?'

'Just like that.'

Now her fingers were enclosing their object, revelling in its size and the thought of having it inside her. Then she moved over him so that she could fit her legs astride him and make him hers in her own way.

She had the glorious sense of being able to do anything she wanted. Everything was right because they were together and did everything together. It was right to celebrate their hearts but also right to celebrate their bodies as they were doing now. So she did as she pleased, confident of pleasing him at the same time, and knew by his expression that she'd outdone herself.

'That was very nice,' she said, luxuriating in his arms afterwards.

'Very nice?' he growled. 'Is that the best you can say?'

'Do you have anything else to suggest?'

'Oh, yes,' he said. 'I have plenty more to suggest. Come here—'

'Suppose I don't want to?'

'You've left it much too late to say that. *Now, come here.*'

Carolling with laughter, she raised her arms over her head and cried, 'Shan't!'

'Oh, yes, you will.'

So she did.

When Lysandros's cellphone began to ring he regarded it for a long time before saying reluctantly, 'I suppose I ought to answer that.'

'I'm amazed you haven't been on the phone more often,' she said. 'In fact I'm amazed it hasn't rung more often.'

'I gave strict instructions to my staff not to disturb me unless it was vital. Linos, my assistant, is pretty good that way.

He's called a couple of times, I've given him instructions for managing without me and so far he's not done too badly. But I suppose—' He sighed.

'We have to get back to the real world.'

He kissed her. 'After this, the real world will be different.' He answered the phone. 'Yes, Linos? Oh, no, what's happened? All right, all right, one thing at a time.'

Sad but resigned, Petra made her way upstairs to start packing. The dream life couldn't last for ever, and now was the time to see if it could be carried into reality. The omens were good.

'I've called the airport,' she said when Lysandros appeared. 'There's a flight to Athens in a couple of hours.'

He sighed and put his arms around her. 'I wish you'd said a couple of years, but I suppose we have to take it. There's a big meeting coming up that Linos says he can't manage without me.'

'It had to happen some time,' she said. 'The sound of battle, summoning you to the fray.'

'It's funny how that doesn't sound so good any more. But you'll be with me, and we can start making plans.'

Her lips twitched. 'Plans for what?'

He rested his forehead against hers. 'Plans for the future, and if I have to explain that to you, then I've been wasting my time recently. Unfortunately, this isn't the moment to make the point. But I think you know what I'm talking about.'

Marriage. He hadn't posed a formal question but he acted as though matters were already settled between them, and she knew it was a sign of their closeness that he felt free to do so.

She went with him upstairs to take a last look at the smashed room he'd shared with Brigitta, but she refused to go with him to the grave.

'You need to say goodbye to her alone,' she said gently. 'If I'm there it will spoil it for her.'

'How can you speak so?' he asked in wonder. 'As though she was real to you, as if you'd met her and talked to her.'

'They say that nobody ever comes back across the River Styx,' she mused, speaking of the river that ran between earth and Hades, as the underworld was often known. 'But I wonder. If someone has something important enough, a message that they simply must deliver—well, let's just say that I think some part of her might still be there. But she wants you to talk to her alone. I don't really belong here.'

He frowned. 'Do you mean not to come back to this house with me?'

'I don't think she wants me to. This is her place. You and I can have somewhere else. Keep this for her, to honour her.'

Her words fell like blessed balm on his soul. He'd been wondering how to solve this conundrum, fearing that the part of his heart that remained loyal to the past might offend her. But she'd understood, as she understood everything about him. He kissed her and walked out into the grounds, offering thanks as he went.

Petra watched him until he disappeared.

The grave lay quiet in the afternoon sun, with only the faintest breeze disturbing the branches of the trees overhead. Lysandros stood there for a long time, listening, but there was only silence.

'Perhaps she imagined it,' he whispered at last, 'or perhaps you really can talk to her and not to me. We never could open our hearts to each other, could we?'

Overhead, the leaves rustled.

'I tried my best. Do you remember how desperately I talked to you as you prepared to cross the eternal river with our child in your arms? But you never looked back, and I knew I'd failed you yet again. That failure will be with me always.

'Petra was right to say that I honour you still, and that will last for ever. This place will always be yours and no other woman's. Nothing can change that.

'But there has been a change in me—can you forgive that, if nothing else? It seems almost wrong to find happiness with her after so much that we could have had, and lost, but I can't help myself. She is everything to me, yet I still—*honour* you.'

He couldn't have said what he was hoping for, but nothing came—no sign, no message, no absolution. Only the wind became stronger until it was gusting fiercely in the trees, shaking the branches. Autumn was still some way off, yet the leaves were falling, seeming to bring the darkness closer.

Suddenly he couldn't bear to stay here. Turning, he hurried back to the light.

At the Villa Lukas the air was buzzing with the news that the bride and groom would soon be home from their honeymoon.

'Such a party there's going to be!' Aminta carolled. '*Everyone* is coming—the press, the television cameras—'

'Any guests?' teased Petra.

'All the most important people,' Aminta said blissfully.

'No, I mean real guests—friends, people the host would want anyway, even if the press have never heard of them.'

Aminta stared at her, baffled. It was clear that after years of working for a billionaire shipping magnate she barely understood the concept of friendship for its own sake, so Petra laughed and went on her way. After all this time as part of a film star's retinue, why was she surprised? Perhaps because her time alone with Lysandros had caused a seismic shift in her perceptions.

As soon as she reached her bedroom there was a call from Estelle, full of excitement at the rumours.

'You and Lysandros were seen together on Corfu, going out in a boat and driving through the streets. Come on, tell!'

'There's nothing to tell,' Petra said primly.

'Hmm! As good as that, eh? We'll invite him to our party and take a good look at you two together.'

'I shall warn him not to come.'

'You won't, you know.' Chuckling, she hung up.

The next call was from Lysandros to say he had to return to Piraeus. 'So it'll be several days before we see each other,' he said with a sigh.

'Just be back for the big party next week. Then it's all going to descend on us.'

He laughed. 'I promise to be there. I don't know how I'm going to manage being away from you.'

'Just come back to me,' she said tenderly.

When the call was over she sat smiling. Looking up, she caught a glimpse of herself in the mirror and laughed.

'I look like an idiot. I feel like an idiot. So I guess that makes me an idiot. I don't care. I didn't know there was this much happiness on earth.'

From the corridor outside came the sound of footsteps. Then the door was flung open and Nikator stood on the threshold. His eyes were bright, his face flushed, his chest heaving, and Petra knew there was going to be trouble.

'Hello, brother, dear,' she said brightly, slightly emphasising 'brother'. But it was useless and she knew it.

'Don't say that,' Nikator hurled at her. 'Oh, Petra, don't say that!'

He dropped to his knees beside her, reaching out to clasp her around the waist, and she had to fight not to recoil. Their last meeting had been two weeks ago, just before she'd gone to Corfu. Nikator had implored her to stay, upset when she refused, desperate when she wouldn't tell him where she was going.

The same exaggerated look was on his face now, making her say soothingly, 'You don't want me to call you "dear"?

All right, I won't, especially as I'm angry with you. How dare you let Lysandros think we'd gone to England together?'

He reached up to seize her in a fumbling grip. She tried to free herself but found there was unexpected steel behind the childish movements.

'I couldn't help it. I love you so much I'm not responsible for my actions. I wanted to save you from Demetriou—'

'But I didn't want to be saved,' she said, trying to introduce a note of common sense. 'I love him. Try to understand that. I love *him*, not you.'

'That's because you don't know what he's like. You think you do. You believe what he told you about Brigitta, but there was no need for her to die. If he hadn't bullied her mercilessly she wouldn't have been alone when—'

He pulled himself up far enough to sit on the bed beside her, his hands gripping her shoulders.

'He's fooled you,' he gasped. 'He only wants you because you're mine. He has to take everything that's mine. It's been that way all my life.'

'Nikki—'

'You don't know what it's been like, always being told that the Demetriou family were lucky because they had a worthy son to take over, but my father only had me. Everyone admires him because he brutalises people into submission. But not me. I can't be brutal.'

'But you can be sneaky, can't you? Grow up, little boy!'

'Don't call me that,' he screamed. 'I'm not a child; I'll show you.'

She tried to push him off but his grip tightened. He rose to his feet, thrusting her back against the bed and hurling himself on top of her. Next thing, his mouth was over hers and he was trying to thrust his tongue between her lips.

Frantically she twisted her head away, trying to put up a hand to protect her mouth and writhing this way and that to avoid him.

'Get off me,' she gasped. 'Nikki, do you hear? *Get off me!*'

'Don't fight me. Let me love you—let me save you—'

With a last heave she managed to get out from under him, shoving him so hard that he fell to the floor. In a flash she was on her feet, dashing to the door, yanking it open.

'Clear out and don't come back!' she snapped.

But he made another lunge, forcing her to take drastic action with her knee. A yowl broke from him and he clutched himself between the legs, stumbling out into the corridor under the interested eyes of several maids.

He got to his feet, his eyes burning.

'You'll regret that,' he said softly.

'Not half as much as you'll regret it if you bother me again,' she snapped.

He threw a look of pure hatred at the servants and hurried away.

'Thanks, miss,' one of the maids said.

From which Petra deduced that several of them had been longing to do the very same thing.

Returning to her room, she tried to calm down. She'd known Nikator could be unpleasant but he was worse than she'd imagined.

In her agitation she forgot to wonder how he knew that Lysandros had told her about Brigitta.

CHAPTER ELEVEN

Two days later Homer and Estelle made a grand and glorious return, under the gaze of carefully arranged cameras. Plans for the party started at once, although first Aminta had a servant problem to deal with. Nikator had made certain accusations against the maids, who pleaded with Petra for help, which she gave.

'I'm sorry, Homer, I don't want to quarrel with you or your son,' she said, 'but Nikator was limping when he left and I'm afraid the maids saw. So now he has a grudge against them.'

Homer was a wise man and he knew his son's bad side. He believed her, thanked her, told Nikator to stop talking nonsense and made him apologise to Petra. Instead of the explosion of temper she'd feared, Nikator seemed to be in a chastened mood.

'Which means he's more dangerous than ever,' Lysandros said as they dined together. 'The sooner you're out of there the better. In the meantime I'll have a quiet word with him.'

'No, don't,' she begged. 'I'm quite capable of having my own quiet word, as he's already discovered. I'm only afraid he'll spin you some silly story about him and me—'

'Which you think I'll be stupid enough to believe?' Lysandros queried wryly. 'Credit me with more intelligence than that.'

Nikator seemed to be making an effort. She went downstairs once to find him with a large painting that he'd bought as a gift for his father. It depicted the Furies, terrifying creatures with snakes for hair and blood dripping from their eyes. Petra studied the picture with interest. She'd been conscious of the Furies recently, but now she felt free from them.

'The point was, they never let up,' Nikator said. 'Once they started on you, they'd hound you for ever.'

She wondered if he was sending a message that he would never forgive her for offending him. He would harm her or Lysandros if he could, she was sure of it. But they were both on the watch for him, and surely there was nothing in his power.

The party was going to be the society event of the season. Fellow film stars from Hollywood were flying in to dance, sing and raise their glasses in the fake Parthenon. Every businessman in Athens would be there, hoping to meet a film star, plus some film makers hoping to secure backing from rich men.

When the night came there was no sign of Nikator. Homer grumbled about the disrespect to his bride, but Petra also thought she detected a note of relief.

'Maybe when you and Lysandros are formally engaged it might be easier,' her mother said quietly. 'He'll have to accept it then. Just don't take too long about it. It might be the best thing for everyone.'

'But surely Lysandros is the foe?'

'A rival, not a foe. If the two families could come together Homer thinks it might be wonderful.'

'What about Nikator? Surely Homer wouldn't cut his son out?'

'Not out of his life or his heart, but out of the shipping business, yes. He could buy him a gaming house, or something else that would give him a good life without threatening people's jobs in the shipyard.'

It seemed the perfect solution, but Petra wondered if it would offend Nikator's pride and increase his hatred of Lysandros. Mentally she put it aside to be worried about later. For now all she cared about was the coming evening, when she would see her lover again and dance in his arms.

She'd chosen a dress of blue satin, so dark that it was almost black. It was a tight fit, emphasising her perfect shape, but with a modest neckline, to please Lysandros.

How handsome he was, she thought, watching him approach. Homer greeted him enthusiastically; he replied with smiles and expressions of civility. Petra remembered how Lysandros had cleared Homer of any involvement in Brigitta's tragedy, saying, 'To do him justice, he's a fairly decent man, a lot better than many in this business.'

So it was true what Estelle had suggested. Her marriage to Lysandros might signal a new dawn in the Greek shipping business, and everyone knew it. Including Nikator.

Lysandros did the usual networking with Petra on his arm, and everyone had the chance to study them as a couple.

'Has anyone told you what they're all thinking?' he murmured as they danced.

'They were lining up to tell me,' she said with a laugh. 'We were watched in Corfu. Estelle says we were seen together, driving through the streets and on the boat.'

He shrugged. 'They're public places. People were bound to see us. When we marry, I suppose that will be in public as well—' He smiled and added softly, 'At least, the first part of it will.'

'Oh, really?' she murmured. 'I don't remember getting a proposal.'

'You've had a proposal every minute of the last few days and you know it,' he said firmly. He rather spoilt the autocratic sound of this by murmuring, 'Siren,' so softly that his breath on her cheek was almost all she knew.

'Don't I get an answer?' he asked.

'You had your answer the first time we made love,' she said. 'And you hadn't even asked me.'

'But now I've asked and you've answered, we might tell them,' he suggested.

'Tell this crowd? I thought you'd hate to be stared at.'

'As long as they see what I want them to see, that's all right. If they watch me walking off with the most beautiful woman in the room, I can live with that.'

He tightened his arm around her waist, swirling her around and around while everyone laughed and applauded. Petra remembered that later because it was almost her last moment of unclouded joy.

As they came out of the swirl and her head began to clear she saw something that made her sigh. Even so, she didn't realise that disaster had walked in. Disaster was called Nikator, and he had a smile on his face. It was a cold, tense smile, but even so it gave no sign of what was about to crash down on her.

'What's he up to?' she asked as he embraced Homer and Estelle.

'Trying to win forgiveness for turning up late,' Lysandros remarked. 'Pretend he doesn't exist, as I'm doing.'

His words reminded her of how hard it must be for him to appear at ease in Nikator's presence, and she smiled at him in reassurance.

'Better still,' Lysandros said, 'let's show him exactly where he stands.'

Before she knew what he meant to do, he'd pulled her closer and laid his mouth on hers in a long kiss, whose meaning left nothing to the imagination.

Now he'd made his declaration to the world. This man, who'd spent so long hiding his true self behind protective bolts and bars, had finally managed to throw them aside and break out to freedom because the one special woman had given him the key. He no longer cared who could look into his soul because her love had made him invincible.

As the kiss ended and he raised his head, his manner was that of a victor. A hero, driving his chariot across the battlefield where his enemies lay defeated, might have worn that air of triumph.

'Let him do what he likes,' he murmured to her. 'Nothing can touch us now.'

She was to remember those words long after.

'Ah!' cried Nikator. 'Isn't love charming?'

His caustic voice shattered her dream and made her shudder. Nikator had marched across the floor and stood regarding them sardonically, while Homer hurried behind and laid an urgent hand on his son's arm. Nikator threw it off.

'Leave me, Father; there are things that have to be said and I'm going to enjoy saying them.' He grinned straight at Lysandros. 'I never thought the day would come when I'd have a good laugh at you. You, of all men, to be taken in by a designing woman!'

'Give up,' Lysandros advised him gently. 'It's no use, Nikator.'

'But that's what's so funny,' Nikator yelped. 'How easily you were fooled when you fancied yourself so armoured. *But the armour doesn't cover the heel, does it?*'

Even this jibe didn't seem to affect Lysandros, who continued to regard Nikator with pity and contempt.

'And your "heel" was that you believed in her,' Nikator said, jabbing a finger at Petra. 'You're too stupid to realise that she's been playing you for a sucker because there's something she wanted.'

'Hey, you!' Estelle thumped him hard on the shoulder. 'If you're suggesting my daughter has to marry for money, let me tell you—'

'Not money!' Nikator spat. 'Glory. Anything for a good story, eh?'

'What the hell are you talking about?' Lysandros demanded. 'There's no story.'

'Of course there is. It's what she lives by, her reputation, getting a new angle on things that nobody else can get. And, oh, boy, did she get it this time!'

Even then they didn't see the danger. Lysandros sighed, shaking his head as if being patient with a tiresome infant.

'You won't laugh when you know what she's been doing,' Nikator jeered. 'Getting onto the press, telling them your secrets, repeating what you said to her—'

'That's a lie!' Petra cried.

'Of course it's a lie,' Lysandros said.

The smiling confidence had vanished from his face and his voice had the deadly quiet of a man who was fighting shock, but he was still uttering the right words.

'Be careful what you say,' he told Nikator coldly. 'I won't have her slandered.'

'Oh, you think it's a slander, do you? Then how does the press know what you said to her at the Achilleion? How do they know you showed her Brigitta's grave and told her how often you'd stood there and begged Brigitta's forgiveness? Have you ever repeated that? No, I thought not. But someone has.'

'Not me,' Petra said, aghast. 'I would never—you can't believe that!'

She flung the last words at Lysandros, who turned and said quickly, 'Of course not.'

But his manner was strained. Gone was the relaxed joy of only a few minutes ago. Only two of them knew what he had said to her at that grave.

'It's about time you saw this,' Nikator said.

Nobody had noticed the bag he'd brought with him and dropped at his feet. Now he leaned down and began to pull out the contents, distributing them to the fascinated crowd.

They were newspapers, carrying the banner headline, *The Truth About Achilles: How She Made Him Talk*, and telling the story of the well-known historian Petra Radnor, who'd first come to prominence when, little more than a girl, she'd published *Greek Heroes of the Past*.

The book had been such a success that it had been revised for a school edition and was now being considered for a further revision. This time the angle would be more glamorous and romantic, as Ms Radnor considered Greek men today and whether they really lived up to their classical reputation. For the moment she was working on Achilles.

There followed a detailed description of the last few weeks—their first meeting at the wedding, at which *Ms Radnor exerted all her charms to entice her prey*, the evening they had spent together dancing in the streets, and finally their time on Corfu in the villa where 'Achilles' had once lived with his other lover, who was buried there.

> *Together they visited the Archilleion, where they stood before the great picture of the first Achilles dragging the lifeless body of his enemy behind his chariot, and the modern Achilles explained that he was raised to do it to them before they did it to him.*

Which was exactly what he'd said, Petra thought in numb horror.

It went on and on. Somehow the people behind this had learned every private detail of their time together at the villa, and were parading it for amusement. 'Achilles' had been trapped, deluded, made a fool of by a woman who was always one step ahead of him. That was the message, and those who secretly feared and hated him would love every moment of it.

All around she could see people trying to smother their amusement. Homer was scowling and the older guests feared him too much to laugh aloud, but they were covering their mouths, turning their heads away. The younger ones were less cautious.

'Even you,' Nikator jeered at Lysandros. 'Even you weren't as clever as you reckoned. You thought you had it all sussed, didn't you? But she saw through you, and oh, what a story she's going to get out of it, *Achilles!*'

Lysandros didn't move. He seemed to have been turned to stone.

Nikator swung his attention around to Petra.

'Not that you've been so clever yourself, *my dear deluded sister.*'

Estelle gave a little shriek and Homer grabbed his son.

'That's enough,' he snapped. 'Leave here at once.'

But Nikator threw him off again. Possessed by bitter fury, he could defy even his father. He went closer to Petra, almost hissing in her face.

'He's a fool if he believed you, but you're a fool if you believed him. There are a hundred women in this room right now who trusted him and discovered their mistake too late. You're just another.'

Somehow she forced herself to speak.

'No, Nikator, that's not true. I know you want to believe it, but it's not true.'

'You're deluded,' he said contemptuously.

'No, it's you who are deluded,' she retorted at once.

'Have you no eyes?'

'Yes, I have eyes, but eyes can deceive you. What matters

isn't what your eyes tell you, but what your heart tells you. And my heart says that this is the man I trust with all of me.' She lifted her head and spoke loudly. 'Whatever Lysandros tells me, that is the truth.'

She stepped close to him and took his hand. It was cold as ice.

'Let's go, my dearest,' she said. 'We don't belong here.'

The crowd parted for them as they walked away together into the starry night. Now the onlookers were almost silent, but it was a terrible silence, full of horror and derision.

On and on they walked, into the dark part of the grounds. Here there were only a few stragglers and they fell away when they saw them coming, awed, or perhaps made fearful, by the sight of two faces that seemed to be looking into a different world.

At last they came to a small wooden bridge over a river and went to stand in the centre, gazing out over the water. Still he didn't look at her, but at last he spoke in a low, almost despairing voice.

'Thank you for what you said about always believing me.'

'It was only what you said to me first,' she said fervently. 'I was glad to return it. I meant it every bit as much as you did. Nikator is lying. Yes, there was a book, years ago, but I told you about that myself, and about the reissue.'

'And the new version?'

'I knew they were thinking of bringing it out again, but not in detail. And it certainly isn't going to be anything like Nikator said. Lysandros, you can't believe all that stuff about my "working on Achilles" and pursuing you to make use of you. It isn't true. I swear it isn't.'

'Of course it isn't,' he said quietly. 'But—'

The silence was almost tangible, full of jagged pain.

'But what?' she asked, not daring to believe the suspicions rioting in her brain.

'How did they discover what we said?' he asked in a rasping, tortured voice. 'That's all I want to know.'

'And I can't tell you because I don't know. It wasn't me. Maybe someone was standing behind us at the Achilleion—'

'Someone who knew who we were? And the grave? How do they know about that?'

'I don't know,' she whispered. 'I don't know. I never repeated anything to anybody. *Lysandros, you have got to believe me.*'

She looked up into his face and spoke with all the passion at her command.

'Can't you see that we've come to the crossroads? This is it. This is where we find out if it all meant anything. I am telling you the truth. Nobody in the world matters more to me than you, and I would never, ever lie to you. For pity's sake, say that you believe me, *please*.'

The terrible silence was a thousand fathoms deep. Then he stammered, 'Of course…I do believe you…' But there was agony in his voice and she could hear the effort he put into forcing himself.

'You don't,' she said explosively as the shattering truth hit her. 'All that about trusting me—it was just words.'

'No, I—*no!*'

'Yes!'

'I tried to mean them, I wanted to, but—'

Her heart almost failed her, for there on his face was the look she'd seen before, on the statue at the Achilleion, when Achilles tried to draw the arrow from his foot, his expression full of despair as he realised there was no way to escape his fate.

'Yes—*but*,' she said bitterly. 'I should have known there'd be a "but".'

'Nobody else knows about that grave,' he said hoarsely. 'I can't get past that.'

'Perhaps Nikator does know. Perhaps he had someone following us—'

'That wouldn't help them find the grave. It's deep in the grounds; you can't see it from outside. I've never told anyone else. You're the one person I've ever trusted enough to…to…'

As the words died he groaned and reached for her. It would have been simple to go into his arms and try to rediscover each other that way, but a spurt of anger made her step back, staring at him with hard eyes.

'And that's the worst thing you can do to anyone,' she said emphatically. 'The more you trust someone, the worse it is when they betray you.'

He stared at her like a man lost in a mist, vainly trying to understand distant echoes. 'What did you say?' he whispered.

'Don't you recognise your own words, Lysandros? Words you said to me in Las Vegas. I'll remind you of some more. "Nobody is ever as good as you think they are, and sooner or later the truth is always there. Better to have no illusions, and be strong." You really meant that, didn't you? I didn't realise until now just how much you meant it.'

'Don't remind me of that time,' he shouted. 'It's over.'

'It'll never be over because you carry it with you, and all the hatred and suspicion that was in you then is there still. You just hide it better, but then something happens and it speaks, telling you to play safe and think the worst of everyone. Even me. Look into your heart and be honest. Suddenly I look just like all the others, don't I? Lying, scheming—'

'Shut up!' he roared. 'Don't talk like that. I forbid it.'

'Why, because it comes too close to the truth? And who are you to forbid me?'

If his mind had been clearer he could have told her that he was the man whose fate she held in her hands, but the clearheadedness for which he was famed seemed to have deserted him now and everything was in a whirl of confusion.

'I *want* to believe you; can't you understand that?' He gripped her shoulders tightly, almost shaking her. 'But tell me how. Show me a way. *Tell me!*'

His misery was desperate. If her own heart hadn't been breaking, she would have been filled with pity for him.

'I can't tell you,' she said. 'That's one thing you must find for yourself.'

'Petra—please—try to understand—'

'But I do. I only wish I didn't. I understand that nothing has changed. We thought things could be different now. I love you and I hoped you loved me—'

'But I do, you know that—'

'No, even *you* don't know that. The barriers are still there, shutting you off from the world, from me. I thought I could break them down, but I can't.'

'If you can't, nobody can,' he said despairingly. Then something seemed to happen to him. His hands fell, he stepped back, and when he spoke again it was with the calm of despair. 'And perhaps that's all there is to be said.'

There was a noise from the distance, lights; the party was breaking up. People streamed out into the garden and now the laughter could be clearly heard, rising on the night air.

And the derision would torture him as well as the loss of his faith in her. Bleakly she wondered which one troubled him more.

'I'll be in touch,' he told her. 'There are ways of getting to the bottom of this.'

'Of course,' she said formally, waiting for his kiss.

Briefly he rested his fingertips against her cheek, but apart from that he departed without touching her.

* * *

The detective work was relatively easy. It didn't take long to establish that the 'newspaper copies' were forgeries, specially printed at Nikator's orders, the text written to Nikator's dictation.

But that helped little. It was the overheard conversations that were really damaging, the fact that they couldn't be explained, and the fact that hundreds of people at the party had read them.

Calling her publishers, Petra told them to abandon plans for a reissue of her book. They were dismayed.

'But we've heard such exciting stories—'

'None of them are true,' she snapped. 'Forget it.'

She and Lysandros were still in touch, but only just. They exchanged polite text messages, and she understood. He was avoiding her and she knew why. If they had met face to face he wouldn't have known what to say to her. He was back stranded again in the sea of desolation, unable to reach out to the one person who'd helped him in the past.

Or perhaps he just didn't know how to tell her that the break was coming and there was no escape.

It might have been different, she knew. By quarrelling, they had done exactly what Nikator had wanted.

But it went deeper than that. However it looked, Nikator hadn't really caused the chasm between them; he'd merely revealed its existence. Sooner or later the crack in their relationship would have come to light.

Sometimes she blamed herself for the anger that had made her attack him when he was wretched, but in her heart she knew it changed nothing. He was the man he was, and the hope she'd briefly glimpsed was no more than an illusion.

In her present bitter mood she wondered how much of her view of him had been real, and how much she'd shaped him to fit her own desires. Had he really needed her so much, or had she just refused to see that he was self-contained, needing neither her nor anyone else? It was suddenly easy to believe that, and to feel alone and unwanted as never before in her life.

'Surplus to requirements,' she thought angrily as she lay in bed one night. 'A silly woman who reshaped her image of a man to suit herself. And got her just deserts.'

In a fury of despair and frustration, she began to bang her head on the pillow and only stopped when she realised that she was mirroring his movements. She wished he were there so that she could share it with him.

But would he ever be with her again?

In Homer's library she found her own volume, the one on which Nikator had built his attacks.

'Now I know where he got the idea,' she thought wryly, turning to the Achilles section and reading her own text.

His name had been linked with many women, but the one for whose love he'd given his life was Polyxena, daughter of King Priam of Troy. His love for her had held out the hope of a peace treaty between the Greeks and the Trojans, and an end to the war. But Paris was enraged. Such a treaty would have meant he had to return Helen to her husband, and that he was determined not to do.

Through his spies he knew that Achilles could only be destroyed through his heel and he haunted the temple, waiting for the wedding. When Achilles appeared Paris shot him in the heel with a poisoned arrow.

In a further twist to the tale, Achilles' ghost was reputed to have spoken from the grave, demanding that Polyxena be sacrificed and forced to join him in death. Whereupon she was dragged to the altar and slain.

And what happened after that? Petra wondered. Had he met

her in a boat on the River Styx, ready to convey her to the underworld? Had she told him that he couldn't really have loved her or he would have behaved more generously? Or had he accused her of betraying him, giving that as his reason for condemning her to death? One way or another, it had ended badly, as many love affairs did.

Or was the story wrong? Had he not forced her to join him in death, but merely implored her, knowing that she would be glad to join him? When they met at the Styx had he held out his arms to her, and had she run to him?

I'm going crazy, she thought. I've got to stop thinking like this.

Stop thinking about him. That was all it would take.

It would never happen unless they could find some point of closure. And she could think of nothing that would provide a definite answer.

Unless…

Slowly she straightened up in her seat, staring into the distance, seeing nothing but the inspiration that had come to her.

That's what it needs, she thought. Of course! *Why didn't I think of that before?*

CHAPTER TWELVE

THE text message was simple and heartfelt.

I need to talk to you. Why have you stopped replying? L

He hesitated before sending it, afflicted by a feeling that the world had turned on its head. He'd received so many texts like this, but never before had he sent one. Would she reply to him as hc had so often replied to the others? The thought sent him cold with alarm. But he must do this. He could no longer endure the silence between them. He pressed the button.

Her reply was quick.

I'm sorry. I needed to be alone to think. P

He answered, *I thought that, but it's a mistake. We must do our thinking together. L*

She texted back, *We only hurt each other.*

This time he sent her only one word. *Please.*

She called back and he heard her voice.

'Please, Lysandros, it's better if we don't talk for a while.'

'No,' he said stubbornly. 'It isn't. There's a way out of this—'

'Not if you don't believe me. And in your heart you don't. Goodbye—my dearest.'

As she hung up he passed a hand over his eyes, troubled

by something he'd heard in the background, something he couldn't quite place—something—

He bounded to his feet, swearing. A tannoy announcement. That was what he'd heard. She was at the airport.

Frantically he called back, but she'd switched off. Neither speech nor text could reach her now. She was on her way back to England.

The world was coming down about his ears. Once she was gone he'd lose her for ever; he knew that well. And then everything would end.

He moved like lightning, calling his private pilot. A moment later he was rushing through the grounds to the landing stage where his helicopter waited, and a few minutes after that they were in the air.

While the pilot radioed ahead to the airport, arranging for a landing and a car to meet them, he called Information to check the next flight to England. It would take off in half an hour. He groaned.

The pilot was skilful and made Athens Airport in the fastest possible time. The car was waiting, taking him to the main building. As he stared out of the window he prayed for a delay, something that would give him the chance to get her off the plane. But then he saw it, rising into the sky, higher and higher, taking his life with it.

Even so, he clung to hope until the last minute. Only the word *Departed* on the board forced him to accept the brutal truth. She had gone. He'd lost her. His life was over. He almost reeled away from the desk, blinded by misery, wanting to howl up to heaven.

He was pulled up short by a collision. Two arms went around him, supporting him as they had so often done before. He tried to pull himself together.

'I'm sorry, I—*Petra*!'

She was clinging to him, staring up into his face, hardly able to believe what was happening.

'What's the matter?' she asked quickly. 'Why are you here?'

'To stop you leaving. I thought you'd be on that plane for England that just took off. You can't go like this.'

'Like this?' she asked hopefully.

'Not until we've settled things.'

She didn't know what to make of that. It might almost have been business-speak, but he was trembling in her arms.

'I'm not going back to England,' she said. 'That's not why I'm here. Please calm down. You worry me.'

He was taking huge gulps of air as relief shuddered through him.

'Let's find somewhere to sit,' she said, 'and I'll explain.'

Over a drink she said quietly, 'I was going to Corfu. I've been thinking a lot about how Nikator knew what we said, and it seems to me that he must have known a lot more about Priam House than he's ever let anyone know; enough to have bugged the place, even long ago. So I was going to see what I could find.'

'Yes,' he said. 'That's it. We'll find the answer. But why didn't you tell me?'

'I wasn't sure how you'd—well, anyway, I meant to go alone, but when I got here I realised I should tell you first. Because if I find bugs, I need you to be there, don't I? Otherwise—' she gave a wan smile '—otherwise, how will you know I didn't plant them, to clear myself?'

'Don't,' he whispered.

'Anyway, I was just about to leave the airport. I was going to come to you and tell you what I was thinking, but here you are. What brought you here?'

'You. I heard an announcement in the background and I thought you were leaving the country. I had to come and stop you. Look, it doesn't matter about all the other things. I can't let you go.'

'Even though you still doubt me?' she asked wryly. 'No, never mind. We'll worry later. We can't tell how this is going to work out.'

'My helicopter's here. It can take us straight on to Corfu, and we'll find all the answers we need there.'

Petra didn't reply. She knew that everything was far more complicated than he'd understood. They might find some answers, but not all and there were still obstacles to overcome. But this wasn't the time to say so.

For the moment she would enjoy the happiness of seeing him again, even though that happiness was tinged with bitterness and the threat of future misery.

An hour later the helicopter set them down on Corfu. As they covered the last few miles she wondered if this was just a forlorn hope and they were chasing it to avoid facing the truth.

'Does anyone know where Nikator is?' he asked suddenly. 'I've been looking for him, but he seems to have vanished.'

'Nobody's seen him for days.'

'How wise of him to avoid me. It was always the way when he was in trouble,' Lysandros said. 'He never did stick around to face things.'

'You do know that he did this, don't you?'

'I've been finding out. And when we know this last thing—'

Then you'll trust me, she thought. But not until then.

Was she making too much of it? she wondered. He'd come looking for her, desperate to stop her leaving him. Wasn't that enough?

But it wasn't. What still lived in her mind was the look that had fleetingly been on his face when disaster had struck. It had been a look of appalled betrayal, saying that she was no different from all the others. Now something must happen to wipe it out, but she had a terrible fear that nothing ever could.

The house was as they had left it, except that then it had been infused with joy. That had vanished now and its silence was the deadly silence of fear.

Lysandros wasted no time. Gathering tools from the shed, he strode out, through the grounds, under the trees, to the place where Brigitta and her child lay, incongruously at peace. Somehow Brigitta seemed a very real presence now, crying out to Lysandros to remember only her love and forget all else.

In the end he'd managed to do that. But too late.

'Why is he doing this?' Petra asked her spirit. 'Can he really only love and trust me when he has something tangible to hold? Isn't there anything deep inside him that tells him the truth? Those times when our hearts were so close that we were like one, do they count for nothing now?'

She thought she could hear Brigitta's melancholy cry, echoing from Hades, the underworld, across the River Styx and down the centuries. There was no hope in that sound.

'That's it!'

Lysandros's shout broke into her thoughts. He'd been hard at work, digging, scrabbling around the grave. Now there was a look of triumph in his eyes.

'Got them,' he said, holding something up.

'What have you found?' she asked.

'Bugs. Tiny microphones powerful enough to pick up anything, including what we said to each other.'

So she was cleared. She waited for the surge of joy that this should have brought her, but nothing happened.

'So this place was bugged,' she said.

But her heart was still waiting for him to say that he would have believed in her anyway, even if he'd found nothing. Desperately hoping, she nudged him in the right direction.

'But how do you know that I didn't come here earlier and put them there?'

If only he would say, *Because I know you wouldn't do that.*

Instead, beaming and oblivious to the undercurrents, he said, 'Of course you didn't. Look at them, they're old. They've been here for years. Nikator must have had spies that told him about this place and bugged it long ago. He's just been waiting for his moment.'

'Ah, I see. So the evidence clears me.'

'Of course it does.'

He scrambled up out of the grave and seized her shoulders.

'Darling, can't you see how wonderful this is? It makes everything right.'

'Does it?' she whispered.

He barely heard her words and totally missed her meaning.

'Come here,' he said, pulling her to him, kissing her fiercely. 'Now nothing can part us again.'

He seized her hand and began to run back to the house, his face shining with happiness. Upstairs, he kicked in the door of his bedroom and drew her swiftly down on the bed. She had a split second to make up her mind, whether or not to go through with this, for she knew that they were coming to the end. But for that very reason she would allow herself this one last time.

She made love to him as never before, giving him not just her body, but a heart infused with sorrow. Everything in her belonged to him. Soul and spirit were his, and there would never be anyone else. He had spoiled all other men for her, and she would live with that. But she could no longer live with him.

With every tender gesture, every whispered word, she bid him farewell. Each caress was a plea for him to remember always that she had loved him utterly and always would, even though their ways must now lie apart.

They reached their moment together and she saw him smiling down at her in triumph and relief, something that had always been her peak of joy. Afterwards he held her tenderly, protectively, and she had to struggle not to weep.

'Thank goodness,' he said fervently. 'We so nearly lost each other.'

To him it was all so simple. He hadn't faced the inevitable yet, but she must face it for both of them.

'Lysandros—'

'What is it, my darling?'

'Don't you realise that we *have* lost each other?'

'No, how can we? We know how it was all done now. The whole newspaper thing was fake, he had us followed to the Achilleion by someone who eavesdropped on what we said, and now we've found the evidence that clears you.'

As soon as he said the last words he knew what he'd done. She saw it in the sudden dismay that swept over his face.

'Yes,' she said sadly, 'you needed evidence to clear me because my word alone wasn't enough.'

'Don't,' he interrupted her hurriedly. 'Don't say it.'

'I have to. I'm going away—at least for a little while.'

'No. I won't let you go. I'll make you stay until you see sense—' He heard himself and screwed up his eyes in dismay. 'I didn't mean it like that.'

'It's all right. I love it that you want me, but perhaps it isn't right for us. If you only knew how much I've longed for you to believe in me anyway, in the face of all the evidence. Now it's too late.'

'But we've just made everything right.'

'My dearest, we've made nothing right. Can't you see that? We made love, and it was beautiful, but real love is so much more than passion. I know what to do when I'm in your arms. I know the caresses you can't resist, just as you know the ones that affect me. We know how to tempt each other on and on until we explode with desire, and for a while that seems enough. But it soon passes, and then we have to see the distance between us.'

'It doesn't have to be there,' he said harshly. 'We can overcome it.'

She loved him for his stubborn belief. She would have given anything to yield to it and it broke her heart to refuse, knowing that she was breaking his heart in the process.

She remembered how he'd raced to the airport to stop her leaving, caring nothing for her guilt or innocence as long as he kept her with him. Surely that was enough? But he was an acquisitive man. What was his had to remain his. There might be no more in his possessiveness than that. It wasn't enough to build on.

If only, she thought desperately, there was still something that could happen—something that could give them hope for the future—but the last chance had gone. He had the evidence in his hands now, and evidence made blind trust unnecessary.

It was too late. Nothing could happen now.

'You're saying that I've failed you,' he grated. 'You can't forgive me.'

'There's nothing to forgive,' she said passionately. 'What was done to you was terrible, and it's not your fault that it's scarred you. But it has. You can't really believe in anyone now, even me. I thought I could help you but I can't. Please try to understand.'

A dead look came into his eyes.

'Yes,' he said at last. 'Of course you must go, because I let you down, didn't I? Get out while you can. Get out before I destroy you as I did her.'

He dressed hurriedly and walked out without looking back.

Shattered, she stared after him. This was what she'd planned, but now it was here it was terrible. Throwing on her clothes, she hurried out after him.

As soon as she reached the head of the stairs she knew that something had happened. The door to the cellar stood open. Through it she could see a light and hear voices.

She knew who would be there before she entered. Lysandros stood by the far wall, his eyes fixed on Nikator, who aimed a small pistol at him.

'Get out,' Lysandros shouted to her. 'Go now.'

'Oh, I don't think so,' Nikator said, pointing the pistol at her. 'I've waited so long to get you both together. Come down, my dear, and let's all three have a talk.'

She'd thought she knew the worst of Nikator. But now his eyes were bright as if he was high on something and his most dreadful side was on display. This man could kill, she was sure of it. And now only one thing mattered.

'How do you come to be here, Nikki?' she asked, trying to sound casual.

'It wasn't hard. I knew you'd both arrive soon.'

'Let her go,' Lysandros said. 'I'm the one you want.'

'But she's also the one I want. She always has been. And now I'm tired of waiting. If not one way, then another. Isn't that so?'

'Then you can have me,' Petra said. 'Let Lysandros go and I'm all yours, Nikki.'

'No!' Lysandros's howl of rage and despair seemed to hit the ceiling, causing some dust and wood flakes to float down.

'It makes no difference to you,' she told him, smiling. 'We'd decided to part anyway. I never stay with any man for long. What do you say, Nikki?'

She was still on the stairs and he reached up to take her hand and draw her down beside him.

'You mean you'd stay with me—?'

'If you let Lysandros go.'

Nikator laughed softly, horribly.

'Oh, darling, I so much want to believe you, but you're lying. You're still in love with him. After all the things I've heard you say to him—'

'You mean—?'

'Yes, I heard it all. It's not just the gardens that are bugged. Everywhere. I bugged it years ago. Years and years I've been waiting. I've been with the two of you all the time.'

Lysandros's roar filled the air. The next moment he'd launched himself onto Nikator. There was an explosion as the pistol went off and the next moment the whole place was shaking as the bullet hit the old ceiling, which began to disintegrate.

'It's coming down,' Lysandros said hoarsely. 'Get out fast.'

But the wooden stairs were collapsing and the next moment the ceiling began to descend on them. She saw it getting closer, then it was blocked out by Lysandros's head, and then there was darkness.

He was in the place that had always been waiting for him. Before him stretched the Styx, the river that ran between the living and the dead. He'd known in his heart that the final choice was out of his hands, and now that he was here he would go wherever the river took him.

Had there ever been a choice? He'd seen the roof coming down on the woman he loved, and he'd lunged forward to put himself between her and danger. There had been no time to think, only the knowledge that without her life was unbearable. He would die with her, or instead of her. Either way, he was content.

He ached all over from the weight of the ceiling on his

back, pinning him against her as she lay beneath him, so frighteningly still that he feared the worst.

'Not yet,' he whispered. 'Wait for me, and we'll cross the river together.'

Incredibly, he sensed a tremor beneath him. Then a soft breath broke from her.

'Petra, Petra,' he said urgently. 'Are you alive? Speak to me.'

'Aaaah—' The word was so soft he hardly heard it.

'Can you hear me?'

Her eyes opened a little way, fixed on him. 'What happened?'

'The roof fell on us. We're trapped here. There's no way out unless someone up there sees what's happened.'

And nobody would, they both realised. They were underground, in a part of the house not visible from the road. They could stay here, undiscovered, for days, perhaps longer.

'You saved me,' she murmured.

'I only wish I had.'

'You took the weight of the rafters to protect me. You could have got out—'

'And live without you? Do you think I want that? It's together or nothing.'

She managed to turn her head. There were tears in her eyes. 'Darling, are you very much hurt?'

'No, but I can't move, and I can't get you out.'

They both knew that if he tried to move he would bring the rest of the place down on them both.

'Together or nothing,' she murmured.

'There's just one thing I could try,' he said.

Taking a deep breath, he gave a shout, but immediately there was an ominous sound overhead and plaster began to pour down. They clung together, seeking refuge in each other.

'Dear God!' he said. 'I neglected this place and let it get in such bad condition. This is my fault.'

'Or maybe it's my fault,' she said softly. 'I came excavating here without thinking of safety. Who knows what damage I might have done?'

'Don't try to spare me,' he said savagely. '*I* did this. *I* harmed you. *I killed you.*'

'Darling, it doesn't matter now. Just hold me.'

'For ever,' he said fiercely, managing to get his arms about her. 'And perhaps help will come in time. We must hold on to that, Petra—Petra?'

Her eyes had closed and her breathing had become faint.

'Petra! Listen to me. For pity's sake, wake up.'

But she didn't open her eyes, and he knew that the boat was waiting for her; she was embarking on the last journey, leaving him behind.

'Not yet,' he begged. 'Not until you've heard me—forgiven me. I shouldn't have doubted you—say that you understand—that it won't part us for ever—'

Once before he'd implored forgiveness from a woman as she'd begun the journey across the river, but she hadn't heard him. Her face had been implacable as she'd climbed into the boat with her child in her arms, not seeing or hearing him, never knowing of his grief and contrition.

Now it was happening a second time, unless he could find a way to prevent it.

'Forgive me,' he whispered. 'Make some sign that you forgive me—'

For he knew that without her forgiveness they could not make the final journey together. He'd betrayed their love with his mistrust; a crime that would keep them apart for all eternity and only her blessing could wipe that out.

But she was drifting beyond him, to a place he couldn't follow.

Now he understood the face of the statue, raised in despair, calling on the gods of Olympus to grant his last request, helpless, hopeless.

'Wake up,' he begged. 'Just for a moment, *please*.'

But there was only stillness and the sound of her breathing, growing fainter.

As he saw her slipping away Achilles lifted his face to the heavens, silently imploring,

'Take me, not her! Let her live! Take me!'

She was in another world. There was the Styx, the river that led to the underworld and from which there was no return, save as a spirit. She looked back at the earth from which she'd come, but it was too late. She had left it for ever.

Then, coming towards her across the water, she saw a boat, with a man standing in the prow. He was tall and magnificent and all the lesser creatures fell away before him, but he had no eyes for them. He was searching for something, and when he saw her his eyes brightened and his hands reached out, imploring.

Now she knew him. He was the man who had chosen to die for her, and was asking if she was ready to follow him.

'I wasn't sure you'd come,' he said. 'It could only happen if you were willing.'

'How could I be unwilling to spend my eternity with you?' she asked.

She went towards him and he lifted her into the boat.

'Eternity,' he whispered.

The boat turned and began to make its way back across the water, until it vanished.

'My darling, wake up, please!'

Slowly she opened her eyes, frowning a little. The underworld didn't look as she'd expected. It looked more like a hospital room.

'How did I get here?'

'They came in time,' Lysandros said from where he was seated beside her bed. 'Somebody heard the gun go off and raised the alarm. Rescuers got us out.'

Now she could see him more clearly. His head was bandaged and his arm was in a sling.

'How badly are you hurt?' she asked.

'Not much; it looks worse than it is. The doctor says we're both badly bruised, but no worse.'

'What about Nikator?'

'He's alive. I got a message to Homer, and he's taking him away to a special hospital where I think he'll need to stay for some time. I've told everyone it was an accident. Nobody else needs to know the truth. Never mind him. I was afraid you weren't going to come round.'

Now she remembered. He had thrown himself between her and the descending roof.

'You saved my life,' she murmured. 'You could have been killed.'

'And so could you. Do you think I'd let you go on alone? I'd have followed, wherever you went, whether you wanted me or not.'

'Of course I'd have wanted you,' she murmured. 'How could I be unwilling to spend my eternity with you?'

'Do you mean that?' he asked anxiously. 'You spoke as though it was all over between us, and I don't blame you, but then—'

But then he had chosen to die rather than live without her. It was the sign she had longed for, his offering on the sacrificial altar. Now she belonged to him in every way, in his way, and in her own.

She had no illusions about their life together. He would

always be a troubled man, but his very troubles called on something in her that yearned to be vitally necessary to him. It would never be easy, but they belonged together.

'I'll never let you go again,' he said, 'not after that time I spent holding you down there, wondering if you were ever going to wake, whether you were going to live or die, whether you'd allow me to go with you.'

'Allow?'

'It was always up to you. You could have gone on ahead without me, or sent me on without you. I could only beg you to show me mercy. While you were unconscious I listened to the things you said, longing to hear something that gave me hope. But your words were strange and confusing.'

'Tell me about them.'

'Once you said, "The story is wrong." What did you mean?'

'The story about Achilles forcing Polyxena to die. He didn't force her. He only asked her to follow him if she was willing. And she was.'

'How do you know?'

'Never mind. I know.'

'Is this another triumphant "find" that will boost your reputation?' he asked tenderly.

'No, I'll never tell anyone else but you. This is our secret.'

He reached out a hand to touch her face with tentative fingers.

'Never leave me,' he said. 'You are my life. I can have no other and I want no other.'

'I'm yours for as long as you need me,' she vowed.

It was a few days before they were both well enough to leave the hospital. They paid a final visit to the villa and wandered through the grounds.

'I'm having it demolished,' he said. 'I could never come here again. We'll make our home somewhere else.'

'What about Brigitta, and your child? We can't leave them here. Let's take them back to Athens and let them rest in the grounds there.'

'You wouldn't mind that?' he asked.

She shook her head. 'She's part of your life, and but for her we might never have met.'

'And if we hadn't met my life would have gone on in the old dead, hopeless way. I have so much to be grateful for. I feared love as a weakness, but I was wrong. Love is strength, and the true weakling is the man who can't love, or the one who fears to let himself love.

'For years I've held myself behind doors that were bolted and barred, refusing to allow anyone through. I thought I was safe from invasion, but in truth I was destroying myself from within. Now I know that there's no true strength except what you give me in your arms, and in your heart.'

She took his face between her hands.

'You're right,' she said. 'It's not a weakness to need people. It's only a weakness if you don't know that you need them, so you don't reach out to them, and you're left floundering alone. But if you reach out, and they reach back, then your strength can defeat worlds.'

'And you did reach back, didn't you?' he asked. 'It wasn't just chance that we met again after so many years.'

'True. I think the ancient gods gave their orders from Mount Olympus.'

'And that's why it's been inevitable between us from the start—if you really feel you can put up with me.'

'How could I disobey the orders of the gods?' she asked him tenderly.

And what the gods ordered, they would protect. Their life together had been ordained, and so it must be. It would be a life of passion and pain, quarrels, reconciliations, heartbreak and joy. But never for one moment would they doubt that they were treading the path that had been preordained for them.

One day the River Styx would be waiting to carry them on, to Eternity.

But that day was not yet.

THE KRISTALLIS BABY

BY
NATALIE RIVERS

Natalie Rivers grew up in the Sussex countryside. As a child she always loved to lose herself in a good book, or in games that gave free rein to her imagination. She went to Sheffield University, where she met her husband in the first week of term. It was love at first sight and they have been together ever since, moving to London after graduating, getting married, and having two wonderful children.

After university Natalie worked in a lab at a medical research charity, and later retrained to be a primary school teacher. Now she is lucky enough to be able to combine her two favourite occupations—being a full-time mum and writing passionate romances.

For my sister, Claire

PROLOGUE

CARRIE stared numbly at the four coffins lined up across the chapel. Apart from little baby Danny, snuggled in her arms, nothing seemed real. How could it be real? How could four people she loved be dead?

She and Danny were alone in the front pew. She shifted him on her lap so that she could look into his face, and the moment they made eye contact a massive grin lit up his features. She smiled back at him tremulously and let the priest's words wash over her. If she listened to what he was saying she knew she'd start weeping.

She couldn't let herself think about her beloved cousin Sophie and her husband Leonidas, or about the aunt and uncle who had brought her up. She couldn't think about the terrible motorway accident that had killed them all and left Danny an orphan or she knew her grief would overwhelm her. If she gave in to it now she might never stop crying. For Danny's sake she had to be strong.

He was all that she had now.

Slowly she became aware that organ music was playing, and she realised the service was over. She stood up stiffly and walked out of the chapel, holding Danny close to her chest. At twenty-five years old, the only other funeral Carrie had ever attended was her mother's, but she'd been very young at the time and had no memory of it now.

Making the arrangements for today had been a daunting prospect, and she'd had to do it all on her own. Her father hadn't helped her. He hadn't bothered to come when she'd told him about the accident, and later, when she'd called to tell him the time of the funeral, he'd almost seemed surprised.

'I can't get away at the moment,' he'd said. 'I'm completely tied up with work.'

'But it's family,' Carrie gasped. She'd learnt not to expect much from her father, but his intention to stay away from the funeral genuinely shocked her.

'Your mother's family, not mine,' he replied.

'My family, too.' She heard her voice break as she spoke. 'When you left after Mum died, they were all I had.'

'Look, it sounds like you've got everything organised,' he said, refusing to be drawn by her comments. 'You don't need me there. I'm sorry about the accident, but whether or not I come to the funeral won't make any difference to them now.'

'It would make a difference to me,' Carrie had said to the silent telephone after her father had rung off. If, just once in her life, he'd been there for her it would have meant something.

She'd wanted to tell him about her intention to care for Sophie's baby, six-month-old Danny. But how could a man who'd abandoned his own daughter as a baby understand?

She stood outside the chapel in the chill November air and clutched Danny to her. Most of the mourners had drifted away now, and the few that still lingered were talking quietly in groups. She bent her head down to press her cheek against the soft baby curls on the top of Danny's head and let out a long, shaky sigh. Soon she would be able to leave, take him away from this place of sadness.

She hadn't thought beyond the funeral. There'd been just too much to take in. But one thing she knew for certain was that she'd always love Danny more than words could say. And she would do everything she could to make him happy.

'Miss Thomas?'

Carrie lifted her head and found herself looking at a mature man she had never seen before. He was studying her with an expression so cold and hard that it sent a shudder running through her.

'My name is Cosmo Kristallis.' His voice was deep and heavily accented.

Carrie's eyes widened in surprise. It was a shock to realise she was facc to face with the estranged father of Sophie's husband, Leonidas. This man was Danny's grandfather.

'I'm so sorry about the death of your son,' she said, instinctively reaching out a hand to touch his arm.

The moment her fingers brushed the heavy woollen sleeve of his long winter overcoat she knew she'd made a mistake. Her sympathy wasn't welcome, and neither was her impudent touch.

'My son was already dead to me.' Disdain dripped from Cosmo's voice as he looked down at her hand on his sleeve. He didn't withdraw his arm or bother to shrug off her fingers. It wasn't necessary. She was already snatching her hand away, but not before she felt her fingers turn to ice.

'Then why are you here?' Carrie held her voice steady despite the unpleasant emotions that were churning through her. If he really thought so little of his own son, why had he bothered to travel from Greece to be at his funeral?

'When you contacted me to tell me about the funeral I realised there were some things I had to make plain to you,' Cosmo said. 'Specifically concerning the child you are holding.'

'Danny?' Carrie took a step backwards and wrapped her arms even tighter about the baby. What could he want with Danny?

'As I said, my son was dead to me a long time ago. I will never acknowledge that child as a Kristallis heir,' Cosmo said, his hand gesturing towards Danny. 'That brat will never see any of my money.'

'Your money?' Carrie repeated, confused and horrified by what she was hearing. Danny was an innocent baby who had just lost both his parents. Why was this man so hostile, and why was he talking about money?

'Your cousin was a scheming little gold-digger,' Cosmo said. 'All she wanted was to get her hands on my fortune.'

'Sophie didn't want your money. All she ever wanted was to live happily with the man she loved and raise a family,' Carrie said, feeling her eyes swim with sudden tears at the thought that her cousin would never be able to live that dream now. She'd never see her child grow up.

She blinked furiously, determined not to start crying, and stared at Cosmo Kristallis coldly. Sophie and Leonidas weren't here to defend themselves, so she would have to do it. They had been good people and she'd loved them both. She wouldn't let him slander them any more.

'That child is not my grandson,' Cosmo said flatly.

'Yes, he is,' Carrie said. 'The thought that *you* are his grandfather makes me feel sick, but nevertheless he is your grandson, and I won't let you tell any more horrible lies about Sophie or Leonidas.'

'I will never acknowledge him,' Cosmo said. 'And if you ever contact my family again you will live to regret it.' Then, without giving Carrie a chance to respond, he turned and strode away.

She stared after him, realising she was shaking. She'd

heard many unpleasant things about Leonidas's Greek family, but until that moment she'd never really understood why he had hated his father so much.

'It's all right. You'll never have to see that horrible man again,' she murmured into Danny's curly brown hair. Her words were to comfort herself as much as the baby. 'We've got each other and we'll do just fine.'

CHAPTER ONE

Six months later

'PLEASE, Carrie, you've got to do this for me,' Lulu begged, streams of mascara-stained tears running down her crumpled face. 'If Darren listens to that message he'll throw me out!'

'I want to help. You know that,' Carrie said, looking at her weeping friend with concern. 'But wouldn't it be better if you did it? After all, no one's going to think twice if you walk into your husband's study and take his phone.'

'I told you—everyone heard us arguing. Anyway, I can't go down there like this,' Lulu wailed, indicating her ruined make-up with a theatrical gesture. 'But if I don't delete that message I'm going to be in such big trouble.'

'Well, *I'm* hardly going to blend in with the party.' Carrie glanced down at the sports gear she was wearing. She was Lulu's personal trainer, not one of her footballer husband's fancy party set. 'And you know I've got to leave soon or I'll be late picking up Danny.'

'It won't take long.' Lulu suddenly lunged towards her and pulled at her T-shirt. 'Quick—get these things off. You can wear one of my dresses.'

Five minutes later Carrie emerged from Lulu's bedroom,

dressed for her mission and feeling decidedly self-conscious. After the past six months of caring for Danny and coming to terms with her grief, it was an unsettling experience to dress up for a glitzy celebrity party. Even before her life had changed so dramatically she wouldn't have felt at ease in such dangerously high stiletto heels and a dress so tight she could hardly breathe. But there simply hadn't been time to sift through Lulu's wardrobe to find something she'd feel better wearing.

She left her backpack, which was stuffed rather haphazardly with her training gear, by the front door, and started moving through the house towards Darren's study. Lulu just needed his phone long enough to delete the voicemail she had left in a fit of jealousy. Then Carrie's task would be over.

She took a glass of champagne from a passing waiter and knocked back a recklessly large swallow of the sparkling liquid. An explosion of bubbles fizzed against the roof of her mouth, making her throat tighten uncomfortably and her eyes start to water. She coughed quietly, and blinked to clear her vision as she glanced quickly round the room.

Despite the early hour, the party was already in full swing. A photographer was making the rounds, finding no shortage of guests willing to pose for him—no doubt hoping to find their photos inside the glossy pages of well-known celebrity lifestyle magazines.

She smoothed the sparkly red dress over her hips in an ineffectual effort to cover a decent amount of thigh. Lulu wasn't known for choosing her wardrobe with modesty in mind, and that coupled with Carrie's considerable extra height meant that she was left with an alarming amount of leg on show. Even more disconcerting was the lack of decent coverage provided by the plunging neckline.

Feeling very self-conscious, she dropped her gaze and

moved across the room. A curtain of sleek black hair fell across her eyes, but she didn't flick it back. She felt better with her face hidden—although no one was actually looking at her *face*, she thought with a shudder.

At last she slipped quietly into the study and closed the door behind her. She ignored the nerves that fluttered in her stomach and crossed to the desk. Putting her champagne glass down, she picked up Darren's jacket from the back of his chair and reached her hand into the pocket.

'Do you make a habit of that?'

Carrie gasped and spun round to see who had spoken, clutching the jacket tightly to her chest.

A stranger stood just inside the study. Tall and imposing, with an unmistakable air of power about him, he was standing perfectly still, calmly watching her every move.

Her eyes flew to his face, and as their gazes met she sucked in a startled breath. He was utterly gorgeous. Dark brown hair and bronzed skin made his appearance classically Mediterranean, apart from his eyes, which were an arresting shade of blue.

She looked at him, taking in his incredible bone structure and perfect features. He was unbelievably good-looking, but there was something disconcerting about him. She had the strangest feeling that she ought to know who he was. She bit her lip and studied him, momentarily forgetting that she was still holding the incriminating jacket.

It worried her that she couldn't place him. Many of the guests at the party were celebrities—easily recognisable people that for an instant you thought you knew, until suddenly you realised who they were. Carrie was used to that, with several of her clients being celebrities of one kind or another. But there was something about this man that unnerved her.

He was studying her in return. She felt a shiver of sexual awareness prickle across her skin as his gaze swept arrogantly over her. The intensity in his glittering blue eyes made her suddenly acutely aware of her body, and of the revealing dress she was wearing. It was an unfamiliar sensation.

For the past six months she had been totally absorbed in her new way of life. She had discovered the bittersweet joys of caring for Danny whilst dealing with the loss of so many loved ones and had learned to cope with the everyday stresses of looking after a child.

With all of that going on, she simply wasn't used to thinking of herself as an attractive woman that men might fight desirable.

A wave of heat washed across her exposed skin, but it was unsettling and she did her best to ignore it. She couldn't let herself be thrown off kilter by her unexpected feelings. After all, she still had to get Darren's phone for Lulu, and then leave in time to pick up Danny.

'Can I help you?' she asked, deliberately making her voice sound as indifferent as she could. 'Are you lost, or were you looking for Darren?'

'You didn't answer *my* question,' the stranger said. 'I asked if you made a habit of that.'

Carrie's heart skipped a beat. He'd seen what she'd been up to.

'I don't know what you mean,' she said, in an attempt to brazen it out. She let the jacket fall back onto the chair, closing her fingers round the mobile phone just as her hand slid from the pocket. She tossed her silky hair away from her face and stared squarely back at him.

'I meant do you often creep into other people's studies and steal their mobile phones?' His voice was deep and resonant, with the hint of an accent that Carrie couldn't place.

'I didn't creep anywhere.' Trying to sound cool, she let her gaze slide down across his powerful body. She was impressed by what she saw. Lean and athletic, he looked amazing in his dark designer suit, but she had no doubt he'd look equally good dressed in the more revealing exercise gear that, because of her job as a trainer, she was used to seeing men wear. 'And I haven't stolen anything. This is Lulu's phone. I was fetching it for her.'

'You should really work on your story more,' he said.

'I work for Lulu.' She shrugged, trying to ignore the mocking note to his tone. Maybe she could still bluff her way out of the situation. 'She asked me to fetch it.'

'Really?' he asked, running his eyes insultingly over her, starting from the tips of her toes and working his way up in a leisurely fashion. 'Are they your work clothes?' he finished, letting his gaze linger on her almost indecently exposed breasts.

'I'm Lulu's personal trainer,' she said, trying to ignore the way her skin was burning from his perusal. It was strangely exciting, yet utterly unnerving, to feel the way her body was responding to the touch of his eyes. 'Now, please excuse me. I really must get back to her.' She took a step towards the door.

Suddenly the sound of Darren's voice right outside the study caught her attention.

Her eyes flicked nervously to the door. She still had his phone in her hand, and there was nowhere in the ridiculously skimpy outfit she was wearing to hide it. She'd made Lulu a promise, but now she wasn't going to get away with it.

She looked back at her uninvited companion. Would he give her away? Reveal that he'd caught her red-handed in the act of stealing the mobile phone?

At that moment he started walking towards her. Her heart lurched and she clutched the phone tightly, staring at him. She was paralysed like a rabbit in the glare of an approaching juggernaut. What was he going to do? Take the phone from her and tell Darren exactly what he'd seen?

His movements seemed quite unhurried, but there was a purposeful glint in his blue eyes that sent an icy tingle skittering down Carrie's spine. Then suddenly she realised he was standing right in front of her, effectively shielding her from anyone who came into the room.

Startled by his sudden proximity, she stared up at him with wide eyes. At five foot eight inches she was tall, but even with the added height of Lulu's four-inch stiletto-heeled sandals she had to tip her head back to look at him.

The expression on his face made her heart beat erratically. His glittering blue eyes darkened, and he looked so deeply into her eyes that it felt as if he could see right into her soul. Then he tipped his head slightly to one side, as if he was about to kiss her!

'So lovely,' he murmured, resting his hands gently on the bare skin of her upper arms.

Carrie was transfixed. She simply couldn't tear her gaze away from his face. He was absolutely gorgeous. Everything about his features seemed perfect, from the deep blue eyes fringed with sinfully long lashes to the wide, expressive mouth. And he was looking at her and seeing a desirable woman.

Suddenly she became aware of the sensuous slide of his hand down her arm, skimming lightly over her skin in a way that made the hairs stand up and goosebumps prickle over her exposed flesh. His hand closed over the phone, taking it from her grasp, then in the next second his other arm moved around her, pulling her hard against his muscular frame.

She gasped as her body bumped against his, the skimpy dress doing nothing to shield her from the hot-blooded strength of his powerful masculine form. Her heart was beating so loudly it blocked out all other sounds, and her stomach was turning somersaults. What was he going to do now? He couldn't really mean to kiss her, could he? He didn't even know her!

Somewhere deep inside her mind a tiny rational thought told her to push him off, to back away and get out of there while she still could. But her body was ignoring the niggle of common sense, overriding her instinct for self-preservation. She simply didn't want to do the sensible thing.

She stared up at him, unable to speak or move. Then the moment of no return passed and his mouth came down on hers.

The sensual movement of his lips against hers set her body trembling, and she clung to him, utterly lost in the moment.

Her legs felt weak, and her arms seemed to slide around his broad shoulders of their own volition as she felt her body meld itself to his. He placed one strong hand between her shoulder blades to support her, and by leaning forward pushed her back over the desk. A moment later his other hand found her waist and tugged her tightly to him.

Her hips were pressed against his, and her spine was arched back, pushing her breasts upwards. It was an undeniably erotic position, and a rush of sexual excitement stormed through her body, starting an insistent throbbing of desire deep within her. Then, with unexpected abruptness, he pulled back from the kiss.

She stared at him in startled silence. All she could hear was the sound of her own breathing and the rapid beating of her heart. All she could see was his face, his expression intense but unreadable. He still held her close, but not so tightly as before.

'Carrie?' A man's voice coming from behind the stranger broke through into her awareness. 'I didn't know you were coming this evening.'

Darren! She'd forgotten all about him. Suddenly she remembered she'd taken his mobile phone—then an instant later realised it was no longer in her hand.

'Lulu…Lulu asked me to stay for the party,' she stammered distractedly, hardly able to tear her gaze away from the stranger's face to glance at Darren.

'What are you doing in here?' There was a hint of suspicion colouring his voice as he looked down at his jacket. It was lying rather haphazardly on the chair where Carrie had dropped it. 'Well, I can see *what* you're doing—but why are you doing it in my study?' he added.

'I needed a moment alone with Carrie.' The stranger suddenly spoke, turning his head to look at Darren. From the calm assurance and air of authority he exuded, anyone would think it was his study rather than Darren's.

Carrie's eyes opened wide with shock. How did he know her name—was he simply repeating what he'd just heard Darren call her? And why had he said he wanted to be alone with her? An uncomfortable mixture of emotions rattled through her as she stared at his strong profile. Had he simply followed her into the room with the intention of making a pass at her?

'Nik!' Darren exclaimed. 'Long time no see. You didn't tell me you were coming.'

Carrie frowned in confusion. For some reason she was surprised that Darren knew the stranger, but after all this was his party, and all the people here were his guests. And he'd called the stranger by name—Nik.

'It was a last-minute decision,' Nik said. 'I've just come straight from the airport.'

'I can see you didn't waste any time getting straight down to business, you old dog!' Darren laughed, slapping him soundly on the back. The action bumped Nik hard into Carrie, sending shockwaves of desire ricocheting through her sensitised body. 'And, Carrie,' he added approvingly, 'you dark horse!'

With another jolt she realised that she was still almost indecently entwined with the stranger. His muscled leg was pressing intimately between her thighs, pulling the fabric of her dress taut across her hips and causing it to ride up even higher.

'Well, don't let me interrupt you, mate.' Darren spoke to Nik as leant past them to pick up his jacket. 'I can see you've got things to do,' he added with a knowing grin as he pulled the mobile phone out of the pocket. 'I've got a phone call to make, so I'll leave you to it. Lock the room if you want,' he finished, closing the door behind him as he left the study.

Carrie stared after him with her mind spinning, then turned back to look into Nik's face, which was still only inches from her own. She was confused and embarrassed by her response to his kiss, but she was also angry with him for putting her in that position in the first place.

'What on earth do you think you were doing?' she demanded, pushing him away from her. She stood up straight, wobbling slightly on her high heels before she found her balance, but then she planted her hands firmly on her hips and stared at him indignantly.

'I would have thought it was obvious,' he drawled, looking completely unmoved as he straightened his tie and tugged at the cuffs of his shirt so that once again he looked immaculate. 'I was replacing the stolen phone, of course.'

'Oh!' Carrie was completely thrown. How could he be so matter-of-fact about what had just happened between them? Had he really only kissed her to provide a distraction while he put the phone back?

The kiss had lasted only moments, but it had had a profound impact on her both physically and mentally. For half a year her identity as an individual with hopes and desires had been locked away. She hadn't thought of herself as a woman with natural needs and passions. Now she had suddenly let go, in a way that even shocked herself.

She'd been so wrapped up in the kiss that she'd been totally oblivious to what was going on around her. Nik, on the other hand, seemed completely unaffected by the experience, and had even been able to concentrate on an entirely different agenda. He'd simply been creating a smokescreen so Darren wouldn't notice him putting the phone back in his jacket pocket.

'I thought you'd be grateful,' he said, his sensual lips curving up in evident amusement at her obvious confusion and discomfort. 'In fact, I got the impression you rather enjoyed it.'

'I didn't enjoy it!' Carrie felt her cheeks blazing at her barefaced lie. 'And you certainly didn't need to kiss me like that!' she added.

'It's what they always do in the movies. I had to bend you back like that to reach the jacket,' Nik said, with a smile that didn't reach his eyes. 'Besides, you looked like a frightened little rabbit. If I'd stuck out my leg and tripped Darren up, I doubt that you would've had the wit to use the diversion to put his phone back unnoticed.'

'I didn't ask you to help me,' she said, suddenly riled by Nik's casual insult, and by the way he was treating the whole thing as a joke. 'I would have simply explained to Darren that Lulu needed the phone.'

'I'm not going to apologise for kissing you, if that's what you're angling for,' he said. 'I did what I thought was necessary at the time, and that's all there is to it. I wasn't exactly delighted with the situation myself, but I'm not asking for your apologies.'

'I've got nothing to say sorry for!' Carrie protested, her emotions see-sawing horribly. She'd found the kiss totally mind-blowing, yet Nik apparently had a very different view of the whole thing. 'I didn't ask you to kiss me. It's not my fault you found it so awful!'

'I wasn't talking about the kiss, of course. Why are women always so insecure about these things?' he asked, with an exaggerated lift of his eyebrows. 'I meant that I wasn't thrilled to discover you're a thief. I'd hoped that you were a reasonable, honest person.'

'What?' she gasped, struggling to understand the implication of his words. Why did he care what sort of person she was? Suddenly she remembered him telling Darren that he needed a moment alone with her. Who *was* he?

'First impressions count for a lot,' he continued, letting his gaze drift slowly down her body, lingering meaningfully on the fullness of her breasts before skimming down to her narrow waist.

'Who are you?' She held herself straight and refused to fidget under his blatant scrutiny. 'And what do you want from me?'

He didn't answer immediately, and, still not making eye contact, rudely let his gaze sweep lower, moving over the swell of her hips and down her long exposed legs to the tips of her toes. She was just about to repeat her question when his eyes snapped up to meet hers.

'My name is Nikos Kristallis,' he said coldly. 'And I have come to discuss arrangements for my nephew.'

CHAPTER TWO

CARRIE couldn't speak. She was so shocked she could hardly think.

She simply stared at him. Nikos Kristallis. He was the younger brother of Sophie's husband, Leonidas. The favoured son of the proud and arrogant Cosmo Kristallis. He was Danny's uncle.

A nasty sensation of dread settled in her stomach, but she took a deep breath to steady herself. She tried not to think about her distressing encounter with Cosmo Kristallis at the funeral, which suddenly loomed up in the front of her mind. It had been a horrible experience, and her memories of the occasion were inseparable from the soul-wrenching grief for her loved ones.

'What are you doing here?' When she finally managed to speak, her voice was no more than a scratchy whisper.

Nik watched the profound impact of his words on Carrie Thomas with a strange sense of satisfaction. The colour drained from her face with startling speed and for a moment she appeared totally stunned.

He was pleased. Not that he liked to inflict pain on people as a general rule, but Carrie Thomas was different. She had taken something that belonged to him, and he would do whatever it took to get it back!

'I have come to discuss my nephew,' Nik replied. 'Now I have identified myself to you, I would have thought that was obvious.'

'I have nothing to say to you about Danny,' Carrie said. Her face was very white against her black hair, but the spark was suddenly back in her green eyes. 'We have nothing to discuss.' She stalked across to the door and walked out.

Nik made no attempt to stop her leaving.

It suited him to get her away from the crowds at this footballer's party. It was too public for what he had to do, and there were definitely too many photographers about.

Nik's eyes narrowed as he watched Carrie weave her way through the crowds of partygoers. She was a gorgeous creature. His investigators had provided him with photos, so he'd known she would be attractive, but those photos had done nothing to reveal the incredible full-blooded impact of her presence.

She was making rapid progress across the room, stepping lightly in her strappy sandals, the extraordinary height of the heels creating a delicious tension in her shapely legs. Every man present was looking at her as she passed. Every man present was picturing those long, long legs wrapped around him. Or maybe it was just Nik. Certainly he couldn't shake the thought of kissing her again. Kissing her and more, much more.

Her silky black hair hung loose past her shoulders, swinging alluringly in time with her step. He wanted to slip his hands under that shimmering black curtain and brush it aside to expose the naked skin of her back, to reveal the zip that ran skin-tight down her spine.

He imagined easing that zip down and running his hands all over that sexy body, teasing and caressing her, removing all her clothes until she was naked and ready for him. He knew she wouldn't be a passive lover. He longed to look deep into those green eyes as she writhed beneath him, as he took her to the brink of ecstasy.

Suddenly he realised she was almost at the door. Pushing his erotic thoughts about her aside, he stirred himself to follow. He knew where she was going, but it would be wise to keep her in his sights.

Carrie picked up her denim jacket and sporty backpack from an alcove by the front door, then stopped and scanned the room for Lulu. She was desperate to get out of there, but she couldn't forget about her friend—especially when she had been so upset earlier. She spotted her almost immediately, hurrying down the staircase looking determined, in freshly applied make-up and dressed to kill in a slinky silver cocktail dress.

'I'm really sorry,' Carrie said, as soon as Lulu reached her. 'I couldn't get the phone.'

'Don't worry about it,' Lulu said, sounding remarkably calm considering her previous histrionics. She was looking across at Darren, who was talking and joking with a group of men. 'I'll get it myself. He can't have listened to the message yet, or he wouldn't be looking so happy.'

Then, without another word for Carrie, she walked across the room towards her husband. Carrie looked after Lulu for a moment, hoping everything would turn out all right, but she couldn't stay any longer. Apart from her desire to get as far away from Nikos Kristallis as possible, she had to hurry—because she was already late picking up Danny. She turned and left through the front door.

The blast of cool air on her face felt good, and she took a

deep breath as she hurried down the marble steps of the swanky London town house to the street below.

It was a relief to be out of there, away from the piercing gaze of Nikos Kristallis. She'd felt his eyes burning a hole in her back all the way across the room. She shivered, imagining the predatory intensity in his expression as he'd watched her walking away from him.

She set off down the street quickly, her heels clicking on the pavement as she walked. Her fingers were surprisingly shaky as she buttoned up her denim jacket, and she had to resist the urge to look behind her to see if Nikos Kristallis had also left the party.

Why was he in London? Had he come to finish off what his father had started at the funeral? Maybe he wanted her to sign legal documents saying she would never pursue a connection with the Kristallis family?

She shook herself sharply and forced herself to put it all out of her mind for now. She couldn't be upset when she picked up Danny. It wouldn't be fair on him.

It was a long walk to his nursery, but with any luck she'd be able to hail a black cab. She turned the corner onto the main road and, amazingly, the first taxi she tried for pulled over. She gave the driver directions and climbed inside, suddenly uncomfortably aware of his eyes on her exposed legs. No wonder she'd got a cab so easily.

A few minutes later she paid the driver and jumped out into the crowd of London commuters hurrying along the pavement. She ducked into a doorway and pressed the buzzer.

'It's Carrie Thomas,' she said into the metal grille. 'I'm so sorry I'm late.'

With a long low buzz the lock released and she was into the building. Up one flight of stairs, and another security door later she was into Danny's nursery.

'Danny!' she cried, dashing over and picking the baby up.

Tears suddenly pricked in her eyes. It felt wonderful to hug him tight. She was sure she couldn't love him any more than she did, even if he was her own son.

Nikos Kristallis had wasted his time coming to London. Leonidas had always said he never wanted Danny to have anything to do with his Greek family. He had even made Sophie promise that if anything ever happened to him she'd never let them get their hands on him. Now, after meeting Cosmo and Nik, it was easy for Carrie to understand his reasons. And the least she could do for Sophie was to keep the promise she'd made to her husband before they were killed.

'Sorry I'm late,' she said, kissing the top of Danny's head and looking over his tousled brown hair into the face of the nursery assistant who had been sharing a picture book with him.

'That's all right,' the girl said. 'We've been having a nice story—haven't we, Danny?'

'You'll find the penalty for a late pick-up added to your bill, Miss Thomas.'

Carrie winced at the sound of the nursery manager's voice, but she plastered a smile onto her face before she looked round. She could hardly afford the nursery bill as it was.

'I'm sorry, Mrs Plewman,' she said. 'I got held up.'

'Hmm.' Mrs Plewman was unimpressed, making no attempt to hide her disapproval as she took in the short skirt of the sparkly red dress and the high-heeled sandals Carrie was still wearing. It was lucky she'd buttoned her denim jacket up to hide the low-cut front. 'I'm not running a charity here, Miss Thomas. Make sure it doesn't happen again. I've got my staff to think about, you know, but I'll waive the penalty payment just this once.'

'Thank you very much, Mrs Plewman. Have a nice

evening.' Carrie swung Danny's bag onto her back, along with her own backpack, and retrieved his buggy from the cupboard in the hallway. She couldn't wait to get home, to the safety and comfort of her flat.

Nik stood outside the building, frowning as an unexpected knot of anticipation twisted deep inside his gut. It was an unfamiliar sensation. He was about to lay eyes on his orphaned nephew for the first time—but why should that make him feel so unsettled?

He'd tried to picture the baby, but he just couldn't imagine what he was going to look like. He must have seen hundreds of babies in his life, but he'd never really looked at one properly. It would be very strange, returning to Greece with a child.

At last he saw Carrie Thomas emerge from the building, a dark-haired baby balanced on her hip and a folded buggy in her other hand. She glanced up and down the street, but the crowds of passing commuters hid him from her view.

His eyes fixed on the baby, his dead brother's son, and a peculiar numbness crept over him. That baby was his family. That baby was all his estranged brother Leonidas had left behind.

He started walking mechanically across the wide London pavement towards them, watching Carrie open the buggy with a practised flick of her wrist and snap the safety catch into place with her foot. All the time she was holding the baby tightly, engaging his attention with a constant stream of chatter and smiles.

'In you go, Danny,' she said, securing the child in the seat with the harness. 'Off we go—tube or bus? What do you think?' She glanced down the street at the queue by the bus stop.

'We still need to talk,' Nik said, coming up beside her.

She gasped in surprise. But the change in her body language made him sure she had recognised his voice before she looked round.

'Anyone would think you were stalking me!' She flicked her silky black fringe out of her eyes as she turned to him.

Nik looked down at her upturned face. Her almond-shaped eyes were a dazzling green, framed by arching brows and accentuated by long black lashes. He saw no sign of any make-up, and her flawless skin was incredibly pale, but it was lit somehow by a shimmering vitality.

It suddenly struck him as odd that she wasn't wearing any make-up. Surely that natural look didn't usually accompany the style of outfit she was wearing? But then, the denim jacket buttoned up to her chin and the sporty backpack seemed somewhat incongruous, too.

'You left before we finished our conversation,' Nik said.

'I don't have anything to say to you,' Carrie said. She looked so cool, standing there, but he knew from experience that her nubile body was anything but.

'Really?' Nik asked coldly. 'Tell me, why did you steal my brother's baby?'

'I… I…' Carrie stammered. She gripped the handles of the buggy tightly and took a step backwards across the pavement. 'I didn't *steal* Danny.'

She stared at him with wide, frightened eyes, suddenly looking even paler than before, if that was possible. She looked genuinely shocked by his words. Maybe she hadn't expected him to cut to the chase so quickly.

'What else would you call taking a baby that doesn't belong to you?' Nik asked. She couldn't really be surprised by his question, could she? In a moment she'd probably recover herself and start spouting a prepared speech in her defence.

'Babies don't belong *to* people!' Carrie gasped. 'They belong *with* the people who love them.'

'They belong with their family,' Nik said, hearing an edge of menace in his own voice as he took a step closer to her. 'And, like I said, you stole that baby from his family.'

'I didn't steal Danny,' Carrie said. 'When his parents were killed in the accident no one else wanted him.'

'No one else was given the chance,' Nik said.

'Your father—'

'My father is dead,' Nik interrupted coldly.

She drew in a sharp breath and stared up at him with puzzled green eyes. He had clearly startled her again, yet as he watched an expression of genuine sympathy passed across her face.

'I'm sorry,' she said. 'I—'

'No.' He cut her off abruptly with an impatient gesture. Her sympathy was the last thing he wanted.

His father had died suddenly just two months ago—four months after Leonidas had been killed in the motorway accident. Nik had had a heavy couple of months, taking over the areas of the family business that his father had still controlled, but things had finally been coming into order when he'd made an astonishing discovery amongst his father's personal papers. Leonidas had left behind an orphaned baby boy.

His gaze dropped to study the baby sitting in the buggy beside him—his brother's son—then he looked back up at the woman who had taken him.

She swallowed convulsively as their eyes met, obviously unnerved by him, and took an awkward step backwards into the crowd of commuters.

'Oi! Watch out!' a young man shouted as he careered into her back, nearly knocking her off her feet. Her stiletto heels didn't help, and she staggered forward, ramming the buggy hard into Nik's shins.

He swore in Greek. 'We need to get off the street,' he grated, hauling Carrie and the buggy sideways, into the relative safety of a café doorway. 'I'll signal my driver.'

'I'm not getting into a car with you.' Carrie shrugged his hand off her arm and bobbed down to check on Danny. 'I hardly know you,' she said, rising to her full heel-enhanced height and meeting his eye.

'We have to talk, and the street is not the place for it,' Nik said categorically. 'We'll go in here.' He indicated the stylish Italian café they were standing beside.

Carrie hesitated, biting her lip as she thought about it. She knew she'd have to talk to Nikos Kristallis some time, and quite honestly she'd rather get it over with.

'All right, but I'm not staying long.' She stooped to lift Danny out of his buggy. 'He'll be getting tired soon.'

A few minutes later they were sitting at a table in a quiet corner at the back of the café. Danny was balanced on Carrie's lap, making alarming lunges for her cappuccino.

She edged her chair away from the table, automatically shifting Danny out of reach of the hot drink, and glanced surreptitiously at Nik. She couldn't let herself believe that he really wanted to take Danny from her. It was six months since she'd contacted his family with news of Leonidas's death, and if Nik had genuinely intended to take Danny he wouldn't have waited so long to seek her out.

She was anxious to know what he really wanted, but she resisted the urge to ask him straight out. She wanted him to put his cards on the table first, to give her a chance to process what he said. But he'd hardly spoken since they'd sat down, and now he sipped his espresso in silence.

She couldn't help letting her eyes run over him, drinking in his amazing good looks. His designer suit hung immaculately on his lean, athletic body, emphasising the powerful width of his shoulders and the strong hard planes of his chest. The crisp white shirt he wore was the perfect foil for his bronzed skin, which glowed with an attractive health and vigour.

'I'm sorry about your father.' She was still wary of Nik, but she couldn't stand sitting in silence any longer. 'It must have been awful to lose him so soon after Leonidas.'

'Thank you for your concern,' Nik said, putting his espresso cup down and lifting cold blue eyes to meet hers. 'But I didn't come here to discuss my recent bereavement. I'm here to make arrangements regarding the child.'

'What do you mean?' A bolt of alarm shot through Carrie, making her heart lurch and her stomach churn unpleasantly.

'Danny belongs in Greece with me.'

Carrie swayed back in her chair, clutching Danny tightly as she stared at Nik in disbelief. It couldn't be true. He didn't really want Danny, did he?

'I'm sorry for your loss,' she said tautly. 'But Danny is staying with me.'

'No,' Nik said. 'Danny will return to Greece with me.'

'I understand you're upset, losing your brother and then your father so soon afterwards,' Carrie said, desperately holding on to her control. She mustn't let him see how upset she was rapidly becoming as the fact that he might be serious about taking Danny away from her started to sink in. 'But you didn't want Danny six months ago. You can't just decide to look after a child when it suits you.'

'Don't insult me,' Nik said, looking at her squarely. 'This isn't about me—it's about Danny's right to be part of his real family.'

'Are you saying I'm not his real family?' Carrie gasped.

'You're not his immediate family,' Nik said. 'And you are clearly not a suitable guardian.'

'What's that supposed to mean?' Carrie was shocked. 'You don't even know me!'

'I know that I caught you stealing,' he said.

'I wasn't stealing,' Carrie protested, thinking about Lulu's plaintive cry for help. She wasn't ashamed of trying to help her friend. It was none of Nik's business, but suddenly she decided to tell him everything. It would be better than having him speculate about what she'd been doing. 'Lulu asked me to do it. She was worried Darren would start a row with her over a message she'd left on his phone, so she wanted to delete it.'

She looked at Nik, to see if he'd accepted her explanation, but his expression was still unreadable.

'I realise it can't have been easy, looking after a baby on your own,' Nik said, abruptly changing the subject back to Danny. 'But—'

'It's been perfectly all right,' Carrie said quickly. 'Wonderful, in fact!' There was no way she'd ever admit how hard she'd found it looking after the baby alone, juggling work commitments and trying to make ends meet financially.

'I'm his uncle,' Nik said flatly. 'You are his cousin.'

'What difference does that make?' Carrie demanded. 'I was there when he needed someone. Nobody else wanted him then. Your father called him a brat…' She hesitated, looking down at the cold grey marble tabletop. She didn't want to remember her horrible meeting with Cosmo Kristallis. It was too hurtful to think about the way Danny's grandfather had viewed him.

'You met my father?' Nik asked sharply. 'When?'

Something in the tone of his voice made Carrie's eyes fly

back to his face. A muscle pulsed at his jaw and a line of tension creased his brow.

'He came to the funeral,' Carrie replied carefully. At that moment she felt more than a little afraid of how he might react.

'Last November,' Nik said, after a slight pause.

'Yes.' Carrie looked at him warily, wondering whether talking about his father and brother was painful for him. He hadn't shown any sign of it, but it was impossible to know what was going on behind his implacable expression.

'What did my father say to you?' Nik asked.

'Not much,' Carrie replied cautiously. 'He simply said that he felt it would be in Danny's best interests if he remained in England with his mother's family.'

'Really?' Nik gave a sudden ironic burst of laughter. 'I knew my father, and I doubt very much that those were his exact words.'

'What your father said wasn't funny.' How could he be laughing at a time like this?

'I'm sure it wasn't.' There was a hard glint in his blue eyes. 'But listening to you putting such measured, almost caring words into his mouth is amusing.'

'Your father didn't care about Danny at all!' Carrie said. 'He wished Danny had never been born!'

'Probably,' said Nik. 'But I do not share his view on that.'

'If that's the case, where were you after the accident? You didn't care enough to come then!' She was so upset that she didn't realise her voice was rising. Suddenly Danny made another lunge for her cappuccino.

'Careful, Danny!' She pulled him back, but in her haste her own elbow caught against the cup. It rattled in the saucer, and a moment later the table was awash with foamy coffee.

She jumped to her feet to avoid the flood of coffee, quickly checking none of the scalding liquid had come anywhere near Danny.

'Hot drinks and babies—not a good combination,' Nik remarked smoothly. He turned and lifted a commanding hand to catch the attention of the girl behind the counter. 'We need a cloth here.'

Carrie hugged Danny and looked at the mess she'd made. Nik had got her so upset that she hardly knew what to think or say. She dabbed her paper napkin into the flood of liquid, but it was saturated in a second, and it didn't stop the coffee running off the marble tabletop onto the café floor.

'I have to go.' She bent to pick up her bag, barely registering that it was sitting in a pool of coffee, and turned to retrieve the buggy—but Nik was already holding it. 'I'm really sorry about the mess,' she said, as the waitress appeared with a large cloth.

She turned and made her way outside.

'We haven't finished this conversation yet,' Nik said, joining her back on the busy London pavement.

'Yes, we have.' She tugged the buggy away from him before he could react. 'I'm taking Danny home.'

'I'll drive you,' Nik said.

'No, thank you.' She glanced up the road, and relief washed over her as she saw a bus approaching. 'Here's my bus now. Danny likes the bus.'

Without waiting for a reply she hoisted the buggy up under her arm and, hanging on to Danny tightly, made a dash for the bus stop.

He laughed, and settled on her lap happily as the bus pulled away. Out of the corner of her eye Carrie could still see Nik, standing on the pavement. She stared straight ahead, resisting the urge to look. A shiver ran down her spine as the bus rumbled to a halt alongside him.

It was true that Danny liked the bus, but she could think of many nicer things than sitting cramped, with a buggy gripped awkwardly between her knees, trying to keep a wriggling baby out of the damp patch of coffee on her short red dress, all the while knowing that those piercing Greek eyes were fixed on her from behind the grimy window of a London bus.

She knew she should have stayed longer—to find out exactly how serious Nikos Kristallis was about taking Danny. But right now all she wanted was to be as far away from him as possible.

Nik watched the bus labouring through the heavy traffic. He knew that Carrie was aware of him, standing there, but she was looking forward, refusing to acknowledge his presence.

It was only a couple of hours since he'd met her, but already Carrie Thomas had become strangely significant in his life. She had known Leonidas while he'd been lost to Nik. She'd even met his father. And now she had his nephew.

Nik saw that Danny had spotted him standing there. He had no hesitation at all in staring right back at Nik. His bright button eyes were fixed on him, and he turned his head and leant forward to keep him in view as long as possible when the bus finally moved off into the stream of traffic.

That baby boy was all that was left of Leonidas. Carrie Thomas could take the child home tonight, but it wouldn't be long before he was taking him home to Greece.

CHAPTER THREE

CARRIE hurried along the street towards Danny's nursery. It had been an exhausting day, and all she could think about was collecting Danny and taking him safely back to the refuge of her flat. Normally she loved her work, but she was so tired and stressed, after a sleepless night worrying about what Nikos Kristallis meant to do, that the day had seemed endless.

She told herself that Nik didn't really mean to take Danny away from her. After all, if he was genuinely interested in Danny, surely he would have made an appearance before now? And even if he really did want Danny, he couldn't just take him. He might be rich and powerful, but he would still have to make arrangements through the proper channels—otherwise it would be kidnapping.

She was starting to regret leaving the previous evening before anything had been resolved. Not knowing Nik's intentions was killing her, and she'd been on edge all day, half expecting Nik to contact her at any moment. Every time the phone had rung she'd nearly jumped out of her skin. Her thoughts had kept turning to Danny, and how much she loved him, and by the end of the afternoon her nerves had been in shreds. Now, as she made her way quickly through the crowds of commuters hurrying along the street, she was desperate to reach Danny and wrap him safely in her arms.

Suddenly she stopped in her tracks. She stared across the wide London street, momentarily unable to believe what she saw.

Nikos Kristallis was standing on the doorstep of Danny's nursery, leaning forward slightly as if he was talking into the intercom.

Buses and taxis flashed across her line of vision, making it hard to see clearly. She couldn't be right. She was so stressed her eyes were playing tricks on her.

No, it was real. The heavy door was swinging closed behind Nikos Kristallis, but just before it slammed shut she saw him heading swiftly up the stairs. He was going to take Danny!

Carrie's heart thudded in her chest and she broke into a run, weaving in and out of people as she sprinted along the pavement towards the crossing. The lights were just changing from red to amber, and four lanes of traffic started revving up as the last pedestrians cleared the road. She dashed out anyway, ignoring the angry shouts and blaring horns as she focussed on the nursery door. If Nik came back out carrying Danny she had to reach him quickly. She could not lose him in the crowd.

She skidded to a halt at the doorway and pressed impatiently on the buzzer, panting for breath.

'It's Carrie Thomas!' she gasped. 'Please let me in.'

She was already leaning heavily on the door, and the instant the lock released she was through, bounding up the stairs two at a time. She couldn't let Nikos Kristallis get to Danny.

She burst through the door at the top of the stairs and dashed along the corridor to the baby room. Danny was there on the play mat—safe and sound.

She called his name and he looked round, but the moment his eyes found her his little face crumpled into tears.

'Up you come, poppet,' the young nursery assistant said, picking him up before Carrie was able to unlatch the child safety gate and get into the room. 'He hasn't been himself today,' she continued, speaking to Carrie. 'Been a bit grizzly all day. I think he might be teething.'

'Poor little thing,' Carrie said, holding out her arms to take Danny from the young woman. She hugged him tightly, feeling some of her anxiety ease as she pressed her face against his hair. Then she held him away from her and looked at him carefully. His cheeks were flushed, but he had already stopped crying.

Voices coming along the corridor suddenly caught her attention, and she remembered with a sick feeling that Nikos Kristallis was in the building.

'And this is our baby unit,' she heard Mrs Plewman saying right behind her. 'It has excellent facilities, and most importantly one member of staff for every two babies.'

Carrie turned on the spot and found herself staring up into the face of Nikos Kristallis. He looked completely indifferent to the fact that she had discovered him at the nursery—a place he had no reasonable reason to be—and her concern over his presence suddenly switched to anger. He was so arrogant that he thought normal rules didn't apply to him.

'What are you doing here?' She rounded on him. 'You have no right to be anywhere near Danny!'

'Mrs Plewman has been kind enough to give me a tour of the nursery,' he replied smoothly, throwing the nursery manager a charming smile.

'I don't want this man anywhere near Danny.' She spoke urgently to Mrs Plewman. 'I don't trust him—he wants to take Danny away, back to Greece with him.'

'I have a right to see where my nephew is being cared for,' Nik replied.

'But that's not why you're here,' Carrie said, hugging Danny protectively and glaring up at him.

'Your nephew?' Mrs Plewman said. Her deferential manner indicated that up until that point she had been impressed by Nik, but now Carrie's reaction had given her pause for thought.

'Yes, Danny is my nephew,' Nik confirmed, but his sharp blue eyes were fixed on Carrie. 'What other reason have I got to come here?'

'To take Danny,' Carrie said. 'To get your hands on him when I'm not around.'

'You really are overreacting,' Nik said with infuriating blandness. 'As Mrs Plewman will tell you, unauthorised people are not permitted to collect the children left in her care. And, quite apart from that, if that was my intention why would I choose to come at the exact time you are due to arrive?'

'So that the staff see us together? To make yourself seem familiar? To give you credibility?' Carrie rattled off the first things that came into her mind.

'Being seen with you would give me *credibility*?' Nik repeated. His eyes swept across her disparagingly, and his disdainful expression made it all too clear what he thought of that idea.

'I'm taking Danny home now,' Carrie said stiffly. 'And just to be sure you understand—you are not to come here again. In fact, I don't want you bothering us at all.'

Carrie didn't wait for a reply. She knew she ought to talk to Mrs Plewman properly, to make it absolutely clear that no one but her should ever collect Danny. But at that moment she simply had to get away.

She let the door swing shut as she walked through and bent to pull the buggy out of the cupboard. Suddenly Nik was beside her again, taking it out of her hand.

'Let me,' he said. 'It's rather dangerous to carry so much on the stairs at once.'

'I've got it, thank you,' Carrie snapped, reaching out for the buggy.

'I'm here, and I can help,' Nik said firmly. 'What's the point of needlessly risking your neck, and more importantly my nephew's neck, when you don't have to?'

'I'm not risking anyone's neck,' Carrie said, but she turned and started down the stairs. The sooner she got outside, the sooner she could catch the bus home.

'I'll give you a lift home,' Nik said, once they'd stepped out onto the street.

'Are you mad?' Carrie gasped, pulling the buggy out of his grasp and flicking it open with an angry gesture that revealed all her pent-up emotions. 'I'm not going anywhere with you!'

'We still have to talk,' Nik replied. 'You ran off before we'd finished yesterday. I know when you collect Danny, and it seemed an appropriate time and place to meet.'

'You had no right to go into his nursery.' Carrie hugged the one-year-old protectively. 'And Mrs Plewman had no business letting you in!' She knew that wasn't exactly fair to the nursery manager. But even as she tried to reassure herself that Mrs Plewman would never have let a stranger take Danny a shiver ran down her spine. Nik had clearly been doing an excellent job of charming her. There was no way to tell what would have happened if Carrie hadn't arrived when she had.

'My nephew has no business being in that appalling place,' Nik replied. 'I wanted to see for myself what kind of care he's been receiving, and frankly I was not impressed. He will certainly not be spending any more time in that dreadful environment. That is not the way a Kristallis child is cared for.'

'His name may be Kristallis,' Carrie said, bristling at his

harsh judgement of the nursery she had so carefully chosen for Danny. 'But Sophie and Leonidas didn't want him brought up like a Kristallis.'

'His parents are dead. He is my responsibility now,' Nik stated, his expression hard and unreadable.

'Now? He's nearly one!' Carrie exclaimed. 'How very responsible of you to miss the first year of his life!'

She knew she had hit a nerve the second the words were out of her mouth.

A change came over Nik so profound it made her blood suddenly run cold.

'I don't intend to miss any more of his life,' Nik grated. 'Now, we need to find somewhere to talk.'

'Danny needs to go home.' Carrie looked at his flushed face and smoothed his hair back from his forehead. It felt uncomfortably warm. 'It's not fair to keep him out if he's feeling under the weather.'

'Then I'll give you a lift home.' Nik indicated a sleek black limousine that was just pulling up next to the pavement. 'When the child is settled, we can talk.'

'I don't need a lift, thank you,' Carrie said. 'We'll be perfectly all right on the bus, just the same as every other day.'

'Don't be ridiculous,' Nik said. 'Just because you seem to have taken an irrational dislike to me, it doesn't mean my nephew has to suffer the unnecessary discomfort of a public bus.'

'There's nothing wrong with buses. Not everyone has a private limo, you know.' She glanced down and caught sight of her reflection in the tinted window of the long black car.

Suddenly she remembered seeing Nik going in to the nursery. If he had taken Danny and put him into that car she might never have seen him again. They could have driven right past her and she'd never have known Danny was hidden from view behind that sinister dark glass. 'I'm not getting into a car with you. I hardly know you.'

'The child doesn't look well,' Nik said. 'Don't let your pride and petty dislike of me make you ignore what is best for Danny.'

'He's not sick.' Carrie bit her lip as she studied Danny and pressed her hand against his face again. 'Teething can make babies hot and bothered, but it doesn't mean he's sick.'

Just at that moment the heavens opened, and it began to pour with rain. Danny howled as the first huge drops started to splash his face, and Carrie looked around in dismay. Rush hour was in full swing, and the thought of a crowded bus or tube train full of disgruntled commuters with dripping umbrellas, jostling her and tripping over Danny's buggy, was simply awful.

But she couldn't accept a lift with Nik. It was true that she hardly knew him, and she was still suspicious as to his motives for going into the nursery. Then Danny began to cry more loudly, and when she touched his cheek to soothe him it felt even hotter. She really ought to get him home quickly.

'I'm giving you a lift home whether you like it or not. Tell my driver where you live.'

Despite her protestations Nik swept Danny out of her arms and stooped to secure him in a child's car seat, which was already in position in the back of the limousine. Carrie bit her lip, wondering what to do. It was pouring with rain and Danny needed to get home. She'd be with him all the time in the limousine, and it would be a lot quicker than the bus.

The driver had the buggy and was struggling to fold it. Carrie took it from him and collapsed it down with a couple of swift and practised gestures. She didn't want the driver to pinch his fingers. Though if it had been Nik trying to fold it that would have been a different matter.

A minute later she was riding in comfort in the back of the luxury limousine with Nik. Danny was crying at the top of his lungs, and nothing she did seemed to make him feel any better.

The nursery staff had thought Danny was teething. They had years of experience with babies and always seemed to know what they were talking about. But Carrie was beginning to worry that Danny might be ill. He really didn't look right. But then it had probably been unsettling for him to see her arguing with Nik.

'You shouldn't have gone into the nursery.' Carrie spoke suddenly. 'You should have waited for me. You knew I'd only be a couple of minutes.'

'You wouldn't have taken me inside,' Nik replied. 'I didn't like seeing him in that place, being cared for by strangers,' he added. 'He should be looked after by family.'

'Those people aren't strangers to Danny,' Carrie said, pulling a toy out of her bag and trying in vain to cheer the baby up. 'The nursery might be a bit old and shabby, but I chose it because you can tell that the staff really love the children. Also, they have a fantastic ratio of staff to children—much better than any of the other places I looked at.'

'It's not the same as being with his family,' Nik insisted.

'You may be a blood relation to Danny,' Carrie said, 'but you're the stranger to him—not the nursery ladies.'

'That's something that's going to change,' Nik said.

Carrie looked at him sharply. Something in his tone of voice made her nervous. The nursery didn't seem such a safe place any more—how could she know it was safe to leave Danny there when she had to work?

Suddenly Danny upped the volume of his wailing, and all her attention flipped back to him. Poor child. She couldn't bear to think of him sick. And if he was poorly, rather than teething, she wouldn't be able to travel with him to Spain tomorrow with a client. She hated letting anyone down, especially a valued friend and client like Elaine, but Danny was more important than anything else.

'Here.' Nik picked up a bag of baby toys and handed them to Carrie.

She took the bag and pulled out a colourful rattle that seemed to be battery operated, with flashing lights and music. Danny usually enjoyed noisy toys.

To Carrie's relief, after a last couple of sobs he fell silent, reached out a chubby little hand and took the rattle. She pushed the 'on' button, starting the flashing and music.

Danny began howling instantly.

'Maybe not the best choice of toy.' A patronising edge to Nik's voice set Carrie's nerves on edge. 'I don't imagine all that noise and flashing is very good if he has a headache.'

Carrie gritted her teeth and leant forward to switch off the wretched device. Danny wasn't the only one with a headache. She could feel the tension starting to clamp round her head and shoulders like a steel vice.

'There's no "off" switch!' she said in exasperation. 'Oh! I hate noisy toys you can't stop once they've started.'

'I'm sure he'll enjoy it when he's feeling better.' Nik was infuriatingly calm as he bent forward and studied Danny.

His face was only a few inches away from Danny's and although he wasn't doing anything but looking intently at the baby he seemed to catch his attention. The baby stopped crying, and while he didn't look exactly happy, he wasn't getting himself into a frenzy any more.

Carrie tried to ignore the feeling of foreboding that crept over her as she watched Nik and Danny staring at each other. The sudden silence as the musical rattle finally reached the end of its song seemed horribly ominous.

'Danny can't go back to that place.' Nik spoke without turning to look at her, but that didn't weaken the impact of his words.

'He has to—so I can go to work.' Carrie had to earn a living. It was as simple as that. She straightened her shoulders, refusing to let herself be intimidated by Nikos Kristallis and his self-important attitude.

'What happened to the rest of your family?' he asked.

The question caught her off-guard. For some reason she had assumed he knew all about how she had ended up alone with Danny.

'My mother died when I was very young.' She spoke steadily, knowing it was best to be open with him, but she was determined not to let any emotion show in her voice. She didn't need to lay her heartfelt feelings out for him to scrutinise.

'And your father?' he prompted.

'My father couldn't cope.' She thought unhappily how he hadn't even managed to come to the funeral six months ago. 'He left me with my aunt and uncle and their daughter, Sophie.'

'And you grew up as part of their family?'

'Sophie was like a sister to me.' Tears suddenly pricked in Carrie's eyes and she dropped her gaze slightly, determined not to let Nik see. Her relationship with her aunt and uncle had never been warm. Somehow the infrequent but unsettling appearances of her father bringing them money for her upkeep had seen to that. But she had loved Sophie.

'You lost a great deal in that car accident.'

Something in Nik's voice made her look up. Their eyes met and a tremor ran through her. For a long moment she couldn't look away, despite the knowledge that he'd seen the tears swimming in her eyes.

Then Danny made a sound, and suddenly the spell was broken.

She looked back at the baby, and the love she felt for him welled up inside her. She wouldn't let Nik take him from her. She couldn't be parted from Danny now.

She'd loved him from the moment she saw him, and had revelled in their time together since then—even though hardly anyone had been truly supportive about her decision to take on an orphaned baby. Sometimes it felt as if they were all watching her, waiting to see how she would perform.

Her friends from the small town where she had grown up kept telling her to return home, where there were people who could help her out if she needed it. They told her it was irresponsible to try bringing up a baby alone in the city, especially as she had no experience and no one to help her. But Carrie had worked very hard to escape her painful roots, and she'd do almost anything to avoid going back.

She'd made a very different life for herself in London. She had been enjoying her new lifestyle, and found a real sense of achievement from her increasingly successful career as a personal trainer. Her London friends knew nothing about her childhood, and that was how she wanted it, but it meant they had no way to understand why looking after her orphaned cousin was so important to her.

Danny looked a bit better now. His cheeks were still flushed, and his wispy brown fringe was sticking damply to his forehead, but for the moment he was all right. They'd be home very soon, and she had to admit—to herself, anyway—that this way of travelling was better for a grizzly child than crowded, unreliable public transport.

Looking at Danny, comfy and secure in the car seat, she suddenly wondered why Nik had a car seat in his limousine. The thought that he might be married with children made her stomach lurch. Surely a family man wanting to adopt his nephew would have a better chance in court than a bachelor businessman?

'Do you and your wife have children?' Carrie asked abruptly.

'Why do you ask?' Nik said, the expression on his face telling Carrie he had misinterpreted her interest.

'You have a car seat,' she said flatly. She had no intention of letting him see how much the meaningful gleam in his eyes had suddenly made her heart beat faster. No doubt Nikos Kristallis was used to women throwing themselves at him—but she had more to think about than just herself.

He might be the most gorgeous man she'd ever seen, and there was no question that she had found him overwhelmingly attractive at first, but that had been before she'd learned his identity. That kiss in Darren's study had been extraordinary for her—she was inexperienced and had had no idea a kiss could affect her so profoundly—but at that point she hadn't discovered the threat he posed to her and Danny.

'I am not married, and do not at present have children.' Nik spoke smoothly, but his deep blue eyes were narrowed and fixed on her altogether too sharply. 'However, we can continue our discussion about my marital status later.'

'I thought the discussion was already finished.' The last thing Carrie wanted was for Nikos Kristallis to start getting ideas. Or, even worse, to think that she was getting ideas! 'Your marital status is of no interest to me,' she added quickly.

'Really?' Nik drawled, 'I thought you asked for a reason—a more pressing one than why I have a child's car seat in my limousine.'

'What possible reason could I have?' she replied. 'I was just making conversation.'

Nik smiled. It was a supercilious smile, with an infuriating lift to his straight black eyebrows. She turned to look out through the tinted window at the rainy street outside the limousine, and was desperately trying to think of a suitably cutting remark to put him in his place when his sudden movement towards Danny took her by surprise.

'What are you doing? Don't undo his seatbelt—it isn't safe!' she gasped.

'How else will we take him inside?' Nik sounded genuinely surprised. 'I assume that my driver has brought us to the correct address.'

Carrie realised with a shock that the limousine had stopped moving. She glanced back through the tinted glass of the window and saw that the street she had been looking at was her own! They were parked outside her home.

'Thank you for the ride,' she said, trying to sound cool even though she suddenly felt very silly. 'I'll take Danny now.'

'All right,' Nik said. 'I'll bring your things.'

A gust of cold rainy wind blew into the limousine as the driver opened her door. She lifted Danny up, slid across the black leather seat, and stepped out onto the wet pavement.

'Thank you very much,' she said to the driver.

'We need to get Danny inside, where it's warm and dry,' Nik said. 'Then we can decide on the best thing to do—whether he needs to see a doctor or—'

'*We?*' Carrie echoed, her hackles instantly rising at his arrogant assumption that he was coming inside with her to decide what was best for Danny. She was his guardian. Nikos Kristallis didn't even know him. '*I'll* take him inside,' she said firmly. 'There's no need for you to go to any more trouble. Thank you for your help,' she added, in a voice she knew didn't sound convincingly grateful.

She reached out to take the pushchair from Nik, but he held it out of her reach.

'I'm not going anywhere until I make sure my nephew is all right,' Nik said flatly. 'Now, stop wasting time and let's get Danny inside.'

Nik sat in the only armchair and watched Carrie tidying her flat with quick efficiency. She was still dressed in the tight-fitting exercise gear that must be what she wore for work. He felt his body stir with pure male appreciation as he admired her long-limbed yet curvaceous feminine shape.

There was no doubt that she was very well toned, and there was something incredibly sexy about her swift and supple movements as she worked systematically around the single space that seemed to serve as kitchen, dining area and living room.

The area was small, but as Carrie put Danny's things away Nik saw that it was very well organised. The stylish design of the place still spoke of Carrie's carefree days as a young single woman, without any attachments or responsibilities, but the child's things were fitted in neatly and looked as if they belonged.

Danny was sleeping in the bedroom. A dose of infant pain-killer, a drink of warm milk and a long cuddle were all that it had taken to send him off into what looked like a very peaceful sleep. Carrie had spoken of the everyday ailments that babies sometimes suffered from—quick to come and equally quick to go. She'd seemed to know what she was talking about.

Nik had deliberately kept out of her way while she took care of the baby, giving her the space and time she needed. He had been impressed, and rather surprised by what he'd seen.

Since his first meeting with Carrie she'd seemed quite jumpy, and full of nervous energy. He hadn't expected her to be so calm and loving towards the child. Somehow he just hadn't taken her for the warm, motherly type.

But recognising that Carrie did have some good points as

a carer did not change Nik's plan. This was not the way he wanted his nephew to be brought up. No matter how well intentioned Carrie was, she was on her own, and she still worked full time. How could she possibly give the child what he, with all the might of Kristallis Industries behind him, could give?

For instance, this flat was so small, and there was only one bedroom. The cot took up most of the available floor space, and there was no chance that an additional bed, even a child-sized one, could be squeezed in next to Carrie's double bed when Danny got older.

His blood stirred at the thought of Carrie's bed—or rather at the image of Carrie lying in it. It was a small double, but a double none the less, and that meant it was made for sharing. He flexed his fingers to prevent his hands clenching at the suddenly intolerable thought of Carrie sharing that bed with anyone.

'That'll do for now,' she said, startling him out of his thoughts as she paused for a moment with her hands resting on the curve of her hips. 'Coffee?'

'That would be perfect,' Nik replied smoothly, despite being caught deep in thought, and watched as she turned to fill the kettle with water.

God, but she was gorgeous! With her back still towards him, she stretched up into a high cupboard for the mugs. The simple action made her top ride up, separating from the black stretch pants that clung so alluringly to her shapely bottom and legs. Several inches of pale skin were suddenly revealed, and hot desire for her slammed into him, hard and unexpected.

Of course she was a good-looking woman. He was a red-blooded male and he'd been aware of that from the second he'd laid eyes on her. But suddenly he wanted her with a power that knocked the breath right out of him.

He remembered the way that pale skin had felt beneath his

fingers, the way that supple body had melded so electrifyingly to his. He thought about yesterday's kiss, and instantly his heart was thumping powerfully in his chest.

He hadn't meant that kiss to be more than a simple distraction to enable him to replace the mobile phone in Darren's pocket. But once he'd been holding her lithe body in his arms, and she had moulded herself to him like a second skin, his animal desire had threatened to take over.

And if he didn't get himself under control soon, the urge to seize her and kiss her again might take over now.

But would that be such a bad thing? The rational part of his mind told him to avoid making a difficult situation more complicated. There was more at stake here than a passing fling with a gorgeous woman.

But Nik wasn't known for playing it safe. His instinct told him to pull her into his arms and kiss her senseless. She wouldn't object if he did. He'd seen her looking at him with those sexy green eyes, and felt the way she'd responded to him the previous day.

'It's only instant coffee, I'm afraid,' Carrie said, twisting round to look over her shoulder at him.

She sucked in a startled breath and stared at him warily. The raw intensity of his expression made her pulse start to race. He looked dangerous. He looked ready to spring up out of the chair and come towards her. What did he mean to do?

'Instant is fine.' Nik's eyes skimmed over her in a way that made her skin start to heat up alarmingly.

Carrie gripped the edge of the counter and turned back to the coffee, trying to ignore the mixture of anxiety and excitement that was suddenly coursing through her.

Why was he looking at her like that? A shiver ran down the length of her spine and she fought the urge to fidget. She knew she was being silly, overreacting like a teenager. But she still felt self-conscious. She could feel his eyes burning a trail over every part of her body.

'Do you take milk and sugar?' she asked, without looking round.

'No, thank you,' Nik replied.

She needed milk for her own coffee, and she stepped across the tiny kitchenette to the fridge, acutely conscious of his gaze following every movement she made.

It was ridiculous! She was a fitness instructor—used to people watching her body. Every day people focussed on the way she moved, and studied the precise alignment of her anatomy.

But as she bent down to pull a carton of milk out of the fridge she was aware of her own body in a way she never had been before. The feel of his eyes on her made every action seem loaded with sexuality.

She knew he wasn't watching her with his attention on her posture or her muscle recruitment. She knew he was thinking about sex. Her whole body started to tremble.

She straightened up and turned back to the counter to pour a dash of milk into her mug, but her feverish body didn't co-operate with its usual precision. The carton slipped from her fingers and jolted against the counter, splashing milk over her hand and up her arm.

'Let me help,' Nik said, suddenly coming up behind her.

'It's all right,' Carrie said huskily, staring almost blankly at her milky hand. She was completely aware of Nik standing behind her. He was so close. If she reached for a paper towel she'd collide with his chest. His arms would close around her and they'd be kissing with all the fire of their first encounter.

He'd caught her unawares in Darren's study, and her own body had shocked her by responding so fervently. She knew it would be crazy to let it happen again, but an intoxicating yearning was building deep inside her. If he pulled her into his arms again she feared she'd be lost to reason.

'Let me see,' Nik said, taking a step closer and placing his hands gently on either side of her waist.

Carrie gasped and spun round to face him. As she turned his hands skimmed the circumference of her waist, tracing the narrow band of exposed skin. The sensation of his fingers brushing against her bare flesh set off a chain reaction of tremors quaking through her body, and she couldn't stop shaking. She knew he must be able to feel it because he was still touching her waist.

She was holding her milky hand out in front of her gingerly, almost as if it was injured. Her palm was facing upwards with the fingers curled over, instinctively trying to contain the spilt liquid.

She swayed as Nik released his hold on her waist, but almost immediately his hands moved to support her again. He placed one gently under her forearm and the other he brought up carefully to cup her milky hand.

Carrie stared down at his bronze fingers curling round her. He was only holding her hand, but somehow it seemed too intimate. A knot of anticipation tightened deep within her and she licked her lips nervously.

'The paper towels are over there,' she said, hardly recognising the husky tones of her own voice.

'It's only a bit of milk,' he murmured. 'We don't need a towel.'

Slowly, ever so slowly, he lifted her hand up to his lips. She followed the movement with her eyes, hardly daring to think what he meant to do.

Suddenly she found herself looking across her palm,

straight into his vibrant blue eyes. She could feel his hot breath on the skin of her hand and she swallowed hard.

His lips parted and, still ensnared by his burning gaze, she watched his tongue emerge to lick a drop of milk from a finger.

She sucked in a startled breath and thought vaguely of pulling her hand away. But before her whirling thoughts had a chance to settle he drew the finger slowly into his mouth.

Sensation flooded her, and the heat of his mouth seemed to radiate through her whole body. The sinuous feel of his tongue moving against her skin sent a tidal wave of longing crashing over her. Without realising what she was doing her own lips parted and a small sigh escaped.

Nik's eyes were fixed on her, registering her response, and immediately he pulled her closer. He released her finger and moved his open mouth over the skin of her palm, nibbling and teasing with his lips and tongue.

Carrie trembled. She didn't want Nik to know the effect he was having on her over-excited nerve-endings, but it was more than she could do to tug her hand out of her grasp. He pulled her closer and brought his lips to the sensitive skin on the inside of her wrist, flicking the tip of his tongue over the beating point of her pulse.

Her breathing quickened, echoing her racing heart, and she closed her eyes, trying to shut out the reaction that was rapidly taking over her whole body. But, instead of grounding her, the action left her completely cut off from any reality apart from Nikos Kristallis. She was only aware of how he was making her feel.

She wanted him to kiss her! She wanted to feel his hot mouth covering hers, feel his tongue moving against hers.

Her breath was coming in short sharp gasps, and although she tried, she just couldn't think about anything else. Suddenly she realised he had let go of her hand. Her eyes flew open, and she saw his face was only inches from her own.

The moment seemed frozen in time, yet only lasted a second. In slow motion she saw him lift his hands to cup her cheeks and incline his head slightly, ready to kiss her.

Then his mouth closed over hers, and her world exploded into a startling frenzy of desire.

Her lips were already parted as his mouth came down to kiss her, and their tongues were suddenly writhing together in an erotic dance. Her body trembled and she clung to his strong arms for support, overwhelmed by the blood singing wildly in her ears, the fervent uprising of excitement that threatened to completely engulf her.

She had one last coherent thought—she hadn't imagined the effect of his kiss yesterday. Then she closed her eyes and was lost as a rush of sensations powered through her boneless body.

Her hands slipped up to his broad shoulders and she pressed herself close to him. His body felt so good, so hard and strong against hers. Her arms reached further round and she let her hands slide slowly across his strong back, feeling the heat of his body through the fabric of his shirt. She yearned to touch his naked skin, feel the play of his muscles beneath her questing fingertips.

All the time they kept on kissing, an ardent expression of their mutual desire, but she was getting increasingly breathless and her head was starting to spin. At last he pulled away from her lips, and she heard his breathing was as ragged as hers.

She opened her eyes to find herself staring into Nik's face, and suddenly plummeted back to the real world with a sickening jolt. Had she completely lost her mind? Why had she let Nik kiss her like that?

'What are you doing?' she gasped, hearing her voice rise with a hint of panic.

'Nothing you didn't like, that's for sure,' Nik replied, his cheeks darkening with strong emotion.

'I didn't like it.' Carrie took a step backwards and bumped hard into the kitchen counter. What was happening to her? She'd never let herself get so carried away before. She'd had no idea it was possible to be so utterly overcome by naked desire that she lost track of the world around her.

'You did like it,' Nik said, his blue eyes burning dangerously. 'And you'd like it if I did it again. Don't lie to me, Carrie. I know what I felt—what we felt. The chemistry between us is incredibly powerful.'

'There's nothing between us,' Carrie said.

She stared at him, battling with conflicting thoughts and emotions. She didn't *want* there to be anything between them. After all, Nik had barged into her life upsetting her and threatening to take Danny. But at the same time all she wanted to do was step back into his arms and let him kiss her again—let him do anything he wanted with her.

No man had ever had such a powerful physical effect on her. But it wasn't just physical. She'd had no idea that her body could respond with such raw sexual energy to a man, but her mind was overwhelmed, too. When she was in his arms all she could think about was how good it was, how incredible he was making her feel.

'A moment ago you wanted that just as much as I did,' Nik said.

'You're wrong,' Carrie muttered, leaning back against the counter and looking down at the floor. Oh, *why* had she let him kiss her?

'I'm not wrong.' He took a step closer and brushed his hand against her cheek.

An instant response shivered through her, but she straightened her shoulders and stared back at him defiantly, refusing to give in to her body's desires.

'You're crazy!' she said. 'Crazy and arrogant and…and I think it's time you left.'

'I'm not leaving yet,' Nik said flatly. 'We still have things to discuss.'

'I'm not talking about it any more,' Carrie said. 'It was a mistake and it will never happen again.'

'Why are you making such a big deal out of it?' Nik asked. 'I told you I'm not married, and neither are you. Do you have a boyfriend?' he added suddenly, looking at her sharply. 'Is that why you're so upset?'

'No!' she squeaked. 'But that's none of your business. Besides, I already told you—your marital status is of no interest to me.'

'You don't care whether your lovers are married?' he asked.

'Of course I do,' she said, thinking it would be a big mistake to let Nik know she was a virgin. 'But, since you are never going to be my lover, why should I care whether you are married or not?' She felt a dark prickle of excitement skitter through her body at the idea of being in bed with him, but she shied away from the thought in horror, appalled at her body's reaction.

'Don't be so sure about that. We both know what we felt just now,' he said. 'Besides, in the car you asked me straight out whether or not I was married. So I think I can be forgiven for assuming you were interested.'

'I just thought you must have children,' Carrie said quickly, thinking back to the awkward journey in the limousine. 'What with the car seat and the toys. That's all.'

'They were for Danny, of course.' Nik seemed surprised. 'How can you think I would come unprepared for him?'

'Prepared for what?' Carrie said in alarm. 'You went to Danny's nursery without my permission. You were planning to kidnap him! That's why you had those things!'

'You really have the most overactive imagination.' Nik's smile didn't reach his eyes.

'Then how come you were discussing who could take children out of the nursery with Mrs Plewman?' Carrie demanded in a stiff and quiet voice. 'She obviously told you an unauthorised person couldn't take a child—so you must have asked about it.'

'I already told you—I wanted to see where he was cared for,' Nik replied. 'I wanted to assess how safe he was there.'

'You *were* going to take him away!' Carrie gasped, convinced that had been Nik's intention all along. What if he really had driven Danny away in the limousine before she'd got there? Her chest felt so tight she could barely breathe, and her stomach churned in horror. 'You were going to abduct him and take him back to Greece!'

She'd been suspicious of Nikos Kristallis from the start, but he'd deliberately distracted and confused her with his magnetic sex appeal. Now the threat to Danny seemed all too real. Next to that, nothing else was important.

'I'll never let you have him!' she cried.

'I would not take the child without your knowledge,' Nik said, his glittering blue eyes darkening with anger. 'What kind of man do you take me for?'

'The kind of man who seduces someone just to get close to her baby!' Carrie declared.

'Danny is *not* your baby,' Nik said. 'And what happened between us had nothing to do with the child.'

'You have no more right to him than me.' Anger was rising up to take over from the sick horror that still swamped her at the thought of losing Danny. 'You're never going to take him from me!'

She planted her hands on her hips and matched his angry stare. He'd soon discover that she wasn't just going to step aside and give up a child she loved like her own.

'This is ridiculous! Why are you making such a drama out of it?' Nik asked. 'I give you my word that I will not abduct Danny and take him out of the country without your prior knowledge.'

'So you're going to tell me first, then take him?' Carrie asked. 'Great—that makes me feel a lot better!'

'No, I'm still working on the basis that we can behave like adults,' Nik said coldly. 'I assume we can work together to come to an agreement. A mutually beneficial arrangement that we both believe to be in the best interests of Danny.'

'You assume a lot!' Carrie said.

'That we can both behave like adults?' Nik asked, a hint of derision colouring his voice.

'That you can treat Danny like one of your business deals,' Carrie said. 'He's a human being, and we certainly won't be coming to any "mutually beneficial arrangements"—he's not a piece of property!'

CHAPTER FOUR

THE Mediterranean sun was hot on her back as Carrie sat beside the pool, waiting for her client, Elaine, to come out of the villa for her workout. She flipped through the glossy pages of a magazine, trying to keep her thoughts away from Nikos Kristallis. Even after three quiet days on the Spanish island of Menorca she was still on edge.

He couldn't get his hands on Danny here, she thought grimly. Or on her. That thought sent a shiver running down her spine, despite the heat of the sun.

Nik had been furious when he'd left her flat the other night, but when she'd asked him to leave for the second time he'd gone without further comment. Maybe he'd realised he was fighting a losing battle? Maybe he'd figured out that she'd never willingly give up Danny?

But surely that wouldn't stop a man like Nikos Kristallis? Wasn't he the sort who went to any lengths to get what he wanted? Carrie shivered again, wondering just how far Nik would go.

She was glad she'd brought Danny to Menorca. The trip was a work commitment that had been arranged for months, but as far as Carrie was concerned the timing was perfect. Although the situation with Nik was still unresolved, everything had suddenly become too intense. She needed some breathing room.

She'd considered letting Nik know about the trip, but in the end she'd decided against it. Why should she tell him? After all, he'd never shown any consideration for her. His constant assertions that Danny would be returning to Greece with him were really starting to worry her, and she was still horrified by what might have happened if she hadn't arrived at the nursery when she had. Despite the nursery's strict rules about who could collect children, she knew the extent of Nik's charm. There was no doubt he could be very persuasive.

'Here I am,' Elaine said, shrugging off her towelling robe as she hurried over to the table by the pool. 'Sorry to keep you waiting.'

Carrie smiled as her friend sat down. 'Yes, it's been really terrible waiting here for you, in the sunshine, reading a magazine…'

She glanced across to the shady spot under the trees where Elaine's nanny and her ten-year-old twin girls were playing with Danny. She could hear his giggles of delight and see how happy he was.

It was good to be in Menorca. They could both do with a pleasant change from their usual routine. It had been a long hard winter for Carrie and, although it was now early May, warmer weather had seemed reluctant to come to London that year. It was wonderful to escape for a while, and relaxing by a pool in the Spanish sunshine certainly beat pushing Danny's buggy round the dreary pigeon-pecked paths of her local park.

'Danny sounds like he's enjoying himself.' Elaine smiled, looking over at the children, too. 'The girls love having him here. If they get too much, you will tell me, won't you?'

'They've been fantastic,' Carrie said, thinking about the way the girls had been doting on Danny, fussing over him every chance they got. 'You know how much I love being with him, but it's been wonderful to be able to relax and watch him playing with someone else.'

'You don't get much chance for that, do you?' Elaine asked. 'You work too hard, love. I know you have to make ends meet, but time flies by and you can never get this time back again.'

'I know,' Carrie said, suddenly feeling a twinge of guilt for sometimes wishing that life was less exhausting, and that Danny was older and easier to care for. Somehow it seemed as if all she did was work and look after the baby. Her social life had ground to a virtual halt.

'Any juicy gossip?' Elaine asked, leaning over to peer at the magazine.

'I don't know,' Carrie said. 'I wasn't really reading properly.' Her eyes scanned the glossy celebrity photos, automatically looking for familiar faces.

Many of her clients were celebrities, and in the past she'd worked with even more famous people. After she'd started caring for Danny she'd had to drop a lot of her clients. The out-of-hours training sessions required by some of her regulars simply didn't fit in with her childcare arrangements. She'd felt bad about letting people down, but Danny had to come first.

She'd been lucky to find part-time work at a gym, and the rest of the time she devoted to clients like Elaine, who could train during the day, when Danny was at nursery.

'Ooh, look—it's Lulu and Darren,' Elaine said, tugging the magazine out of Carrie's grip. 'Isn't she one of your clients?'

'Yes,' Carrie said, unsettled by how quickly her thoughts had bypassed Lulu and settled on Nikos Kristallis kissing her in Darren's study.

'Maybe not any longer,' Elaine said. 'Look—it says Darren has thrown her out.'

'What?' Carrie gasped, pulling the magazine back and placing it on the table between them. Was that her fault? Had Lulu been right about how strongly Darren would react to the voicemail she'd left him? If only Nik hadn't interrupted her and she'd been able to get to Darren's phone in time.

'It says that she's been having an affair with another footballer!' Elaine said. 'Darren discovered them together last week at a party. There was a terrible scene, ending with him throwing her out!'

'How awful!' Carrie said, feeling torn apart on Lulu's behalf. But she couldn't help wondering exactly what had really been going on when Lulu had begged her to get the phone.

They both looked at the photographic evidence in front of them—a sequence of shots that apparently showed Darren and Lulu arguing, followed by pictures of Lulu leaving the house in tears.

There were lots of other photos of guests at the party. Some of them were celebrities, some were not well known, but all of them seemed happy to be photographed at the glitzy party. Carrie frowned, thinking how fickle the media was—happy to build you up when it suited them, and even happier to drag you down if it made a better story.

'Good grief—look at this!' Elaine hooted, pointing to a photo of a couple kissing. Their faces were pressed together, keeping their identities hidden, but there was no hiding the way the couple's bodies were intimately entwined in a position that was frankly sexual. The man's leg was pressed between the woman's thighs, pushing her skimpy red skirt up revealingly, and her back was arched so that her breasts were more than half exposed, and looked as if they were about to explode out of the dress altogether. 'That's positively indecent! Just what kind of party *was* it? Were you invited?' Elaine asked.

'What?' Carrie gasped, feeling her blood run cold as she looked at the photo.

Oh, God! It was a picture of Nik kissing her!

'Makes you wonder what goes on at these celebrity parties,' Elaine said. 'Some people have no shame. They'll do anything to get their photo in one of these magazines. Did you see all this going on?'

'No…no, I didn't stay at the party,' Carrie stammered. Her heart was pounding and she felt sick to her stomach. 'Ready for your workout?' she blurted, hoping Elaine wouldn't notice that she was shaking, and beads of perspiration had broken out on her clammy brow.

Elaine laughed and tossed the magazine back on the table. 'That's why I love you!' She smiled. 'You're so focussed. You never let me waste my workout time.'

'I think you'll enjoy the routine I've got planned,' Carrie said, inwardly wincing because she certainly wasn't focussed on Elaine at that moment. She continued speaking, trying to sound breezy and natural, when inside she felt like curling up and hiding. 'It's good to take advantage of the pool while we're here.'

'As long as it works,' Elaine said, patting her stomach and looking critically at her thighs. 'I haven't got long to fit into my outfit.'

'Your dress already looks great,' Carrie reminded her. 'And you're so much fitter. You know you've done brilliantly.' She was proud of how well Elaine had got back her fitness after an operation had prevented her from exercising for a while.

Carrie wasn't really concerned with how slim people were;

she just wanted to help them achieve their fitness goals so that they could enjoy life to the full. In her work as a trainer she always put the emphasis on fitness over conforming to stereotyped images of body size and shape. But she understood how important it was for Elaine to feel she looked good at her younger sister's wedding.

'Right—let's do this,' Elaine said, jumping into the pool.

Carrie switched on the portable CD-player, and immediately a funky dance beat filled the air.

'Okay, let's warm up,' she said, slipping into the water beside Elaine. She concentrated on the task at hand, hoping some hard work would burn off the stress adrenaline that was pumping round her body. As long as she didn't let herself think about that appalling photo she'd be all right.

In the past she'd always taught aqua-aerobics from the poolside, where she could keep her eye on a whole class. Earlier, when she'd been planning the session, she'd thought it would be fun to get in to the water and join in properly—now she was grateful for something that required a higher level of concentration from her.

She started off gently, taking Elaine through the unfamiliar moves, but before long both of them were thoroughly involved in the routine. Carrie almost felt disappointed as she came to the end of the cool-down and stretch section of the workout.

'That was really great,' Elaine said, climbing out of the pool and pushing her wet hair out of her eyes.

'I'm glad you enjoyed it. We'll do it again tomorrow,' Carrie said, pulling herself up out of the water. The tiles surrounding the pool felt deliciously hot under her wet feet as she walked across them to pick up a towel from the table.

She lifted the towel to dry her face, but as she closed her

eyes behind the soft warm fabric a shiver suddenly darted down her spine.

Something was wrong. Elaine had started to speak, then suddenly gone quiet.

'What is it?' she asked, glancing quickly over to the children, who were still playing under the tree, and then back to Elaine.

'Who's that—talking to John?' she asked.

Carrie turned and followed Elaine's puzzled gaze across to the drive, where her husband John was talking to a tall, dark-haired man.

It was Nikos Kristallis.

'No! It can't be!' Carrie gasped. 'How did he find me here?'

'Who is it?' Elaine asked, looking at her sharply. 'Are you in some kind of trouble, Carrie?'

'It's… It's…' Carrie croaked, struggling to speak with a suddenly dry mouth. She swallowed hard and twisted the towel tightly in her shaking hands. She was rooted to the spot, hardly able to believe her eyes.

Nik stared at Carrie.

Satisfaction at finding her and the child mixed unpleasantly with a powerful rush of anger. Here she was, apparently having a whale of a time, frolicking around the pool in the sunshine, while he'd had to go to the trouble of ascertaining her whereabouts from her colleagues at the gym and then follow her to Spain. That wasn't how things worked in his world.

He turned and scanned the garden quickly. His eyes settled on Danny, who was sitting on a rug under a tree, with two older girls and a young woman who appeared to be looking after all three children. The girls were laughing and building a tower of blocks in front of him, and the young woman leant forward and adjusted the hat that had slipped down over Danny's eyes.

He seemed to be happy and well cared for, but that didn't excuse the fact that Carrie had taken him out of the country without informing him. He knew she was here to work, but as far as he was concerned that made no difference. The sharp pain from his fingernails digging into his palms told him he was clenching his fists too fiercely.

He turned his attention back to Carrie, and suddenly the memory of their last evening together flashed unexpectedly through his mind. To make matters worse she appeared to have just stepped out of the pool. His body's hot response was out of his conscious control as he took in the sight of her, wet and glistening, dressed in a tiny clingy bikini.

'I need to speak to Miss Thomas.' He spoke briskly to the British gentleman who owned the villa, knowing his tone didn't leave room for debate.

Carrie was looking across the pool at him. He had seen her reel under the shock of seeing him, but now she was talking to the other woman and glancing across at the children.

He deliberately uncurled his fingers and forced himself to release some of the tension gripping his tightly coiled muscles. He took a few quick strides and suddenly he was standing right in front of her. Two hectic spots of colour danced on her pale cheeks, but she stood her ground and stared straight up into his face.

'What do you think you are doing here?' she demanded, planting her hands firmly on her hips and tossing her sleek black hair back from her face with a shower of droplets. Next to the wet blackness of her hair, her skin looked paler than ever, almost shimmering with the sheen of moisture that still clung to it. 'How did you find us?'

'Your colleagues at the gym were most helpful,' Nik said, thinking how it hadn't taken much to loosen their tongues.

'They had no right to tell you,' she said through gritted teeth. 'And you have no right to barge your way into my client's house. I'm working,' she added.

'I have every right to be concerned over the welfare of my nephew,' Nik replied, keeping his eyes firmly on her face and not giving in to the desire to run his gaze down over her exquisite body.

'Well, as you can see, he's perfectly fine.' Carrie folded her arms across her chest. 'Not that it's any of your business. I look after him and I decide what's best for him.'

She glared up at him, determined to keep her cool, but it wasn't easy when she was standing there in nothing but a bikini. He was so tall that standing in her bare feet, she had to tip her head right back to look at him properly.

It was hot beside the pool, but the heat of the Spanish sun was insignificant compared to the burn of his gaze. She couldn't help fidgeting slightly, curling her toes against the hot tiles, then dropping her arms down to her sides before promptly folding them again.

'You may be Danny's guardian at the moment,' Nik said. 'But pull any more stunts like that and you'll soon find out who you're up against.'

'You think I'll just roll over and let you do whatever you want?' Carrie gasped. 'Danny means everything to me. Do you think I'd care if I found myself up against you?'

As soon as the words had left her mouth she realised how they sounded. Or maybe it was only to her own ears. But she couldn't stop her gaze sliding down and taking in the broad expanse of his chest. She knew exactly what it felt like to be pressed up against him, and she couldn't stop her body responding to the memory.

She knew all about 'muscle memory', where muscle

groups seemed to have their own recall of a sequence of movements in dance or exercise. But she'd never heard of 'body memory'—which was surely what she was experiencing now. Her whole being seemed to be buzzing with the memory of their bodies pressed together and bending as one as he pushed her back over Darren's desk. If she wasn't careful she'd find her body stepping forward of its own volition and melding provocatively to his.

Nik narrowed his eyes and a smile flashed across his tanned face.

'In fact, I can see you definitely *would* care to come up against me—again.' He tilted his head and let his deep blue eyes sweep suggestively down her exposed body.

The touch of his gaze was almost as potent as the touch of his hands. It felt as if he'd run his fingertips across her skin, leaving a sizzling trail of sensation in their wake and starting a slow-burning fire deep within her body.

Carrie sucked in a shaky breath and hugged her arms defensively over her breasts. But she knew she hadn't stopped him noticing the sudden tightening of her nipples beneath the wet bikini. And she couldn't hide the hot flush which was creeping across her bare skin.

She simply wasn't used to her body reacting like this, and she didn't know how to handle it. She'd never realised that she could experience such powerful and confusing sexual feelings.

'Should I ask this man to leave?' Elaine asked crisply. She had been standing politely to one side, to give Carrie some space, but now she stepped closer and handed Carrie her own towelling robe. 'John and I certainly won't put up with anyone bothering you while you are in our home.'

Carrie turned away slightly and gratefully pulled the robe on. She belted it tightly and made herself look back up into

Nik's face with a confidence she didn't really feel. She wanted Elaine and her husband to make him leave, but she knew they had to sort this out now. Besides, somehow she doubted whether *anyone* could actually make Nik leave if he wasn't ready to.

'Miss Thomas and I have not finished our discussion yet,' Nik said arrogantly. 'And we would appreciate a little privacy, if that would be convenient for you.'

'Just hold on a minute—' Elaine started to bluster.

'It's all right.' Carrie spoke to her friend, making her voice sound bright and confident. 'There are some issues that Mr Kristallis and I really do need to clarify.'

'I'll be just inside with John,' Elaine said. 'Call me if you need anything.' She gave Nik a hard stare, then turned reluctantly and headed across the lawn to gather up the children and the nanny.

Carrie looked back at Nik. He was watching Elaine pick up Danny and carry him away into the villa. The intense expression on his face made her shudder.

He continued to stare into the dark interior of the villa for a few moments longer, then suddenly his piercing blue gaze turned back to her. But she was ready for him and spoke before he had a chance.

'Let's get this straight,' Carrie said firmly. 'You have no right to storm in here and demand explanations from me. I am under no obligation to report my plans to you.'

'No, you're not. At least *not yet*,' Nik added. 'But what about common decency?'

'Decency!' Carrie gasped. 'That's rich, coming from you—the man who forcibly kisses total strangers just because he feels like it, and who barges uninvited into other people's homes whenever it suits him!'

'And you're so perfect?' Nik asked. 'By taking Danny

out of the country you've done exactly what you accused *me* of planning.'

'I haven't abducted him,' Carrie said. 'It's up to me to decide where I want to take him.'

'And to do whatever you want without any regard for other people?' Nik demanded. 'I gave my word never to take Danny anywhere without your knowledge. And even as I made that promise you were planning to get on a plane with him a few hours later!'

'That's different—' Carrie started.

'Perhaps you would be so good as to tell me your plans now?' Nik interrupted coldly, as if whatever reasons and explanations she was about to offer were completely immaterial to him. 'How long are you staying in Menorca and where are you intending to go when you leave here?'

'I shall be staying here with Elaine's family until Friday,' Carrie said quietly. Suddenly there didn't seem to be any point in making things more difficult between them. 'And then I shall return to my flat in London and carry on like normal.'

'All right,' Nik said. 'You may stay here and honour your work agreement. But that is on the strict understanding that you will not agree to any similar undertakings in the future.'

'My work is none of your business. I don't need your permission,' Carrie said in exasperation. 'I keep telling you that.'

'But where you and Danny go and who you see *is* my concern,' Nik said. 'I keep telling *you* that, but since you seem to have difficulty accepting it, I shall be leaving my assistant here in Menorca while I return to London to complete some business.'

'You're going to leave someone here to keep an eye on me?' Carrie gasped. 'Who do you think you are?'

'You know who I am. I've never tried to conceal my identity from you or mislead you about my intentions,' Nik said. 'You, on the other hand, don't have such a shining record. Let's not forget what you were up to when we first met.'

'I wasn't up to anything,' Carrie said, feeling her cheeks blaze. A rush of images spiralled horribly through her mind—Nik catching her red-handed in Darren's study, Nik kissing her, the appalling photograph of them kissing that she'd just seen in the magazine.

She gritted her teeth and stared up at him, refusing to let her thoughts continue down that path. She flicked her damp fringe out of her eyes and tried to look confident and unperturbed by his comments.

'I know what you told me,' Nik said. 'Surely you don't think it's wise to get involved with that sort of thing?'

'I was doing a favour for Lulu,' Carrie said. 'What's wrong with helping a friend out?'

'Considering what Lulu was up to under her husband's roof, with one of his best friends, I'd say the answer to that question hinges on your attitude to adultery,' Nik said.

'You don't know the whole story,' Carrie said defensively, actually wishing that she'd known what was going on before she'd agreed to do Lulu's dirty work. But there was no way she'd admit that to Nik. 'There are always two sides to these things.'

'Maybe more than two sides,' Nik said. 'After all, you were in Darren's study. Perhaps you were there for a secret liaison with him.'

'Now you're being ridiculous,' Carrie said. 'Anyway, I thought he was your friend. That's not exactly very loyal of you.'

'Acquaintance rather than friend,' Nik replied. 'But I do know what he's like, and it's fair to say he can give Lulu a run for her money. And, as I said, it was Darren's study and you were certainly dressed to impress.'

'If that's the case, why didn't he mind when *you* kissed me?' Carrie threw at him.

'He recognised he'd met his match?' Nik asked.

'He was virtually cheering you on!' Carrie snapped. 'It was humiliating!'

'Is that how you found it?' Nik asked.

'Of course it was humiliating to see my photo in that trashy magazine!' The awful full-colour image that she'd seen on those glossy pages flashed nauseatingly through her mind.

'Oh, you saw that?' Nik drawled, as if seeing himself portrayed like that meant nothing to him.

'You had no right to put me in that position.' She suddenly felt her cheeks blaze as she remembered exactly how she'd felt as he pushed her back over the desk, his leg pressed intimately between her thighs while he kissed her.

'I got the impression that position turned you on.' The corner of his expressive mouth twitched, as if he found her embarrassment amusing. 'I thought you found our little encounter quite stimulating.'

'That's not what I meant.' Carrie glared at him, despite the overwhelming urge to turn away and hide her blazing cheeks. 'You had no right to drag me into your sordid little celebrity scandals!'

'As I recall, it was your ill-advised foray into Darren's study that led to our little clinch in the first place,' Nik said dryly. 'I hope you've learned your lesson and now realise it's not very sensible to get involved with that kind of thing.'

'Don't you dare patronise me!' Carrie gasped. 'If I choose to do a favour for one of my friends, it's none of your business!'

'While you are caring for my nephew, everything you do is my business,' Nik said.

'And what about you?' Carrie demanded. 'It was your outrageous behaviour that resulted in that appalling photo. Who knows what other unsuitable activities you might have been indulging in?'

'I do not need to make an account of myself to you,' Nik said.

'But you think I need to explain myself to you?' Her eyes flew over him with irritation, standing there so cool and perfect in his immaculate designer suit. He oozed wealth and power, from the top of his arrogant head to the leather soles of his handmade Italian shoes. 'You've had life so easy. You have no idea what it's like for the rest of us—having to question our actions, worrying whether we made the right decisions.'

'Of course I question my actions,' Nik said coldly. 'Having money doesn't make you immune to difficult decisions.'

'No, but it makes it a whole lot easier.'

'I have to live with bad choices I've made, just like everybody else.' Nik pushed his fingers roughly through his dark brown hair.

'Poor little rich boy,' Carrie said. 'Do you expect me to feel sorry for you?'

'Okay, let's just stop it!' He took off his jacket and slung it over his shoulder. 'I didn't come here to argue with you. I only wanted to ascertain where you and Danny were.'

Carrie stared up at Nik, suddenly breathing very quickly. His outburst had startled her, making her stomach feel fluttery.

He was studying her again. His full lips were pressed together and his brows were drawn down, casting his blue eyes into deep shadow. The muscles in his face were tense, pulling his bronzed skin taut across his high cheekbones and around the strong, darkly stubbled curve of his jaw line.

'What time is your flight back to London?' he asked, suddenly businesslike.

'Late Friday morning,' Carrie said warily. 'We are all flying back together.'

'My assistant, Spiro, will stay with you until then, to make sure you and Danny are all right,' Nik said. 'Unfortunately I have to return to London to sort out some business.'

'He can't stay here,' Carrie said. 'This isn't my place, you know. I won't have you ruin Elaine's family holiday by leaving someone here to…to stalk me!'

'Believe me, it's not my first choice,' Nik said. 'But it will have to do. If you try to evade Spiro I shall return at once and place both you and Danny under my care, in a location where you can be closely supervised.'

'Are you threatening to abduct us?' Carrie gasped. It was a nasty reminder that dealing with Nikos Kristallis was dangerous. There was so much at stake.

'Still so over-dramatic,' Nik said calmly. 'Just don't do anything stupid in the next few days. I have to try and salvage something from a business deal that collapsed when you pulled your disappearing act.'

'Why are you doing this? You don't care about Danny at all!' Carrie burst out. 'He's just a big inconvenience because you had to choose between him and clinching a business deal!'

'Don't talk about Danny as if he means no more to me than some kind of acquisition,' he said. 'Even though you seem unable to accept it, he is my nephew and I care about him.'

'Then why did it take you six months after your brother died to come and find his orphaned baby boy?' Carrie demanded. 'You just thought it would be more convenient to wait until a business trip brought you to London anyway.'

'I didn't know he existed,' Nik grated. 'Until very recently I didn't know he existed.'

A flash of raw emotion passed across his face for a split

second and Carrie stared at him in surprise. Was he telling the truth? She wanted to know how it was possible that he hadn't known about Danny, but then a movement from the villa caught her eye. Elaine was approaching, with a bottle of mineral water and two glasses.

'I thought you might need some refreshment,' she called out as she came towards them.

'Thank you for your concern.' Nik turned to speak to Elaine. 'But it's not necessary. I was just about to leave.'

'But…' Carrie was suddenly lost for words, still wondering about what Nik had just said.

'I'll meet your plane when you return to London next week,' Nik said, turning on his heel and striding away towards the wrought-iron gate at the villa driveway.

'You look like you need a long cool drink,' Elaine said, pouring water into a glass.

'Thank you,' Carrie said, with only part of her attention on her friend. She was watching the tall dark figure of Nikos Kristallis as he climbed into the back of his black limousine.

He had frightened her with his announcement that he'd only learned about Danny's existence recently. The fact that he hadn't waited six months to seek out his nephew but instead had come virtually straight away was unnerving. It seemed to make it even more certain he really *did* plan to take Danny from her.

She was glad that he had gone, but a nasty cold feeling of dread crept over her.

CHAPTER FIVE

THE appalling heat in the underground car park was the final straw as Carrie searched in every corner of her bag for the keys to the hire car. She'd looked and looked, even emptied the contents of the bag out onto the dusty bonnet of the car—but the keys simply weren't there.

Danny had come down with a case of chickenpox, and was screaming agonisingly in her ear. Her head was spinning and tears pricked behind her eyes as she desperately tried to think what to do next.

Only one thing was clear. She had to get Danny out of that car park quickly, before his fever got dangerously high. The poor little thing was burning up, and if she couldn't find the keys to the hire car she'd have to find some other way to get him somewhere more comfortable, where she could try to cool him down.

She started stuffing things back into her shoulder bag with one hand while she held Danny in her other arm, trying not to rub his irritated skin or press him too close to her hot and sticky body. It wasn't an easy task, especially with her eyes blurring with unshed tears and a lump of anxiety constricting her throat. What if she couldn't cope? What if she couldn't take care of Danny properly, make him well again?

The nightmare had started that morning, when they'd got ready to leave for the airport. Danny had seemed grizzly, and then one of Elaine's girls had noticed the small red spots. Carrie hadn't known what they were, but Elaine had recognised them immediately. Chickenpox.

The airline doctor had agreed with Elaine and refused to let Danny fly home.

At first Carrie had felt quite calm. She'd just have to stay in Elaine's villa with Danny until he wasn't infectious. It would be fine. She knew where everything was. There was food in the freezer and there was a small grocery shop a few metres along the road.

Elaine had been more worried, fretting and saying she'd stay behind, too. But she had her sister's wedding, and Carrie knew how much that meant to her. Then John had offered to stay instead, but Carrie had insisted she'd be all right on her own with Danny. After all, she looked after him on her own at home.

She'd done such a good job sounding confident and convincing for Elaine and her family that she had more or less convinced herself, too. Luckily she had her driving licence with her, and John had just had time to hire a car for her before their flight left. And then they'd had to go, leaving her alone with Danny and the keys of the villa.

He had seemed all right while she drove away from the airport, and she'd been proud of herself for staying so calm. When she'd caught sight of Nik's assistant's car in her rearview mirror she had smiled grimly and thought to herself that she wasn't exactly alone anyway. No doubt he'd already called Nik to let him know she wasn't on the plane.

She'd decided to stop in town to buy some infant painkiller, just in case she needed more and they didn't stock it in the village shop near the villa. That was when everything had started going badly.

Danny had become increasingly distressed, and by the time she'd got back to the stifling underground car park he'd been far too hot and screaming at the top of his lungs.

For the first time that week Nik's assistant had disappeared, so she couldn't even ask him for help. She was feeling so desperate she would have asked almost anyone around. But the car park was deserted.

Oh, why had she assured everyone she'd be all right on her own? She didn't feel all right, and Danny certainly didn't look or sound all right.

She grabbed a tube of suncream just as it slid off the car bonnet and tried to get it into her bag, but the strap of her bag had started to slip off her shoulder. A moment later her bag and all its contents were scattered on the grimy concrete floor of the car park.

She stared at the mess in utter dismay. It was too much! But somehow she had to get through it because Danny needed her.

'It's all right, Danny,' she said, in a falsely high and squeaky voice. Her words didn't reassure him or stop him crying at the top of his lungs.

'It'll be okay,' she said again. But as she spoke she heard her own voice crack. She pressed her quivering lips together and squeezed her eyes shut to stop the tears from falling.

She couldn't bear to hear Danny in such distress. She had to keep it together and think of what to do next.

She squatted down next to the car and started picking up the essentials, like her purse, Danny's water bottle and the keys to the villa. The suncream and rest of the stuff would just have to roll around under the car until she could deal with it.

The most important thing was to get Danny out into the

fresh air, give him some infant painkiller and get him to drink something. Then she would think what to do after that.

'What the hell are you doing?' a deep voice behind her grated. 'Why didn't you get on the plane with the others?'

She recognised the voice immediately. It was Nikos Kristallis.

'Oh, thank God you're here!' Carrie said, standing up and turning round to face him. Despite the harsh tone of his voice, she had never been more grateful to see anyone. She felt tears of relief swim in her eyes, and she spoke quickly before she really started crying. 'Danny's sick, and they wouldn't let me take him on the plane. He's burning up, and I need to get him out of this sweltering car park, but I've lost the car keys.'

'What's wrong with him?' Nik asked sharply, reaching out to take the child.

'Chickenpox,' Carrie replied, letting him take Danny without objecting. She was too hot and sticky, and she knew it was making the fevered baby feel even worse. 'The first thing we have to do is get him out of here and cool him down.'

'Come on,' Nik barked, instantly striding towards the exit. He shot a series of comments in Greek to his assistant. 'Leave your things. Spiro will bring them.'

Carrie hurried along beside Nik, keeping close enough so that Danny could easily see her. But he wasn't really looking. He'd stopped howling and his head was lolling against Nik's shoulder. She didn't think that was a good sign.

'We'll go to a hotel and call a doctor,' Nik said. 'I saw a hotel just down here.'

Carrie was almost running to keep up with his long stride, and it seemed as if only moments passed before they were marching into the foyer of the hotel. Carrie was watching Danny so closely that she hardly registered Nik's rapid conversation with the receptionist, but they were quickly shown into a large hotel room.

'The doctor will be here very soon,' Nik said, turning to face Carrie. She was looking at Danny and biting her lip anxiously. 'What do we do now, before he gets here?'

She stared up at him with wide green eyes, and for a moment she seemed almost surprised that he had asked her what to do. Then her gaze flicked straight back to Danny.

'Try to cool him down,' she said quickly. 'Get him to sip some water, and it's time to give him another dose of painkiller.'

Nik laid Danny carefully on the bed and sat beside him to take off his shorts and T-shirt. He stared at him in shock, appalled at the sight of his little body covered with red spots.

It was unacceptable! No Kristallis baby should have to endure this. No nephew of his should be dragged around hot and crowded public places while he was sick. God knows what Carrie would have done if he hadn't arrived when he had.

'Oh, no!' He heard Carrie's sharp intake of breath. 'There's twice as many spots as this morning.'

'He doesn't feel so hot as when I first took him.' Nik lifted Danny and placed him awkwardly on his knee. 'It's air-conditioned in here. Maybe that's helping.'

'I'm sure it is,' Carrie said, kneeling down beside them and tearing open a sachet of painkiller. She started to squeeze out the syrupy liquid onto a spoon. 'It's very cool in here. That car park was unbearably hot.'

'Yes,' Nik said dourly. He didn't need reminding. Danny should never have been in a place like that in his condition.

'Here you go.' Carrie popped a spoonful of pink medicine into Danny's mouth. 'That will make you feel better. Now, a few sips of water to wash it down, that's a good boy.'

Carrie sat back on her heels and studied Danny thoughtfully. She was starting to feel less anxious.

'He seems a bit better,' she said after a moment. She reached out and took him carefully from Nik. 'I mean, of course he's still sick, but his temperature is not dangerously high any more, and he's looking at me now and trying to smile a bit. I was so frightened when he wouldn't respond.'

She hugged him gently, pressing her face against his curls, and looked at Nik, who was still sitting on the bed.

'Thank you,' she said. 'Thanks for helping us out like this.'

'There's no need for thanks.' Nik stood up abruptly. 'Danny is my nephew. Naturally I would do whatever I can for him.'

'Well, you turning up when you did certainly made things easier,' Carrie said. She was grateful for his help, but at that moment an uncomfortable wariness crept over her. Would he find a way to use this against her? Would he say it proved she was an unsuitable guardian for Danny? 'Of course we would have managed on our own,' she added. 'I just needed to get Danny somewhere cooler.'

She looked up at him, standing over her, and a shiver prickled between her shoulderblades. Suddenly he seemed incredibly tall, incredibly powerful. He was looking down at her with an unnerving intensity that made her wish she wasn't kneeling on the floor.

'Where's that doctor?' he asked impatiently. He glanced at his watch and strode across the room. 'He should be here by now.'

'He'll be here in a minute,' Carrie said, to reassure herself as much as anything. She stood up and moved away to the other side of the room. Waiting with Nik was making her feel jittery. Thankfully at that moment there was a knock on the door, announcing the arrival of the doctor.

* * *

Carrie hesitated by the door that linked the two hotel rooms and looked at Nik. He was sitting at a little table, working on his laptop computer. He hadn't noticed her come in, and that gave her a moment just to look at him.

The jacket of his suit and his silk tie were lying on the bed, and he had rolled up the sleeves of his white shirt and undone the top button while he worked. He was completely absorbed in his task, and his tanned fingers were flying over the computer keys with a speed that surprised her.

He looked so rigidly focussed that he reminded Carrie of an athlete, centering himself before a crucial event. For a second she envied him. He always seemed so sure of himself, so certain of what he wanted and what to do next.

She had been so relieved to see him when he'd turned up in the car park, and was truly grateful for the decisive way he had taken control, bringing them to the hotel and calling the doctor. However, things did not seem so straightforward now. He'd been very helpful, but there had been an edge to his manner that made her feel anxious. What would he expect in return?

She glanced around the hotel room and frowned. Nik had the only chair, which meant she'd have to sit on the bed or stand about looking awkward. Or tiptoe back into the other hotel room, where Danny had finally fallen asleep.

She hadn't realised at first that Nik had booked adjoining hotel rooms for them. She didn't know what he intended, but all she wanted to do was return to the villa and wait until she could take Danny home.

The doctor had confirmed the previous diagnosis of chick-enpox and told her what to expect over the next few days and what to do to keep Danny comfortable. It shouldn't be too long until he wasn't infectious and would be allowed to fly.

Suddenly Nik turned round and caught her watching him.

A smile flashed across his face so quickly she thought she might have imagined it, and then she felt his brilliant blue eyes ensnare her. She was fixed in his gaze, and it almost felt as if he was tugging her towards him.

She'd been studying him a moment ago, but now the tables were turned and she was the one being watched. She felt her pulse leap and her senses move onto red alert.

'Danny's sleeping now,' she said quickly, unsettled by how breathless her voice sounded. 'I'll leave this door open a fraction so we'll be sure to hear if he wakes up.'

'Come and sit down,' Nik said quietly, careful not to disturb the sleeping child. 'We need to discuss our immediate plans.'

Carrie walked across the room, feeling absurdly self-conscious, and sat down. She didn't want to sit on his bed, but she wasn't about to make a big deal out of it.

'Spiro brought your things up while you were with Danny,' Nik said, closing his laptop and lifting his chair round so he could look at her straight on.

'Thank you,' Carrie said, glancing behind her to the pile of things Nik had indicated. 'Oh, my suitcase and everything! That was locked in the boot.'

'Spiro found the keys on the ground under the car. They must have fallen out of your bag,' Nik explained, lifting one hand to unconsciously massage the back of his neck.

'That's a relief,' Carrie said, watching him roll his head from side to side. She knew he was acting instinctively, to relieve the stiffness in his neck, but the incredible sensuality of the movement suddenly caught her deep down inside.

Her heart started to race, her legs felt shaky and her mouth ran dry. It was an unfamiliar feeling for her, but even so she recognised it for what it was. Pure sexual attraction.

Nikos Kristallis was the sexiest man she had ever seen—

and it wasn't just his gorgeous good looks. The way he moved his body affected her in the most alarming way. The sinuous roll of his head from one powerful shoulder to the other. The way he flexed his muscles and tilted his head as he lifted his hand to rub his neck.

Her fingers itched to touch him—touch him in a way she had never touched any man before. She wanted to slide her hands down over the contours of his hard muscled chest, feel the heat of his body, lean forward and press her face against his skin and inhale his masculine scent.

'That's all taken care of now,' Nik said.

'I'm sorry?' Carrie said, shaking her head sharply to clear her mind. She shook her hair back from her face and focussed on Nik carefully, concentrating on what he was saying. She didn't like realising she had lost the thread of the conversation while her mind ran away with such blatantly sensual thoughts about Nik. 'What's taken care of?'

'Spiro is returning the hire-car to the airport. You won't be needing it any more.'

'He can't take it back. I *do* still need it!' Carrie exclaimed, suddenly completely back in the moment. 'I need it to drive to the villa, and to get about until Danny's given the all-clear to travel.'

'That's what I wanted to talk to you about,' Nik said. 'I can take you home.'

'Danny can't fly,' Carrie said.

'He can't fly on a public flight while he's infectious,' Nik agreed. 'Luckily, I have my own plane.'

'Your own plane!' Carrie echoed Nik's words in surprise. Just how rich *was* Nikos Kristallis? 'Is that how you got to Menorca so quickly when I didn't get on the flight home?'

'No, I simply jumped on the first flight to Menorca out of

London Gatwick,' Nik said. 'It was quicker than getting to my own plane, which was at another airport. I don't usually use major airports—too many people, too many delays.'

'Oh,' Carrie said, not quite sure how to respond to the information that Nik was obviously even wealthier than she had thought. 'Sorry you had to rough it by travelling with the public.' She looked down and her eyes settled on the tie Nik had left lying on the bed. Without thinking she picked it up and smoothed her fingers along it. 'Anyway, if you left your plane at another airport, how can you offer us a ride home?'

'It will be here later this evening,' Nik said, letting his gaze drop to her lap, where she was unconsciously tracing the pattern on his tie as it lay across her thighs. 'Until then you can rest in the hotel.'

'It's not necessary.' Carrie slid the silky fabric of his tie between her hands. It was tempting to accept his offer, but she didn't want to be even more indebted to him than she already was. He was still dangerous to her, and she mustn't let herself forget it just because he had helped her out of a difficult situation. 'Danny and I will be quite all right staying at Elaine's villa.'

'I think it's best if I take you home,' Nik replied, his eyes still fixed on her hands. God, she was turning him on! Watching the sensual movements of her fingers playing with his tie was pure erotic torture. If he didn't feel those sexy hands on his body soon he was going to explode. 'I can't stay here. I have work I must do.'

'I didn't ask you to stay here!' Something in her voice made him look up, and the expression on her flushed face told him she had finally realised what she'd been doing with his tie. And that she'd seen him watching her sensual actions.

Her heated cheeks revealed that she knew how it was affecting him, and as that fact sank in her own body was responding in kind. She wanted him as much as he wanted her.

She tossed her head in a gesture of denial and stood up jerkily, dropping the tie as if it had suddenly burnt her fingers.

'I'm grateful you came when you did, but now we'll be perfectly all right on our own.' She folded her arms defensively, but lifted her gaze to meet his.

'There's no point taking chances.' Nik stood up and moved a step closer to her. He wanted to feel her hands on his body, caressing him the way she had caressed his tie. 'I'm going to take you home tonight.'

'So when you said that we needed to discuss *our* plans, you meant you needed to tell me *your* plan?' Carrie placed her hands firmly on her hips. She stood her ground and looked him squarely in the eye.

Another bolt of desire ripped through Nik as he looked down at her. She seemed unaware that her defiant posture was thrusting her breasts towards him in a way that was almost impossible to resist.

'If you have another idea that is better, I'll listen to it before I make a decision.' Nik narrowed his eyes and tilted his head slightly as he studied her.

There was an enticing naïveté about her sexuality that experienced women didn't normally have. Oh, he was quite sure she'd had her share of lovers—how could such a sensual creature not have experienced physical love?—but there was still a freshness about her actions that drew him.

'Don't think for a moment I'm going to leave you alone in a strange country with no one to watch over you, though,' he added.

Carrie swallowed, and unconsciously drew her lower lip into her mouth as if she was struggling to maintain eye contact with him. Her teeth pressed gently into her lip as she concentrated, but her gaze slipped down and he guessed she was staring at the vee of bronzed skin at the open neck of his white shirt.

She was looking at him as if he was irresistible, and that turned him on like nothing else before. He was used to women falling all over him, but there was something different about this. She wanted him, but she was fighting it. It was the biggest aphrodisiac he had ever experienced.

Nik lifted his brows slightly as he continued to look at her. 'Do you have another course of action to suggest?'

'What?' Carrie asked, blinking as if to clear her mind. She looked up at him, clearly trying to appear as cool and collected as she could. 'I'm sorry. I lost my train of thought. I was miles away for a moment.'

'Not that far away,' Nik spoke quietly, deliberately letting his voice drop to a deep, seductive tone. 'You were right here all the time—with me.' A buzz of anticipated conquest ran through him. Despite her resistance she was going to be so easy to seduce.

'I'm tired,' Carrie said. She tossed her fringe back and tried to stare him down, even though she could feel herself blushing furiously. She had to brazen it out. She couldn't let him know just how much he was affecting her. 'It's been a long day, but I'm still capable of making my own decisions.'

'What do you suggest?' Nik asked.

Carrie thought hard for a moment.

'Take us home,' she said. 'But don't get any funny ideas about it. I'm only doing what is best for Danny.'

'Funny ideas?' Nik echoed, his Greek accent more pronounced as his gaze skimmed sensually across her body. 'What could be funny about taking you home?'

'You know what I mean,' Carrie insisted, ignoring the wave

of heat that moved through her as his eyes swept over her. 'Nothing is going to happen between us.'

'Even though you want it to?' Nik asked huskily.

Suddenly he seemed too close. He was an overwhelming physical presence that sent the prickle of goosebumps shivering over her skin and a ripple of undeniable sensual desire washing through her.

She had never felt such a strong attraction to any man before, but she knew she must not let herself be distracted by it. She was tired, she hadn't eaten all day, and she was grateful for his help. But she must never forget the threat Nik posed to her and Danny's happiness

'I *don't* want anything to happen between us.' Carrie folded her arms tightly over her breasts.

Talking about it suddenly filled her with a rush of excitement that sent her pulse soaring and started a quiver of desire deep inside her. Who was she kidding? She couldn't deny the overwhelming need she felt for him—but she knew it made her too vulnerable.

Nikos Kristallis already exerted too much power over her life. Too much was at stake to let him have any more advantages. Her attraction for him frightened her.

She remembered with vivid clarity how her incredible desire for him had almost left her at his mercy that evening in her flat. What if she lost control again?

'I've seen the way you look at me,' Nik said huskily. 'You want me to make love to you.'

'No, I don't!' Normally she appreciated plain-talking people who said what they meant—but Nik's sudden directness left her gasping for breath with her cheeks blazing.

'Are you protected?' Nik continued, as if she hadn't spoken and wasn't going scarlet with embarrassment.

'What?' Carrie's mind was spinning. Why was he talking about protection? She certainly needed something to keep her safe from him—at that moment he seemed just like a deadly predator moving in for the kill.

'For when we make love—are you protected?' he pressed again.

'Oh!' Carrie felt her cheeks heat up even more as she finally realised he was talking about contraception. For a moment she couldn't believe he'd asked her such a thing—how had things gone this far? 'Yes—I mean no! Look, there's no need to worry about that,' she said. She was never going to let things go that far!

'That's good,' Nik said softly, moving even closer. 'I would be honoured to make love to you. But I understand why you're holding back.'

'You arrogant beast!' Carrie gasped, unsuccessfully trying to flick her suddenly damp fringe back from her face and willing her cheeks to cool down. 'I know you must be used to women queuing up to climb into your bed, but some of us are immune to your charms!'

'So you admit I have charms?' Nik's blue eyes glittered with laughter.

'No, I don't,' Carrie said crossly. She pushed back the strands of hair that clung damply to her forehead with a jerky movement, upset that he was making fun of her.

'I'm sorry,' Nik said. 'But you know everything will be all right. After all, we both want the same thing.'

'No, I don't know anything of the sort!' Carrie said. 'We hardly know each other, so stop acting like you know me or what I want!'

'You're scared of yourself,' Nik said quietly. 'You don't want to give in to your feelings for me in case it complicates things.'

'I'm not scared!' Carrie snapped, horrified by how well he had read her. 'And I certainly don't have feelings for you!'

'I think there's more between us than mere sex.' Nik lifted his hand and laid his palm gently against her cheek.

'There isn't... We haven't...' Carrie stammered, unconsciously leaning her blazing cheek into the soothing coolness of his palm.

'The physical expression of our desire is burning between us,' Nik said, slipping his hand round to cup the back of her head and taking a step closer to her. 'We can both feel it surrounding us, pressing us together, buzzing through our bodies like electricity.'

'I can't—' Carrie started, then forgot what she was going to say as Nik leant forward, his lips hovering only a fraction above hers.

His words were spinning through her mind and body as if they were tangible things. She really could feel some kind of energy surrounding her, pressing her closer to Nik.

She was breathing rapidly. Her heart was beating fast. She knew he was going to kiss her. She wanted him to kiss her.

She stared at him with wide eyes. Their faces were so close that he was slipping out of focus and she could feel his breath hot on her skin. His hand behind her head held her firm and she let her eyelids slide down. Then she was only aware of the moment. She was poised, waiting for his lips to find hers.

'I want you to touch me,' Nik murmured against her mouth, the teasing movement of his lips almost, but not quite, a kiss.

Carrie's eyes flew open, but he was still so close that she couldn't see him clearly.

'I want you to touch me,' he repeated, and his lips moved against hers again.

'No—' Carrie started to protest, but as she spoke her lips

brushed tantalisingly against his, making hot liquid desire suddenly pool deep inside her. She wanted to press closer and kiss him properly.

'Touch me—like you were touching my tie,' Nik murmured, every syllable an exquisite, delicate torture. She felt the strong suppleness of his lips, and could imagine the flick of his tongue as he formed the words.

'I don't…' She paused and took a breath. She tried to pull back but he was still holding her head. She closed her eyes—it was impossible to think clearly. All she wanted to do was open her mouth and run her tongue along Nik's lip. All she ought to do was pull away from him decisively—show him that she didn't want this—but she felt too weak to move.

'I know you want me to kiss you, and I will.' His words sent sparks of electricity zinging through her body. 'But first you have to touch me.'

'No.' She wouldn't play his games. It would be playing with fire.

'I know why you don't want to.' His mouth brushed hers. 'You're afraid—afraid that once you start you won't be able to stop. You'll want to tear my clothes off and push me down on the bed. You'll want to press your face against my skin, taste me, lick me, kiss me.'

Carrie made an involuntary sound deep in her throat and screwed her eyes even tighter shut. She'd never ever even thought about licking a man before, but now Nik had said it all she could think about was how his skin would feel under her tongue. What would it taste like? Would it turn him on?

Oh, God! What was happening to her? She didn't want to turn him on! She wanted him to leave her alone.

'Maybe I'm mistaken,' Nik murmured as he moved his free hand and started sliding it down her bare arm. Carrie held her breath. He'd done the same thing in Darren's study right before he kissed her.

He caught her hand in his, lifted it up to his chest, then moved back slightly to allow a little space. She stifled a moan of protest as his lips left hers, but then became aware of the feel of his hot skin beneath her fingertips. He'd undone one more button of his shirt and slipped her hand inside.

Carrie stood stiffly, staring in alarm at her own hand that was resting just inside the open collar of Nik's white shirt. She wanted to snatch it away, but at the same time she wanted to glide it across his chest. She couldn't do either, because Nik was still holding her wrist, keeping her hand firmly in place.

'If I'm mistaken, and you're not burning to touch me, then it should be no problem to demonstrate just how indifferent you are,' Nik said. 'But I can feel the chemistry buzzing between us. I know what you want to do.'

'I don't…' Carrie paused, trying to steady her quavering voice. 'I don't know what you mean. What is this supposed to prove?'

'When you were stroking my tie, running your fingers backwards and forwards along it, you were thinking of me, thinking of touching me,' Nik purred.

'I wasn't.' Carrie swallowed, trying desperately to keep her hand still, but she could feel the heat of his skin beneath her fingertips and she wanted to feel more.

'No? Well, maybe it was just me, fantasising about the feel of your hands on my body.' Nik looked at her through long dark lashes. 'Maybe I was projecting my desire onto you.'

Carrie bit her lip, unable to speak. His words seemed too much to take in, but her body was already responding to them. The thought that he'd fantasised about her hands touching him sent her pulse soaring and make her tingle deep inside.

'Show me how you feel,' Nik said. 'Run your hand across my body just like you smoothed it along the silky length of my tie. I want to look into your eyes as you touch me.'

'No, I'm not going to play your games,' Carrie said. She avoided meeting his gaze, but the sight of her hand inside his shirt was almost as unsettling.

'I said you were afraid.' Nik smiled. 'Afraid of the attraction between us.'

'I'm not afraid,' Carrie protested. 'And I don't need to prove anything to you.'

'Indulge me.' Nik's voice was a low, seductive purr that rolled right through her.

She held her breath and looked at him, wondering what to do. His gorgeous face was so close to hers and he was giving her every ounce of his attention. For an absurd moment she felt as if she was the only woman in the world.

He wanted her to touch him, and she wanted the same thing. Alarm bells were ringing in her mind but she ignored them. She could do this. Satisfy her desire to touch him, then pull away and pretend she was indifferent. He had challenged her, and if she didn't rise to the challenge he'd never let it drop.

'All right.' She looked him boldly in the eye as a surge of courage fuelled by excitement stormed through her. 'I'll show you I'm immune to your charms. But are you sure your ego will be able to take it when I don't swoon at your feet?'

Nik said nothing, but dipped his head and focussed on her from beneath half-closed lids. He released his hold on her wrist, leaving her free to withdraw her hand if she wanted.

She didn't want to. She just couldn't resist the temptation to make the most of this opportunity.

She could feel the ridge of his collarbone, and she slipped

her hand along it up to his powerful shoulder. Then she traced her fingertips gently back to the hollow at the base of his throat. His skin felt silky and smooth and she wanted to feel more.

She laid her palm flat and started to slide it downwards across the top part of his pectoral muscle. She'd seen his well-developed pecs through his shirt, and she had an overwhelming desire to feel his muscle swell against her hand and find his nipple with her fingertips.

Suddenly her hand was stuck, her wrist blocked by his next button, which was still tightly fastened.

'I said I wanted to look in your eyes.' Nik's deep voice startled her, then he cupped his hand under her chin and tilted her head towards him. 'Feel free to rip the buttons off, if the desire takes you that way,' he added, his eyes glittering.

'There's no need,' she replied, dismayed by how breathless her voice sounded. She looked up into his deep blue eyes, determined to brazen it out. She had to convince him of her indifference.

She lifted her free hand and undid the next button, and then the next one for good measure.

Her hand glided lower, and the well-defined bulge of his muscle felt as amazing against her palm as she had anticipated. Her fingertips brushed over the taut skin on his chest, and then she found his nipple.

A sudden release of hot melting desire turned her insides to liquid. Her fingers had itched to touch him, but she'd never guessed that stroking him would be as arousing as the feel of his hands touching her.

'Look at me.' Nik's voice rumbled through her, vibrating deep into her feminine centre.

She gasped, startled again by the strength of her desire, by her body's physical response to his voice.

'I said, look at me.' His voice resonated through her again, making her blood sing.

She blinked in confusion, realising that her eyes had slipped out of focus.

She pulled herself together and stared at Nik, overwhelmed by how powerfully she was reacting. His eyes, dark and sultry with obvious sexual need, were fixed on hers. She wondered vaguely if her own eyes were giving her away, but soon her mind was full of her own desire.

She let her fingertips circle his nipple, brushing against it with delicate teasing touches. She felt it stiffen against the pads of her fingers and she rubbed it lightly, then pinched it between her finger and thumb.

All the time she was looking into Nik's eyes. The deep blue colour was growing darker and his lids were sinking lower. There was no doubt as to how he was responding to her caresses, and that thought made her desire sharper still.

'You said you didn't want to touch me,' Nik said, his voice impossibly deep.

'I didn't want to,' Carrie replied, amazed at how steady she managed to keep her voice. 'I was proving a point, like you wanted me to.'

'I think we've proved the point,' Nik said huskily.

'No,' Carrie protested. Then her voice dried up as Nik took a step closer, trapping her hand between them.

'Now I'm going to kiss you,' he said, leaning close so that once again his lips were brushing hers.

'No,' Carrie gasped, but her body was already humming with desire.

'I asked you to touch me,' Nik murmured against her lips. 'And in exchange I said I'd kiss you.'

'It wasn't like that,' Carrie said. 'You're making it sound like…like…'

'Like we're both consenting adults free to express our desires, free to tell each other what we want?' Nik asked. 'Don't worry. I like that in a lover. I want to know your fantasies. I want to know how to satisfy you.'

Carrie's mind was spinning and her body was buzzing with overpowering desire for Nik. But her response to him was suddenly frightening her. She'd thought she could play Nik at his own game, but now she knew she'd been mistaken. He was a confident, sexually experienced man. She'd never even had a serious boyfriend.

She pulled away suddenly, taking a step backwards so that she was pressed up against the door frame.

A knock at the door right beside her head made her jump, and she jerked her hand free of his shirt, popping off several buttons in the process.

'I ordered Room Service,' Nik said, glancing down at his torn shirt. He didn't seem in the least moved by his damaged shirt, or surprised by the sudden intrusion, but he made no move to open the door. 'I thought you probably hadn't eaten today.'

'Room Service?' Carrie echoed in confusion, struggling to pull her thoughts together.

'You should eat,' Nik said, suddenly stepping round her and opening the hotel room door. 'I've got work to do before we leave.'

Carrie blinked as a trolley was wheeled in. She leant against the safety of the wall and took a moment to recover herself, while Nik signed for the food and tipped the waiter.

But she knew it would take more than a moment recover herself. Her legs felt weak and her heart was still racing. Her lips still tingled where he had brushed his against them, and an incredible yearning was building up inside her. She wanted him to kiss her. And that was not all she wanted.

'I didn't know what you'd like,' Nik said, apparently completely oblivious to the way she was feeling as he indicated the trolley that was loaded with a startling amount of food. 'Eat what you want, and if I have time after I finish this work I'll grab a bite as well.'

He'd never meant to kiss her, she realised with a jolt. The thought sent a ghastly weight slamming down to the pit of her stomach. He'd known that Room Service was coming all along—known that they'd soon be interrupted. He'd just been playing with her.

She was still reeling from what had happened between them, yet apparently he had totally switched off. The desire she'd thought she'd seen in his eyes and heard in his voice had completely evaporated.

'I'm not hungry,' she said, feeling the words stick in her dry throat as she moved towards the doorway into the other hotel room. 'I'm going to check on Danny. Then I'll try to get a bit of rest myself.'

Even though she hadn't eaten all day, the thought of food suddenly made her feel sick, and getting away from Nik was the most important thing.

'Before you go—' Nik called her back. 'I'll be needing your passports.'

'What?' Carrie turned and stared at him in confusion.

'To make arrangements,' Nik explained, sitting down at his laptop and opening it up.

'Oh.' Carrie paused. She'd almost forgotten that she'd agreed to Nik taking her and Danny home. 'But I thought we were going in your private plane. We don't need tickets for that.'

'We're still travelling from one country to another.' He

didn't look up from his laptop, and the tone in his voice suggested he was stating something that was blindingly obvious.

'Oh,' Carrie muttered again, going through to get her bag. It wasn't *her* fault she wasn't used to travelling by private jet. He didn't have to treat her like an idiot.

'Here you are.'

He still didn't look up, so she placed the passports on the table next to the laptop and slipped quietly back into Danny's room.

CHAPTER SIX

CARRIE woke up with a start and realised straight away that the plane had landed.

'It's time to go,' Nik said. 'I've already carried Danny out to the car.'

'I'm coming,' she said, getting groggily to her feet. She didn't remember falling asleep, and even now it was a struggle to wake up properly. 'Sorry—I'm a bit wobbly.'

'You've had a difficult day,' Nik said. 'It's not surprising you're exhausted.'

'I suppose so,' Carrie said. She peered out of the plane window and frowned. It was dark, and she couldn't see much, but it didn't look at all familiar.

'This doesn't look like Gatwick,' she said.

'It's not,' Nik said. He picked up Carrie's hand luggage and moved towards the exit.

'Where have you brought us?' Carrie asked. He had already told her he used small airports. This must be one of them.

'Corfu,' Nik said. 'Come. You'll want to be with Danny, in case he wakes up.'

'What?' Carrie gasped in surprise. She couldn't have heard him properly. Even someone as arrogant and controlling as Nik couldn't have brought her to a foreign country without her permission. 'Corfu?' she repeated in sheer disbelief. 'You said you'd take us home!'

'I didn't say your home,' Nik shrugged. 'This is my home, and it is a much more suitable place for Danny to recover.'

'It wasn't your choice!' Carrie cried, hardly able to believe what she was hearing. A terrible day had suddenly got a whole lot worse. 'You deceived me. You've brought us here against my will!'

'It's for the best,' Nik said. 'There's no need for you to be cooped up in that dismal little flat. Obviously you will be more comfortable in my home. You can relax and Danny can have the best care to aid his recovery.'

'I want you to take me home to London,' Carrie said coldly, digging in her heels and refusing to move. 'It's what we agreed, and you know it.'

'Whatever for?' Nik sounded genuinely surprised. 'What is so important in London?'

'My job, Danny's nursery, our home!' Carrie's voice rose as she spoke.

'Danny can't go to nursery while he's sick,' Nik said. 'So you can't work. And don't expect me to believe you'd rather be stuck in that tiny flat than taking it easy in my home.'

'I'm not discussing this with you. It's my decision, not yours,' Carrie said firmly, wishing she felt as confident as her voice sounded. 'I'm getting Danny and taking him home, *to London*, right now.'

'How are you planning to do that?' Nik asked, lifting his dark brows superciliously. 'You'll have no more chance of getting him on a flight here than you did in Menorca. What's more, I'm not going to risk my nephew's well-being by leaving him in your care when you're obviously not thinking straight.'

'I wasn't thinking straight when I trusted you to take us

home,' Carrie snapped. Tears were pricking behind her eyes but she blinked furiously, determined not to let him see how upset and helpless she felt.

Nik paused at the exit and looked back at her, his broad shoulders virtually blocking the view of the airport behind him.

'By now Danny is safely in a car that is ready to take him to my home,' he said. 'Whether you join us is up to you, but Danny is coming home with me tonight.'

He turned calmly and started down the steps to the tarmac below.

Carrie dashed after him, her heart pounding as she burst through the doorway into the warm night air.

'Wait!' she shouted, stumbling prccariously on the top step and grabbing the metal rail to keep her balance. 'You can't do this.'

'Of course I can.' Nik turned and looked up and her, his expression utterly implacable. 'It's already done.'

'But you lied to me!' Carrie cried. 'This is kidnapping!'

Nik studied her for a moment, not even bothering to defend himself, and then he pulled something out of his jacket pocket.

'Here's your passport,' he said, tossing it up to her. She caught it instinctively. He also put her bag down on the step beside him, so she could pick it up as she passed. 'You can do as you wish. Danny stays with me.'

Oh, God! Her stomach plummeted as she stared at the passport in her hand. Nik still had Danny's!

'Wait!' she shouted again, clanking down the steps behind him. 'Give Danny's passport to me right now,' she demanded, snatching up her bag from the step as she passed.

'I'm going home,' Nik said over his shoulder. 'You may do as you wish.'

Carrie stared in dismay as he strode across the tarmac

away from her. Her stomach was churning and she felt horribly sick. She couldn't believe this was happening, but she knew if she didn't follow him he'd soon be driving Danny away into the Greek night without her.

She did the only thing she could. Gripping her shoulder bag tightly, she started to run after him.

Carrie stared out of the window as the limousine made its way swiftly through the one-way system of Corfu Town. It was late at night, but there were still a surprising amount of people about.

She'd never been to Corfu before, but she knew it was a busy tourist spot, popular with the British. If only she could get Danny away from Nikos Kristallis, surely there would be people she could ask for help?

She glanced sideways at Nik. He was leaning forward, watching the sleeping baby with an unsettling intensity.

'I need to stop here in town,' Carrie said suddenly, knocking on the window that separated them from the driver. 'Could you ask your driver to pull over?'

'Whatever you need will be provided at my home,' Nik said, picking up the internal telephone to communicate with the driver. 'There's no need to stop.'

Carrie gritted her teeth and looked through the glass to see the man talking to Nik on the telephone link. She had expected him to slide open the glass that separated them. But she knew without Nik's support she didn't have much chance of persuading his driver to stop for her.

'I need to pick up some things for Danny and for me. I didn't expect to be away from home for so long,' Carrie tried again.

'Don't think about doing something foolish.' Nik turned to look at her. 'I have Danny's passport and a copy of his birth certificate. He is my nephew and my family is well known here. No one will help you take the child out of Corfu without my permission.'

Carrie bit her lip and went back to staring out of the window. They were driving through the countryside now. It was dark, but she could see that the road was winding its way through dense olive groves. She tried to concentrate on remembering the route, so that she could retrace it on her own if she got the opportunity. But all she could think about was how foolish she'd been.

She'd played right into Nik's hands. It would have been very hard for him to take Danny out of England without her consent, but she had done it for him.

Of course she hadn't known Danny would come down with chickenpox, but Nik had been all too quick to turn that to his advantage. She should never have accepted his offer to take her home. And she should definitely not have handed over Danny's passport.

'My home is the other side of this mountain,' Nik said. 'It is quite isolated, so please don't try stumbling about outside. I don't want you falling down a rocky path.'

'Really?' Carrie asked nastily. 'If I broke my neck falling off a mountain, surely that would solve all your problems?'

'Not if you kill yourself on my property,' Nik said coldly. 'I should also warn you that the very best modern security system protects the perimeter of my land. You won't be able to leave with Danny.'

'You mean I'm your prisoner.' Carrie glared at him.

'Not at all. You are quite free to leave any time you choose,' Nik replied.

'No one will try to stop me?' Carrie asked suspiciously.

'My staff will have orders to take you anywhere you want to go,' Nik said. 'But you will not leave with Danny.'

Carrie tossed her hair back and turned to the window. She should be paying attention to her surroundings. The limousine was climbing into the mountains, sliding slowly round an alarming series of hairpin bends.

Surely this couldn't be the same road they had been driving along a minute ago? That one had been narrow and windy enough, but nothing like this hair-raising track. They must have turned off the main road, but she had missed the junction.

The limousine went slowly and carefully, but Carrie couldn't help feeling jittery. She only hoped they didn't meet another car coming the other way.

She glanced at Nik, but he appeared completely oblivious to the fact that the limousine seemed to be clinging precariously to the side of a mountain. Instead he was studying Danny intently, a slight frown creasing his strong forehead.

'He's been asleep a long time,' he said. 'Is that normal?'

Carrie blinked in surprise, caught off kilter by Nik's sudden question.

'I think so,' she said. 'After all, it is his usual bedtime.'

'But he slept a lot of the afternoon, and he hasn't had anything to eat or drink.' Nik leant forward and brushed a gentle hand over the sleeping child's brow.

'No doubt he'll make up for it later.'

Nik was acting like a concerned father, Carrie thought with a worrying stab of anxiety. It was good that he was genuinely concerned about Danny, but it was making her feel uneasy.

'Should we wake him?' Nik turned to look at her.

It was dark inside the limousine, but Carrie could tell his sharp eyes were scrutinising her. Instinct told her that it wouldn't be a good idea to wake Danny, but now Nik and his questions were making her feel worried.

'How long till we arrive at your place?' she asked.

'Only a few minutes now,' Nik said.

'Let's wait and see if he wakes up naturally when we move him,' Carrie said. 'If he doesn't, we can wake him and give him a drink, see if he's hungry.'

'I'll call ahead and have some food prepared.' Nik pulled out his mobile phone. 'What does he eat?'

'It's all right. I have a jar of food in my bag,' Carrie said.

'A *jar*?' Nik repeated incredulously, the disapproval plain in his deep voice. 'Obviously we have very different standards, but don't think for a minute you will feed my nephew mass-prepared convenience food in my home.'

'It's a good brand,' Carrie said, feeling slightly defensive. She cooked fresh food for Danny at weekends if she could, but she did feel a little guilty over giving him shop-bought meals at other times. 'It's organic,' she added, 'and, most importantly, now that he's feeling ill, it's what he's used to, and I know he likes it.'

At that moment Danny made a little murmuring cry. Both pairs of adult eyes were instantly fixed on the infant, who was finally stirring from his long sleep.

Nik stared at Danny in alarm. Was it normal for a baby to howl quite so loudly? He didn't know, but in the confined space of the limousine the noise was almost unbearable.

Fortunately it was only a matter of moments before they arrived at the villa. He led the way swiftly through the building to the suite of rooms that had been prepared for them. A cot had been brought in and placed close to a large bed that Carrie could use.

'Shall I call the housekeeper to help you?' he asked, speaking loudly to be heard over the incredible racket Danny was still making. 'Her English is not good, but she has many grandchildren so she will know what to do. Is there anything else you need?'

'I'm used to managing on my own,' Carrie said, perching on a chair and offering Danny his beaker of water. 'But perhaps someone could warm a little milk?'

'Of course,' Nik said. He took a step backwards, then turned and walked out of the room, issuing orders to his assistant.

He sat down in the adjoining room and opened his laptop. He would use the time to catch up on some work, and also keep an eye on the proceedings in the next room.

It was a long night. After his milk Danny settled down a bit, but not for more than a few minutes. Carrie walked around the room holding him in her arms. She tried laying him down in his cot while playing a gentle melody from a music box. She even tried rocking him in his buggy. The night wore on, but whatever Carrie tried Danny just wouldn't sleep. She was beginning to look dead on her feet, and Nik was starting to think he should call the housekeeper to help.

Then, eventually, Danny's head drooped onto Carrie's shoulder and he was quiet. Nik watched her ease herself carefully down onto the bed, and miraculously Danny didn't stir.

He saw Carrie's eyelids slide down. She was so exhausted that she was asleep in a moment. Danny was sleeping too, nestled snugly against her, although he had slipped down and was supported by the bed, with his little tousled head resting in the crook of her arm.

Nik watched her sleep. He couldn't help but admire her beauty as he looked at her jet-black hair spread out on the white pillow behind her head, her long black lashes making a delicate arc on the pale skin of her cheek.

The grey light of dawn was just forming outside, and it had been a long, tiring night. But it wasn't quite over yet, and when a murmuring whimper caught Nik's ear his gaze instantly flicked back to the baby.

Danny had started to stir again. In a moment he would be fully awake and howling at the top of his lungs.

Nik knew what he had to do. He crossed quickly and silently to the bed where they were lying. In her sleep Carrie had relaxed her hold, and it was easy to slip Danny gently away from her.

CHAPTER SEVEN

THE sun was streaming in through a chink in the curtains when Carrie woke up. She jerked into a sitting position and gazed groggily around the unfamiliar room. Her mind was foggy and for a moment she couldn't remember where she was.

Then the previous day's events came flooding back—Danny coming down with chickenpox, Nik bringing them to Corfu without her knowledge and against her wishes, and then, finally, the long night spent comforting Danny.

Suddenly she realised Danny was gone. She stumbled to her feet and looked wildly round the room, but he was not on the bed or in the cot.

Nik had taken him! He was probably halfway to Athens, or wherever else he had a house, by now.

Maybe not, she thought, forcing herself not to panic. She had to keep her head until she found out what had happened. She hurried to the door, but despite her best efforts to stay calm, her heart was in her mouth as she opened it and burst through into the adjoining room.

She stopped in her tracks and stared.

The room seemed to be full of people gathered round the sofa, where Danny lay on his changing mat, having his nappy changed by an older Greek woman. Carrie guessed she must be Nik's housekeeper, Irene, because she seemed to know what she was doing and was keeping Danny's attention with a lively stream of chatter.

'You're awake,' Nik said, glancing at her briefly before turning his attention back to the sofa, where Irene was slipping Danny's legs smoothly into his sleepsuit and fastening the poppers with a deft hand. 'I'll send for some food.'

He issued a series of orders and a younger woman who had been hovering near the door hurried away. Irene scooped Danny up, then turned and passed him carefully to Carrie before leaving as well.

Carrie's heart-rate had started to ease once she'd seen Danny was safe, but nothing beat having him back in her arms again, and she cuddled him tightly. He was no longer flushed and sweaty, as he'd been last night. He seemed much more settled as he curled up comfortably against her shoulder.

'You frightened me, taking him like that,' Carrie said. 'What happened? Why didn't you wake me?'

'You'd barely had any sleep at all when he woke up,' Nik said.

'I would have managed,' Carrie said, pressing her face into Danny's curly hair. 'That's what looking after a sick child is like. You can get by on hardly any sleep if your baby needs you.'

'It's not necessary for you to risk my nephew's well-being by running yourself into the ground,' Nik replied. 'You're not on your own any more.'

Carrie stared at him crossly. She couldn't stand his arrogant attitude, but she didn't want to start arguing with him right over the top of Danny's head.

'Nevertheless, I want your word that you won't take him from me again when I'm sleeping,' she insisted.

'It was an exceptional circumstance,' Nik said with a shrug.

'Hopefully the child won't keep you up all night again any time soon.'

His glib response was infuriating, but Carrie bit her tongue because at that moment the young woman returned, carrying a tray loaded with food and drink.

'Here is your breakfast,' Nik said, gesturing to the young woman to take the food outside onto the balcony. 'Danny has eaten and taken some milk. Now, if you'll excuse me, there are things I must attend to.'

With that he walked out of the room, leaving her alone with Danny. Carrie stared after him in irritation, then turned and stepped through the open door onto a long balcony that seemed to wrap itself around that end of the villa. The young Greek woman was waiting by the table, which was laid with a generous breakfast.

'Would you like some coffee? Or anything else to eat?' she asked politely.

'No, no, there's more than enough here,' Carrie said, realising just how thirsty she was as her eyes settled on the frosty jug of juice.

'Would you like me to hold the baby while you eat?' the young woman offered.

'No, thank you.' Carrie smiled. 'He can sit on my lap. We'll be fine on our own. Thank you,' she said again, relieved when she took the hint and left them alone.

Carrie sat down at the table and looked at the array of food, feeling slightly overwhelmed. She'd hardly eaten yesterday, and although she was absolutely ravenous she didn't know where to start.

She poured herself a glass of fresh juice and lifted it to drink.

She paused, the glass forgotten halfway to her lips, and stared with wide eyes at the incredible view from the balcony.

Nik had said his house was in the mountains, but Carrie had never imagined the sheer breathtaking beauty of its setting. Verdant wooded slopes, shimmering with the iridescent silver-green leaves of olive trees, dropped dramatically down to a glittering turquoise sea. The tall thin spikes of cypress trees punctuated the landscape, and the rusty brown exposed rock of the mountain across from Nik's house provided a stunning backdrop.

It was a perfect Mediterranean day, and a more beautiful setting would be hard to picture. Carrie stood up and carried the now sleeping Danny nearer to the edge of the balcony, so she could look at the view properly.

For the last seven years she'd lived in London, where the view from her window was the rather dull sight of the flats across the road from her. Before that, at her aunt and uncle's house, she'd had a small side room with a view of their neighbours' garage roof. She couldn't even begin to imagine what it must be like to live somewhere so beautiful.

She took a long drink of the cool juice and looked out at the clear blue sky. The ground fell away sharply beneath the villa, and the tops of the cypress trees undulating gently in the breeze close to the balcony made her feel as if she was in a tree house, suspended above the awe-inspiring terrain.

Awakened by the orange juice, her stomach growled, and Carrie turned back to the table. Her mouth watered at the sight of the succulent fresh figs with their rosy centres, and thick white Greek yoghurt drizzled with amber honey. She sat down and started tucking in to a hearty breakfast, making up for the meals she'd missed the day before.

Carrie took a last bite of a very sweet sticky pastry, covered with chopped nuts and a delicately flavoured orange syrup, then leant back in her chair with a sigh.

The balcony was a very pleasant place to sit, and after all the stress of the previous day it felt good to hold the sleeping baby in her arms, but she really ought to transfer him to his cot.

She stood up, carried Danny inside, and laid him in the travel cot that had been set up in the small living room adjacent to the bedroom. She stood back and held her breath, hoping he wouldn't wake. Then she tiptoed quietly through the bedroom into the *en-suite* bathroom, removed the clothes she'd been wearing for more than twenty-four hours and took a quick shower.

A few minutes later she was just slipping into a clean dress when Nik's voice coming from behind nearly made her jump out of her skin.

'He's asleep,' he said. 'Good. We need to talk.'

She spun round to see Nik standing in the doorway, watching her with an unnerving intensity in his deep blue eyes. He reminded her of a predator, waiting for its moment to strike, and she felt her heart start to beat faster.

'Don't you ever knock?' she asked hotly, quickly buttoning up the front of her dress. She was acutely conscious of how his dark gaze had settled on her exposed cleavage and a wave of heat washed through her body. Suddenly her stomach was fluttering, and she was catapulted straight back to the way he'd made her feel in the hotel room in Menorca. A minute earlier and he'd have caught her in her underwear—or even wearing nothing at all.

'I'm sorry if I startled you.' Nik sounded far from apologetic as he strode right into the bedroom and shut the door. 'I approached quietly, so as not to disturb the child. We should talk without distraction.'

Carrie's eyes flicked to the closed bedroom door and a

sense of danger coiled through her. She wanted to suggest they move to a different room, but she didn't want Nik to realise that she was feeling intimidated by him.

She looked back at him, noticing for the first time that he'd taken the opportunity to freshen up too—his hair was still wet from the shower and he had changed his clothes. The short-sleeved ivory shirt and dark trousers were less formal than his usual sleek designer suits, but they didn't make him seem any less imposing.

'I'm here to discuss Danny's future,' Nik said. 'There are decisions that must be made immediately.'

'Good.' Carrie straightened her shoulders and looked him squarely in the eye. 'I appreciate you getting right to the point, but before we continue there is something I need to make absolutely plain.'

'What is that?' He watched her through narrowed eyes, looking irritated that she had something to say that delayed his personal agenda.

'You are not to do anything without my agreement,' Carrie said. 'Bringing us to Corfu without my permission was unacceptable. I won't be naïve enough to fall for anything like that again.'

'That's behind us now,' Nik said, not giving her the assurance she was after. 'What's already happened is no longer relevant. We're here now, with decisions to make that will affect all our futures.'

'It's relevant to *me*!' Carrie exclaimed. She wasn't ready to let that incident drop yet—not until he'd acknowledged he was in the wrong. 'You blatantly deceived me! You took—'

'You keep saying Danny is important to you,' Nik interrupted. 'If that's the case I suggest you stop delaying our discussion about his future.' The menace in his voice warned

Carrie that he was not going to lose sight of his goal easily. Well, neither was she.

'I will never give Danny up.' She spoke clearly and plainly, hoping it was the best way to make him understand.

'Nor will I,' Nik said. 'That is why I have come to offer you a compromise.'

'A compromise?' Carrie repeated. If he was going to suggest they shared custody she wouldn't agree. She might, at a pinch, agree to visitation rights. But she'd never ever give Danny up, even part time. It wasn't just that she'd promised Sophie and Leonidas, she had grown to love Danny too much to ever let him go—especially to a controlling, duplicitous man like Nikos Kristallis.

'You will marry me,' Nik said. 'And like any other married couple we will share his upbringing.'

Carrie stared at him in shock.

Had she heard him properly? Maybe the sleepless nights were finally catching up with her. That must be it, because he couldn't possibly, in all seriousness, have said she was to marry him.

'What did you say?' she asked, her voice scratching her suddenly dry throat.

'We will be married,' Nik said.

'Are you crazy?' she gasped, staring at him in astonishment.

'Not at all,' he replied. 'Marriage is the only solution if you wish to retain any contact with Danny.'

'I'm not marrying you,' Carrie said, finally realising he really meant it—although she still couldn't believe she was actually having this conversation. 'I've never heard anything so ridiculous in my life. I don't even *like* you!'

'A marriage of convenience is the only compromise I'm prepared to offer you,' Nik said coldly. 'And take note that it is a one-time only offer. You must agree to it now or you will lose Danny for ever.'

'How can you call it a compromise?' Carrie asked, hearing her voice rise with appalled disbelief. 'Unless you mean I am to compromise all my values and beliefs by marrying someone I despise!'

'*I* am making the compromise.' Nik's voice cut like steel through the air. 'Marry me and you will still be part of Danny's life. If you refuse I'll have you escorted off my property today and you will never see him again.'

'You can't do that!' Carrie cried.

'I can do anything I want.' There was a dangerous edge to his words. 'Now, what is your answer?'

'I'll never give up Danny!' Carrie said, horrified to feel tears prick behind her eyes. She blinked them away, refusing to show any weakness in front of Nik. He was detestable, coming to her and making such an unbelievable demand.

'I'll take that as your agreement.' Nik turned to leave. 'I will start the arrangements for our marriage straight away.'

'No!' Carrie flew across the room and seized his arm.

She was strong, and fit from years of exercise, but as she grabbed him he was as solid and unmoving as rock. She held on to him just above his elbow, knowing that he stopped and turned back because he chose to, not because of the pressure she was exerting on his arm.

'You can't marry me without my consent.' She looked up into his face and spoke through gritted teeth.

'I'll have your consent.'

'No, you won't!' Carrie said.

'I'll have *anything* I want.' He let his eyes sweep over her in a way that set her senses on red alert. But, despite the sense of danger, a dark ripple of anticipation shuddered through her.

He moved his arm slightly and Carrie suddenly realised she still had hold of him. His bicep bunched beneath her fingers, strong and powerfully sexy, making the nerves in her hand tingle in response.

'Is this about sex?' Carrie swallowed, letting her hand drop from his arm and taking a step backwards out of his reach. 'Did you propose just to get me into bed?'

'Don't be so naive,' Nik said darkly, edging forward. 'Why would I go to such lengths? You've always been easy prey—you've wanted me since the first moment we met in Darren's study.'

'No…no…that's not true,' Carrie stammered, backing away another step. Her heart was racing and her stomach was turning wild somersaults.

'It's nothing to be ashamed of.' Nik suddenly closed the gap between them and lifted his hands to cup the back of her head. 'It works both ways. I've wanted you since the beginning as well.'

'I don't want you!' Carrie protested, raising both arms to push his hands away from her head.

'Why fight it?' He caught her wrists, one in each hand, and held them above her head. She was locked in position, her arms in the air, her breasts pushing up towards him.

'Because you're a beast!' she cried. She tried to pull her hands down, to escape from his grip, but suddenly she became ultra-aware of how exposed her body felt with her arms above her head. A skitter of excitement ran through her, and her breasts started to throb. 'You lied to me, kidnapped me, and now you're threatening me!'

'But still I turn you on.' His voice, rich and deep, vibrated through her, setting off a reaction through her entire body.

'No!' She denied it passionately, but she couldn't suppress

the compulsion to arch her back, thrusting her breasts closer to his chest. Her nipples felt hard as diamonds and were aching for him.

'Yes, I do,' he purred, leaning forward so that his chest brushed briefly against the points of her nipples, setting them on fire with the slightest contact, then withdrawing to leave them aching with frustration. 'You're desperate for my touch.'

'I'm not.' Her voice was a husky whisper and her body hummed with her pent-up desire for him.

'I'm going to touch you all over,' he said, tugging her towards him so that her breasts rubbed against his chest again and a frisson of sexual excitement buzzed through her. 'I'm going to explore every inch of your body, find all the secret places that are yearning for my touch and make them mine.'

She squeezed her eyes shut, trying to ignore the sensations and desires that were storming her body, but it was impossible. Despite all the reasons why it would be a disaster to let Nikos Kristallis make love to her, there was nothing else in the world she could think about.

She wanted him to make love to her. She was desperate for him to make love to her.

'Don't fight it.' He released his hold on her wrists and started sliding his hands downwards, across the sensitive skin on the underside of her arms. Then his hands slid round to her back, and Carrie knew he was ready to pull her into his tight embrace. 'We both want this and I promise it will be good.'

She stared up at him, seeing his desire for her darkening his blue eyes. Her hands were clutching the front of his shirt, the fabric scrunched in her fists, and she realised she was pulling him towards her rather than pushing him away.

Then there was no more time for thought as his mouth

came down on hers and suddenly he was kissing her with a fierce intensity.

She responded with a passion that equalled his, opening her lips and letting his tongue sweep into her mouth in a sensual invasion that took her breath away. Her mind was spinning and her body was trembling uncontrollably, but she clung to him, locked to his kiss as though nothing else mattered.

Their tongues moved together in a sensual dance, but the effects of the kiss extended far beyond the feelings created by their joined mouths. Waves of sensation washed through her whole body, making her reel from the intensity of it.

It was a soul-shattering kiss, a kiss that delved into her very being and laid bare the shockingly powerful desire she felt for Nik.

She hardly noticed his hands moving as they skimmed across her body, but as they closed over her breasts her centre of awareness shifted immediately.

He held both breasts, cupping them gently in the palms of his hands. Then he started kneading the aching flesh through the fabric of her dress, teasing the jutting nipples with his thumbs.

The muscles in her neck felt weak, and as he pulled away from their kiss she let her head fall back, a sound of pure pleasure sighing from her open lips. It felt so good to feel his hands touching her, stroking her, sending wonderful feelings washing through her. But she yearned for more. She needed more.

Almost of their own volition her hands went to the buttons on her dress, undoing them—one, two, three—until Nik closed his hands over hers and pushed the top of her dress wide open. Her white bra had a front fastening, and in a second her breasts were free.

Nik bent down and took the throbbing peak of one breast in his mouth. She cried out and buried her hands in his hair, pulling him tightly to her. He responded by drawing the nipple deeply into his mouth, sucking harder and increasing the pressure of his caressing tongue.

A torrent of desire stormed through her, making her quiver and moan. An incredible pulsing of pure sexual energy started throbbing at the very core of her femininity, making her moan with pleasure and press her thighs tightly together.

She had never felt anything like it before, and was totally unprepared for the intensity of her own reaction. She felt herself swaying as her legs started to give way.

Nik swept her up into his arms and carried her over to the bed, where he laid her down. He sat beside her, leaning over her and looking down at her with blue eyes that were already dark with his rising passion. Excitement coiled through her and she started to tremble with anticipation. She couldn't just lie there, waiting for him to make a move, so she lifted her hands and grasped his shoulders to pull him down.

His arms were braced on either side of her body, but he let her tug him slowly down until his face hovered only inches above her own. His eyes were intense and he held her gaze for the longest moment, despite the fact that her hands were running wild all over his body, tugging his shirt free of his trousers and slipping underneath to touch his skin.

The heat of his body drew her like a magnetic attraction, and she slid her hands round to the front and started undoing his buttons. She wanted to see him naked, wanted to feel his naked body beneath her palms.

Then he pressed down, trapping her hands between their bodies, and kissed her. It was no gentle kiss, but a fierce and passionate conquest. His tongue plunged masterfully between her lips, thrusting into the soft interior of her mouth. She moved her tongue to meet his, and then they were writhing together in a kiss more erotic than Carrie had ever before experienced.

At last he lifted himself away slightly, allowing her hands to move freely again. She reached round him, smoothing her palms over the strong plains of his back, but he was on the move, suddenly kneeling over her, his hands on either side of her shoulders, one knee between her thighs and the other beside her hip. She was effectively pinned beneath him.

Her breath was coming in small, rapid gasps and she stared up at him hungrily, not caring that her desire for him must be completely obvious. He rocked forward, using his leg to nudge her dress up.

She gasped out loud as his long hard thigh brushed intimately between her legs, sending a jolt of pure sexual excitement thrilling through her. His expression intensified and he moved his leg again, letting it ride up and down between hers, all the time maintaining pressure on the place between her legs that was suddenly the very centre of her awareness.

A pulsing point of desire began to throb insistently where his thigh rubbed against her. She moaned with pleasure and looked up at him. She could see in his eyes that he wanted her, and if that wasn't enough she could feel his arousal, pressing hard and ready through the thin fabric of her summer dress.

She reached for him again, this time her hands finding the buckle of his belt. The leather was soft and flexible and she slipped the end through the loop. Suddenly he straightened up and he pushed her hands aside once more. He jerked the belt undone and quickly removed the rest of his clothes.

He stood naked beside the bed and she gazed up at his magnificent form appreciatively. She was torn between the desire to look and the need to touch, but she didn't have time for either as he quickly bent over her again and grasped her panties in his strong hands. With one swift movement he pulled them down and tossed them away.

Her heart thumped erratically as he knelt between her thighs. Her body was aching with her need for him, but at that last second she felt a rush of nervous energy. She wanted him. But this was something she'd never done before.

She looked up at him, gloriously naked above her, and, inexperienced as she was, her body knew what it wanted.

She needed to feel him moving inside her, and that need was growing greater every moment. She let her knees fall apart and reached to pull him down onto her, into her.

He hesitated, looking at her face as the hard tip of his penis pressed against her. She wriggled, unable to bear the delay, and lifted her hips towards him. At that moment he pressed forward, and as their bodies were finally joined she felt a sharp momentary pain.

He stopped suddenly, as if he had sensed what had happened, and looked down at her with an unreadable expression in his eyes.

The pain passed in a second, and as she felt her body ease to accommodate his hard masculine length she let out a long low moan of satisfaction.

But that was only the start. He began to move, and with each slow thrust a wave of pleasure crashed over her, spiralling out from the core of her womanhood to the tips of her fingers and beyond. It was wonderful. Her whole body trembled with delight, getting fuller and fuller with quivering, singing energy.

She was riding the moment, almost bursting with extraordinary sensation, moving closer and closer to the peak. Instinctively she lifted her knees towards her chest and angled her hips upwards, letting him thrust deeper and deeper into her. With every thrust she cried out, clinging to him, gripping his buttocks and holding him as tight to her as she could. His body was growing damp with sweat and her hands glided over his slick skin.

The pressure was building within her and she felt as if she would explode. She lifted her head, straining towards him, biting down on his neck as his head dipped next to hers.

Suddenly her moment came. Her toes curled, her breath caught in her throat and she felt her climax breaking over her like a tidal wave of sensation, pulsing through her body to every extremity. Her back arched and her head fell onto the pillow as she cried out his name. Aftershocks clenched inside her, and she felt her inner muscles tightening convulsively around his hardness, which was still moving deep inside her. The moment went on and on in an orgasm that was more powerful than anything she'd ever dreamed was possible.

Nik gave a shout and she knew his own climax was upon him. He reared back and was poised above her for a second as his body peaked in its moment of release. Then he collapsed onto her, breathing heavily in long ragged breaths.

She wrapped her arms around him, feeling his heart pounding against her breast, and let her body sink down into the bed, totally satisfied.

Nik lay there for a moment, feeling her body beneath his, feeling her still holding him inside.

He'd been right. Making love to Carrie had been good. No—*good* was not the right word. Incredible was a better way to describe it.

He lifted himself onto his elbows and rolled away so that he was beside her on the bed. He looked at her, waiting for his heart rate to slow, listening to the sound of her panting breaths slowly quieten.

She was lying supine next to him, still wearing her flowery summer dress, which was crumpled and mussed from their lovemaking. The front was slightly open, showing a glimpse of the shadow between her breasts, and the skirt was hiked up to her hips. She must have smoothed the hem down just enough to cover her decency when he moved off her, but her long legs were still gloriously naked.

She looked utterly irresistible, lying there in such wanton disarray, even though most of her body was still covered. In fact, apart from undoing the front of her bra, her panties were the only item of clothing that he'd removed. He remembered tearing them off and tossing them to one side, and was suddenly filled with an urgent desire to ravage her once more.

'Carrie,' he said, as a shaft of refreshed desire mixed with anger ripped through him, 'why didn't you tell me you were a virgin?'

CHAPTER EIGHT

'IT WAS none of your business.' Carrie pushed herself up into a sitting position and stared straight back at him. There was a defiant look on her flushed face, but deep in her green eyes he thought he could detect a glimmer of uncertainty.

'Of course it was,' he said.

An image of her strutting through the footballer's party, wearing that short red dress and those impossibly high-heeled sandals, flashed through his mind. No one who looked that sexy could be a virgin.

'No, it wasn't.' Carrie jumped off the bed and buttoned up the front of her dress. 'I didn't ask you how many lovers you've had before.'

'That's not the same thing,' Nik grated. 'And in any case I never misled you about my experience.'

He remembered all the times he'd kissed her. Her response had always been the same—as hot as hell. No timorous virgin could have been so full of desire for him.

'You're acting like I deprived you of something,' Carrie shot at him, her eyes flashing angrily.

'You lied to me.' He stood up and tugged his trousers on. 'And that will not be acceptable in the future.'

'I never lied,' Carrie said. 'You assumed.'

Nik looked at her, standing with her hands on her hips, staring straight back at him. Knowing that her bra was still undone under her dress and that she wasn't wearing any panties sent a powerful ache burning through him.

She was ripe and ready for picking, and he was the only man ever to have tasted the delights of her body. Now that she'd given herself to him, no other man would ever have her!

'We'll be married immediately,' he said.

'I'm not marrying you!' Carrie gasped. With everything that had just happened between them she'd almost forgotten the unbelievable proposal he'd made earlier. 'I never agreed to marry you!'

She bit her lip as she watched him pulling on his shirt. He couldn't really be serious about getting married, could he?

'I thought you'd understood the offer I made,' Nik said.

'It wasn't an offer,' Carrie replied, keeping her voice level. She had to keep her head and try to find a way out of this. 'It was blackmail.'

'Whatever you call it, the facts remain the same,' he said. 'Marry me and be a part of Danny's life—or leave and never see him again.'

'I'll fight you,' she said, hearing her voice rise as a jolt of panic ran through her. 'I'll get a lawyer.'

'Go ahead.' Nik turned away towards the door. 'Shall I send Irene to help you pack?'

'No!' She dashed across the room after him and was about to grab his arm to stop him when she remembered what had happened the last time she'd done that. At the last second she darted around him and stood with her back pressed against the closed door of the bedroom.

'You don't want to leave?' Nik said. 'I'm glad you're finally coming to your senses. It will be best for everyone.'

'No—we haven't finished our discussion yet,' Carrie said. She held her arms stiffly by her sides and looked up into his face, determined not to feel overwhelmed by him.

But suddenly he seemed very large and powerful in front of her. He was too close for comfort, yet she knew she was the one who had slipped past him, positioning herself in his personal space.

'You know that your choices are severely limited,' Nik said, fixing her with intense blue eyes. 'I will not allow Danny to be taken off my property, which means that if you wish to seek legal representation you will have to leave him with me. I have no problem with that—but I'm surprised you are willing to abandon him. It doesn't add up with the dedication that you've always claimed you have for him.'

'I would never abandon Danny,' Carrie said, feeling her blood run cold at the thought of leaving Danny behind. She knew if she did that she might never see him again.

'Then you must agree to marry me.' He towered over her, making her shrink back against the door.

How had she managed to get in so deep with Nikos Kristallis? There was no way out that she could think of. He was so rich and powerful that she didn't stand a chance against him.

'I don't understand why we have to be married,' Carrie said, stalling for time. Maybe if she went along with him, made him trust her, she would be able to find a way to get Danny away from him. 'We hardly know each other. It wouldn't be a real marriage.'

'It will be real.' His blue eyes bored deep into her, starting a trembling at the very core of her body. 'Make no mistake that it will be a proper marriage in every sense and you will be expected to do *everything* a proper wife would do.'

'But why...?' Carrie faltered, pressing her teeth into her lower lip as she stared up at him with stormy green eyes.

Nik looked at her, watching the shifting emotions play across her beautiful features. She'd be no good at poker—everything she felt was always written on her face.

'Because it's best for my nephew,' he said, satisfied that he was finally getting her where he wanted.

'But what about my job?' Carrie asked in desperation.

'You won't need one once you are my wife,' Nik replied. 'I have more than enough to keep you and Danny in a comfortable lifestyle.'

'I don't understand what's in it for you,' she said, still determined to show she wasn't about to meekly accept whatever he told her.

'It's not about me,' he replied. 'As I just said—it's about what is best for Danny.'

'But how can it be good for him to be cared for by two people who don't even like each other?' she asked, bright spots of colour appearing on her cheeks as she spoke.

'I don't dislike you.' He took a step closer to her and slipped his hand under her hair, which was still slightly damp from her shower. He pushed it back over her shoulder, feeling a shiver run through her.

'It won't be a proper marriage.' She straightened her shoulders and met his eye boldly, but he knew she was thinking about what it would be like sharing a bed with him each and every night. 'People will know.'

'No one will know.' His voice was so low it was almost a growl, and he knew the warning in his words was clear. 'You will never do or say anything to reveal our arrangement. The purpose of our union is to protect Danny—so we will show the world that we are happily married.'

'Even real marriages are not always happy.' Carrie's voice shrank to little more than a whisper, but she continued to match his gaze.

'I don't intend my marriage to be a battlefield. I won't live that way,' he said. 'Be nice—or I may retract my offer.'

A spark of defiance flashed in her eyes at his provocative words, but Nik knew she had accepted the situation. Soon Carrie would be his—signed, sealed and delivered.

Carrie stared at the wedding band on her finger. The civil ceremony was over—she was Nik's wife.

It was two weeks since he'd demanded they be married, and for Carrie that time had passed in a haze of exhaustion and disbelief. At first all her energy had gone into caring for Danny. Then, when he'd got better, she'd tried to talk to Nik—but he'd seemed to work all the time. She'd wanted to be certain that she couldn't persuade him to change his mind, but he'd never been available. And now it was too late. They were husband and wife.

She watched the sunlight glinting off the gold ring, hardly able to believe she was married. Things had happened so quickly, and the only thing she'd had any say in was the choice of her wedding gown. It felt as if her life was totally out of her own control.

'You look beautiful,' Nik said, handing her a glass of champagne.

She glanced up in surprise and realised that they were alone. It was the first time since the day they'd made love. His eyes were intense as he met and held hers, and her heart started to beat faster.

'Thank you.' She knew her cheeks were colouring under his continuing gaze but she didn't look away. They were married now—man and wife. Suddenly everything seemed different, and she felt the flutter of nerves deep inside her.

'I believe there are ways we can make this work,' he said, leaning close to her ear and letting his lips brush tantalisingly against the sensitive skin of her neck.

His warm breath whispered in her hair and she shivered with pleasure, her mind suddenly whirling with memories of Nik making love to her. She'd never imagined that it could be such a totally overwhelming experience—especially not her first time.

'I want to lock the door and make love to you right now,' he murmured, tracing his hand slowly down her spine in a way that made the hairs on the back of her neck stand up and hot liquid desire pool deep inside.

'Wouldn't they all know what we're doing?' Her voice was shaky as she replied, but a powerful feeling of excitement was building up within her as she let herself lean against his hard masculine form.

Her body was suddenly humming with anticipation, longing to enjoy the wonders of Nik's lovemaking again. For the last two weeks she hadn't been able to put thoughts of it out of her mind.

'That wouldn't matter. We're married.' He took her champagne glass away from her, then lifted his hands to gently cup her face. 'But I have to go now.'

'What?'

Carrie pulled back and stared at him in shock. Had he really just said he was going now?

'I have pressing work commitments that I can't ignore,' Nik said.

'But…but surely not today?' Carrie gasped, feeling humiliated. She glanced out of the window as the unmistakable sound of an approaching helicopter filled the air.

'It's not what I would have wanted, but this is important.' He turned away from her and strode to the door.

By the time he was out of the room Nik's body was rigid with the effort needed not to turn back and seize her in his arms. He wanted to cancel his business meeting, even though he was in the final stages of an important acquisition he'd been working on for ever. Right now it seemed less important than taking Carrie to bed.

It wasn't like him. He was a red-blooded male with a healthy appetite for women—but he'd always known when to put business before sex. Somehow Carrie had got under his skin, making him want to do things he wouldn't normally do.

Five days later Nik had still not returned to the villa. Carrie sat on the tree-top balcony, feeding Danny his breakfast and wondered just what she'd got herself into.

Nik had said he wanted to be part of Danny's life, that he wanted their marriage to appear normal—but he wasn't here. What if he never returned? What if he simply left her locked up here, like a princess in a tower?

She frowned, looking out at the pure blue sky and the glittering azure sea in the bay below her. It was time to stop waiting for Nik.

It was a beautiful Mediterranean day and she'd take Danny and go exploring. They'd already investigated every nook and cranny of the villa's beautiful garden, but now she decided to go further afield. She'd take the path that she'd discovered led down to a private beach far below.

She knocked back the last of her juice and lifted Danny out of his highchair.

'Let's go.' She smiled at him. 'Are you going to walk a little bit today?' She held his hands and guided him along in his funny, bouncy tiptoeing walk. He'd been pulling himself up to stand, even 'cruising' around the room, hanging onto the furniture, for a month or so, but he'd shown no real desire to actually walk yet.

Half an hour later Carrie set off along the winding path, finding it a delightful walk down a wooded slope to the beach. The going was steep, and she was glad of the three-wheeler buggy that Irene had produced from somewhere, but the tantalising glimpses of sparkling sea would have drawn her on even if she'd had to carry Danny and the very heavy bag.

It was wonderful to be out and about on her own with Danny, and in hardly any time at all she turned one last bend and there in front of her was a gorgeous curve of beach and the glittering blue sea. But right across the path there was a tall wrought-iron gate, blocking her way.

She stopped in her tracks and stared at it. Was it locked? Would she have to turn back? At that moment the gate swung soundlessly inward on well-oiled hinges, and Carrie noticed the little camera and voice grid mounted on the gatepost.

'Thank you!' she called, looking up at the camera and smiling as she recalled Nik's words about the best security system. No doubt cameras covered the beach as well—their usual purpose being to prevent intruders making their way onto Kristallis property, but on this occasion to stop her trying to flag down a passing boat in an attempt to sail away with Danny.

The idea suddenly struck her as funny. Despite Nik's comment in the limousine she knew that the security system hadn't really been set up to keep her prisoner, but she had the sudden childish impulse to start acting suspiciously for the benefit of the cameras, just to see what would happen.

At that moment Danny squealed, and started wriggling against his harness. She'd never taken him to a beach before, and his eyes were round and bright as he stared out at the exciting terrain.

She pushed the buggy through the gate and found herself at the top of a few steps down to the beach. The steps were wide and sloping and, being constructed of sun-bleached olive wood packed with silvery grey pebbles, were in perfect sympathy with the unspoilt beach. They looked as if they'd been there for years.

Carrie stooped to lift Danny out of his seat, and a moment later she was crunching across the narrow beach towards the sea, with Danny's cries of excitement tickling her cheek.

'Isn't it lovely?' she murmured, quietly absorbing the subtle beauty of the setting. It truly was a charming bay, with a sweeping arc of silver pebbles giving way to a strip of rich golden sand that was gently lapped by the water. At each end of the small bay precipitous ochre cliffs plunged into the peacock-blue sea, and behind her the wooded slopes rose up steeply, enclosing her in a beautiful secluded paradise.

If she'd wanted a shady spot she could have settled under the branches of the wizened old olive trees that edged the beach, but she was enjoying the feel of the sun on her skin too much. She put Danny down and sat beside him, letting her fingers close over a warm flat pebble. All the pebbles seemed to be perfectly smooth, perfectly round—perfect for skimming.

With a dip of her body and a flick of her wrist she flipped the pebble out over the sea. One bounce, two bounces and it disappeared under the water with a plop.

Danny let out an excited squeal and grabbed up a handful of pebbles to launch at the sea himself.

'Oh, dear.' She smiled wryly. 'I probably shouldn't be teaching you to throw stones!' But even though she knew she shouldn't, she just couldn't resist it.

A few minutes later, encouraged by Danny's enthusiastic response, she was standing up and practising her skimming skills. It was ages since she'd skimmed stones, and try as she might she couldn't manage more than two bounces.

Suddenly a stone whizzed past her shoulder and tripped across the water. One, two, three, four, five bounces, before breaking the surface and sinking down into the clear sea.

She gasped and looked round, to see Nik standing on the beach behind her.

He was smiling broadly. It was a heart-stoppingly gorgeous expression she'd never seen him show before, and suddenly butterflies started to flutter in her stomach.

She smiled back, instinctively matching the warmth in his expression, and a surge of excitement ran through her. She'd spent the last five days resenting his absence, but somehow his smile had the power to lift her mood. All at once she was brimming with memories of their lovemaking, and she let her eyes run over him with a buzz of pure pleasure.

He was wearing worn jeans and a tight black T-shirt and he looked simply incredible. He was dressed more casually than she'd ever seen him before, but the look really suited him—the short sleeves showing off the well-defined muscles of his arms, the snug jeans emphasising the lean athletic strength of his long legs.

'Hello,' he said, still smiling. 'How are you? How's Danny?'

'We're fine.' Carrie suddenly found it a challenge to bring her thoughts into any kind of order as his blue eyes caught hold of hers. 'He's full of beans today.'

'That's good,' Nik replied. 'I've always liked it here.' He knelt down next to them and leant forward to catch Danny's attention. 'Hello, what have you been doing?'

Carrie watched them with a curious feeling spreading

through her. As far as she could remember Nik had never spoken directly to Danny before. It seemed as if he actually wanted to engage properly with his nephew for the first time.

'Um…learning to throw stones,' Carrie said awkwardly.

'Everyone likes to throw stones into water,' Nik said with a shrug, still maintaining eye contact with the baby. 'We'll just have to teach you to be careful when people are around, won't we?'

Danny grinned and lifted his arms, as if he wanted Nik to pick him up. Nik glanced over at Carrie, then reached out and swung Danny up into his arms.

'Let's walk.' He stood up and set out along the strip of golden sand that edged the gently lapping water.

Carrie walked behind them, feeling even more unsettled than before. It was good that Nik was making an effort with Danny, wasn't it? So why did she feel so strange about it? She'd married Nik for Danny's sake—she ought to be pleased that he was starting to form a relationship with him.

'I used to skim stones with my brother,' Nik said over his shoulder, slowing down until she fell into step beside him. 'We were always very competitive about it.'

'I'm not very good at it,' Carrie replied, realising that it was the first time Nik had spoken about Leonidas in a personal way. He was full of surprises today—it was making her feel jittery.

'We practised a lot,' Nik said. 'We both wanted to be the best.'

'On this beach?' Carrie asked, wondering about their childhood. Leonidas had been determined that Danny should have a very different childhood from his strict Greek upbringing with his overbearing father.

'No, but it was a very similar beach, on my parents' property on the mainland,' Nik replied. 'I bought this place a few years ago, for times when I need to get away from the city.'

Carrie bit her lip and looked at Nik. Talking about his family had reminded her of something that had been bothering her for some time, but she didn't know how he would react if she brought it up.

'How is it that you didn't know about Danny until just a few weeks ago?' she asked, steeling herself for his response.

Nik stopped abruptly and turned towards her. In the bright morning light his blue eyes were more vibrant than ever, but there was a hint of unknown emotion clouding their depths.

'I hadn't spoken to my brother for some time.' His expression was uncharacteristically troubled. 'I didn't know he had married your cousin, let alone had a child with her. I didn't find out about his death until after the funeral.'

'But your father knew. He came to the funeral,' Carrie said, shuddering at the memory of how unpleasant Cosmo had been. 'And he definitely knew about Danny.'

'He didn't tell me,' Nik said simply. 'He only told me Leonidas had died—and not until after the funeral.'

'I don't understand why he'd keep such important news from you,' Carrie said. But even before she'd finished speaking she knew why. Cosmo had not wanted to acknowledge Danny as a Kristallis. He must have known there would be a chance that Nik would want his brother's son to be part of the family.

'My father was a difficult man,' Nik replied, giving no clue as to whether he had realised his father's motivation in keeping Danny a secret.

Carrie waited, hoping he'd carry on speaking. She wanted to know how their family had got so messed up that two brothers hadn't spoken for years and their father had rejected his own grandson. She knew Leonidas's side of the story—

at least up until he had left Greece—but she wanted to hear Nik explain it.

There was a long pause, but he didn't continue. In the end she broke the silence, hoping that if she shared information about her childhood he would follow suit.

'*My* father isn't easy to get along with,' she said. 'All through my childhood I tried to get to know him, but I always ended up disappointed.'

'What happened?' Nik asked.

Carrie looked at him and thought he seemed genuinely interested to hear about her background. Somehow she had the feeling he usually avoided that sort of personal discussion—but maybe he was prepared to make an exception for his wife.

'When I was growing up he always seemed to take jobs as far away as possible—he's a marine engineer, and his work took him all round the world. My aunt and uncle disapproved, saying he could get a job closer to home if he wanted. They called him a workaholic and said he'd rather put his work before his daughter.' She paused and took a deep breath. 'I knew they never really wanted me, but they gladly banked the cheques Dad sent for my upkeep. I felt like I was being looked after for money.'

'That must have been hard,' Nik said.

'It was.' Carrie gazed at the wooded mountain slope on the other side of the bay, but she was thinking about her childhood in England. 'He let me down so many times. He never remembered my birthday or anything important. I just wanted to talk to him—but he was never there.'

'Do you see him now?' Nik asked.

'Rarely.' Carrie turned back to Nik. His blue eyes were serious. 'It got easier to deal with once I'd left home, once I was independent. When I was eighteen I got a small inheritance from my mother. It was enough for a deposit on my flat in

London, and I started working in the fitness industry. I'd always been keen on sport—it was a good way to escape for a while.'

Nik was still looking at her, listening carefully to what she was saying. She got the feeling he understood how difficult her childhood had been at times.

'My father was always conscious of his duty as a good father. And he made sure Leonidas and I knew our duty as his sons.' Nik took a breath, almost as if he'd startled himself by talking about his family. 'My father never missed any significant dates—I imagine his secretary sent him a memo—but neither of us were ever able to talk to him.'

'Leonidas said he only ever wanted to hear about your successes at school or other achievements that proved you were living up to the Kristallis name,' Carrie said. 'Leonidas didn't want Danny to grow up judged only by how successful he was. It was something I had in common with your brother,' she continued, her voice suddenly shaky. 'We both knew what it was like to have a father who didn't really care about us. Leonidas wanted Danny to grow up knowing he was loved, feeling able to talk about anything.'

She stopped walking and looked across at the child in Nik's arms. She knew Nik had seen her eyes sparkling with tears.

'I share that desire too,' he said quietly. 'That is why I came for Danny—he needs a decent father figure.'

'You still haven't answered the question I asked,' Carrie pressed. She blinked away unshed tears and started to walk along the beach again. 'If your father didn't tell you, how did you find out abut Danny?'

'Going through my father's personal papers after he died,' Nik said. 'There was a lot to sort through, but as soon as I found references to Leonidas's son I turned my attention to following the trail that led to you.'

'I'm glad you did,' Carrie said.

Suddenly she stopped stock-still, aware that she'd just said something momentous.

'I meant…I meant that…' She stumbled over the words. 'I don't mean that I approve of the way you brought us here to Corfu—it was underhand and unacceptable—but I do accept that it's good for Danny to get to know his father's brother.'

Nik stopped abruptly beside her and turned to fix her with a powerful stare. The atmosphere between them was suddenly super-charged.

'Carrie…' His voice throbbed with intensity. 'We have to move past the events that led us to this time and place. We can't change what has happened—but we *can* make a good life for Danny.'

'I know,' she replied, trying to keep the words steady despite the sudden pounding of her heart. They were standing beside the vast open space of a calm sea—but at that moment she felt as if she was enclosed with Nik in a small stormy space.

'If I could go back and change what happened to Leonidas and Sophie I would,' Nik said. 'But that was out of my control. More than anything I wish I had not ignored what was in my control. I should have put things right between us before Leonidas died.'

Carrie stared at him, overwhelmed by the depth of feeling that coloured his voice. He'd always seemed so controlled when talking about his brother, but now he was showing real emotion.

'What happened between you?' she asked in a small voice.

'It was after my mother died,' Nik explained. 'She was the one person who kept our family together. Just like your father, my father lived and breathed his work. Kristallis Industries was everything to him, and he had no time for his family.' He paused and took a breath. 'My mother eased the tensions between us. She softened my father and kept Leonidas from overreacting when he couldn't see eye to eye with him.'

'What happened after she died?' Carrie prompted quietly.

'Leonidas was grief-struck—we all were,' Nik said. 'He had a blazing row with my father—I can't even remember what it was about—which ended with him storming off, saying he wanted nothing more to do with our family.'

'Did you try to talk to him?' Carrie asked gently.

'We argued,' Nik said. 'I accused him of taking the easy way out. I accused him of showing no respect for my mother's memory—she had dedicated years to keeping the family together, and as soon as she was gone he was ready to walk out.'

'It must have been a terrible time,' Carrie said. She knew how forceful and single-minded all three of the Kristallis men could be.

After Leonidas had married her cousin she had grown to love him, but he had always displayed a fiery Greek temper. Her one encounter with Cosmo had told her all she needed to know about *his* personality. And she knew from first-hand experience how ruthlessly Nik operated to get what he wanted.

She shuddered, imagining the fireworks that must have flown when the three Kristallis men had clashed.

'I have to head back to the villa now.' Nik's voice jolted her out of her thoughts.

'But…but you've only just got here,' she stammered, surprising herself with how much she wanted Nik to spend more time with them. 'Why do you have to go so soon?'

'Work,' Nik said shortly, passing Danny over to Carrie. 'It's unavoidable.' He was already crunching away across the pebbles to the gate.

CHAPTER NINE

CARRIE leant over the cot and brushed her fingertips lightly over Danny's hair. He looked blissfully content as he slept, and her heart swelled with her love for him.

She crossed the room and walked onto the balcony overlooking the mountainside that dipped down to the bay. The sun was setting, and she gazed out at a sea that looked like molten gold. It was a beautiful view, but it didn't improve her mood.

She hadn't seen Nik again since that morning—apparently he was still working—and she'd begun to worry about what her life would be like, married to him. She was really starting to feel like a pampered princess locked up in a tower. All the material things she could want were provided for her—but she didn't have her freedom. Danny would need to make friends with other children, and she needed contact with other people. She was missing her job and friends at home.

When it came right down to it, she had to admit that being ignored by Nik was hurting her feelings. That walk along the beach had seemed special to her—it had felt as if they were finally making a connection—but to him it had obviously been just something he had to fit in around his work.

Growing up, it had been hard for Carrie to come to terms with the fact that her occasional visits with her father had had to be fitted in around his work. She didn't like the thought that she was in the same situation with Nik.

She decided then and there that the next time she saw Nik she would challenge him on the subject. She had started to hope that there was a way they could work together to bring up Danny—but if he was never there what was the point of being married at all?

A slight noise coming from inside caught her attention, and she turned to see what it was. Nik was leaning over the cot, looking down at Danny.

A ripple of emotion passed through her and she bit her lip, staring at him. Why did she feel so pleased to see him when she'd spent most of the day feeling angry with him for the way he'd been ignoring her?

He looked up and, seeing her watching him through the open door, he smiled. Before she could help it she'd smiled back, suddenly realising that she had missed him. Why did his smile have the power to make her bad mood drift away?

But as he walked towards her she remembered her intention to make him talk about the future. She folded her arms, determined not to let him charm her with a dazzling smile, and tried to make her expression stern.

'I'm sorry.' He held his hands out in an open gesture as he approached her. 'I've left you alone too long and I want to make it up to you.'

'It's not enough just to say sorry,' Carrie said, determined not to be distracted from her good intentions to sort things out between them. 'I don't want to just sit around here waiting for you to spare us a few minutes out of your work schedule. I need to build a proper life for Danny and me. And that involves going out and meeting people, being part of the community, maybe getting a part-time job as a personal trainer…'

'There's no hurry to talk about that now.' Nik took a step forward and lifted his hand to brush a strand of hair back from her face.

As his fingers touched her skin a tremor ran through her, and suddenly it was hard for her to be aware of anything other than Nik standing right in front of her.

'We can't put this conversation off.' Carrie tried to sound firm, but her words came out in a breathless rush. 'You'll be gone again in the morning, and I won't see you again for days.'

'It'll be all right.' Nik bent to press his lips against the side of her neck. 'My business deal is completed so we can talk about it tomorrow. I'm not going anywhere.'

'But I want to get things sorted out,' Carrie said, sucking in a wobbly breath as Nik opened his mouth against her neck and started trailing his tongue downwards. She was wearing a strappy sundress and his fingers skimmed lightly over the naked skin of her shoulder in a way that made shivers skitter down her spine. She took a step backwards and found the backs of her legs pressed against one of the balcony chairs.

'Tomorrow.' Nik's breath tickled her skin, making little darts of pleasure tremble through her. 'I give you my word, we'll talk properly tomorrow.'

She opened her mouth to speak, but at that moment Nik's mouth closed over hers. His tongue slipped in through her parted lips and all her thoughts were suddenly forgotten.

He kissed her gently, tenderly exploring the soft recesses of her mouth. It wasn't the hot, furious conquest of their previous kisses, but a long, slow-burning seduction.

Despite the change of pace she was soon clinging breathlessly to him, her whole body quivering with reawakened sensations, until at last he pulled back and she gazed up at him wordlessly. The setting sun was behind him, casting his handsome face into shadow, but still he looked incredible.

'I'm going to make love to you,' he said quietly, looking at her with such intensity that a flurry of excitement started deep in her stomach. 'Think of this as the wedding night we didn't have.'

'You're making my legs feel weak.' She'd meant to sound light and breezy, but the words came out as a husky murmur that made his eyes darken with heightened desire.

'Then you'd better sit down,' he said, sweeping her off her feet and lowering her onto a chair. 'Because soon you won't be able to stand.'

Carrie gasped, and was about to protest when he stopped her words with another long languorous kiss. His tongue slid against hers, unhurried and sensuous in its movements, like a sultry slow dance that was simmering with the promise of a passionate release still to come.

He was kneeling beside her chair. One arm was around her shoulders, locking her to his kiss, and the other hand was skimming her body with a light, teasing touch. At last his fingers came to rest quite deliberately under the hem of her dress, halfway up her inner thigh. He pulled back from the kiss to look at her.

Carrie gazed at him, feeling slightly bemused. Her whole being was humming with sexual readiness and all she could think about was what it would feel like when he touched her intimately.

His hand on her leg started to move inexorably upwards, towards the place in her body that was already throbbing out its need for him. Her legs fell apart and she held her breath, waiting for his fingertips to make contact with her aching flesh.

'Last time we made love I was negligent,' he said, finally

reaching the very top of her inner thigh. At the last moment, just when she was poised on the edge of glorious anticipation, waiting to feel his masterful touch, his fingers took a diversion upwards towards her left hip. 'These were the only items of your clothing that I removed.' He hooked his thumb under the elastic of her panties. 'I won't be so rash again. You can rest assured that it will be a long time before I remove these tonight.'

Carrie's breath came out in a shuddering sigh. She hardly had time to react to his announcement before he pushed her dress upwards and dropped his head to scatter kisses on her naked stomach. Somehow he had manoeuvred himself so that he knelt between her parted thighs, and as he leant forward she felt both exposed and overwhelmingly excited.

Once again he pulled away and sat back on his heels, looking up at her. She gazed down at his face, hardly able to believe what was happening. The most gorgeous man in the world—the only man she had ever felt this way about—was kneeling between her legs, making love to her in the most unexpected, marvellous way.

'Your skin is glowing in the sunset,' he murmured, lifting his hands to the front buttons of her dress. 'I want to see your naked breasts touched by the golden sunlight.'

'My skin is glowing because of you,' Carrie breathed, sitting almost mesmerised while he undid her dress and slipped his hands behind her to unfasten the strapless bra she wore.

'You are like a golden goddess.' He cupped her breasts tenderly, looking at her with the most open and adoring expression.

'Normally I'm pale,' Carrie said, brimming with delight at his extravagant flattery. She wasn't used to playing sensual word games, and it filled her with a heady excitement. 'Perhaps you'd prefer a bronzed Greek beauty?' she asked, and suddenly felt a moment's insecurity.

'No, I like your white skin,' he said. 'I want to see it shimmering like a pearl in the moonlight.'

'Don't look now, then,' she teased, filled with an unaccustomed sexual confidence as she arched her back and flourished her breasts at him before pulling her dress closed.

'Oh, yes,' he murmured as he pushed her dress apart again and leant forward to nuzzle her breasts. 'I intend to look at you and touch you and keep you here until the moon is well into the night sky.'

'Someone may come,' she gasped, looking over Nik's head along the darkening balcony.

'No one will disturb us, I promise,' he said. Then his mouth closed over her nipple.

CHAPTER TEN

A SIGH of delight escaped Carrie's parted lips and her head fell back. She gazed with unfocussed eyes at the bougainvillea, sprawling luxuriously over the balcony, the scarlet flowers shining like little Christmas lanterns in the last rays of the setting sun.

Nik's tongue was drawing circles around her nipple, eliciting the most wonderful sensations that spiralled out and filled her whole body with a magical glow. His hand caressed her other breast and his arm was behind her, holding her safe and secure as she sat on the chair.

Her eyelids slid down and she gave herself over completely to Nik's lovemaking. His fingers deftly managed the last of her buttons and she felt the warm evening breeze whispering across her naked skin. His mouth followed, exploring parts of her body that until that moment she had never realised were so sensitive.

She felt herself trembling as the sensations within her slowly built. His touch was so gentle, but her desire for him was growing more and more powerful.

'You're cold,' he said, scooping her up into his strong arms and crossing to the door of her bedroom before his words had fully penetrated the glorious cocoon of sensuality in which he'd wrapped her.

'No,' she said. 'You're keeping me warm.' She smiled up at him languidly as he laid her carefully on the bed.

'You are so beautiful.' His voice was gruff as he looked down at her beneath him, dressed in nothing but her white lacy panties.

'And you are wearing too many clothes,' she responded, marvellously free of inhibition as she rolled onto her side to watch him undress.

'Well, I can soon put that right.' He stripped off his clothes swiftly, all the while letting his eyes roam appreciatively over her naked curves.

Suddenly a feeling of pure sexual excitement shuddered through Carrie. Nik was making love to her, and all the wonderful feelings she had already experienced were only the very start of what was to come.

'Kiss me,' she said huskily, rising to her knees and wrapping her arms around him as soon as he moved within her reach.

His tongue plunged between her lips, and at that moment the tempo of their foreplay increased. He was just as aware of her needs, but gone were the long slow strokes of his fingertips, the gentle feather-light brushes of his lips. Now he was making love to her with an urgency that matched her own heightened arousal.

His lips were demanding on hers, and he pushed her down onto the bed purposefully, his hand sliding across her stomach and under the lace of her panties. Then his fingers dipped deep, finding the place that craved his attention.

At first he stroked gently, circling back and forth with the lightest of touches. Soon she was trembling in his arms, breathing rapidly and yearning for more.

Carrie whimpered as he suddenly increased the intensity of his touch. She closed her eyes and pressed her head back against the soft pillow, giving in to the wonderful feelings that his touch created. Her body arched and vibrated, tingling with an exquisite pleasure that reached every extremity.

His mouth closed, hot and demanding, over her nipple. He worked the aching peak with his tongue and she cried out in surprise as overwhelming sensations coursed through her body.

Her breath was coming in gasps and moans and she writhed on the bed. Nik's fingers still toyed with her, stroking her on to new heights, unrelenting as he followed her movements whilst she bucked her hips and arched her back.

'Oh! Oh!' she gasped. 'I… I…' She couldn't speak as wave after wave of pleasure crashed over her. Her world was rocking and she clung to Nik for support, carried away on the rush of excitement that exploded within her. His arms swooped her up and he held her shuddering body next to his chest.

Slowly she became aware that he was breathing as raggedly as her, then he laid her gently back against the pillows. Her body was still humming from his touch, and as he paused by her feet and kissed her toes she could feel the results of his caresses quivering through her body. Each brush of his hand or touch of his mouth set her body trembling anew.

'I think it's time to remove these.' He let his fingertips trace the patterns on the lace of her panties, but his touch was light and teasing, driving Carrie almost to distraction with her urgent desire for him. She needed to feel him strong and powerful, filling her with his hard male flesh.

'I want you!' she cried out. She couldn't wait any longer. She pulled her panties off herself and reached for him. 'I need you *now*!'

Nik groaned, a deep animal rumble, and quickly moved over her. He paused for a moment, looking down at her with hungry eyes.

She lay beneath him, suddenly desperate to feel him inside her. Her trembling body ached for him. He had made her ready—more than ready—and now she needed him like she'd never needed anything before. She slipped her hands down his back to his hard buttocks and grasped him firmly, urging him on.

He pressed his hips down, his hard male flesh sliding smoothly into the place that was so desperately aching to be filled. Then he began to rock against her, pushing in and pulling out. He took it slowly at first, but each movement sent a delicious wave of pleasure rushing through her.

Carrie moaned and clung to his back, tilting her hips to bring them even closer. She heard his breath coming in short hot gasps that matched her own, each breath escaping in time with every powerful thrust. The intensity was building, his pace increasing. He pushed into her harder and faster, each movement filling her with pleasure.

Overwhelming sensations coursed through her. Her body was quivering, from the tips of her fingers to the ends of her toes. Incredible feelings spiralled within her, shimmering out from the glorious place where they were joined to the tingling peaks of her breasts.

Without breaking his rhythm Nik eased away slightly, allowing space for his hand to slip down between them. His thumb found her sensitive bud, caressed it lightly.

Carrie cried out. Her body splintered into a million points of pleasure that lifted her beyond anything she had ever imagined. Gasping and trembling, she clung to Nik.

A second later she heard him cry out too, shuddering and panting as he reached his explosive climax.

'I'm glad I waited until I had time to spend with you properly,' Nik murmured some time later, as he traced his fingers along her collarbone and leant over to dip his tongue gently into the hollow at the base of her throat.

Carrie smiled when he raised his head to look into her face. She lifted her hand and smoothed her palm against his cheek. Everything seemed different now, she thought, gazing lovingly into the face of the man with whom she had just shared the most magical experience.

A sense of intimacy still lingered between them, as if to prove the act of lovemaking had been more than just a physical experience. Her body glowed with the aftermath of his loving, but she also felt a powerful connection had been forged between them. Surely everything would turn out all right now? Surely they would be able to find a way forward that suited everyone?

'It's been a busy few weeks,' Nik said, lying propped up on his side next to her, gently caressing the swell of her hip with his fingertips. 'But I've worked hard to clear some space for us. There will be time to discuss all the issues you mentioned earlier.'

'Thank you,' Carrie said. She smiled with relief, believing he meant what he said. There was a lot on her mind, and she needed to know where she stood, but at that moment all she could think about was the feel of Nik's fingers on her skin.

'It's important to me that you and Danny feel you belong here,' he said, letting his hand slide upwards until he held her breast softly in his palm. 'This is your home now, and you must have whatever you need.'

The glimmer in his eyes told her exactly what he thought she needed right then. And if that message wasn't clear enough he pulled her back into his arms and kissed her.

The following morning Carrie was in fine spirits as she walked down the winding path to the cove below the villa. Nik was with her. He was pushing Danny's buggy and they were all going to the beach together.

She'd made that same walk with Danny only yesterday, but now everything had changed. The sense of closeness she had felt with Nik the previous night was still there, wrapping her in a warm and comfortable glow. They'd all enjoyed breakfast together on the balcony, and for the first time she felt as if they were truly becoming a family.

'Last night you said there were a lot of things you wanted to talk about.' Nik flashed a smile at her as he spoke, and in the dappled shade under the olive trees he looked utterly gorgeous. He turned his attention back to pushing Danny safely over the uneven ground, but he inclined his head slightly, waiting for her response.

'Yes, there were…I mean there are.' Carrie gazed at him, suddenly finding it difficult to remember what had seemed so pressing the night before. Right then she just wanted to enjoy the moment, with Nik and Danny.

'You mentioned that Danny needs friends his own age,' Nik said. 'I have several cousins with a number of young children.'

'Oh,' Carrie said, thrown slightly off her stride by the discovery that Danny apparently had a lot of Greek relatives.

'But I thought it would be best if *we* spent some time together first—getting to know each other better before rushing into any family gatherings,' Nik said. 'Unless you think he needs contact with other children sooner?'

'No, no.' Carrie felt disproportionately relieved at Nik's intention to wait. 'Your plan not to rush into anything seems sensible.'

'I know he'll need other friends, too,' Nik added with a smile. 'Not just Kristallis children. We'll look into it.'

'Thank you,' Carrie said, just as they turned the corner and arrived at the wrought-iron gate to the beach. The gate swung open without a squeak, and they walked through onto the silver pebble steps.

It was a beautiful Mediterranean day. The sea was a gorgeous peacock-blue beneath a cloudless sky, and the olive trees on the slopes that flanked the bay shimmered in the sunlight.

'Let's go down to the water,' Nik said, lifting Danny out of his buggy and crunching off across the smooth pebbles.

Carrie followed along behind them, having difficulty keeping up with Nik's long stride as Danny's noisy enthusiasm drove him swiftly on towards the sea.

He stopped as he reached the strip of golden sand that edged the water and, kicking his shoes off, turned back to throw her a dazzling smile.

Carrie's heart turned over and she stopped in her tracks. The warmth of his smile spread over her, sinking right into her soul, filling her with happiness. It felt so good just to be standing there—smiling back at him, gazing deeply into his blue eyes.

She'd never felt that way before. She'd never been so absurdly happy just to smile at someone. Never felt someone's smile enfold her like a wonderful embrace.

The moment could have lasted for ever, but suddenly Danny made an unexpected lunge towards the water.

'Whoa! What are you up to?' Nik laughed, breaking eye contact with Carrie and hoisting Danny up more tightly in his arms.

'He likes the water,' Carrie said distractedly. Why had sharing a simple smile with Nik made her feel so strange?

'He wants to get wet!' Nik exclaimed. 'I'll take his shoes off and splash his feet.'

Carrie pushed her fringe back off her face and brought her

attention back to the situation at hand. 'You'll have a hard time only getting his feet wet, but Irene packed a change of clothes, so don't worry too much.'

Nik sat down on the pebbles, rolled up Danny's trousers and pulled off his shoes and socks. He stuffed them into his pockets and rose smoothly to his feet, despite the shifting pebbles beneath him, and started making his way along the water's edge, dipping Danny up and down so that his toes skimmed the water.

Carrie let her eyes run appreciatively across Nik's broad back and powerful shoulders as he lifted Danny easily up and down over the lapping waves. The movement of his well-defined muscles under the tight black fabric of his T-shirt snared her gaze, making her heart start to beat a bit faster. She remembered so well how those muscles felt beneath her questing hands, as he lay on top of her, making love to her.

Her gaze slipped lower and she found herself admiring the athletic grace of his long stride. Then suddenly she was thinking about how those strong legs felt lying between hers. She remembered gripping his buttocks tightly, urging him on, pulling him deeper as he thrust inside her.

Her body trembled as echoes of the sensations that had overwhelmed her so magically rippled through her. She longed to feel that way again, to lie in Nik's arms night after night.

'The water's not that warm yet,' Nik said over his shoulder, speaking loudly to be heard over Danny's squeals of delight. 'But you'll really love it here in the summer. It will be perfect then. In July and August the water is as warm as a bath, but the olive groves are cool and shady.'

Carrie stopped walking and looked at him, feeling momentarily confused. She'd been so preoccupied thinking about making love to Nik that she wasn't entirely sure what he had just said.

He turned, still holding her with his eyes, and retraced his steps so that he was standing right in front of her. He lifted one hand and brushed his fingers across her temple, tucking the loose tendrils of hair back behind her ear. An automatic shiver ran through her, and she inclined her head to rest her cheek against his open palm. She returned his gaze, drifting dreamily in the blue depths of his eyes.

'You look tired,' he said, leaning forward to place a gentle kiss on her lips. 'Sit down and rest for a few minutes while I play with Danny.'

She gazed back at him, pleasantly surprised by the tenderness of his kiss and slightly taken aback by his words. But it was true—she did feel unusually tired.

'All right,' she said. 'Just for a few minutes.' She released his eyes reluctantly and turned to walk back up the beach a few paces, to a place where the smooth pebbles formed a natural mound that looked comfortable for sitting on.

Nik smiled at her, as if her actions pleased him, then went back to dipping Danny up and down over the gently lapping water.

It was an enchanting bay, enclosed on both sides by cliffs and backed by the steep wooded slopes. The sea was a blissful shade of blue and the barest touch of a breeze ruffled her hair deliciously.

But the beautiful view didn't hold her attention. All she wanted to do was feast her eyes on Nik, soaking up everything about the way he looked, the way he moved.

Just watching him made a funny feeling start to spread through her—and she wasn't thinking about making love to him. Just being near him made her feel happy, and seeing him play so naturally with Danny filled her with hope for the future. He'd make a very good father for Danny. And for his own child one day in the future, if things worked out between them.

Carrie gasped and clamped her hand over her mouth. She'd been in Corfu for three weeks and she hadn't had a period. Nik had made love to her the day after they'd arrived and they hadn't used any protection.

She was pregnant!

An icy shiver ran through her and she hugged herself, despite the heat of the Greek sun.

She *might* be pregnant, she told herself sternly, trying to keep calm. She'd buy a pregnancy test, and then she'd know for sure.

But how could she get a pregnancy test? Nik had her locked up here like his prisoner. She wasn't allowed off his property. She couldn't even go to a shop and buy a test.

A nasty mixture of anger and despair coiled through her, making her feel sick to her stomach. That was a sure sign of pregnancy, she thought bitterly, ignoring the fact that she hadn't felt sick a minute earlier.

She'd always wanted a child of her own, and had hoped that one day she'd be able to give Danny a little playmate. But not like this. It was too soon.

Nik controlled everything—Danny's life, her life. He even controlled her ability to discover whether or not she was pregnant. If she had a baby she'd be putting herself more completely under his control.

What if it didn't work out between them? If he wouldn't give up on Danny, his brother's child, he'd never, *ever* give up on his own child. He'd take Carrie's child away from her as brutally as he'd forced her into marrying him to get possession of Danny.

She stared at Nik balefully. A moment ago she'd been filled with happiness while she watched him playing with Danny.

Now her insides were filled with a horrible churning mess of emotions. She had to find out whether or not she was pregnant.

'I need to go shopping,' she called out to Nik. She started to get up, but her legs felt unaccountably weak so she stayed sitting down, staring up at him as he turned and walked towards her.

'I'll take you after lunch.' Nik was studying her carefully through narrowed eyes, a questioning expression on his face.

'I want to go on my own,' she said, squinting up at him in the bright reflected sunlight. She suddenly wished she had her sunglasses on. She didn't like the feeling that he was seeing right through her, that maybe he could tell something was different about her. She held up her arms for him to pass Danny to her.

'I'll take you,' he said, bending to place the baby carefully on her lap. 'If Danny's sleeping we can leave him with Irene.'

'I'm not leaving Danny here alone,' she said stiffly, evading his eyes and staring out to sea.

'Why are you being like this? I thought things were going well between us. Last night—'

'All we did last night was make love—except it wasn't exactly making *love*,' she interrupted, her green eyes snapping back to his. 'We didn't have a proper conversation. Nothing meaningful happened between us.'

'Didn't making love mean anything to you?' he asked.

She stared at him in surprise, startled that he could dare to ask such a question considering the circumstances of their marriage.

'What would mean something to me is a little respect—a little freedom,' she said hotly. 'You've got me here against my wishes and I'm not even permitted to go shopping on my own.'

'What's so important about shopping?' He was keeping his voice level, but Carrie could hear undertones of suspicion hardening it. 'You can have anything you need delivered to the villa at any time you choose.'

'It's not about shopping,' she said, realising it had been a mistake to draw his attention so strongly to that. 'It's just that I don't want to be watched all the time,' she added, pointing up at the camera that was silently sweeping the beach. 'And I don't want to be locked up here all the time.'

'What do you want to buy that I can't see?' he pressed, clearly not thrown off the scent by her attempted diversion. 'I thought we'd agreed to have no secrets between us.'

'No. *We* didn't agree that,' Carrie snapped. She was close to breaking point and she could feel tears pricking her eyes. She pressed her face instinctively against Danny's curls and closed her eyelids for a moment, drawing comfort from the feel of him in her arms. 'Like everything else in this marriage, *you* dictated it. *You* announced that was how it should be.'

Nik stood towering over her. She could feel his anger radiating out despite the rigid way he held himself. He leant down abruptly and took Danny from her, and before she had time to protest he pulled her to her feet and held her firmly in front of him.

'It's time to get back to the villa now.' He fixed her with eyes so cold that an involuntary shudder ran through her.

'Why?' she demanded, shaking his hand roughly off her arm and pulling Danny safely back into her embrace. 'Because *you* say so?'

'Because Danny's getting tired,' Nik said. 'And this conversation has gone as far as it's going to right now.'

Carrie stared at him for a second longer, suddenly feeling as if he'd wrong-footed her. Then she looked at Danny. Nik was right. He did look ready for his nap.

'You don't know he needs to sleep!' Carrie said crossly, irritated that despite their argument Nik had noticed the signs that Danny was getting tired before she did. 'You can't just sweep into his life and assume you know exactly what he needs.'

'We're going back.' Nik took her arm and set a brisk pace across the beach to the buggy.

'You go back if you're so determined to. I'm not going yet,' Carrie said. She fastened Danny securely in the pushchair with the harness, gripped the handles and moved him away from Nik. 'I'll push him into the shade while he sleeps, and then I can enjoy the peace and quiet on my own.'

'You're not staying here alone,' Nik said through gritted teeth. 'Not when you're acting so erratically.'

'Why not? This bay is totally cut off. You don't seriously think I'll try to swim away?' Carrie turned towards the sea and made a sweeping gesture with her arm. Her eyes suddenly settled on a little boat that she hadn't noticed before. Without thinking she raised her arm and waved. 'Perhaps you're worried I'll flag down that boat!' she said.

'Don't be so ridiculous,' Nik grated, grabbing her arm and moving her roughly through the wrought-iron gateway. He followed closely with the buggy, pausing for a moment to bark something in rapid Greek into the intercom system just inside the gateway. Then, before Carrie had a chance to catch her breath, he was striding up the hill, pushing the buggy in front of him.

Her heart was pounding with shock and anger as she heard the heavy gate clang shut behind her. She turned and rattled it, then looked up at the camera, but nothing happened. She spun round and stared at Nik's retreating back.

She was trapped! Locked on his property once again.

And he was leaving with Danny! She started running up the hill immediately. He had a head start, and was already out of her sight, but she ran until her lungs were burning. She rounded the corner by the villa and saw Nik lifting Danny up.

'You're not going to take him away from me!' she cried. 'I'll never let you have him.'

'I was simply bringing him inside for his sleep,' he said. He let her take the baby but there was a lethal calmness in his eyes.

'You were trying to separate us,' she panted, still trying to catch her breath from the steep climb as she hugged Danny. 'Locking the gate and getting him away from me—'

'If I'd wanted to separate you from Danny I'd have locked you *off* my property, not *on* it,' he said witheringly, and he turned and walked away from her.

Nik pushed his chair back from his desk abruptly, stood up and strode across to his study window. The spectacular view across the mountains usually soothed him, made him thankful for this peaceful retreat away from his main residence in Athens. But that afternoon it didn't seem to be having its usual calming effect.

He turned and stalked across to the other window, looked out over the bay. The water glittered turquoise and the sky was still fine—which was more than could be said for his mood. Since they'd returned from the beach his mood had been growing darker and darker.

He thought about Carrie's behaviour that morning. She'd been happy and relaxed at first, but then everything had suddenly changed. It had seemed as if she was deliberately trying to pick a fight with him.

It was unacceptable. He wouldn't put up with that behaviour from anyone—and especially not from Carrie. She had agreed to this marriage and she understood his terms—or at least he'd thought she did.

'We need to talk.'

He turned to see Carrie standing in the doorway of his study. Her face was pale but resolute and her black hair was tied neatly at the nape of her neck. She was wearing the same flowery green dress she'd been wearing earlier. It was the dress she'd been wearing the first time they'd made love. The shade suited her, bringing out the colour of her eyes, and the soft draping fabric skimmed alluringly over her body, accentuating her curves.

'Yes, we do,' he agreed smoothly. Her silent arrival had caught him slightly off guard, but he didn't allow it to show. 'Where's Danny?'

'Irene is playing with him,' she said. 'I don't want any distractions while we talk.'

'Good. Neither do I,' he said. She had calmed down, but he noticed an unusual brittleness underneath the surface of her composure. 'Come in and sit.'

'There's no need. I want to get on with this,' she said, not moving from her spot.

'I'm not having this discussion in a doorway.' Nik took her arm and pulled her into the room. 'Haven't you understood anything I've said to you about being my wife—about discretion?'

'Stop manhandling me!' Carrie wrenched her arm out of his grasp and glared at him. Her eyes were flashing green fire again and her calm composure was starting to crack.

'Then stop deliberately baiting me.' He closed his study door and looked at her meaningfully. 'When you married me you agreed to maintain the appearance of a normal happy marriage.'

'I wasn't baiting you!' Carrie gasped, rubbing her arm where his hand had held her. 'And there was no agreement between us! Like everything else, you *told* me what I had to do!'

'Well, listen carefully to what I'm telling you now,' Nik grated. 'You'll regret it if you try to pick a fight with me in public again. At the beach it was unacceptable—but arguing in front of my household is utterly unthinkable!'

'I wasn't trying to pick a fight,' she said, staring up at him towering over her. It was a large room, but Nik's presence seemed to fill it to capacity, making her shiver apprehensively. 'I was upset.'

Her heart was pounding and she was starting to question whether coming to talk to him now was the right decision. But no matter how much she balked at telling him her fears, in her heart she knew she had to take the initiative. By making the running it felt as if she was taking back some control of her life.

'What have you got to be upset about?' Nik asked, his derisive tone doing nothing to encourage her to tell him the truth. 'I told you—I'm not going to put up with petty squabbles and backbiting.'

She stared at his glowering face and swallowed, wondering how he was going to react. Despite the fact he was already bad-tempered, he couldn't be angry over possible pregnancy—he must know it was a potential outcome of their lovemaking. *She* might have forgotten about contraception, but surely he was far too experienced to have made the same mistake?

'Well?' he barked impatiently. 'Are you going to tell me what's bothering you?'

'I think I might be pregnant,' she blurted.

'What?' Nik stared at her in absolute shock. His chest felt rigid and drawing breath was suddenly hard.

'I...I realised at the beach this morning.' She stared up at him with wide eyes, looking uncertain even though she was the one who'd said the unfathomable thing.

'But you're on the pill,' Nik said. Blood was thudding relentlessly in his temples, making it almost impossible to think straight. 'If you forgot to take it you had a responsibility to tell me.'

'I didn't forget,' Carrie said. 'I'm not on the pill.'

'Then what are you playing at?' he demanded, raking his hands through his hair. 'Why did you tell me you were on the pill?'

'I didn't,' she insisted, shrinking back slightly.

'Did you plan to trap me in some way by getting pregnant with my child?' he growled. A horrible sensation churned in the pit of his stomach and he clenched his teeth, biting back the turmoil that was rising within him.

'Of course not!' Carrie snapped. 'I would *never* do something like that!'

'Then why the pretence?' Nik asked furiously. 'Why did you tell me in Menorca that you were protected?'

'I didn't!' Carrie gasped. Then clamped her hand over her mouth. A look of realisation flashed across her face as she suddenly recalled their conversation in the hotel room.

'You said we didn't have to worry about protection.' Nik stared at her. She looked pale and fragile, but at that moment all he felt was anger.

'I meant that it wasn't a problem because I never planned to sleep with you,' Carrie said, biting her lower lip and meeting his eyes with a cloudy green gaze. 'I'm sorry you misunderstood.'

'It's too late now. The damage is done,' Nik bit out, his voice uncompromisingly severe. 'Are you pregnant or not?'

'How would I know?' Carrie cried. 'It's not entirely my fault, you know! If you hadn't been so relentless this would never have happened.' She paused for breath, pushing her black fringe back from her eyes. 'I'm late—very late. But as I can't go shopping to buy a pregnancy test I can't say for certain.'

'You'll see the doctor this afternoon—as soon as possible,' Nik said, reaching into his pocket to pull out his mobile phone. It was unbearable not knowing.

'No!' Carrie's voice was firm, and she was standing with her hands on her hips in a determined posture. 'I'm not seeing a doctor—not yet. I want the freedom and privacy to find this out for myself.'

Nik put his phone down and looked at her through narrowed eyes.

'I want a home pregnancy test,' she said with conviction.

CHAPTER ELEVEN

AN UNEXPECTED numbness crept over Carrie as she watched the blue line appear on the test strip. But it only confirmed what she already knew in her heart. She was pregnant. She stood up stiffly to go to Nik. There was no reason to delay telling him the result.

She found him in his study. She paused at the open door, watching him standing by the large picture window. He hadn't seen her approach and was staring intently at the mountainous view.

Tension was evident in every line of his body, and in profile his face showed an expression that was as rigid as the rest of him.

Her heart started to patter, and she had the urge to back away, but at that exact moment he turned to look at her.

'Do you have the result?' His eyes were riveted on her and his voice was as hard as his body language

'Yes.' She walked into the study and closed the door. Soon the household would know, but for now she'd protect their privacy.

'Sit down,' he said, indicating two leather armchairs close to the window.

Carrie crossed the room and perched on the edge of one of the chairs. Nik sat down opposite. He drew his brows down so that his eyes were cast into shadow and his long fingers tightened on the arms of his leather chair.

She took a breath and, still holding his gaze, steeled herself to speak.

'It was positive.' She spoke clearly, but there was a slight tremor in her voice. 'I'm pregnant.'

She watched him, waiting for his response—but he said nothing.

A second later he stood up and walked out of the room.

Carrie stared after him in shock.

She'd expected him to be angry—she'd already seen that earlier—but she hadn't expected to glimpse the expression of pure horror that had flashed across his face as he left. He'd looked utterly appalled.

She stared at the empty doorway, feeling curiously detached from the situation. She was pregnant—her life was going to change for ever. And the man she was supposed to share it with had just walked out.

Carrie sat on a log in the shade, under a particularly large and ancient olive tree. The ground was covered with a layer of tiny white star-shaped flowers that had fallen from the gnarled branches, and Danny was picking them up and placing them in her outstretched hand.

It was a magical place for a child to play. The warm shade enclosed them and the lapping water just across the sweeping arc of pebbles glittered with the promise of even more fun still to be had. But Carrie wasn't enjoying herself as much as Danny.

She felt sick and tired, and slightly guilty because she'd gone off without telling Danny's new nanny where to find them, and now she couldn't summon up the will to trek back up the path to the villa.

It wasn't finding the energy for the climb—although she was tired, she was still fit—it was the awful feeling of claustrophobia that swamped her in the villa. She had no freedom, and it felt as if she was being watched all the time.

She hadn't wanted a nanny, but Nik had been immovable on the subject.

'I've hired someone to help with Danny,' he'd said one afternoon, about a week after the confirmation of her pregnancy. 'You need to take better care of yourself.'

'I'm fine,' Carrie replied, feeling resentful that this was the first time he'd come anywhere near her or Danny for days. He hadn't asked how they were—or spoken directly about her pregnancy. 'I don't need any help.'

'A nanny will give you time to rest,' Nik said.

'I'm not giving Danny up for someone else to care for.' She stared at him crossly, suddenly determined to get him to acknowledge the child she was carrying. 'And you know that when this baby is born I will look after it myself.'

'You need to be responsible,' Nik said. 'And that means accepting some help.'

'I don't need any help,' Carrie said stubbornly, irritated that he still hadn't shown any sign that he accepted their unborn child. 'Other parents manage on their own.'

'*You* don't need to,' Nik said categorically. 'I won't allow you to run yourself into the ground. You should rest now—you look tired.'

'Don't patronise me!' Carrie snapped. 'I'm pregnant—not ill.'

'Nevertheless, you need to rest,' Nik said, turning on his heel and striding away.

And that, Carrie reflected, had been the closest he'd come to acknowledging her pregnancy.

She laid her hand on her still flat stomach and looked out

at the peacock-blue sea. She liked this shady olive grove next to the beach; it was the only place she felt at ease, and over the last month she had spent more and more time here. Danny liked it too, and would spend hours happily sorting the silver-grey pebbles or playing by the water.

A movement caught her eye and she saw the nanny, Helen, walking along the beach away from them. She must have come through the gate and turned in the opposite direction.

'I'm over here, Helen!' Carrie called, and waved, hoping to catch her attention. She was a nice Greek girl who spoke perfect English, and despite Carrie's resistance to having a nanny she'd found that she liked her. She didn't want her to needlessly walk all the way to the other end of the bay and back.

'Hello, there!' Helen called, ducking under a low olive branch and grinning at Danny. 'What have you got there?'

He squealed with delight and deposited a handful of crushed olive blossom onto her outstretched palm.

'Sorry you had to search for me,' Carrie said. 'I didn't seem to have the energy to climb the hill.'

'That's all right.' Helen smiled brightly, and Carrie suddenly had the strangest feeling that maybe she was also happy to get away from the villa for an afternoon. Being around Nik was anything but relaxing, and he'd got into the routine of coming to play with Danny during Carrie's afternoon break.

It hadn't occurred to her before, but Nik's presence must be totally overpowering for a young girl—especially considering the black mood he'd been in since the discovery of Carrie's pregnancy.

'May I take him down to the water's edge?' Helen asked.

'Of course,' Carrie replied, putting his hat firmly on his head. 'He loves to splash, and he's already covered with sunblock.'

She watched Helen take Danny down to the lapping waves and sighed. Sometimes it was hard to believe how different her life had become from her life spent in London, doing two jobs just to make ends meet. Despite the hard work, she'd been happy then. Now she wasn't so sure.

In her mind there was no doubt that Danny was enjoying being here. But she couldn't help thinking about herself and the child she was carrying. Was this the right place for *them*?

Nik seemed to be actively avoiding her. He hadn't spent any time with her during the day and he never came to her at night. Was this how her life was going to be? Totally isolated, with a husband who didn't want to know her, didn't want to know the child she was carrying?

A movement caught her eye and she glanced up to see Nik. He was standing in the sunshine just below her, on the edge of the beach.

He looked amazing. His dark hair gleamed in the sunlight and his bronze skin glowed with vitality, but her gaze slid straight to the expression on his face.

He hadn't spotted her under the trees. All his attention was focussed on Danny. An incredible smile spread across his handsome features and she felt her heart skip a beat.

If only he would look at *her* like that.

She sucked in a startled breath and frowned as she looked at Nik. Why should she care how he looked at her?

Because being ignored by him hurt her feelings. No, it was worse than that. She kept remembering the horrified expression he'd had when she'd told him she was pregnant. He hadn't been able to get out of the room quickly enough, but she'd still seen his face. That horrified look still haunted her.

He'd started playing with Danny now, and Helen stood awkwardly to one side. As Carrie watched them heading along the water's edge together, splashing as they went, she felt a cloud of misery settle over her.

Now Nik was on the beach there was nothing else to look at. Whenever he was around she found her gaze drawn to him like a bee to a honey pot. She noticed his hair had been trimmed, and his skin was a shade darker. His bronze skin obviously tanned easily in the Greek sun, despite the number of hours he spent inside on the telephone or his computer.

She wondered who had cut his hair. She'd been away from home so long that her own fringe was in desperate need of a trim. She bit her lip and frowned—*this* was her home now, and she needed to start thinking of it that way.

She drew her knees up to her chest and wondered why she felt so unhappy. Nik had come down to the beach to see Danny, and that was good. But that was just it—he obviously couldn't stand to see *her*. He always came to see Danny when he was with Helen, because he simply couldn't bear to spend any time with her.

Suddenly her vision blurred with tears. Her eyes filled up as she watched Nik playing with Danny and no one knew or cared. She hugged her knees tightly, suddenly overtaken by sadness. Why did she long for Nik to come under the olive tree and talk to her?

She remembered how happy she'd felt the night he'd come back from his business trip. He'd made love to her and it had been truly wonderful. The following morning she'd been filled with happiness and everything had felt perfect. But that had been just a hollow illusion that had quickly fallen apart.

She gazed at Nik through a haze of tears, wishing she could have that feeling back. For such a short time she had been full of happiness, full of love.

She sucked in a startled breath and stared at Nik with wide, shocked eyes.

She loved him.

Somehow she had fallen in love with Nik.

Her heart started to thump in her chest and her mouth suddenly felt dry. It couldn't be true. She couldn't have fallen in love without realising it.

She pressed her front teeth into her lower lip to stop her jaw trembling. How was it possible? Did she really love him or was she just imagining it? She pushed shaking fingers through her hair, brushing her long fringe back from her eyes, and looking at Nik.

It was true. She loved him.

She could feel her love for him flowing though her, making her chest ache, causing a tremor to run through her from the tips of her fingers to the ends of her toes.

But wasn't being in love supposed to be a good thing? If she was in love with Nik, why did watching him make her feel so bad?

She knew the answer.

Because he didn't love her.

CHAPTER TWELVE

BY THE time Danny was bathed and ready for bed that night Carrie felt utterly drained. It had been a difficult day—and realising that she'd fallen in love with Nik had made everything seem so much harder.

She sat on the rug with Danny before bed, and an overwhelming feeling of loneliness welled up inside her. The time she spent alone with Danny had always been precious to her, but now it was all she had.

She felt like a traitor—to herself, to Danny, and also to her unborn child. She was locked in a marriage with a man who would never love her. Surely they all deserved more than that?

Without her compliance none of this could have happened—yet what choice had she had? There was no doubt that Nik would have kept his word to take Danny away from her if she hadn't married him. And now her innocent unborn child would be part of this appalling charade as well.

Suddenly an impatient cry cut through her thoughts. It was Danny.

She lifted her head to see him standing on the other side of the room, waving a large toy at her.

'Sorry, Danny,' she said. 'Was I ignoring you?'

With her attention now firmly fixed on him, Danny

squealed with delight and threw the toy down. Then, with a totally mischievous look on his cute little face, he took a step towards her. Then another. Then one more.

'You're walking!' Carrie breathed, her worries momentarily blotted out as a smile of wonder spread over her face. She held out her arms towards him. 'Come on,' she called in encouragement. 'You can do it!'

Danny squealed again and took three more steps towards her, before losing his balance and veering off to one side.

'You can walk!' She swung him up into her arms and hugged him tightly. 'Clever, *clever* boy!'

She beamed at him and ruffled his hair. His button eyes were shining and he looked as proud of his achievement as she was.

She sank down onto the cream sofa and smiled at him. It was incredible—Danny was walking. It was one of those all-important milestones. She should go and tell Nik—he would be so proud, too.

She stopped and bit her lip.

She couldn't go to Nik. He'd made it crystal-clear that he didn't want to see her. He might be interested in Danny's achievement, but she wasn't to be the one to tell him. Now he asked Helen how Danny was getting on. She would pass on the information tomorrow.

Suddenly tears welled up in her eyes. She wanted someone to share her joy over Danny's milestone. And she wanted someone to share her unborn baby's milestones.

Tomorrow she was going to the hospital for her first scan. Nik knew about it—he'd seen the appointment letter—but he'd never even bothered to mention it to her. He simply didn't care.

Carrie felt cold inside. Cold and numb.

She lay down on the sofa, hoping for sleep to block out her

misery, but the sleep she craved would not come. The leather was cool and ungiving beneath the skin of her cheek and it seemed to draw out the heat of her body through the thin cotton of her dress. She hugged a cushion, but it provided no warmth or comfort.

She couldn't believe things had come to this. She'd just wanted to do what was best for Danny, to make sure his future was secure, but as she looked into her own future all she could see was darkness. She felt as if she was being sucked into a black hole and the life was being slowly crushed out of her.

Nik stood on the balcony and stared out to sea. There wasn't another human being in sight, which was normally how he liked it when he had the opportunity to take a break from work. But today it seemed curiously empty.

He'd grown used to having Carrie and Danny around the villa, and even though he'd kept his distance he liked to have some idea where they were.

He started back towards his study, but then heard Danny's happy cries coming from the garden at the front of the villa. He looked out of a window and saw him playing with his nanny. He frowned and headed out to the garden.

'Why do you have Danny now?' Nik called, walking quickly towards them. 'This is not the time of day you normally spend with him.'

'Mrs Kristallis has gone to the hospital,' Helen said. 'Her appointment letter said that they prefer you not to take children with you when you go for your scan.'

Nik stopped and stared at Helen.

'The scan is this morning?'

'Yes,' Helen said. 'I thought you knew.'

Without another word Nik turned and strode away across the lawn.

The radiographer rolled a hand-held probe across the gel on Carrie's stomach and strange echoey noises started coming from the ultrasound machine. Carrie stared at the monitor, trying to see her baby, but she didn't understand the shifting black and white images that flashed before her.

Where was her baby? Was it supposed to take this long to get a picture of her baby on the screen?

'Is everything all right?' she asked.

The radiographer didn't reply, and Carrie belatedly remembered what she'd discovered earlier—she didn't speak English. Instead she kept frowning at the monitor with a look of intense concentration on her face and continued to move the probe across Carrie's stomach.

She lay still as stone, trying to keep calm, but horrible fears were building inside her. She tried to make her mind go blank, to relax, but it was impossible. How long was it supposed to take to see her baby on the screen? She knew it had only been moments, but it seemed like an age.

She wished she wasn't alone. She wished the radiographer spoke English.

She wished she knew her baby was all right.

Suddenly the door opened and Nik came into the room. He took one startled look at her face, then was by her side in two powerful strides.

'What's wrong?' he asked, taking her shaking hand in his.

'I don't know. Nothing, maybe.' Carrie's voice trembled as she spoke and she felt tears prick in her eyes. 'She doesn't speak English, and I haven't seen my baby on the screen yet.'

Nik swore in Greek, then spoke rapidly to the radiographer.

'It sometimes takes a moment to get the probe in the right position.' Nik translated what the radiographer said to him. His voice was comforting and he squeezed her hand reassuringly, but Carrie saw from his body language that he was tense.

At that moment the whomp, whomp, whomp of a heartbeat filled the room.

'Look—there's the baby, and there's the heart beating.' The relief in Nik's voice reverberated through her, but she had to see for herself.

She stared at the screen with wide eyes, desperately trying to make out the shape of the baby, then suddenly she saw its tiny beating heart, pulsing like a little beacon on the fuzzy black and white screen.

Her lip quivered and she squeezed her eyes shut to stop the tears of relief from falling. For a moment she'd been really scared that something was wrong.

'The radiographer has to make some measurements,' Nik said, holding her hand in both of his.

He looked at the screen, watching the little body come in and out of focus as the radiographer moved the probe about, trying to get the best angle for her measurements.

Suddenly it struck him like a thunderbolt out of the blue—he was looking at his baby!

His heart thudded powerfully in his chest.

He was going to be a father. It was the first time that fact had really sunk in. When Carrie had told him she was pregnant he'd been so shocked he hadn't known what to do. He'd understood it in his mind—although he'd shied away from thinking about it—but now he felt it in his heart. That little figure wriggling on the screen was his baby, and he already loved him.

'Look—I can see its head,' Carrie breathed. 'And its little arms and legs.'

'It's incredible,' Nik agreed, studying his baby intently. 'Look—he's really moving, and kicking his legs about. Can you feel that?'

'No,' Carrie paused and looked down at her still flat stomach. 'You don't feel them moving till later. And we don't know what sex it is yet.'

Nik watched her as she turned her attention back to the monitor. The moment he'd come into the room and seen her stark white face and frightened green eyes he'd been racked with guilt. She shouldn't have come to the scan alone—he should have been with her. It was his responsibility.

But now his feelings ran deeper than guilt and responsibility. Suddenly he was feeling an unprecedented wave of protectiveness towards her. Despite the tremulous smile on her face she looked so vulnerable that it made his chest ache. She was even paler than before, if that was possible, and there were dark circles under her eyes.

'I'm sorry,' Nik said. 'I should have been here with you from the start.'

'I thought you weren't interested in coming.' The haunted look in her eyes as she turned to meet his gaze sent a shudder running through him. 'You never even mentioned the scan, even though I know you knew about my appointment.'

'I didn't intend for you to come alone,' Nik said, breaking eye contact and looking back at the screen. 'I just didn't realise it was so soon.'

Carrie looked at Nik. He was staring at the baby on the screen with a look of awe on his face. She was used to seeing intense expressions on his face—he was a man who felt things passionately and didn't mind her knowing the strength of his feelings—but his expression of open wonder as he gazed at the image of the baby—*their* baby—was strangely affecting.

A mixture of emotions stirred inside her. He did care about the baby. He might not care enough about her to remember the scan appointment—but he *did* care about the baby.

He was still holding her hand, and for a moment his grip was strong and warm. If he cared about the baby she had something to hang on to—something to give her strength.

She looked at the screen but the image was gone, and suddenly she realised that the radiographer had put the probe down. She wanted to catch one last look at her baby, but the radiographer was speaking to Nik, holding out a small printed photo.

'Everything is fine.' He handed the photo of their baby to her. 'You'll need another scan later on, but for now everything looks good.'

Carrie stared at the little black and white photo. It was her baby. It was real.

'We can go when you're ready,' Nik said, taking the wad of tissue the radiographer was holding out and gently smoothing it over Carrie's stomach, wiping off the lubricating gel that had been used for the scan.

Carrie lay still, surprised by the tenderness of his actions. He'd touched her before, but his touches had always been loaded with sensuality. Now he was smoothing the tissue softly over her skin in a tender, caring way.

A frisson of disappointment surprised her. Did that mean that now she was to be the mother of his child she no longer interested him on a sexual level? She wasn't feeling very sexy—she was tired and nauseous most of the time—but the idea that Nik no longer thought of her in that way was horribly upsetting.

'I'll drive you home,' Nik said, gently pulling her blouse down into position and sliding his arm behind her shoulders to help her up into a sitting position. 'Unless there is anywhere else you'd like to go now we're out?'

'Home is fine,' Carrie said.

Nik's arm was still around her shoulders and she leant against his strong chest, letting the heat of his body warm her.

The scan photo was in her hand, and as she looked at the image of her baby she felt Nik's arm tighten protectively round her. For a moment she let herself imagine that they were a normal loving couple, sharing in the experience of seeing their baby for the first time.

It had been awesome to see the baby, and she knew Nik had been affected by it, too. It was amazing to think there was a baby growing inside her

But for Carrie it was overshadowed by stress and sadness.

She loved Nik so much that being close to him, knowing he didn't return her feelings, was like a physical pain. Leaning into his embrace was a bittersweet mixture of joy and regret.

'Let's go to the car if you're ready?' Nik said.

'All right.' She stood up, and they walked outside to the car park together.

'You sit down and rest a moment,' Nik said, opening the door of an open-topped black sports car that Carrie had never seen before. 'I'll tell Spiro to head back on his own.'

Carrie slid into the passenger seat of Nik's car, feeling more alone than ever. She missed the comfort of his arm around her shoulder, and suddenly she hated the fact that she'd never even seen his car before. She'd only ever been in the limousine with Spiro, and it had never occurred to her that Nik had a personal car that he drove on his own.

This morning was the first time Nik had spent more than

a couple of minutes with her since she'd told him she was pregnant, and she had realised two things.

She loved Nik, and she craved his company even more than she'd thought.

Being with him, especially with him acting as if he cared about her and her unborn child, was a kind of torture. A succession of emotions churned through her, knotting painfully inside her chest and tightening her throat so that she could hardly breathe. Tears welled up in her eyes and there was nothing she could do to stop them falling.

Nik walked back towards his convertible, thinking how lucky he'd been not to have missed the scan altogether. Seeing his baby on the screen had been simply amazing—but because of his reluctance to accept how fast his life was changing he'd almost been too late. He wouldn't let anything like that happen again.

Suddenly he caught sight of Carrie's face in the rearview mirror of his car. What he saw stopped him in his tracks.

She was staring at the ultrasound picture with tears rolling silently down her cheeks. She shivered slightly while she wept, but it wasn't her tears that wrenched his heart so cruelly—it was the look of utter desolation on her face.

Almost without realising it, he started walking towards her. She turned her head slightly as he approached, and he caught a glimpse of her tear-stained face, but then she wiped her hands quickly over her cheeks and pulled her sunglasses down from on top of her head to hide her red eyes. Her hand was shaking and there was a fragility about her that tore at him painfully.

It hurt that she didn't want him to know how she was feeling—but he knew it was his fault. He had driven a wedge between them, and now they were so far apart emotionally that she couldn't bear him to see her upset.

But he had to find out what was wrong. She was holding the scan picture. It had never occurred to him to wonder whether she was happy to be pregnant.

He opened the passenger door and knelt beside the low-slung car, taking her hand in his.

'I'm sorry,' he said. 'I'm so sorry I wasn't here for you.'

'It's all right.' Carrie's voice was quiet, but steady. If he hadn't seen the tears for himself he would never have guessed that he'd caught her crying. 'I'm glad you managed to come when you did.'

'You gave me a shock when you told me you were pregnant,' Nik said. 'I'm sorry I reacted the way I did, but I realised today how happy I am to be having a child.'

Carrie didn't speak. She looked small and wretched—a million miles away from the fiery woman she'd been when they first met. And it was *his* doing.

The muscle of his heart clenched and his throat tightened painfully. He couldn't be responsible for making Carrie so miserable.

But he'd married her for a good reason. This was all about doing what was right for his brother's son. And now for his own unborn child.

Or was it?

Realisation hit him like a blow. It was about Carrie. Ever since the day they'd met, it had always been about Carrie.

Of course he'd wanted her, from the moment he laid eyes on her in that skimpy red dress. She'd been pure sex on legs—enough to make any man's libido shoot into overdrive. But each time he'd seen her after that the need to possess her had deepened, and now he knew it wasn't just sexual.

She was an extraordinary person. She did and felt everything with such passion. Her inherent vitality had drawn him to her from the start, and beneath her sparkling personality he'd been aware of the depths of love and devotion she felt for Danny. She had given up a lot to look after him, and even though it was a challenge, both financially and practically, she had thrown herself into it with the energy that characterised everything she did.

The more he thought about it, the more he realised that every decision he'd made, every action he'd taken, had been about Carrie, about how to make sure she became part of his life.

And now he had won her. She was his wife. She was having his baby.

Why did her unhappiness cut him so cruelly?

Because he loved her!

His heart hammered in his chest and he felt the prickle of sweat break out on his brow. He had fallen in love with Carrie.

He stared at her beautiful face in shock, hardly able to comprehend what he'd just realised—then suddenly he saw a teardrop trickle out from under her dark glasses.

'Oh, my love,' he cried, lifting her sunglasses gently away and cupping her face so that he could make eye contact. 'Please don't cry.'

Carrie stared at him in bewilderment. Tears blurred her vision, but Nik's expression seemed to reflect the agony she felt.

'I'm sorry,' she gulped. 'I didn't mean to… I can't…'

'I'm the one who's sorry,' Nik said. 'I've done this to you. I've made you so unhappy.'

Suddenly he leant forward and started showering her face with gentle kisses. His hands slid down to her shoulders and he knelt before her, supporting her tenderly with his strong arms.

Carrie closed her eyes and gave herself over to the feelings his kisses evoked. One last time she would allow herself to believe it meant something to him. One last time she would blot out the world and just be there with Nik, her lover.

'I can't bear that I've caused you so much pain,' he burst out. 'I love you!'

'What?' Carrie gasped. Surely she couldn't have heard correctly.

'Please forgive me for putting you through so much.' He held her away from him so that he could fix her in his intense gaze.

'What did you say?' Carrie asked, her voice hardly more than a whisper.

'I'm sorry for hurting you,' he said. 'And I'm sorry you're having a baby before you're ready for it.'

'Before that,' she said. Her heart was racing, but she couldn't let herself believe she'd heard correctly.

'I love you,' Nik said.

Carrie stared at him in bewilderment. A glimmer of hope was growing in her heart, but she wouldn't give free rein to it—not yet. Nik had said he loved her—which was unimaginably wonderful—but for some reason he seemed upset about it.

'I have fallen in love with you,' Nik said simply. 'And I can't bear that I've caused you so much misery.'

Carrie finally let the happiness swell inside her.

She smiled with wonder as things fell into place at last, and she lifted her hands to cup his face tenderly.

'You were so sad.' Nik's expression was still troubled. 'It was marrying me and getting pregnant that made you miserable.'

'I was sad because I love *you* so much and I thought you'd never love me,' Carrie said tentatively. 'I was always happy to be having your baby. I just wished our marriage was real.'

'You love *me*?' Nik asked, a look of almost incredulous joy slowly lighting his face.

She nodded and smiled up at him tremulously, her happiness overflowing as at last they understood each other.

Nik gave a shout of pure joy and seized her in a rough embrace, bounding to his feet with an exuberance that lifted her clean out of the car. Once again her eyes were misty, but this time they were tears of happiness, and she didn't try to hide them. He kissed her fiercely, then swung her round and round before setting her down, still encircled by his arms.

She laughed, thinking she had never seen him look more handsome. He was incredible. The love he felt was written all over his face, animating his features and lighting him from within. At that instant she knew it was real. He loved her as much as she loved him.

She gazed up at him, basking in his adoration, never wanting him to release her.

'You are so amazing!' Nik seized her and almost crushed her in his enthusiasm.

'So are you,' Carrie gasped, thinking how true that was, from the very bottom of her heart.

'You've given me my life,' he said suddenly. 'Before I met you my life was hollow. I was hollow.'

'That's how I felt last night,' Carrie admitted quietly. 'And during the scan. I love you so much that I could hardly bear to be with you, knowing that you didn't return my feelings—but I couldn't even stand to think about life without you.'

'We'll never be apart.' Nik's voice was suddenly gruff as he pulled her down into the sports car with him. 'You and Danny are everything to me and we will always be together.'

Carrie sank down against the comfort of Nik's steady heartbeat, revelling in the strength of his arms embracing her. For the first time in her life she felt as if she'd finally come home.

'The three of us will always be together,' she repeated, smiling dreamily up into the face of the man she loved. 'Well, the four of us,' she added, resting her hand gently on her stomach.

Nik looked down at her, an incredible feeling of love and pride spreading through him.

'Maybe we'll spend a few moments on our own,' he answered, a mischievous twinkle in his eyes. 'Just the two of us.'

Step into

THE ROYAL HOUSE OF KAREDES…

TWO CROWNS, TWO ISLANDS, ONE LEGACY

One royal family, torn apart by pride and its lust for power, reunited by purity and passion

Now available as a complete collection at: www.millsandboon.co.uk

0414/MB467